# HAWKEYE RIDGE

BOOK 1

G. D. COVERT

# 1

## PRESENT-DAY

***Friday, September 8, 2017, 8 A.M.***
***Student Union Food Court***
***Chemeketa Community College***

Julia felt a pair of eyes upon her. Feeling compelled, she turned. She made eye contact with a tall, handsome man who nodded his head. It was instinctive to return the nod.

It was another sunny September morning in Salem. The temperature would hit the low 80s, although, at 8 A.M., it was still a little brisk. The leaves were turning color and starting to drop. It was beautiful, but scary since they were dropping, not from frost, but drought. Oregon's weather's reputation was that it was wet and drizzling all the time. During typical mild winters, this proved true. It was also what produced the lush forests, ferns, and greenery everywhere. Summers, however, were spectacular. A little rainfall, but not a lot, is the norm, with blue skies and warm, but not hot, temperatures. This summer, however, there had been no rain in over three months. The forest fire danger was extreme.

~

ROMAN DRUMMED his fingers on his thigh in the long line while waiting to order his morning coffee. The student union at Chemeketa Community College was buzzing, with boys flirting with girls. The girls pretended not to notice as they wore their skimpy outfits, which begged for attention.

Roman's eyes scanned the crowded room. Always moving, they paused on an attractive young woman. She appeared more poised, better dressed, and more confident than the girls who were just a few years younger. She radiated with charisma. As their eyes connected, he had that "male knowing" if the circumstances in his life were different; this was a woman he would like to meet. He nodded at their eye contact, feeling a powerful attraction.

Without being obvious, he watched her texting on her phone and chatting with a small group. He thought, "I'd bet she's just a few years younger than me, maybe 28." Dressed in expensive, but classic, white shorts, and a royal blue designer top, she wore them with style.

He thought, "Gorgeous, she may have gotten that tan on those long legs sitting at a pool with a bikini, but she'd never go to a tanning booth. With those legs and her style, she'd always look like she was on her way to a photoshoot."

It was hard to tell at a distance, but he guessed she was 5'8", maybe 5'9" tall. She had a thick mane of honey-blond hair that hung to her shoulders. Her face was oval, with a slender nose and thick, well-shaped eyebrows. She tossed her hair with her hand in a move, which with others would appear an affectation, but with her, seemed to be natural.

He couldn't help thinking, "If I ever get to where I can be with a woman again, I'd like to find one like her. She looks like she would be fun. She's beautiful and exudes class. I wonder if she has the personality and brains to match her looks."

Observing what he perceived as a classic loser approach and start flirting with her, his interest turned into disgust. He wondered for the umpteenth time what drew so many women to the "bad boys," the abusive, addicted users.

The coffee barista, Bob said, "Thanks again for the conversation this morning, sir. It's nice to talk to someone who has experienced the nightmares and flashbacks I'm going through."

Roman said, "It's not past tense for me either, Bob. I still get them. On the 4th of July, a kid at the park tossed off a firecracker, and I dove under the picnic table. What's worse was I tossed my beer and hamburger on the ground, diving for safety." He and Bob laughed at the fragility of their shared experiences.

As Roman got his coffee, he was no longer thinking of the girl across the room. He was thinking of his sister, Alexia, and her most recent relationship fiasco. He loved his sister. Alexia was 27 and had a build similar to the girl across the way. Alexia was a slender 5'9" raven-haired beauty with a magnificent smile and great personality. Roman couldn't help thinking both women were tall and slim, and they both had that magnetic spark that jumped across a room to catch all the men's eyes.

In her broadcasting job, Alexia met many successful people. However, she seemed to have nothing but short-term relationships with men who ended up being abusive. Roman couldn't understand it.

Lost in thinking over the problems of Alexia's love life, he waited at the coffee bar to doctor his drink. Absorbed in his thoughts, he reacted out of instinct to the bump he felt on his back. His reflexes forgot he was in the coffee shop. He responded as if he were under attack in Somalia, 9000 miles away. The attacker was an enemy sentry with a knife. Even as his training had him spinning, taking down the person attacking from the rear and delivering the killing blow, his senses picked up her fragrance, her softness, and her terrified green eyes.

Pulling his attack at the last second wasn't easy. Roman stared into the green eyes as they dropped to the floor. As he fell, he twisted, so she fell onto him instead of being crushed by his automatic response to what he perceived as a knife coming from the dark. Both of them broke free and jumped to their feet as the scalding coffee spilled all over them.

# 2

PRESENT-DAY

***Friday, September 8, 2017, 8 A.M.***
***Student Union Food Court***
***Chemeketa Community College***

Each week Julia's photography class went to a local scenic area for real-life photography experience. They'd already hiked and photographed the ten magnificent waterfalls at Silver Falls State Park, with its towering Douglas firs. She loved South Falls, the waterfall you could walk behind. She had taken a series of great photos standing behind the falling waters.

Next, Willamette Valley Vineyards had volunteered its property, with its idyllic views, to the class, followed by wine sampling for those who were old enough. Or, at least those that had ID's that said they were old enough to drink. Today's class, a raft trip on the Santiam River, had her most excited.

A week after the class started, a late registrant, Charlie, started talking about a once-in-a-lifetime opportunity to raft and photograph the Santiam River Canyon, as Detroit Dam was being drawn down for inspection. He explained to everyone he had been away in the Navy for four years overseas and was looking forward to getting back on a river he had fished as a child. Charlie made the trip sound exciting, a great photographic opportunity, and easy enough for beginning rafters. The first time or two, Julia met Charlie; she sensed his interest in her.

Charlie was about her height, swarthy, longish hair, and had a small earring. He always wore a long-sleeved shirt, but she thought she glimpsed well-muscled arms covered in tattoos. She was pleasant to him, but couldn't identify why he made her feel uneasy.

Since she was up earlier than usual, she stopped in the food court at the Student Union for caffeine. She felt eyes upon her. Turning, she made eye contact and felt a connection to a tall, athletic man across the way. He was a little over 6 feet, with short wavy black hair. Not skinny, he looked a fit 190 pounds.

Trying to be discrete, she checked him out and saw faded jeans and a sports shirt. She didn't see any tattoos, which, in her mind, was a plus. Looking closer, she thought, "Maybe he's got a small tat on his right wrist."

Taking another discrete glance, she saw well worn, Danner desert colored combat boots and a leather jacket carried over his shoulder. Her guess was he had ridden a motorcycle to the campus.

She observed him for the next few minutes and saw he appeared known to and respected by several people in the room. His presence seemed to fill the coffee shop.

She asked herself, "Why can't I ever meet a guy like him?" She couldn't contain a grin as she realized he was checking her out.

While waiting for her latte, she thought of her last few boyfriends. They all fit the same pattern. They were fun and easy going when she met them. But, as she got to know them better, they all became aggressive and controlling. Julia knew she was a strong woman and wouldn't allow herself to be abused. What she didn't understand was why she seemed to always find overbearing men attractive.

Recognizing her relationships were all with flawed men, she had withdrawn inside herself and started questioning what caused her attraction to men of this type.

She didn't want to think she attracted the men into her previous relationships because of her wealth and connections. Julia recognized she was becoming cynical about men. She wondered if there were any men out there who were strong enough in their sense of self that they didn't need to prove it by being overbearing and controlling. Her relationship insecurities had kept her out of a relationship for a year and a half. She was feeling lonely, but she was also feeling an intense sexual need, which she didn't want to satisfy with a one-night stand.

Julia asked herself, "Where can I meet a man who wants me for who I am, and not how much money I have, or who my father is?"

As she took the first sip of her latte, Charlie stepped up to her and said, "You better hurry. The carpool will leave soon."

He started shepherding her photography friends out the door and urging her to come along.

While she was talking to Charlie, the man who made eye contact with her had a disgusted look on his face.

Surprised, she wondered, "Hmm, what's that look all about?"

She answered her internal question with, "I guess it doesn't matter."

After a pause, she thought, "Maybe it matters if he's the kind of guy I want to meet."

Without worrying about how she would come across, she decided to ask him. She remembered wondering what she would say as she tapped his back to get his attention.

The next instant, she was falling backwards. One hand savagely gripped her breast, pressing her back and down while another had a death grip on her throat. She knew as she fell, she was looking into the intense black eyes of death's messenger, the angel Gabriel.

As they were falling, his face and eyes transformed with a look of horror. They hit the floor with his hands still attached to Julia's breast and throat. He bounced like a cat and lifted her to her feet, apologizing, and trying to brush her spilled latte off her blouse and white shorts. Which produced an anxious moment as he pulled his hands back from her breasts one more time.

# 3

## THREE YEARS AGO

*August 2014*
*The Philippines*

Sweltering in the mangrove forests' ninety-degree tropical heat and humidity, Lt. Commander Roman Nelson, watching from the darkness, saw the screaming rebels racing their pickups for the bridge. The driver of a beat-up yellow bus filled with terrified, crying schoolchildren led the way. The honor of crossing the river first was at stake, as was his martyrdom. Wearing night-vision goggles, Roman could also see most of the beleaguered SEAL team. They were wearing jungle camo and had their exposed faces and hands painted with green, brown, and black stripes to break up their shape. The team leader was in clear sight hiding in a ditch with the team medic. The bodies of two SEALS and one female sailor lay in the ditch with them.

Dreading the decision the leader of the outnumbered SEAL team must soon make to stop the school bus, Roman knew the necessity. Hiding in dense tropical foliage, he knew it was common practice around the world for combatants to use children as shields. He suspected the rebels kidnapped the children from the local village, and a suicidal rebel was driving an explosive-laden bus. The ambush with its murderous automatic weapons fire kept Chief Warrant Officer Jimmy Stockade and his team pinned down while the guerilla reinforcements were racing for the bridge.

Roman was tight-jawed, waiting on his friend, Chief Jimmy Stockade, to fire. He was thinking, "Jimmy, you gotta do it. You gotta do it."

The school bus reached the middle of the bridge spanning the narrow gorge, as the timer on Petty Officer Jim Bridger's bomb reached zero. With a massive explosion, the wreck of the bus dropped into the river a hundred feet below. With horror written on his face, Bridger stood screaming at the disappearing children, "No, No, OH NO!"

Hurtling out of the dark, a blood-covered Commander Nelson knocked Bridger down and covered him with his body. A grenade exploded near them, peppering Roman's back and legs with shrapnel wounds while his body danced and jerked from the sniper fire hitting it. Roman earned his nickname, "The Ghost," in the Middle East and North Africa. Tonight, his bravery in action behind enemy lines earned him near-legendary status among the SEALS.

Roman had, without help, dispatched most of the enemy force. He did it unseen, in the darkness, in total silence, one rebel at a time, and did it with a knife.

# 4

**The Philippines**
*A short while later*

Opening his eyes, Roman saw Chief Jimmy Stockades face. The chief's eyes were wide, and his jaw clenched. Roman thought his best friends' hands were shaking. As though he had cotton in his ears, Roman could hear Jimmy saying, "Stay with us, Roman. Stay awake."

The medic, Petty Officer Andy Baker, huddled over Roman, placing pressure bandages on the open wounds, injecting him with morphine, and starting an IV for a plasma drip. Chief Stockade was functioning at hyper speed. Jimmy was cutting away Roman's uniform and applying additional bandages on wounds that pulsed with every beat of his heart. He was yelling, "Medic, we need another medic. Get over here."

Command was instinctive for Roman. He knew he was fading and attempted to snap rapid-fire orders. His voice, however, came out shallow and raspy. "Chief, you're in command. Lt. Erwin, in command of platoon 2, was killed in the fight on the road near the beach. They're experiencing heavy casualties. Platoons 3 and 4 should reach the beach in minutes and secure the area for withdrawal. Make sure we leave no American bodies behind, including those of the admiral and the ambassador. There can be no evidence we were here. Secure the money and burn the villa to ashes. Take no prisoners, allow no wounded to leave, and put all enemy bodies in the villa to burn."

With searing fire racing through his body, Roman whispered, "Make sure no one on the team goes anywhere on their own. Always travel in twos and threes. There are no other witnesses, so guard your backs. It would be easy to eliminate our team and have no witnesses."

The morphine began kicking in. Roman felt woozy. The pain was no longer excruciating, but he fought to stay awake.

The medic was yelling, "I need help with the stretcher."

With his vision fading, Roman could hear Chief Stockade assuming command, "No, Petty Officer Baker. You can't move the commander until I say so. I understand he needs evacuating. Again, I say no, not until I have a team member available to function as his bodyguard. You can't go with him, Baker. We have other wounded who need you."

"Chief, we gotta get him out of here. How about Roger?"

In a commanding voice, Chief Stockade said, "Harper, get over here."

Petty Officer First Class Roger Harper raced to the stretcher holding the commander, "Yes, Chief."

"Petty Officer Harper, go with the commander. Watch his back. Don't give up your weapons for anyone until I get there. Keep your eyes on everyone who approaches the commander. If their activities look suspicious, stop them. Shoot them if necessary. I don't care who they are or what their rank."

They loaded Roman in the Zodiac and rushed him to the ship. Drifting in and out of consciousness, he kept thinking of Amber and knew that was a memory fraught with pain. In his drug-induced unconsciousness, everything was foggy. He struggled to focus on how he got wounded and why.

# 5

## TEN MONTHS EARLIER

***October 2013***
***Sydney, Australia***

Amber sat fidgeting in her seat, waiting on the crowded aisle to clear. She gathered her bags to unload from the plane. She texted, "On grnd, r u here? c u n baggage?"

Roman texted back, "Yes," with a series of emoji's blowing her kisses.

She took a deep breath, knowing she was nervous over this trip. There was no need to question the reason for her jitters. She knew the reason, "It's because this could be the last time I see the man I love. I hope not, but I'm sure that's a possibility."

Meeting in baggage, Amber melted into Roman's arms, saying, "It's so good to see you." She scratched her fingernails on his neck as they kissed. Opening her eyes to see a passerby grinning, she broke the kiss.

Keeping her wrapped in his arms, Roman replied, "You too. I got here three hours ago. I've gotten my bags and rented the car. Are you hungry? Shall we get a bite to eat before we head to the resort?"

"The bite I want to eat is you. Why don't we go to our room and take care of first things first?"

Squeezing her hand, he carried her bags and stored them in the backseat of a deep red Camaro convertible. The sun was shining, and the temperature was in the mid-eighties. It was perfect convertible weather. He had the top down already.

She laughed. "You almost always rent convertibles."

LT. COMMANDER ROMAN NELSON AND LT. COMMANDER AMBER SABATINO wore their Navy uniforms as they drove to the resort from Sydney's Kingsford Smith Airport.

Laying her hand in his lap, she brushed her fingertips across his thigh. "You're driving. You need both hands on the wheel. Can you keep your eyes open for people with cameras, or should I keep my hands off you?"

"How about I drive faster? I'm sure neither of our admirals wants to see photos of us going viral."

Amber asked, "How is it, we see each other two or three times a year for a few days, maybe for a week or two, yet whenever we get together, it seems like the time apart didn't happen. We always pick up right where we left off."

# 6

## ANNAPOLIS PARTY

*Nine Years earlier*

They were friends and occasional lovers since their days at Annapolis. In his third year at Annapolis, Roman felt the crushing pressure of an elite military school. The training, education, expectations, and discipline were rigorous. Midway through the year, a friend invited him to a weekend party at a home he'd rented at the beach.

Walking into the party with the obligatory bottle of tequila for the bar, Roman made eye contact with a striking woman he'd seen in classes at Annapolis. Roman suspected her heritage was Italian with her darker skin and thick black hair. She wore it short as required of all cadets, but it looked chic on her.

She was wearing a tight aqua tank top, which covered her from her long neck to just above her indented bellybutton. Her large upright breasts strained the knitted fabric's ability to contain her and accentuated her well defined-abs.

Approaching her, he said, "I don't think we've met, but I know I've seen you in the Leadership class at Annapolis. I'm Roman."

"I'm Amber, and yes, I've seen you in the Leadership class."

Holding up the bottle, he asked, "Tequila?"

"Not straight shots. I came here to drink too much and unwind from the pressure, but I can't do straight shots. Can you make a margarita?"

Two margaritas later, Roman asked, "What do you think about finishing the night together at the Marriott down the road?"

Leaning into him for a kiss, Amber said, "Only if we can order a bottle of wine from room service, and you promise to service me all weekend."

# 7

## NINE YEARS EARLIER

*Post Annapolis party*

Checking into their room didn't take long since they had no luggage. The clerk at the front desk smiled and gave them a suite with a king-sized bed. Other than the bed, it was a basic upscale motel room. Neither Roman nor Amber worried about the room. Moments after closing the door, it was a contest to see who could remove the other's clothing the fastest.

Looking at Amber naked, he caught his breath. "Oh my God, you're so beautiful. How do you hide a body like that in a cadet's uniform?"

~

MAKING LOVE EVERY COUPLE HOURS, walking on the beach, and eating soft shell crab where the locals ate made the weekend fly. Roman and Amber became infatuated with each other.

She worried, "I hope you don't think I'm a tramp and just jump in the sack with every guy I meet an hour or two later."

"I didn't think that at all. You could say the same for me."

"This weekend, and you were just what I needed."

"It has been perfect."

Amber said, "I needed to feel like a woman again. The pressure at Annapolis has been unrelenting. The schoolwork, the military indoctrination, the physical exhaustion, coupled with being a woman in a male military institution, has been overwhelming. I needed this weekend with you. Thank you."

During the next year, they spent their weekends together. They were not only lovers, but they were also great friends. All subjects were open for discussion. They talked about the difficulty of securing a congressional appointment to Annapolis, the hell of the initial plebe summer, their loneliness, and their families. Every free moment they spent together. They talked about their hopes and dreams. But they spoke about love just once.

Roman took Amber out for a birthday dinner a few months before graduation. He treated her like the proverbial princess.

She said, "I can't imagine what it will be like when we graduate. The possibility of not seeing you again devastates me. I can't envision life without you."

Roman massaged the back of his neck. "We've never talked about it, but I hope you know I love you. That won't do us much good for a lot of years. We are both committed to the Navy for a minimum of five years upon graduation and commissioning. We both have career paths in the service which will send us worldwide. Odds are we'll be on opposite sides of the world, which is no way to build a relationship or have a future together at this point in our lives. Whatever our feelings are, they'll not matter to the powers that control our destiny for years."

Pinching her lips together, while shaking her head, Amber asked, "How can you be so matter of fact? You tell me you love me and then tell me that will not do us any good. Don't you think it would be nice to separate those two comments by at least a few minutes?"

A flush began to creep across Roman's cheeks. "I'm sorry. You know romance is not my strong suit. I love you, but I don't see any path forward for us at this point. I don't think we've ever defined our relationship, or even said we are in a relationship. What I know is I don't want to lose touch with you. Let's keep doing what we've been doing to the extent our assignments allow it. We can try to connect as often as we can and coordinate our leave time. We'll see what happens."

Lowering her head, Amber frowned at Roman as she took a deep breath and let it out to a count of ten.

Roman found his career path in covert operations with the Navy SEALS. Amber's background was accounting, but she drifted into political affairs. She became an aide to Admiral Hayes, serving on an aircraft carrier in the South Pacific.

# 8

OCTOBER 2013

*The Malaya*
*Sydney, Australia*

Roman and Amber lingered over a fabulous dinner at The Malaya on King Street Wharf. With seats overlooking Sydney's harbor and the yachts anchored next door, their table on the terrace was private. Well dressed as befitted their rank, Roman was wearing khaki slacks with a short-sleeved, lightweight, teal-colored shirt. Amber wore a blue, ankle-length sheath, with a slit up to the left thigh. Sleeveless, it showed the definition in her arms. Both exuded a charismatic presence. It wasn't what they were wearing. It was how they were wearing it.

They feasted on the salt and pepper scampi, which were battered, deep-fried, and tossed in fresh chili, salt, cracked black pepper, and shallots. Their waiter recommended a fine Australian wine, but knowing the fire in their upcoming meal, they opted for a local microbrew beer.

Amber fidgeted, raking her fingers through her hair and taking deep, relaxing breaths. As they talked, she chased a Brussels sprout around and around on her plate, but never ate it.

Roman asked, "What's up? You seem tense and distracted."

"I'm sorry. I guess I'm not good company tonight."

"You're always good company, but I can tell something's bothering you. Anything you want to talk about?"

Glancing around at the closest tables, she lowered her voice. "Two things are going on. One's personal and one's work."

Roman was smart enough to suggest she tell him what was bothering her at work first.

Again looking around at the servers and neighboring tables, she lowered her voice, "I can't tell you any details of what's bothering me. I happened into Admiral Hayes's office one day and saw something I should not have seen. I shouldn't even be telling you this since he said what I saw was top-secret. What made me suspicious was his alluding to career advancements for me if I could be discrete about what I saw. I assured him I could be."

"You can tell me, you know I've got a top-secret clearance," Roman said.

"No, Sweetie, this isn't something you can do your male SEAL thing with, and come in and fix it for me. I feel like I stumbled into something serious. I can't say anything, but I feel like I need to. The problem is I don't know who to tell. It feels like I'm taking part in something illicit, illegal, or dirty. The way Admiral Hayes looked at me when he saw me standing there gave me chills," saying that, she shivered.

"Are you sure I can't help," Roman asked, "even if it's just to listen?"

Amber gave him a sad look. "No, Roman, I don't think you can wave your testosterone wand at this problem and fix it. I wish you could."

He frowned. "Know if there's anything I can do to help, I will. You've got me nervous for you."

"That's sweet, but I think this one is on me to solve."

"OK, if I can't help with that issue, what's going on with you? Are we ok?"

Amber looked Roman in the eyes while tapping her fork on her plate. "I'm thinking of not re-upping when my enlistment is up next year. I'm disenchanted with what I'm doing, but I'm also approaching the age where my biological clock is ticking louder every year. I want to get married, have kids, and settle down to a normal life. Which won't happen while I'm cruising all around the world."

Readjusting himself in his chair, and signaling the waiter to remove their plates, gave Roman a moment to process what he had heard. "I think you've been thinking of many of the same issues which are bothering me. I was waiting to talk to you about this."

"What's going on for you?"

"First, I understand what you're saying." Folding his napkin and placing it on the table, he continued. "I think getting out of the Navy when this tour is up, is on both our minds. We should both be getting out about the same time. You know my father died a few years ago. Finances have been hard at home for my mother ever since. I think I need to get out of the service and go help in the family businesses. Dad lost everything in the market crash in 2008 that wasn't in the trust. It's time for me to step up and be the man of the family."

Amber focused on Roman's face as he continued, "When I went to Annapolis, I never thought I'd be gone from home this long. I never intended to be a 'lifer.' I didn't want to be a career Navy man in for the twenty or thirty-year retirement program. That's not what I wanted."

Being honest with himself, he didn't like the idea of Amber having a child with anyone else, either. His stomach roiled at that thought.

Amber jiggled her foot on the floor and rocked her wineglass back and forth, waiting for him to continue.

"The Navy provided me with many great experiences. I've learned a lot about leadership and myself. Which I know will be valuable in civilian life. There have also been a lot of experiences I hope don't come back to haunt me. Most of the action I've seen was rather grim."

Amber held his hand and said, "You've never talked about it, but I've seen the change in you over the years. You've gotten quieter and more withdrawn. I can see you looking at the thoughts inside yourself. You're too young to have those stress lines around your eyes. I've never asked because I know everything you do is classified, but I'm here for you. You know that."

"Thanks, Honey. No, I can't talk about any of it. On the personal front, everyone from my high school class is on their third kid or their second marriage. I have nothing in common with my friends from home."

Amber nodded her head. "I know. I may be ready to settle down and have a family, but it's not that easy. I don't have any family connections at home. There will be no one waiting to introduce me to a special guy. I don't want to go shopping for a husband on the internet. I don't even know how you go about meeting anyone, let alone falling in love with them."

Her eyes never left Roman's as she waited on his reaction.

"Well, you and I get along pretty well," Roman said, looking her in the eyes and picking up her hand. "We've got the same values, and we want a lot of the same things. We've shared a lot of great times. I think we've both loved each other for years but at a distance."

Amber took a breath and held it. She continued to hold his gaze.

Reaching into his pocket, Roman pulled out a small ring box, gave her a lopsided grin, and said, "I know I love you. Let's get out of the Navy, settle down, and get married. What do you think, Amber? Will you marry me?"

# 9

With a squeal of surprise and tears in her eyes, she threw her arms around him to the delight of everyone in the restaurant. They ordered another bottle of wine and started planning their wedding.

The timeline they settled on was to submit their requests to resign their commissions at the end of their current tours of duty in a year.

They agreed to meet in Bali in nine months for a pre-wedding honeymoon. A significant perk of the military was the ability to accrue two-and-a-half days leave time each month. They would each accumulate three weeks' leave time before they got back together. Three weeks in Bali sounded terrific.

They agreed, once they were both out of the service, Roman would meet Amber and take her to Oregon to meet his family and get married. Amber's parents died in a car wreck when she was a teenager. None of her extended family of aunts and uncles wanted to take in another child. Amber bounced around in the foster home system until a local senator gave her a "hardship" appointment to Annapolis, where she excelled.

"From my side," Amber said, "the wedding planning will be easy. I have no family that I care to have at my wedding. If my aunts and uncles couldn't take me in when I was a teenage girl, I don't feel any desire to invite them to my wedding."

"In that case, we can get married on Hawkeye Ridge. It's a mountain top which my family owns with an incredible view."

They were both excited at no longer having the strain of being vacation buddies with no emotional connection. For the first time, they both felt free to express their emotions. Although they were on different ships, in different oceans, they could email each other every day. Their conversation, even though by email, was at a depth they'd never experienced.

# 10

MAY 2014

*Bali, Indonesia*

The relaxed young lovers walked down the beach in Bali in the dusk. It was still warm, and the humidity was high. Even though the sun was setting, the bird sounds surrounded them.

Since graduating from Annapolis, besides their last get together in Sydney, their previous vacations included beaches in the Azores, the Italian Rivera, Thailand, and Hawaii.

On this pre-wedding honeymoon, they rented a thatched-roof bungalow with a private beach in Bali. Their bungalow sat on stilts, with the high tide lapping below them. The beach was wide and white, and the cottages were all a minimum of fifty yards apart on lush winding paths. Brilliant oranges and blues covered the horizon as the sun sank into the Pacific. A blazing red sun nudged into the ocean, and black descended upon them.

Tonight was their first night together in months. The temperature was warm, and Amber was wearing a skimpy pale yellow bikini. It excited them to think about a few weeks of uninterrupted joy and sex.

"Sweetie, I have big news," she said.

"What's that?"

"Well, we've been engaged since our last vacation," she answered. "I've turned in my intent to not re-up when my enlistment is up in 90 days, just like we talked about."

"I know all that, what's the news?"

"My biological alarm clock is ringing. We're getting married as soon as I'm out of uniform. I want our first baby right away."

Roman's gasp was almost audible. Turning his head to look at her, he held onto her arm as he processed that thought. With a tentative smile which built as the surprise sank in, he said, "That's great, I'm ready." Roman kissed her and led her into the water.

Walking deeper into the warm ocean with the sandy bottom, she put her legs around his waist and slipping aside her bikini bottom, guided him into her. She moaned deep in her throat as they moved buoyantly with the ebb and flow of the water. She smiled. "I hope you're ready because I went off the pill, and I intend to milk you dry this trip."

They spent the next three weeks relaxing on the beach and experiencing all the delights their bedroom could offer. As they wrapped up their leave time, they focused on the wedding. Roman said, "I haven't told my mother that we're engaged or planning on a child right away."

"Why not?"

Roman explained, "I thought we could show up together, get our marriage license, and a day later take a minister to the top of the mountain, and get married. If I tell Mom now, she'll freak out planning a big wedding. I don't want that. I just want to get married and settle down."

Amber nodded. "I don't have anyone to invite. All my friends are in the Navy, and they couldn't come. It's no big deal for me. But, you better plan on having a pregnant bride. I don't know for sure, but if I'm not pregnant, it's not for our lack of trying. I keep track of my cycles, and I know we were trying at the right time."

They were both excited, and for the next few weeks, emailed each other every day. As expected, her cycle was late.

She sent Roman an email. "I'm late, Yippee. I'll go to the pharmacy later today and get a pregnancy test kit. I know I'm carrying our son."

ROMAN HAD NEVER THOUGHT about having a family. It was in the back of his mind as a natural event that would always happen. Now that it was happening, he was beside himself with excitement. He told his best friend, Jimmy. Roman and Amber emailed every morning on the question of the baby's name and whether she should do an ultrasound to determine the baby's sex.

Roman and Amber started counting down the days until their discharge from the Navy and the upcoming wedding. It was a race each morning to see who sent the first email. For the first time in their careers, they were in the same time zone.

All at once, Amber's emails stopped coming.

# 11

## THE SOUTH PACIFIC

*August 2014*

On a destroyer in the South Pacific, Roman and Chief Warrant Officer James Stockade were stripped to their trunks and going hard at it on the exercise mats. Their hand to hand combat practice always drew spectators from around the ship. Roman was six feet tall, one hundred and ninety pounds. He wore his black hair military short, but it still looked styled. Every move he made flowed without effort. Jimmy Stockade was 5'11" with short blond hair parted on the left, and he exuded controlled violence. Equal in skill, the edge, if there was one, wasn't definable. It was more of an emotional edge. Their fellow SEALS joked about the need for killer instincts. Roman's instincts were superb. He was unbeatable in knife fighting.

Other SEALS gathered watching as the two worked up a sweat keeping their combat skills sharp. They were each pockmarked with scars which those watching could identify as knife wounds, bullet wounds, or shrapnel from various engagements. They had each saved each other's life several times, and regardless of the difference in rank, were best friends.

A seaman with an order for Roman to report to the flight deck wearing his full dress uniform at his earliest convenience interrupted their workout. A helicopter was waiting for him.

Roman showered, jumped into his uniform, and raced for the flight deck. A pilot was sitting in the cockpit, waving him in. As he strapped into the seat, the pilot was already lifting off the destroyer. "Sir, I have orders to get you to the fleet aircraft carrier ASAP and to await your immediate return."

When they landed on the flight deck of the aircraft carrier, ten minutes later, another seaman was there to escort him to the skipper of the carrier, Captain Barnes. The captain himself was the person who escorted Roman to another door. Before they entered, the captain required Roman to sign a document attesting to the fact he had no paper, writing utensils, or recording devices on his person. Roman signed, and the captain ushered him into a small room lined with communication devices and a TV screen that blanketed one wall.

Captain Barnes said, "Lt. Commander Nelson, this is a secure room with a lead lining. All communication in or out is encrypted. There will be no record of this conversation. Is that clear?"

"Yes, sir."

The captain left, and within a minute, the new President of the United States, Alex Myers, was on the screen talking to Roman.

# 12

Roman jumped to his feet and snapped to attention. "Mr. President."

"Good Morning, Lt. Commander, stand 'At Ease.'"

Roman continued to stand ramrod straight. He snapped his left foot out ten inches and placed one hand on top of the other in the center of his back. His thumbs were locked together, centered on his belt. Roman's perception was the president was in the Situation Room at the White House. He appeared alone and was pacing back and forth. Roman could move his eyes and follow the president as he paced on the large screen. He was tall, with thinning hair. He was an average weight, wearing dress slacks and an open-throated long-sleeved shirt.

President Myers said, "I asked the Chairman of the Joint Chiefs of Staff, Admiral Seastrand, for his recommendation of an individual to handle a tricky situation we've got going on. This is irregular. There isn't an easy solution. Let me give you the background. You must understand the urgency and delicacy of the upcoming mission."

President Myers continued to pace as he spoke, "My predecessor, President Potts, was a loud, blustering, posturing, blowhard who knew nothing about diplomacy and harmed our image overseas. About a year ago, a new leader, President Duerte, took over in the Philippines. President Duerte could be a twin of President Potts. He is also a loud, blustering, posturing, blowhard who knows nothing about diplomacy. But in the Filipino culture, he adds in the need to exhibit machismo."

Seating himself at his desk, President Myers continued, "In 1992, the Philippines didn't renew the United States lease of Subic Bay Naval Station or Clark Air Force Base. Losing those bases was devastating for the United States' ability to project its military presence in Asian waters. Today, with the issues with North Korea, Russia, and China heating up, it is becoming imperative we re-sign those bases."

Looking at Roman's image on his screen, he asked, "Any questions so far, Commander?"

"No, sir."

President Myers shifted his vision from the television monitor of Commander Nelson. Looking back at the video camera continued. "For the last couple of years, the U.S. has been negotiating to once again sign a long-term lease of Subic Bay for our Navy. When President Duerte took over the Filipino Presidency, the lease negotiations stopped. Duerte claims the U.S. has been funding the rebels who oppose his party and his policies. Former President Potts insulted Duerte's machismo while swearing we weren't supporting the insurgents."

Examining the president's image, Roman saw his jaw clench, and his lips tightened for a moment. "Former President Potts got himself into a 'pissing match' with President Duerte. They were like two little boys on the playground, yelling insults at each other. Except the big prize being tossed back and forth was our lease of Subic Bay. President Duerte accused the U.S. of funneling money to his rebel opposition. He accused us of providing the funds for them to buy munitions on the black market. President Potts denied the accusation and did it in a way that was demeaning to President Duerte. After the election, President Potts told me we had not been funding the rebels. I believed him."

Drumming his fingers on his desk, the president sighed. “I should have known better. Potts lied.”

# 13

Once again, looking at the television screen showing Roman, President Myers sipped his coffee. Roman seemed relaxed in the military's strict definition of standing "at ease." His eyes looked straight into the video camera, filming him.

President Myers said, "With a change of presidential leadership and a shift in style, President Duerte met with me four months ago. Based on the assurances of President Potts, I told Duerte we had never funded his opposition. I also told him I had sent an order to all South Pacific commanders to cease any activities they may have going on in support of the rebels. I shook his hand and gave him my word, man to man. We are in the final stages of signing a lease for both Subic Bay and Clark Air Force Base."

Roman watched the president as he looked down at a paper on his desk and slightly shook his head. Roman thought, "The President looks worried. I guess that's why I'm here."

"Our regaining the use of Subic Bay and Clark Air Force Base is vital to U.S. interests in Southeast Asia. Our ability to stage our fleet and our long-range bombers in the Philippines opens our range of options as we confront the aggression of Russia, China, and North

Korea. All of that, Lt. Commander, was to bring you up to date on the big picture. Now here is the issue. This week we've had a message from an informant on Admiral Hayes' staff, which sent panic throughout the Joint Chiefs of Staff."

Standing "At Ease," Roman's unseen hands behind his back clenched. His fingernails began biting into his palms.

President Myers said, "My people vetted that message, Commander. Once they knew what was going on, and where to look, it was simple for my team to validate the informant. I found out, over the last few years, President Potts was funneling money to the rebels. Everyone thinks cash leaves no trail, but it does. Each month, Admiral Hayes received a separate container of cash at the same time as the regular cash shipments went to the aircraft carrier. That separate container of cash doesn't show on any of the ship's record books."

Roman continued to stand "At Ease," but was breathing rapidly. Forcing himself to slow his breaths, he wanted to drag information from President Myers at a faster pace.

"Admiral Hayes skimmed a portion off the top and sent it to our ambassador to the Philippines, Ambassador Knapp, in a diplomatic courier pouch. The ambassador deposited part of it into secret bank accounts for the two of them. They would give the more substantial portion each month to a courier of Admiral Hayes. That money was hand-delivered to a rebel leader Ambassador Knapp would identify. The process should have stopped several months ago when I became president and issued the order to cease all activities of support of the rebels. Not only did they not stop, but the process has sped up. I have proof that the latest shipment, is for a $50 million payment to the rebel leader Juan Alvarez to assassinate President Duerte. The admiral and the ambassador will deliver it in a few days."

Holding the briefing paper from his desk, the president was again pacing the room. "We've intercepted communications between Juan Alvarez, Admiral Hayes, and Ambassador Knapp. They'll all be attending a dinner and delivering the $50 million. Juan Alvarez has agreed to assassinate President Duerte and assume command of the Philippines. I believe the assumption which started this whole process more than a year ago was that once Alvarez was president of the Philippines, he would lease us Subic Bay."

President Myers paused for another sip of coffee and looking at Roman's compressed lips, and clenched jaw asked, "Before we go further, Commander, do you have any questions?"

As the president was speaking, Roman developed a knot in his stomach. His fingernails were slicing into his palms. Roman now said, "Yes, sir, my fiancée, Lt. Commander Amber Sabatino, is on Admiral Hayes staff. I'm wondering if she is your informant. She has not been responding to emails for a few days."

President Myers was quiet for a moment. His brow furrowed as he sat and looked at the papers on his desk. Roman wondered if he would get an answer.

After a long pause, President Myers said, "Well, crap. This gets touchier and touchier. Yes, she is our informant. I hope she is ok. There's nothing we can do to verify her status right now without jeopardizing the mission I'm about to give you."

Taking another deep breath, he said, "Commander, I have read the record of you and your SEAL Team. Your team is our preeminent hostage rescue team. I know in the process of those rescues, you have penetrated enemy encampments around the world and eliminated many enemies for us in the past. I also know you have never killed prominent American citizens, which is what I must ask you to do. I have redirected your fleet to get you closer to the island where the dinner meeting will be. You now have operational control of your destroyer's resources for this mission. The skipper will remain in naval command and will have orders to support your mission."

The President stood and walked to look into the video camera, "Commander, I want you to infiltrate that dinner, when you're certain the parties I have discussed are there, you're to eliminate them all. I want no one able to tell tales. No one can whisper that we were supporting the rebels. Questions, Commander?"

"Yes, sir, I assume that is except for your informant, Lt. Commander Sabatino?" Roman asked.

President Myers looked at Roman's image on his television monitor. He saw Roman's tight jaw and rapid breathing. "At the moment, I have no reason to believe she will be there. If she is there, it would be at Admiral Hayes's orders, yes, protect her life. She has earned that."

Roman's hands unclenched as he took a deep breath. He could feel his heart rate return to normal.

"For clarity, sir, so there's no possibility of miscommunication. You want Admiral Hayes, Ambassador Knapp, Juan Alvarez, and all staff killed. Correct?" Roman asked.

"I read that you were a lawyer, Commander. Yes, I want no witnesses and no bodies left behind."

"What about the $50 million?" Roman continued to question.

"I'm not concerned with the $50 million. I'm concerned with eliminating a major problem for this country, and getting all of your team out of there unharmed," President Myers snapped. "Understood?"

Roman jumped back to attention. "Yes, sir." He presented a sharp salute, did an about-face, and walked out of the room.

# 14

A seaman was waiting to escort him back to Captain Barnes, the skipper of the aircraft carrier. Captain Barnes handed him a sealed envelope with new orders addressed to the skipper of Roman's destroyer.

Captain Barnes said, "Give the envelope to your skipper, Lt. Commander. I still have command of my fleet, but I understand all fleet resources are under your operational orders for whatever your mission is. Our fleet has new sailing orders to position us for your assistance. Your helicopter is waiting. I understand encrypted maps, etc. are being forwarded to your destroyer as we speak."

Standing at attention, he replied, "Yes, sir. Could you forward a message to Chief Warrant Officer James Stockade to meet me in the SEAL ready room?" With that, Roman turned and ran for the helicopter.

While in the helicopter, Roman replayed the conversation in his mind. "Did I hear what I think I heard? The mission is straightforward. No more complicated than a dozen others we've been on. Penetrate in the dark, kill the bad guys, and get the hell out of there. Try to do all that while letting no one know you were there. The tricky piece is killing the ambassador and the admiral, which would be political suicide for President Myers if it were discovered."

Worry over Amber kept infiltrating his thoughts of the mission. "What kind of mess did Amber get into? I hope she's ok, but if she is, why isn't she responding to my emails? I have a bad feeling about her admiral."

Looking out the helicopter window, he watched the aircraft carrier disappear. "If I'm not mistaken, I think the president just told me we could have the $50 million if we can get it out of there. Hmmm, why? Is that what he meant, he just couldn't say it? Could I be misinterpreting what I heard? Jimmy and I need to talk about this."

# 15

Roman arrived in the SEAL's ready room to find Chief James Stockade waiting for him. He gave Jimmy an outline of the mission and said, "While I get out of my dress uniform, you can start the preliminary planning of what platoons and equipment we will need. Before anyone else gets here, we need to talk about something else."

Roman discussed the intent of the president's comment about the $50 million.

"Are you serious?" Jimmy asked. "That's what he said?"

"Word for word."

"Why would he want us to get the $50 million? All he has to do is tell us what to do. We can go kill those guys without his bribing us."

Roman said, "Let's think about it from his perspective. He wants the mission accomplished. What better way to assure our secrecy than to bribe us with enough money to keep our mouths shut? Only killing our entire team would be more effective. I guess killing our team might be a good option for the president. Damm, we gotta watch our backs on this one."

"Holy shit," Jimmy said. "Do you think the president is positioning another SEAL team to take us out?"

"SEALS, CIA, Rangers, I hope not. We need to figure out why he offered it to us."

Jimmy said, "Ok, what reasons would he have for not caring about the money? If we shoot the place up and leave, even if the place is on fire, the money may or may not all get burned up. If it doesn't burn, then the locals would have $50 million, and that would for sure start rumors. Is that it?"

"No, I don't think so."

Then nodding his and head and with a look of certainty on his face, Roman said, "I got it. The admiral and the ambassador got that much money, plus whatever went before this, as untraceable cash. However, they did it doesn't matter to us. It's all 'off the books' money. If we return it to my superiors up the chain of command, money that doesn't exist will demand an explanation. I know that's it. The president doesn't want to explain the money. He wants us to make the evidence go away. If we can get it out of there, we can have it. I think he would prefer we get it out of there, that way he knows what happens to it."

"Unbelievable, it's hard to accept the president wants us to take the money."

"I know," Roman replied. "He was cagey about what he said. The president never said the money is yours if you can get it. But he made sure I knew about the money and that it was untraceable with no records. He emphasized he wasn't concerned about the $50 million."

"It sure sounds like he wants us to take it but not tell anybody about it. If we can figure out how to get it, I think we'd be crazy just to burn it up."

"Let's talk about this later when no one's around, but I agree."

As Roman was turning to go, Jimmy commented, "You know who needs to watch their back?"

Roman cocked his head with a raised eyebrow as Jimmy said, "The guys who figured out how to get all the cash to the admiral in the first place."

Roman pursed his lips in thought and then nodded his head.

# 16

## Shipboard Planning Session

Jimmy started the preliminary planning as Roman changed out of his full dress uniform and picked up the encrypted maps and the packet of logistical information. Based on the information in the package, Roman could decide how many platoons would be necessary. The officers in charge of each platoon could help plan.

Thirty minutes later, Roman was back in the SEAL's ready room. He posted a seaman at the door to keep everyone out. Asking all the team officers to stand by for a meeting, Jimmy and Roman first reviewed what they knew. They pulled up a computer projection of a large-scale map showing their current location, and the site of the rebel-held island where the dinner meeting would be. Flipping to the next slide, they saw a color satellite photograph of their target area. The detail was so precise, they could see chickens on the grounds, and they could read a license plate number.

In the package of information provided to him by the skipper of the aircraft carrier was further information on the location of the dinner meeting and estimates of enemy strength. The rebels of Juan

Alvarez were a ragtag guerrilla force armed with older Kalashnikov rifles and Norinco Type 69 RPGs, rocket-propelled grenade launchers. Both the Kalashnikovs and RPGs were available on the black market. They also had a few captured Humvees and light cargo trucks for troop hauling. They didn't appear to have any heavy weaponry but had an encampment in the mountains with several hundred guerrillas.

From the information, they would hold the meeting at a villa about a half-mile from the ocean's white sandy beach. The dinner was scheduled for 8 p.m. local time. Satellite photos showed it as a large compound with a beautiful villa inside the compound walls.

The compound was part of an old pineapple plantation abandoned by Dole. Dole had decided that the political conditions were too tenuous and had moved all their pineapple plantations to Thailand. Native jungle foliage overgrew the four-foot-high pineapple bushes in cultivated rows. The estate bordered a wild mangrove forest laced with winding creeks and ocean inlets. The tidewater where the salt and fresh water mixed was an impenetrable jungle marsh laced with fish, snakes, and saltwater crocodiles.

Rebel forces occupied a small village about two miles up the mountainous country. The villagers were allowed to flee, leaving their huts to the rebels, however, the young women were forced to stay for obvious reasons.

After reviewing all the intelligence and photos, Roman decided he would need two sixteen man platoons in the mission. Each platoon contained two squads. He ordered Lt. Gloss of platoon 1 and Lt. Erwin of platoon 2 in for planning while telling the lieutenants of platoons 3 and 4 to stand down for now.

Leaving the large-scale photo of the villa on the projector for everyone to see, Roman briefed the two lieutenants.

# 17

**Shipboard Planning Session Continues**

"This conversation is classified. Our fellow SEALS can't know about it. I'm operating on special orders from President Alexander Myers. This entire mission is top-secret for presidential eyes only. I am compartmentalizing the mission plans. Each platoon will only know its portion of the mission. The two of you and Chief Stockade will be the ones with the overall knowledge of the mission. I will task the lieutenants leading platoons 3 and 4 with assisting in our withdrawal from a hostile situation. They'll not be knowledgeable about what our mission is. When we undertake the mission, platoons 3 and 4 can stand by in combat-ready mode. Both shipboard platoons can race for the beach if needed in less than a minute. They can then assist in the shore team's withdrawal if it is under enemy fire. Is that clear?"

Lt.'s Erwin and Gloss both nodded and said, "Yes, sir."

Roman said, "As our plans evolve, I'll tell you what our mission is. For this phase of our planning, you need to know our mission requires us to take a hostile action inside this villa and withdraw in secrecy."

Lt. Erwin asked, "I assume this is a nighttime operation?"

Roman said, "The action will be about 8. p.m."

Lt. Erwin said, "That's good, sunset should be full dark at 5:30, we're lucky we are in the dry season. Otherwise, we'd be planning on getting soaked."

Lt. Gloss commented, "The white beach isn't good, it will be low tide at that hour of the day. The beach at low tide is two hundred yards wide. Our Zodiacs and SEALS in black camo will stick out like a sore thumb."

Chief Stockade and Commander Nelson drank coffee and listened to the two lieutenants discuss the operation.

Lt. Erwin said, "I think the landing needs to be up the creek bordering the plantation. We could take the zodiacs up to within a hundred yards of the villa, unload the team, and then withdraw to a stationary position just off the beach for a quick exit if needed. The tide will turn, so the longer the action takes, the shorter the beach crossing to the zodiacs."

Chief Stockade said, "Better not forget about buwaya in your planning or the bulls."

Lt. Gloss said, "What is buwaya?"

The chief replied, "It's Tagalog, the native language, for a salt-water crocodile. I'll bet you've got some monsters lying up on those muddy creek banks."

Everyone's eyes widened.

Lt. Erwin waited a moment and said, "Ok, I'll bite. I've never had to plan on bulls before. What are you talking about?"

The chief answered, "Look at the photos." Standing near the projection photo on the wall, he pointed to it. "These creatures are water buffalo. Farmers use them instead of tractors. The cows are placid. The kids ride them to pull their loads to market. However, it looks like they are not held in fences. They might even be wild. With this many cows wandering around, I'll bet there are a few bulls. The bulls are not placid."

Lt. Erwin said, "Ah shit. I got chased by a bull on my grandfather's farm when I was a kid. I'd rather take out a human sentry."

Roman let the discussion move forward as long as new planning points came up. He didn't speak until the conversation slowed. "Ok, I think we've got our general outline. Lt. Gloss, I want you to stay on board the destroyer as part of the headquarters team. You'll be in the loop of all planning, so you'll know what's going on. I will task the headquarters team with our support, but they won't know what we are doing. You will. If things go bad, you may have to make command-level decisions. Which is why you need to know the whole plan. Understood?"

"Yes, sir."

"Lt. Erwin, you'll lead platoon 2. Your mission is to secure the beach and coastal highway for our withdrawal under fire. Understood?"

"Yes, sir."

"Good, I want both of you to work together to further the plans for your area of responsibility. Chief Stockade and I will use platoon 1 at the Villa. We will develop the plans for our portion of the operation."

"Yes, sir."

Roman said, "As we move into the next phase of planning, you need to know what our mission is. On presidential orders, we are to kill everyone attending an upcoming dinner of rebel leaders at the villa shown on the screen. The two primary targets will be my responsibility. Intelligence is unclear if a female sailor, Lt. Commander Amber Sabatino, will attend that dinner against her will. She isn't responding to email communications to verify her status. If she is at the dinner, she is the sole exception. Protect her life. That is my request, and it is a presidential order."

Roman then added, "Amber is my fiancée, and is expecting our child."

At that news, the silence in the room was palpable.

Roman didn't tell them about the $50 million.

# 18

**Two nights later**

Platoons 1 and 2 loaded into six low profile Zodiac F470 Combat Rubber Raiding Craft. Each Zodiac could hold 10 SEALS. Roman and Jimmy had each Zodiac carry half capacity, so there would be room to retrieve the money.

Cloud cover darkened the waxing moon, and the ocean swells were running two to three feet as the Zodiacs raced for the shore.

The destroyer was staying far enough offshore that it was below the sea horizon. The Zodiacs rushed to the beach until they were within the hearing range of the shore, at which point the SEALS switched to paddles. Navigating to the creek closest to the villa, they were invisible and soundless. The stream had a strong ebb tide and required a team effort to make headway up the channel. The SEALS were wearing black, and their gear and weapons were all matte black. They were comfortable in the dark with their digital night vision goggles.

A SEAL was in the prow of each Zodiac, scanning the creek and its banks with his weapon poised. Sniffing the putrid smell of rotting vegetation and river gas, Lt. Erwin murmured into the CommNet, "Does anyone know what a crocodile smells like?"

"No, No, and No," was the whispered response.

As soon as the Zodiacs hit the muddy creek bank, the SEALS unloaded and disappeared towards their objectives.

Two men stayed with each of the Zodiacs and paddled them offshore. Bobbing with the ocean swells, they were invisible. They rode the surf up and down in silence. The SEALS in the Zodiacs positioned themselves for a rapid pickup of the team on the beach.

Roman stayed with platoon 1 as it infiltrated the compound. Searching in silence, the team located the security guards and dispatched each without making a sound. Roman earned his nickname of "The Ghost" with his proficiency in silent killing in hand to hand combat situations. He'd spent hundreds of shipboard training hours with his team on a silent attack with the knife. His entire team was proficient.

Each platoon contained two squads of eight men. Chief Stockade kept squad 1 with him and Roman at the villa and sent squad 2 to set up a defensive perimeter around the villa. Lt. Erwin took the sixteen men of platoon 2 to set up the defense of the beach exit point. He needed to guard against reinforcements arriving on the coastal highway, which paralleled the beach.

A ROOSTER CROWED, and other chickens started cackling. Roman whispered into the CommNet, "I don't know who woke up the rooster but watch out for the damn chickens. I thought they were sleeping at this hour."

Jimmy muttered into his microphone. "The windows are greasy, you need to clean a spot before attaching the suction cups for the mics, or they won't stick."

With the exterior of the compound secured and suction cup receivers placed on all the windows, Roman could hear the conversations throughout the house. It was easy to pinpoint the dining room.

The SEALS held their positions surrounding the house. Roman and Chief Warrant Officer Stockade could hear everything. They were invisible to anyone more than a few feet away.

Chief Stockade spoke into the CommNet, "Heads up, cars coming."

Expensive cars started to arrive. Mercedes sedans were the cars of preference with a driver and two bodyguards. Staff escorted a series of guests to the dining room. Drifting from window to window and peering in from the dark, Roman saw Ambassador Knapp and Admiral Hayes escorted to the library.

"Son of a bitch, I'm glad I'm the guy who gets to kill that bastard," said Roman, seeing Lt. Commander Sabatino and two sailors carrying chest after chest into the library. When the crates were delivered, Juan Alvarez joined them.

Juan Alvarez was 5'8" and two hundred pounds. He wore the excess weight in a large belly in his white suit. His black hair and black mustache glistened with pomade. He was in an exuberant mood as he paced back and forth in front of the chests of money.

## 19

Happy the conversation was in English, Roman and Jimmy watching through the fly speckled windows heard everything.

After all the greetings, Alvarez said, "Tonight is a momentous night. I will make certain it is in my country's history books. Thank you both for your contributions to our cause over the last year. They have enabled me to pay my army, buy the weapons we needed, and grease the right palms. Your payment tonight will allow us to do as you requested, assassinate the pig, President Duerte."

Jimmy murmured into his mic, "President Myers was right. Who's the bigger bastard, Alvarez, or our two guys?"

Roman said, "They are all a bunch of crooks, we gotta get Amber out of there."

"Yeah, and the two sailors look like they are here against their will."

Alvarez continued, "I'm sure you have diverted your share of the money from those chests before you brought them. You have made yourself wealthy in the last year, skimming a little. I have not minded. There's enough for all. You also sent a contribution to my accounts in Switzerland each month, which I appreciate. All of that is peanuts compared to what we'll make when I assume the Presidency. Ambassador Knapp, you have assured me the U.S. will sign a lease for Subic Bay. I trust you'll continue to divert some of those funds to each of our accounts before the deposits flow to my country?"

"Yes, with great discretion," the ambassador replied.

"Good," Juan Alvarez continued. "I have changed our dinner plans. In the other room, I have invited the leaders of my opposition to join us. I want to show my power to them. I want them to meet you and to see fifty million dollars. I'm sure after meeting you and the power which you represent, along with seeing the money, they'll all swear loyalty to me. If not, they'll not leave our dinner. In either case, all opposition will end tonight, and our plans can move forward."

Admiral Hayes interrupted, "Before we join the others, Mr. Alvarez, I hope you remember our requirement that there are no witnesses. I'm sure Ambassador Knapp and I can make an exception for your dinner partners. However, there are a few others." He nodded to the two sailors who had carried in the chests of money and were standing at attention next to them. His nod also encompassed Lt. Commander Sabatino.

Juan Alvarez nodded, pulled his pistol, and shot the sailors in their foreheads. "I didn't forget Admiral."

Roman did his best not to gasp as the wall behind each of the sailors was dripping with the blood and brain matter of the two sailors. Jimmy said, "We've killed lots of guys, but that was cold-blooded murder. How could the Admiral allow it?"

"Money and greed. He's going down."

Juan Alvarez continued to hold his pistol on Amber as his men secured her. He said to his men, "I think she deserves an opportunity to entertain my troops before she dies. Take her to the camp as a gift."

All the team heard Roman's, "Aw shit."

With her wrists tied, Amber was struggling, kicking, and contorting her body. Afraid to take a shot to free her, Roman watched as she was drug from the house and thrown in a car. He feared in her struggles; he might shoot her instead of her captors.

Roman wanted to rush to rescue Amber, but his responsibility was to the mission. The anguish caused by that internal conflict was manifest in the strain in Roman's voice.

He commanded Jimmy, "Take half of platoon 1 and rescue Amber. I'll keep the other half here to accomplish the mission.

## 20

Jimmy took off at a run, calling out the names of who was to go with him after Amber. Within minutes, Jimmy heard on the CommNet in his ear, Lt. Gloss from the SEAL headquarters team on the destroyer, announcing, "Multiple boogies arriving on all roads. Ten miles out." His viewpoint was an Unmanned Aerial Vehicle with lookdown cameras.

Jimmy heard Roman speaking into his jaw microphone, commanding, "Platoons 3 and 4 get moving. Start your run in from the destroyer. Position yourself just offshore in case platoons 1 and 2 need help."

Knowing the trust Roman placed in him, Jimmy focused on the mission in front of his team, rescuing Amber. The Mercedes carrying her was moving at a slow pace up the bumpy dirt road. Every few moments, Jimmy let Roman know what was happening. He knew Roman would keep pace with his rescue team, envisioning each step of the process.

~

JIMMY'S TEAM followed the guards who were holding Amber to the rebel camp two miles up the road to the mountains. The car holding Amber on the rough dirt road wasn't much faster than Jimmy's team as they jogged in the rear. As Jimmy's team ran past the perimeter post, he picked up half of squad 2 to go with him to rescue Amber.

Jimmy ordered, "Petty Officer Bridger, set explosives on this bridge. We may need to retreat in a hurry. If we are, we may need to blow the bridge."

Jimmy now had eight SEALS with him. The car which had brought Amber and her captors parked in front of a small hut. Twenty guerillas were outside surrounding her. Two men were holding her arms as she struggled, while another was slicing off her uniform.

The team could see Amber struggling against her captors. She was yelling, attempting to claw them with her tied hands, and spitting in their faces.

She yelled, "Roman if you can hear me in this life or the next, I love you."

Jimmy's team surrounded the guerillas. The intention was to kill them all in a quick blast of gunfire since they outnumbered his team twenty to eight.

There was a loud explosion on the coastal road, and gunfire erupted in the distance.

THE REBELS all stopped and ran for their weapons, except for the leader of the small group. He pulled his pistol, put it against Ambers' head, and shot her. Jimmy's shot killing the rebel leader was a second too late. The SEALS became engaged in a brutal firefight.

The SEALS had the advantage, even with the numerical odds against them. Wearing their black on black clothing and digital night vision goggles, they were all but invisible. The rebels appeared in their goggles as though it were bright daylight. The SEALS sniper skills were decimating the insurgents as Jimmy sped in, picked up

Amber, and raced out with her in his arms. Covering fire from his team killed anyone foolish enough to shoot at them.

Jimmy's team retreated across the bridge with Amber's body. As they exited the bridge, the Rebels opened fire with automatic weapons. Returning fire, Jimmy's team dove for cover. The ambush immobilized them.

Lt. Gloss leading the shipboard Headquarters team monitoring the UAV (drone) informed the team that guerilla reinforcements were two miles out.

Platoon 2, providing perimeter defense on the coastal highway, fired the first shots. Warned by the drone of the approach of a column of rebels, they lined the road with landmines and set up their positions to cover the spot at which the mines would explode. They didn't expect to stop the lead vehicle of a full convoy of troops. Platoon 2 dug in for a fierce firefight, and Lt. Erwin called for reinforcements.

# 21

Watching through the grimy windows from the darkness, Roman saw the admiral, the ambassador, and Juan Alvarez move into the dining room. The opposition leaders and their bodyguards were all standing. With hands-on their weapons, they had jumped to their feet at the sound of gunfire in the room next door.

Roman paid close attention as Juan Alvarez speaking in both Filipino and English minimized the shooting and introduced everyone.

Juan said to his aide, "Bring in the money."

His staff scurried to carry in the containers. It was an impressive sight. Five thousand packets of $100 bills in shrink-wrapped bundles of $10,000 each.

Roman ghosted into the library through a patio door. He positioned a shooter at the dining room window, and another shooter followed over his left shoulder. Roman proceeded through the library, down the hallway to the dining room.

Roman clenched his jaw. His eyes were cold and hard as he seethed over Amber and her unknown fate. He knew Jimmy would do everything possible to save her. Roman also knew it was an operation where nothing was certain. His fury with Admiral Hayes knew no bounds.

In his ear, he heard Lt. Erwin, "The ball starts in two minutes, a huge convoy of troops approaching on the coast road."

Roman murmured into his jaw mic. "Be ready. Remember, the admiral and the ambassador are mine."

He was vibrating with suppressed rage. His nerves were strung like taunt piano wires waiting on the explosion and eruption of gunfire from the coastal road to thunder through the villa. When it did, Roman fired the first shot. Seconds later, he looked around the room and saw the only ones left alive were Admiral Hayes and Ambassador Knapp. They were unharmed. They both dove under the heavy mahogany table at the first shot.

Ambassador Knapp soiled himself in his fear. "I'm an American ambassador. I have diplomatic immunity. Let me talk to your leader."

Admiral Hayes stood up with relief when he recognized Roman as a Navy SEAL.

Jimmy was in Roman's ear, "Commander, there's no good way to say this. Amber was killed, and our squad is retreating under heavy fire."

Roman closed his eyes for a brief second and felt a piece of his emotions die inside him. Rage filled his eyes. His neck corded with tension. With his lips pulled back, baring his teeth, Roman turned to his team, who had heard the same message. He ordered them out of the room. He wanted no witnesses.

Ambassador Knapp was standing as Roman looked at him and said, "President Myers has a message for you, Mr. Ambassador." The ambassador looked hopeful as Roman threw a heavy knife across the room and into the ambassador's heart.

Looking Admiral Hayes in the eyes, he stalked across the room. No matter which way Admiral Hayes turned, Roman hounded him. There was no escape, the doors and windows were all closed with SEAL's guarding the exit points. No one could enter or leave.

Roman cornered the admiral, "And this is for Amber and my son."

He snapped the admiral's neck.

Roman was numb and functioning on autopilot. He struggled to focus his fury on the mission. He knew that this evening's event was forever etched in his heart. Roman walked outside to his team. "Petty Officer Sanchez, remember the orders. Leave no survivors in the villa. Get the admiral, the ambassador, and the money out of there before you torch the place. Make sure the money goes in the waterproof body bags. I'll go assist the Chief."

# 22

Chief Warrant Officer James Stockade and his team were hiding in a ditch. Secure from the searching machine gun fire, they could not move.

Jimmy was taking short, fast breaths. He felt the skin on his forehead tightening as he huddled in a ditch with the medic, Andy Baker. The thick jungle kept them hidden as they peered at ground level, looking for their ambushers' legs. He was trying to focus on the immediate problem, but it was impossible.

"I've heard, 'ego goes before a fall.' I thought I was this hotshot team leader. I sure f'd up tonight. We should have set a faster pace chasing that car, they'd never have seen us following. I should have attacked quicker instead of getting everyone in a perfect position. Oh my God, what a horrible way to tell Roman. How can I ever face him again? He trusted me to save her."

Jimmy could hear continuous small arms fire from the perimeter team on the river road. There had been a short but sharp spate of gunfire from the villa, and then all was quiet there.

"And now this, I led us right into an ambush. Out of the f'ing frying pan and into the fire."

"Knock it off Chief, you're the best, but we need you focused right now." Andy said, "We all did everything we could do for Amber, and none of us saw this ambush coming. Quit playing the 'woulda, shoulda, coulda' game in your head and start thinking about how the hell we're gonna get out of this mess alive."

"You're right. Roman can kick my ass later."

Using the team's local communication network, Jimmy tried to contact Roman for reinforcements. Radio silence was the response, and then Jimmy heard an agonizing scream from behind enemy lines. The chief knew that was his answer. His reinforcements were in place. He whispered to the team, "Be certain of a shot before taking it. The commander is behind enemy lines."

Over the next few minutes, the enemy fire facing them diminished. He contacted Jim Bridger, "How are you doing on the bridge?"

Bridger responded, "I'm just setting the timer, Chief. What do you want the time set for?"

"Make it three minutes, Bridger, and get your butt out of there."

Moments later, Jimmy could see a dark shape crawling from under the bridge and disappearing into the shadows. The enemy fire facing them diminished. Racing towards them on the other side of the bridge was a small convoy of pickups with machine guns mounted to their roofs.

Packed with screaming rebels, the trucks raced for the bridge. Just as the first vehicle in the convoy reached the bridge, Jimmy realized it was a beat-up school bus loaded with crying children. Bridger's bomb exploded, dropping the wreck of the bus into the river. Bridger jumped to his feet and, Jimmy heard a screech emanating from Bridger's throat. He knew he would listen to that sound in his nightmares for years to come, "No, No, OH NO!"

Hurtling out of the dark, a blood-covered Commander Nelson, knocked Bridger down and covered him with his body. Roman's body jerked again and again from sniper fire as the shrapnel from an exploding grenade peppered his body.

# 23

30 YEARS EARLIER

*April 1987*
*The Miller Family*

Donald Miller told anyone who asked, "I moved my family to Oregon to take advantage of the construction boom in the Portland area. Times are hard in Alabama what with the 'coloreds' getting all the jobs."

He knew he wasn't supposed to call them that or the other, even more offensive, names he used. He knew he should call them African Americans or Blacks. But when they'd work for peanuts, and take your jobs, he'd keep calling them what his family had always called them.

No one called Donald a racist to his face, but he knew everyone in Oregon thought he was one. He didn't care.

Donald had experienced difficulties for years in Alabama with a black neighbor. The neighbor was a quiet older man. He, however, turned a complaint in at least once a month to the local police about Donald running cockfights and dogfights on the back of his property. The police did nothing about the complaints, but Donald got fed up with it. He assaulted his neighbor when he saw him in town. There were plenty of witnesses demanding justice. The investigating officer gave him a ticket for disorderly conduct. It infuriated Donald.

A few weeks later, the neighbor disappeared. All the local people assumed Donald had killed him and fed him to the 'gators.'

The uproar in the community wouldn't die down. Donald's cousin, who was the sheriff and head of the local Klan, suggested, "Donald, it might be a good idea for you to leave the area. If you stick around here, we may have open race riots in the county. Now, you and I wouldn't care, except it would draw federal attention. I think it might be a good idea for you to git the hell outa here. Maybe go across the country where nobodies heard about what happened. When you go, I don't think you should come back for a long time. Allow the uproar to die down."

Donald said, "I can't afford to pack up and leave. Everything I own is here, my family is here, my home's here, and my job's here."

His cousin said, "I asked all the boys in the Klan to open up their pocketbooks. We've raised enough money to buy your property and give you enough to restart in Oregon. Jobs are plentiful out there, and the property is cheap. You need to do this. None of us want the damn feds down here, poking around looking for your neighbor. Who knows what else they'd find."

All four of his young sons went with him.

# 24

Donald was short, and he preferred to say stocky instead of fat. He had a full head of dirty brown hair, which he kept cut short, just long enough for a part. Going to the cheapest barber he could find, Donald didn't care if his barber gave him a good haircut or a bad one. He just wanted it cut like he wanted his fingernails cut.

Winter or summer, Donald always wore bib overalls, the one-piece kind with the built-in suspenders. If he wanted to wear a shirt, he could, and if the weather was hot, he didn't have too. Donald liked the overalls, though, instead of regular jeans. That way, if he didn't wear a shirt, no one could see his 'man boobs' or his 'plumbers crack' when he was on his knees working. His overalls always had tears and snags in them. Every set of 'bibs' had holes in the knees.

Donald settled twenty miles outside of Portland in a forested area. He picked up thirty acres with an old beat-up shack on it and a large old barn. He and his boys caravanned from Mobile. They had five trailers set up out in the forest where no one could see them.

Not being seen was perfect. Donald brought with him his prize-winning fighting gamecocks. Setting up bleachers in the barn and building a central pit for 'blood sports,' he planned on picking up half a dozen pit bulls. Donald figured Oregon was ripe for a little 'gaming' action, and nobody ever welched on a gambling debt to him.

If anyone tried to leave without paying their debt, Donald had his boys beat them until they were unconscious. They would then throw the welcher out of a car on a distant highway. The broke loser would no sooner get out of the hospital before Donald and his boys would show up to collect the debt. Donald knew he only needed to put one welcher through the collection process before all his friends would scramble to pay their gambling debts.

Donald and his four boys, Charlie, Bruce, Hank, and Larry, all worked in construction. They saw no sense in wasting their money with building permits or zoning restrictions. None of them saw any reason to pay the state for a contractor's license, either.

Bruce said, "That's just the damn state trying to suck the money out of a working man's wallet." If no one saw what they were doing, they could keep building extensions onto the shack and or putting a wood frame carport structure over the trailers and closing them in.

Donald explained to the boys, "Why do we need to get permits and permission to build? I oughta be able to do what I want on my own property."

# 25

**Donald Miller compound**

Mary Beth was shivering and sniffling. The trailer was damp and leaked. Little Charlie cried all the time. She had always gone to her mother, who would sneak her food when Little Charlie was hungry. She couldn't do that now. Her momma was clear across the country. She knew she looked like hell. She wasn't tall and had never been heavy. Now she was skinny, her dark hair was greasy, and none of her clothes fit. She'd lost weight taking food off her plate to dice into baby food for Little Charlie.

Marriage to Charlie differed from what she expected. Daddy and her older brother started crawling into her bed when she turned thirteen. She started working at the family truck stop when she was fourteen and accepting money for favors in the trucks when she was fifteen. When she met Charlie, he was kind to her. She was infatuated and married him a month after meeting him.

When they met, Charlie worked with his family in construction. He always seemed to have money on him to buy his chewing tobacco or a six-pack of beer. She thought Charlie was handsome with his 'good ol' boy ways. He was 5'9" tall, skinny, and had swarthy skin. His hair was dark brown, and she liked his muscular arms. He was ten years older than her and, by her standards, well dressed in his overalls, which didn't have ragged holes. She didn't know that it was his best dress pair and his only pair without tears.

While they were dating, Charlie also kept himself clean. He always showed up showered and shaved. Charlie taught her that sex could be fun. She was happy and became pregnant in just a few months. She thought she was the luckiest girl she knew.

Now, Mary Beth hesitated to say anything to Charlie about the food or damp trailer. Since they had moved to Oregon, he had beaten her for the smallest reason, and then he would be apologetic and try to make it up to her in bed. She hated the rest of the family, seeing her with a black eye or a fat lip.

When Charlie arrived, the small child's whimpering and crying irritated him. "What's wrong with the kid?"

Mary Beth hesitated and then said, "He's hungry, and he's cold."

Charlie started to take offense, and then said, "It's been harder than we expected to find work. They have all these stupid laws about licenses for us to bid on jobs, and if we try to work for another contractor, we're competing with the blacks and Mexicans. They don't have as many Negra's as we had, but they have a boatload of Mexican's."

Mary Beth came up and rubbed his neck. "What are we gonna do, Honey? Little Charlie has to eat."

"I know, I know... Maybe I can make a bunch of money tonight."

Later, he took a snub nose thirty-eight caliber revolver out of his drawer and put it in his jacket pocket as he walked out the door.

# 26

Charlie wasn't sure where to go. This wasn't 'Bama where he knew where the nice homes were. He'd heard of Lake Oswego and West Linn, and he'd heard the rich people lived there. He figured he'd go check them out. Driving his beat-up old pickup with Alabama plates, he headed for Lake Oswego first.

As he drove around the town, he couldn't help but wonder, "What do all the people living here do to make the money to afford homes like these? I've never seen mansions like these. I gotta bring Mary Beth back and drive her around. These homes are like the ones we see in movies. I'm gonna strike gold tonight."

Once it was dark, he drifted into a quiet cul-de-sac and parked his car. All the lights were off in the neighborhood as he moved to the back of the home he'd chosen as his target.

Charlie thought, "I may not have the experience they want up here in a contractor, but I still know how to get into a home. I'm sure glad I didn't leave my housebreaking skills behind."

He was inside the dark home in less than a minute.

The house was huge and filled with elegant furniture and art. Charlie stood there looking around for a moment, and then he moved towards the bedrooms. He had always had success in finding the wallet and purse in the bedroom. Charlie was interested in cash. He didn't want to steal anything he had to fence or pawn. If he could find Mary Beth a beautiful piece of jewelry, that would be a plus.

The lights flipped on. Standing in front of Charlie was the biggest damn black man he'd ever seen. He thought, "That bastard's about 6'8", must weigh 275 pounds, and I think I'm about to get my ass kicked."

"What's you doin' in my house, you young punk?"

"Your house? What's a black bastard like you doing with a house like this?" said Charlie as he pulled out his revolver and shot the homeowner dead.

Screaming, a beautiful black woman ran out of the bathroom towards her husband. Charlie shot her. A child started screaming as Charlie raced for the door. As he opened the door, he was looking down the barrel of a Glock 9mm. The hole in the gun barrel looked an inch across as three cops grabbed him, cuffed him, and started reading him his rights. Blue lights were flashing on the police cars, and behind them, he saw a private security car. It was then he also saw on all the lawns, signs warning that the premises all had security alarms and patrols.

# 27

MARCH 1988

*Lake Oswego Courthouse*

A black-robed judge asked, "Madam Chairman, Have you reached a verdict?"

"Yes, your honor. We find the defendant guilty on all counts."

The judge asked Charlie to rise, sentenced him to death, and asked the bailiff to escort Charlie to the Oregon Correctional Institute in Salem until he exhausted all possible appeals of his death sentence.

Charlie's wife, Mary Beth, broke down and started crying out loud, "I'm sorry, Charlie, I'm so sorry."

Bailiffs held the arms of his brothers, who were yelling threats at the judge and both the prosecuting and defense attorneys. A smell of urine exuded from Charlie's damp pants, as another bailiff held him upright.

Donald Miller, however, sank onto his knees and raising his arms to the heavens, exhorted God. "I call forth Jehovah's hellfire and eternal damnation on anyone who harms my son. Let that curse strike through the third generation, and may that damnation strike them on this earth and in the next."

Donald issued his commandments to God in a loud booming voice and finished by collapsing on the floor in a seizure with saliva drooling from his mouth.

# 28

ONE DAY LATER

***Oregon Correctional Institute***

Biggie was in for life with no parole. Prior to his arrest, he was the big man in Portland's gang-driven crime. He had his fingers in prostitution, drugs, and stolen cars. In addition, any gang member who needed weapons could get one from Biggie. The informer who set him up for a Portland Police sting operation didn't live to see Biggie reach the prison.

Prison didn't seem to bother Biggie much. Continuing to run his operation from inside prison, he always seemed to have access to whatever he needed inside his cell. He had a clean bed, all the food he could eat, and didn't have to pay membership fees at the gymnasium. The guards made sure he also had a constant supply of fresh "sweet cheeks."

The corporal of the guard paused at Biggie's cell, "I'm gonna have you a new friend later today, Biggie."

"Thank you, Corporal. I heard the sergeant say your sister was having a hard time. You let her know I think about her now and again. I'm gonna have a friend drop a little care package off for her."

"I'm sure she will be grateful, Biggie."

~

LATER IN THE AFTERNOON, the corporal escorted Charlie to his new cell. Whistles and catcalls followed them as the inmates pantomimed blowing kisses. "Hey guys, look at this." "Fresh meat." "Hi, Cutie."

Charlie pretended not to hear them and acted insulted about having to share a cell with a black man. In truth, his mouth was dry, and his heart was racing. They terrified him. He wondered if all black men in Oregon were big. His cellmate was tall and had his shirt off. His upper body looked like a photo Charlie had seen of weightlifters. He had muscles on top of his muscles. He struck a bodybuilding pose Charlie had seen in magazines. His chest muscles rippled and danced.

Charlie figured he better get the upper hand right away. He started running his mouth about having to share a cell with a black man.

~

BIGGIE WAITED until the guard walked away, and then he spun around and, with an open hand, smacked Charlie across the face, knocking him across the cell. Biggie stalked after Charlie, who crawled backward until he reached the wall.

Biggie towered over Charlie. Reaching down with a hand the size of a small ham, he seized Charlie by the shoulders. Lifting him and pinning him against the wall, he allowed Charlie's feet to dangle in the air.

Charlie could smell Biggie's sweaty musk and tobacco laden breath. His ears were ringing, and blood was dripping from his cut lip. His eyes were unblinking in fear.

Biggie spoke in a low deep growl, "Now Charlie, you and I are gonna share this cell for a long time. I won't hurt you unless I have to. If I have to, I promise no one will hear you scream except me, and I'll enjoy it. Now what we're gonna do is change your name to 'Sweet Cheeks.' That's all anyone in here is gonna know you by. I'm gonna protect you from that riffraff out there. You won't need to worry about bending over in the shower or having someone standing behind you in the food line. All you need to worry about is keeping me happy. Right now, I'm gonna walk across the cell to our bunk. I want you to take a moment to think. If I tell you to come, you come. If I tell you to sit, you sit. If I tell you to do anything else, you do it. Understood?"

Frozen in place, Charlie's eyes bulged. His breath was coming in rapid, shallow gasps. Biggie reached up his hand and taking a vice-like grip on Charlie's jaw, nodded it up and down. "And bitch, when I ask you a question, you answer. Understand?"

Charlie nodded.

Biggie grinned, then holding a dinner plate-sized hand in front of Charlie's face, said, "Stay." Biggie then walked to the bunk and turned around. Charlie hadn't moved.

Biggie grinned again and said, "Good, you can learn. Now you git over here. It's time for you to make me happy. When we git finished, I'll take you down to the weight room and introduce you around, let everybody know your 'sweet cheeks' belong to me and to keep their hands off your candy ass. We'll design your exercise program. Right now, you look'n a little puny. We gonna get you bulked up and look'n real purty."

He dropped his pants, saying, "Now you see why they call me Biggie."

Charlie whimpered in fear. There was no one around, and the guard had locked the cell door.

Biggie crooked a finger and in an authoritative voice, said, "Come."

Charlie's feet inched forward.

~

LATER THAT NIGHT, when the lights were out, Charlie lay in his bunk crying. He remembered the first time he met Mary Beth and thought she was the cutest little gal he'd ever seen. When he'd heard there was a young girl turning tricks at the truck stop, he'd gone there to check her out and spend money for her services.

Instead, he sat at the lunch counter and ate dinner. Every time Mary Beth walked past with plates on her arm, he flirted with her. He knew he could buy her services for an hour, but instead, he asked her to go to the movies. She accepted.

As the evening finished, she took care of his other needs but refused his money. He asked her to go out with him the following weekend.

Returning home, his brothers asked, "Tell us about her Charlie, is she any good?"

His brother, Bruce asked, "Should I take my money and go buy a poke tomorrow night, or did you wear her out tonight."

Charlie told them, "You're bigger than me and older than me, but if you do, I'll take a club to you while you're asleep."

A month later, they married.

Lying on his prison bunk, unable to sleep from the raw tears in his flesh, scenes from his life played behind his eyeballs. He remembered his first home burglary. He was thirteen. His father told him he was old enough to help the family make money. Charlie stood lookout while Donald entered an empty home. If anyone came home, Charlie was to whistle.

After that, Charlie started helping in the home construction and remodeling business. As part of that, Donald taught him how to install windows and doors. He also taught Charlie how to come back later and open the locked windows and doors.

## 29

APRIL 1988

Mary Beth was holding Little Charlie in one arm while placing a pot on the floor under a leaking roof. Looking out the window at the rain, she could see Donald walking up the path from his home. Donald opened the travel trailer door and walked in. He poured himself a cup of coffee, sat at the small built-in table, and looking at Mary Beth said, "It's time we talk."

Still holding her son, she backed up against the stove. She hated that her voice had a tremor. "What about?"

"Charlie ain't gonna be coming back. It was just his frigging luck to shoot a Portland Trailblazer. A big black bastard, they made out he was the second coming of Christ at the trial. I don't think the public defender tried too hard. He couldn't even get the death penalty off the table. I got the family down in 'Bama raising money for appeals, etc., but I think the best we can hope is to get the sentence reduced to life in prison."

Squeezing her son in one arm, she fed him Cheerios with her other hand and cried, "I know."

"Which brings us back to you and Little Charlie. We've been letting you live back here in the trailer. We've been giving you food and trying to do right by you. It's been hard to do since it was your whining, which drove Charlie to attempt robbing that house without the family. Here's the deal, if you want to go back to your family, I'll get you a bus ticket. But, if you do, Little Charlie stays here with me. If you want to remain here with Little Charlie, then it's time for you to move into the house and start helping out. Momma's not been well for quite a while. Being as fat as she is, it's hard for her to perform all the duties of a wife. I think you would make her a good 'sister wife.' You can help her in a lot of ways. Starting tonight. Understood?"

"I can't do that. You're my father-in-law. I don't love you that way."

"Then you can go home to your family, but Little Charlie stays. You think about it, Mary Beth, it's your decision, but those are your only two choices. I'll come back in an hour. If you want to go home, you have your goodbyes said and your clothes packed. We can get you downtown in time to catch the three o'clock bus."

He paused a moment then said, "If you're staying, you might as well move your stuff over this afternoon. Momma's excited about your help. She's already moved into the new little room we added on. You can move into the bedroom with me. Little Charlie can sleep with Momma."

Giving her a sharp look, he said, "If you stay, I don't want to hear any whining and crying. I'll expect your willing participation in all your 'duties.' Starting tonight."

AFTER HE LEFT, Mary Beth cuddled Charlie and cried racking sobs of desperation.

She thought, "I can stay here near my boy, and for the rest of my life, I have to have sex with a stinky old man who will beat me. Or, I go home where Daddy will put me back to work in the diner. Then, if Daddy's not crawling into my bed himself, he'll have me out in the parking lot turning tricks with the truckers."

She sat and sobbed, trying to figure out what she should do.

"It's a hell of a choice on my 18th birthday."

# 30

When Little Charlie was thirteen years old, his grandmother, Donald's first wife, died in her bedroom. It took six firefighters and a lot of equipment to get her obese body out of the bedroom and to the mortuary.

Mary Beth went to the prison to tell Charlie his mother had died. Whenever she came to visit Charlie, his cellmate was on the phone in the visitor's booth next door, while Mary Beth talked to Charlie on his visitor's phone. Although he was always there on the phone, there was never a visitor. Charlie never told her what occurred between him and Biggie, but said Biggie protected him and kept him safe. Mary Beth assumed there was a cost for that safety.

On this visit, she watched Charlie sobbing for a while about his mother before she interrupted, "We need to talk about our situation."

Charlie looked up and wiped his eyes. "With your mother gone, you and I need to get a divorce. If I need to sleep with your dirty old father as a price to stay near my son, I'll do it. But the least he can do at this point is marry me. That way, I can look people in the eye and tell them I'm at least married to the fat s.o.b."

Charlie protested, but Mary Beth was adamant. "I deserve self-respect even if I don't get respect from anyone else."

She stood up to leave. Biggie knocked on the glass partition for her to pick up the phone to talk to him. That's when she learned Biggie could always hear her conversations with Charlie.

Biggie said, "You've stood by Charlie for ten years while he's been in here. Lots of women wouldn't do that. I've seen his father. He is a dirty old racist 'cracker.' I hate to think of you having to sleep with him to stay with your son. It ain't right."

Charlie said, "He's not that bad."

"He's a bigoted old redneck. Mary Beth deserves better."

Quiet for a moment, Biggie tapped his fingers on the counter thinking. Looking at Mary Beth, Biggie continued, "Charlie's reacting to losing his mother and you saying you want a divorce. But it is the right thing to do. I'm gonna have a man contact you. He'll be a black brother, but you trust him. He'll do your paperwork to get divorced from Charlie, and I'll have Charlie sign everything. There won't be any problems. I'll have him do a will for Charlie also, leaving everything to you, even if you're divorced."

In a wide-eyed surprise, Mary Beth said, "Thank you for understanding."

"You gonna have to suck it up for a while and sweet talk that old man into marrying you and doing a will. That way, there are no questions when he dies. I'm locked up in here, but I still know what's going on out there. That thirty acres his old man owns is gonna be worth a lot of money in a few years. The city is moving out to him."

Mary Beth started to ask a question. Biggie held up his hand to stop her and continued talking, "Whenever Donald dies, call my attorney friend. He'll have some brothers from my old group show up and guard you. Donald's relatives may not be happy when they find out you inherit everything. I'll talk to him about evicting all the family off your property. He'll also be able to help you subdivide it and sell the lots for you."

Mary Beth was shocked, "Why are you doing this for me?"

Biggie replied, "Because I respect you. Life dealt you and Charlie hard hands. Neither of you has whined or complained. Both of you are doing what you need to do to survive."

Mary Beth asked, "When's your birthday? If you can do all that for me, I'll bake you a birthday cake every year for the rest of your life."

Biggie face split in a wide toothy grin, "You do that, that's a fair trade. Make it a chocolate layer cake and take it to that attorney. He'll git it to me the same day."

# 31

Later in the week, the family arrived from Alabama for Mama's funeral. There were lots of stories of remembrance as the men hung out in the cockfighting barn and drank moonshine. Donald Miller told Charlie to ask his mother how many chickens she needed for that night's dinner. He added, "Whatever she needs, you get her that many and cut their heads off for her. She and the women can clean them, but you're big enough to kill em now."

Charlie said, "I've never killed chickens. Mom has never let me watch."

Shaking his head, Donald asked, "How old are you, thirteen?"

"Yes, sir."

"Ridiculous, mollycoddling you like that. I've gotta talk to that woman. Hank, go show Charlie how the chicken gets on the table."

Hank and Charlie went to the hen house. They collected four fat hens and took them into the woods to a chopping block. The chopping block was a big old stump with two large nails driven into the top.

Charlie stepped back to watch, and Hank said, "Oh no, I know how to do this. I've butchered hundreds of birds in my time. I don't intend to get all bloody for the funeral wake."

Hank told Charlie, "Take the bird by its feet and stretch it out with its neck between the two nails. Bend the nails over the chicken's neck so it can't get away. When you've done that, all you have to do is whack off its head with the hatchet."

Just as Charlie raised the hatchet, Hank said, "Get a good grip on those feet, and start spinning as soon as you whack her."

With one chop, Charlie took the chicken's head off and started screaming and spinning in circles. The headless chicken was flapping its wings and spewing blood out its neck. Charlie kept spinning and yelling until the bird had lost all its blood and quit flopping. He then dropped it into the waiting bucket and turned to his uncle, Hank.

Hank was howling in laughter. "Charlie, when you're done, you'll need a shower and fresh clothes. You're covered in blood."

Continuing to laugh, he pointed at Charlie and said, "And, it looks like you got something growing inside those trousers."

Charlie blushed as he looked down at his erection.

Hank said, "You need to let the cute girl I see flirting with you at the school bus stop, show you what to do with that little pecker."

Hank left Charlie to butcher the rest of the chickens.

# 32

A few weeks later, Mary Beth revisited Charlie and Biggie. She thanked Biggie for having his attorney friend draft all the paperwork. She'd divorced Charlie and married his father. There had been no celebration or honeymoon. She convinced Donald to stand in front of the local justice of the peace by the age-old method of threatening to withhold sex.

Making conversation, she told Charlie about the teasing Little Charlie was getting for getting an erection while butchering chickens. She mentioned he seemed to enjoy the butchering since he was always asking if they needed any chickens for dinner.

Charlie and Biggie both jumped out of their chairs. Biggie was pacing around the small visitors' area, and Charlie was pounding his fist into the wall while cursing. The guard entered the room, and Biggie waved him off.

Frowning, Mary Beth asked, "What's the big deal? You guys are acting like a thirteen-year-old boy getting a 'hard-on' is a horrible crime."

Charlie said, "You've got to get control of him while you can. This facility is full of serial rapists and serial murderers. What they have in common was torturing small animals while they were children, and using that torture as sexual stimulation. You have got to have an iron control of him and my family who is around him. Put an end to all of the teasing, and don't let him do any more butchering. Don't let him go back to the barn for the cockfights or dog fights. Dad will think you're turning him into a sissy, but you've got to do it."

Mary Beth did just that and turned into a controlling mother. She ceased complying with Donald and his boys. She was like a ferocious mother bear protecting her cub. The family all thought she was a bitch, and she didn't give a damn.

NOTHING WORKED. When Little Charlie was fifteen, he convinced a neighbor girl to come look at their pretty chickens. He told her they were prize-winning fighting cocks and were beautiful. While he had her in the barn, he attacked her. He appeared more interested in beating her than he was in raping her, although, he raped her while she was unconscious. When Mary Beth found them, he was attempting to burn the girl with a soldering iron.

Mary Beth called 911 for both the police and an ambulance. Little Charlie received ten years in the Oregon Youth Correctional Facility. When he turned 18, they agreed to parole him for good behavior if he would go straight into the Navy. The problem was the Navy had gotten picky about accepting enlistees with a serious criminal record. Mary Beth helped him work through the appeal processes for six months before she found a recruiter who needed to meet his quota. The recruiter helped Charlie fudge on his records.

# 33

AUGUST 2014

*Rebel Villa, the Philippines*

The villa on the former pineapple plantation was on fire. Sporadic gunfire occurred on the coast road and the country road to the guerrilla camp. The SEALS were mopping up all resistance. The presidential command had been no prisoners and no witnesses.

Roman's last words to Jimmy before fading into unconsciousness were for the team to watch its back. Jimmy knew Roman was worried, other than the team itself; there were no witnesses to the action which had occurred. If the members of their unit died, there would be no witnesses to the secret battle and assassinations.

The medic, Andy Baker, said, "Chief, we gotta get him out of here. If we aren't careful, he's gonna bleed out. It's gonna be touch and go as it is. We can't wait."

Jimmy, however, remembered Roman's remarks, "Petty Officer Harper, get over here. Go with the commander. Watch his back. Don't give up your weapons for anyone until I get there. Keep your eyes on everyone who approaches him. If their activities look suspicious, no matter who they are, stop them. If they don't stop, shoot them."

Looking at the medic, he asked both he and Petty Officer Harper, "Are my orders understood?"

They both responded with a crisp, "Yes, Chief." Four team members carried Roman's litter to the shore for evacuation.

Jimmy next ordered all the members of platoons 1 and 2 who had taken part in the action at the villa and the bridge, to always be with a fellow squad member when they returned to the ship.

JIMMY GOT the bodies in the body retrieval bags to the morgue and secured the money, placing it in chests. The chests were identical to other containers of SEAL equipment. Jimmy hid them in plain sight in the SEAL ready room with exercise mats on them.

Jimmy placed a sticker on them, which said, Top Secret, Eyes Only, Lt. Commander Nelson. There was always an off-duty SEAL sitting on the containers. It was an impressive sight at 1100 pounds of cash.

The bodies of the admiral and the ambassador, along with Amber and the fallen SEALS, went to the shipboard morgue. The team securing the coastal road faced overwhelming odds and sustained huge losses. Jimmy was happy the responsibility of explaining those deaths belonged to an individual with a higher pay grade than his own.

JIMMY RETURNED to the ship moments behind Roman. He delegated the cleanup chores to the surviving members of platoons 1 and 2. They locked the doors of the ready room and stood guard until his return.

Jimmy raced into the small shipboard hospital just as a doctor was preparing an IV for Roman. The doctor looked up at a black-garbed SEAL, with his hand on a knife. Jimmy had streaks of black grease on his face, and blood covered him although he had no visible wounds. He reeked of gun smoke.

Chief Stockade spoke in a cold threatening voice, "Doctor, I hope what you're about to do is legitimate. I assume it is. I will also assume there are no air bubbles in that syringe. Let me be clear if Lt. Commander Nelson dies, so do you. Do we understand each other?"

The doctor stepped back with wide eyes. He looked at Jimmy, "I'll do my best. I want him to him live, Chief." He started an IV solution of normal saline. "However, his injuries are life-threatening. He needs airlifted to the carrier and flown stateside. I cannot guarantee he will live."

Jimmy opened the hospital door, grabbed the nearest sailor walking past, and demanded, "Sailor, do you recognize me?"

Standing at rigid attention with his back to the wall, the sailor stammered, "Yes, Chief Warrant Officer."

"Good, you have got just five minutes to get Master Chief Petty Officer O'Brien and Sergeant Major Hamilton down here. Do I make myself clear?"

"Yes, Chief," the sailor said, frozen in place. Respect and fear both tinged his voice.

"Then why are you still here? Get going." Chief Stockade roared.

# 34

Chief O'Brien was the top-ranking member of the Navy enlisted personnel on board ship, and Sergeant Major Hamilton was the highest-ranking enlisted Marine on board ship. They were not officers, but as paygrades E-9, they earned more than junior officers, and senior officers deferred to their experience.

As the doctor and corpsmen readied Roman for his flight, Chief O'Brien walked in the door.

"What's going on, Jimmy, my boy, that you scared the crap out of my sailor?" While asking that, he walked over to Roman, and stroked his forehead, "Is the scuttlebutt I heard true, then?"

Jimmy and Chief O'Brien walked to a corner of the room and held a quiet conversation. "Not to worry, Jimmy. I'll have his back till he can watch it himself. The chief's network will take care of him."

The Sergeant Major of the Marine contingent on the destroyer, Wayne Hamilton, barged in the door. "What's up? What's the hell's so urgent?"

Moments later, the corpsmen placed Roman on the medevac helicopter for the flight to the carrier. An armed Marine gunnery sergeant stood by his side, watching every action taken with the unconscious SEAL. In the gunnery sergeant's left hand was a locked athletic bag which he placed next to Roman. He put an elastic wrist band with the key on Roman's wrist. What the sergeant didn't know was that in the bag was $100,000 of contraband money and a tape recorder Jimmy recovered from Amber's body.

At each transfer point, a new set of guards with no official orders stepped forward. Roman's transfer from the destroyer to the aircraft carrier and to the medevac plane taking him to his final destination of Bethesda Naval Hospital was flawless. The chief's good old boy network provided a guard every step of the way. If anyone asked, they were informed it was an honor guard. The guards also volunteered, they were providing the service on their own leave time.

# 35

SEPTEMBER 2014

*Bethesda Naval Hospital*

Roman was recovering. Six of the SEALS in his command died in the action, with their deaths reported as a 'training accident.' Amber and their child were gone forever. Bridger, from all reports, was a wreck over the children who died when his bomb destroyed the bridge containing the school bus with both militants and children.

Roman's team had resisted efforts to break them up and reassign them into other units. They were, for now, still intact as a unit. The Navy redirected their destroyer to Pearl Harbor. Jimmy had moved the money out of the containers into 15 backpacks, one for himself and each member of his team who survived the fight. As soon as the ship docked, he lined them up in a formation and marched them off. Jimmy had a bus waiting, which conveyed them to a Brinks Armored Car office in Honolulu. He met with the manager and sent all 15 backpacks to the Brinks office nearest the Bethesda Hospital. He marked the shipment for pickup by Commander Nelson.

The team then returned and re-boarded the ship. No one besides Jimmy knew where he shipped the bags. He was prepared to explain that their departure and return from the ship had been the final step of a top-secret mission and that he was following the orders of Commander Nelson to complete the mission. No questions were asked.

THE MEDICAL DOCTORS and therapists at Bethesda had been excellent. Yet, without a word being said, Roman knew he had an ever-present, around the clock, guard. They could call themselves an honor guard, but everyone knew armed guard duty when they saw it.

One evening, ten days after Roman's arrival, there was noise down the hallway from his private room, which caught his attention. He could hear a small group being escorted down the hall and stopping in front of his room. Looking out his open doorway, he realized his armed guard was nose to nose with another armed guard.

That guard, however, appeared to be Secret Service. Four men in dark suits and wearing earbuds were standing outside the door. The one in command requested that Roman's guard step aside and surrender his weapon. The demand was refused.

Roman struggled to his feet and tried to stand at attention, facing the door. His hospital gown was open in the rear with no way for him to close it. He heard a voice with a Texas twang say, "Why doesn't everyone stand easy?"

Speaking to the Secret Service agent, the voice said, "Vince, I think this gentleman is ok keeping his weapon. I'm sure with all the ribbons on his chest; he's on our side."

"Yes, sir."

# 36

**Roman's hospital room**

Roman struggled to stand at attention. His face pinched with pain as he reached a halfway vertical position. He knew anyone passing his window on the outside could look in and see his bare ass. There was nothing he could do about that. He watched, President Alex Myers, slip past all the guards and walk-in. He looked tired.

President Myers said, "Sit, Commander, sit before you fall. I came by to chat with you and see how you're doing."

Roman's crisp, "I'm well, sir," wasn't congruent with his fragile appearance.

President Myers looked long and hard at Roman, "No, you aren't well. You may get better, but you aren't well now. You're bent over and shaky just standing there, and you've got pain lines around your eyes. Let's both sit. I want to chat with you, and I don't feel like standing and don't think you can. The way you are shaking, I think you've got two more minutes before you fall down." Saying that President Myers sat and waved Roman to a chair.

With relief, Roman eased himself into a chair close to the bed.

"First, Commander, I came by to thank you in person. Your mission, which cost so many lives, was vital to U.S. interests abroad. You may have heard President Duerte signed a long-term lease for the return of Subic Bay Naval Station and Clark Air Force Base. He was ecstatic when I informed him we became aware of a meeting attended by all the rebel leaders. I told him we took action on his behalf and wiped out all his opposition. We are now on excellent terms, and I have high hopes for improved relations between our two countries."

Roman nodded and said, "I heard on television that you met with President Duerte again and signed the leases. That was good news."

The president said, "Your country cannot know what happened, but I've read the debriefing of everyone involved, including your own. I understand you're now a legend in the SEALS. No one appears to know the exact reason, or what you did, but I know you're spoken of with awe."

Glancing out the door, the president could see the two sets of guards glaring at each other. "I've heard about your 'honor guard.' I hear you have had members of all the services Special Operations teams standing outside your door. That says a lot about you as a person and the respect you have across all branches of the military. I understand how and why the members of your team worried about your safety. You need to know you aren't at risk from me."

Roman responded, "I hope not, sir."

"Is there anything I should know about your mission that didn't make it into your written report?" President Myers asked.

Roman replied, "Yes, sir, there was."

"What was that?" President Myers asked frowning.

# 37

"Chief Warrant Officer Stockade found this taped to Lt. Commander Amber Sabatino's abdomen," Roman said, pulling out a digital body recorder. He pushed play, and together they listened to the voice of the admiral, the ambassador, and the rebel leader Alvarez linking the President of the United States to the assassination planning and payment of the $50 million. From the recording, it was impossible to tell if they were referencing former President Potts or the current President Myers.

"Not clear who they are talking about, is it, Commander?" The president asked.

"No, sir."

With a little hesitation, President Myers asked again, "Was there anything else that didn't make it into your report, Commander?"

Roman paused as he took a breath and said, "Yes, sir."

"I'm afraid to ask what that might be."

Roman reached behind him, and from the athletic bag, removed a shrink-wrapped package of one hundred $100 bills. Ten thousand dollars was in the package, and the bag appeared to contain several similar packets. He handed the bundle to President Myers, who pursed his lips as he looked at it.

Roman answered, "I know you ordered me to not worry about the $50 million, sir. But, we recovered the money. It didn't burn in the villa fire. It is secure, guarded, and awaiting your orders of what to do with it. I was hesitant to report it up my normal chain of command. I feared it might lead to too many unanswerable questions. What would you like me to do with it, sir? It is non-traceable, unaccounted for money, isn't it?"

The president sat back in his chair and looked Roman in the eyes. Roman returned the look with no emotion crossing his face. After a moment, the president grinned at Roman. "You know you're a true son-of-a-bitch, don't you?"

"Yes, sir, I've heard that before, sir."

President Myers continued looking at Roman, who knew he was being sized up by a world leader. The president said, "I know it's hard to keep your composure in that silly hospital gown, but you're doing a good job."

Roman did his best not to grin, although the president was.

The president continued, "Ok, you've done a lot of thinking on this. What do you think we should do with this money that doesn't exist?"

Roman said, "Well, sir, I think this would be a good time to disband my SEAL team, at least platoons 1 and 2 who took part in the action in the villa itself. It would be difficult to stay in the SEALS and keep a secret of this magnitude. It was a significant firefight. I think you should advance everyone in rank to their twenty-year retirement point and then give them a Medical Discharge today with full benefits.

"I'm not a lawyer, but I think a presidential executive order could distribute the nonexistent money as a tax-free medical severance package. That way, no one would have an issue with trying to explain to the IRS, or anyone else, where the money came from. Which I'm sure we can agree, no one needs to hear about."

The president sat there for a long time looking at Roman, who looked back at him with no expression. The president sighed, "You know, you're an s.o.b., but I like you. I wouldn't want to play poker against you. I've dealt with world leaders who were easier to read than you are."

The president thought for another minute then said, "I'll order your team back here to Bethesda for pre-retirement physicals. I need you to impress on your team what top-secret and classified mean. Understood?"

Roman nodded, "Yes, sir."

# 38

ONE WEEK LATER

Roman's SEAL team had arrived at Bethesda Naval Hospital.

Andy, Roger, and Bridger were talking to Jimmy, "Come on, Chief. None of us believe you don't know why the entire team is at Bethesda. You always know everything. What's up? The only issue we've all got is Bridger's hangover."

He replied, "No clue. I'll see the Commander in a few minutes. I'm sure he'll know what's going on."

Everyone clamored to see Roman.

Jimmy said, holding up a hand to quiet them, "No, I need to see him alone first and talk to him about Amber."

Everyone was silent at that.

A short time later, Jimmy walked into Roman's room and closed the door behind him. Roman used his cane to help himself stand. It surprised him to see Jimmy coming to hug him with tears in his eyes.

Jimmy said, "I'm sorry, Roman, I screwed up. I let you down. I let Amber down. My doing everything by the book cost Amber her life. I don't know if you'll ever be able to forgive me. I know I won't be able to forgive myself."

Roman said, "Don't give me that crap. I've read all the reports from everyone on the team. You and I both know there was nothing more you could've done. You and the team were following all the proper protocols. One more minute and you would have saved her life. You had no control over the explosion on the coast road, which triggered the action."

With a sad look on his face, he continued, "There's more than enough guilt to go around over Amber, but you are not guilty of her death. I, however, failed to tell her years ago, I loved her. We should have married and gotten out of the service a long time ago. I was having too much fun playing war games all over the world. I've learned a brutal lesson at Amber's expense. In the future, if I care for a woman, I'll tell her right away, and not just assume we have all the time in the world."

They discussed Roman's health for a while, and then Roman explained the upcoming retirement process he'd negotiated with the president.

Jimmy said, "Let me get this straight, we're getting released from the service now, but with the rank, we would hold if we stayed in until our twenty-year retirement point? We get a medical discharge with full benefits and full retirement pay? And we get a tax free severance package paid out of the money we captured?"

"Yes," Roman agreed.

"Hot shit, that's great," Jimmy said with his eyes lighting up. He processed what that would mean in his life, "All we've to do is stay classified forever? If that's true, I'm in. I can't wait to get new threads. How do we divide up the money?"

Roman replied, "I don't care."

"Don't be stupid. Let me talk to the guys about it. Fourteen guys survived the fight, plus you and me. No matter how you slice it, it will be a lot of money. I'll get team consensus and explain the program to everyone."

# 39

The team met in a conference room at the hospital. Petty Officer First Class Roger Harper explained to Roman that the consensus was to establish a ratio based not on future pay grades, like the retirement pay Roman had negotiated for them, but on their current pay rates. Petty Officer Harper was the team's "bean counter." He was taking a series of online college courses working towards his degree in accounting. Anytime anyone on the team had an issue with money or budgeting, they would turn to Roger for his help.

Using the formula Petty Officer Roger Harper devised, those making the highest pay, like Roman and Jimmy, would get the largest percentage of the money. However, the unanimous decision of the team was, $10 million was to come off the top for Lt. Commander Nelson, and $1 million for Chief Stockade before Roger applied the percentages.

When Roman protested, Bridger stood up and said, "Sir, with all due respect, half the team wanted to give it all to you. We wouldn't be here if you hadn't done what you did. There's no question you saved my life. We've not talked with you about it, but we all owe you our lives. They ambushed us and surrounded us at the bridge. In another few minutes, we would have all been dead. A little extra in your kitty is ok with all of us. You deserve it. Besides, even the newest, youngest men, with the smallest percentage, get to retire now with full retirement pay, and a minimum of a seven-figure severance package. Get real. We owe you big time. Nobody begrudges you the money, and none of us would feel right if we don't do it this way. "

The conversation continued long into the night. At last, Roman got everyone's attention. "Your family and friends will ask how, and why, you're home. They'll want to know why you're receiving retirement pay at such a young age and where you got all the money. Tell them the reason is 'classified.' You know what that means. Think about a great big red TOP SECRET stamp right in the middle of your forehead. Joke about it with whoever asks, but remember, what we did will remain classified, top-secret, for your entire lives because of national security concerns. Got it?" He asked.

Everyone around the table nodded or said, "Yes, sir."

"Remember, part of the TOP SECRET stamp is not telling anyone how much money you're coming home with. It's ok to tell them you're getting a medical early retirement discharge. You can't tell them anything about the cash. I'm concerned many of you will go wild, spending money you have never had before. I've got a friend I'll be talking to. I have confidence he knows more about money than any of us. If any of you want to talk to him about how to invest it, I'll get you his phone number."

Pain filtered across Roman's face as he shifted in his chair, "We have been through a lot of hairy times together. We will all have emotional issues to deal with. If you would like to retire to a laid back area, I'd invite you to come to visit me. I live in a remote canyon country in Oregon with green forests and running rivers. We get cell phone coverage about half the time, and our internet runs at the speed of molasses pouring out of a jar. You might like the old-time country feel, and we could all support each other. My door is open to you."

Bridger said, "I'm in. I have nowhere else to go and no one to do it with. You guys are my family. I'll come. I think I'll catch a little R and R first, and then I'll show up."

Anthony Baker also piped up, "Thanks for the invitation. I think Brutus and I'll visit my folks for a while, but they'll tire of me in a few months. I think after that, Brutus and I might enjoy Oregon. Whenever you talk about it, you make it sound wonderful. I grew up a city kid in Pittsburg, but I don't think that's a place a big dog like Brutus would be happy. With the Attack and Search training Brutus has, he'd be taking down all the gangbangers and dealers who are carrying concealed weapons. But I'll bet he'd like the forests and farmland you talk about. Expect us to show up at least for a visit."

Several of the others said they would come for a visit, if not to relocate.

Bridger piped up, "You guys will always be the brothers I never had. So we never lose track of who we are I think we should all get a team tattoo. I got mine today; the artist did a great job. What I told him was I wanted something which every time I look at it, it will remind me of who I am at my core, what I have done, and what I'm capable of."

Smoke said, "Let's see it. What'd you get?"

Bridger rolled up his right sleeve. On the inside of his right forearm, where a long sleeve shirt would cover it, was a small tattoo in vivid reds and blues. It showed a seal in blue, the seal's right flipper turned into an arm with a clenched fist holding a dagger. The dagger was bright red and dripping blood.

Smoke said, "I like it. I'm in."

The rest of the team was enthusiastic. Roman said, "I never saw myself with a tattoo in my life, but we're a team forever. If the team wants Bridger's tat, I'll go to the parlor as soon as I can get an afternoon pass out of the hospital."

# 40

NOVEMBER 1, 2014

The entire team stood at attention in the Oval Office as the president presented a Unit Citation to each member. Each of those wounded in action also received a Purple Heart. He then pinned the Silver Star on Chief Stockade and presented Lt. Commander Nelson the Presidential Medal of Honor. He thanked them for their activities in the Philippines and their overall careers in the service.

As the president finished, he commented, "If any of you get bored in retirement, I've got another department which could use your skills."

Jimmy asked, "What department, and doing what?"

The president replied, "Special duty in the U.S. Marshal's Office."

"Interesting," Jimmy thought about it for a moment and said, "Give me a few months to see if I get bored."

The official White House photographer wandered around the room, snapping casual photos. He made sure everyone had a photo of the president pinning on their medal and shaking his hand. Roman tried to hide his cane whenever the photographer came by. Moving to a reception area, a discrete staff served the team petite finger foods and desserts. President Myers came over and shook Roman's hand.

THE PRESIDENT SAID, "I'm grateful for what you and your team did. I know it was a great sacrifice for you and your team, and I'm sorry for your personal loss."

Roman replied, "Thank you, sir."

"You need to know I do not begrudge you the money." President Myers said, "I'm, however, concerned. Is there anything you or your team needs which will help you or them reintegrate back into your communities?"

Roman replied, "Yes, sir, if you're offering, there are several areas we could use your help. Each of us will have a lot of cash. The challenge will be how to get that into our bank accounts. You can't just walk into a bank and open an account with the amounts of cash we have without warning bells going off. Also, I'm concerned they'll go crazy spending money which will raise questions and be a waste. I'd like help in getting investment accounts opened for them, which will keep their principal intact and give them lifetime income. But I think the biggest immediate hurdle for most of us is getting the initial deposits into a bank account."

Roman gave a lopsided grin, "It may seem strange, but for myself, I'd like to find out how I go about buying old gold coins."

"How many?"

"I don't know, sir. I suppose about the size of a lunch bucket. The rumor is my grandfather, before he died, hid a lunch bucket of gold coins in the walls of our old warehouse. I want to 'find Grandpa Bill's gold.'"

President Myers roared with laughter.

# 41

The next day Assistant Secretary of the Treasury McMahon came by Roman's hospital room with a personal banker from the Pentagon Federal Credit Union to open a bank account. They agreed Roman would send his team in to see the banker in the following days to open their accounts. Once all the accounts were open, Brinks could deliver the money for a deposit. The banker also agreed to their use of a secure area at the credit union, which would have a machine to count the money. Petty Officer Roger Harper was in charge of dividing up the money. He'd already computed the agreed-upon ratios and percentages. Everyone knew what percentage of the funds each would get. The problem was they didn't have an actual count of the money. Once Brinks delivered the money to a secure room at the credit union, they would count it, divide it up, and make deposits to everyone's accounts.

When the banker left, the assistant secretary McMahon said, with a little frost to his voice, "I understand I'm also to sell you, $100,000 in old gold coins. I'm not sure how you got the president to agree to do this. I have never heard of this happening before. We are selling you the coins for what they are valued at on our books, $100,000. If you were to sell them at today's prices, the value is $2.4 Million."

Roman's voice rose, "What? I don't understand."

"I would say the president must like you, except this goes beyond liking you. This is unheard of, I don't understand why he would do this, but he has."

Roman said, "I don't know either."

"My job is to follow presidential orders, not second guess his decisions. Would you like to accept delivery at the credit union for access to a safe deposit box, or would you prefer Brinks? It will weigh about 180 pounds. You also must give me a check for $100,000 payable to the U.S. Treasury."

Roman was in a daze. "Brinks at 10 a.m. tomorrow will be fine."

ROMAN COULDN'T WRAP his head around his wealth. He knew at one level his family timber business, Nelson Timber, owned thousands of acres of timber. His share of that was in the millions, but that wasn't anything he considered wealth. Those were trees and land. You couldn't spend them as his father had learned when the real estate bubble collapsed in 2008.

What he had now, however, was real money, spendable money. Roman tried to add it up. He knew he was getting $10 million off the top of the "Discharge Bonus," but his share of the rest was another $4 million. Which would be $14 million. He had never expected the president to authorize his purchasing, at book value, the gold coins worth another $2.4 million. Altogether, he now had $16.4 million.

In anguish, he put his head in his hands. He wanted to cry but couldn't. He thought, "Not bad for a poor country boy, but I'd trade it all in a heartbeat if it would bring Amber and our child back and erase my guilt."

Not able to sleep, he pulled out a yellow legal pad and started thinking about what could go wrong and how to protect himself against those issues. Grandfather Bill had explained to Roman that to avoid the loss of purchasing power due to inflation, he needed to invest the money. From those mountain top conversations, Roman also knew that depositing the money in the bank on interest was a guaranteed loss of purchasing power after inflation and taxes.

Ruling out individual stocks or bonds as being more risk than he wanted to take. Roman decided on an investment in mutual funds. He didn't need growth out of his investments. He wanted a reasonable income, but his primary goal was the safety of his principal. Thinking about that brought him to bond mutual funds. The problem he could see with those, however, was even a small return would produce a huge tax bill with the volume of money he had.

He looked at his watch. It was close to midnight. Pulling up the internet on his laptop, he searched for a high school friend, Greg. Roman had bumped into him half a dozen times since graduation. According to his mother, Greg was now a branch manager with a large financial services company.

Roman found Greg's number and thought, "Its 9 p.m. in Oregon, and for the amount of money I'm talking about, I'm sure it's not too late to call."

"Hello, this is Greg," said the voice on the phone.

"Hey Greg, It's Roman."

"Roman, it's been years. I haven't seen you since your dad's funeral. Where you at? Are you home? What's going on?"

His friend fired questions without giving Roman a chance to answer. Roman laughed at hearing a friendly non-military voice who knew him so well. They chatted for a while, and then Roman got to the point.

"I'll be home to stay soon. I have come into a large sum of money. It's more money than I'll ever need and needs to be invested. Nothing risky. The principal needs protected, and I want it to produce steady income."

"What income tax bracket are you in?"

"I'll be in the highest tax bracket. What would you suggest?"

Greg paused a moment before asking, "When you say home to stay, does that mean here in Oregon, or just home to the states? Where will your official residence be?"

"I'll be coming home to Gates."

"Great, I look forward to having you over for dinner and meeting my wife and kids. To answer your question, I'd suggest a mutual fund which invests in municipal bonds issued inside the State of Oregon. That would make all the income free of both federal and state tax. Translating that into normal language, you would have no taxes on your income. None. Can you access the internet?"

Roman replied, "Yes."

Greg said, "I'll text you the website of the fund I'm thinking of. We can both jump on the same site so you can see what I'm talking about."

Roman said, "Got it, and is what I see correct? Has this fund averaged what I'm seeing for the last thirty years? Are those returns really free of tax?"

Greg answered, "Yup, shocking, huh? Now it hasn't done that the last few years, with what's been going on in the economy. You can see the ten-year record. But remember, that's Double Tax-Free income, which means no taxes to pay, nothing to the State of Oregon or IRS."

Roman thought for a minute and said, "Excellent, can you handle it for me?"

Greg said, "Absolutely."

"Good, I'll let you know when I'm arriving. It will be a few weeks yet," said Roman.

Roman continued his planning. He thought, "I'll keep the $10 Million intact. I'll invest it with Greg in Salem. If the fund he's talking about produces anywhere close to what it has done in the past, it should send me a check for $25,000 to $50,000 per month tax-free, on top of my military retirement. If I don't get stupid like my dad did and mortgage our property, I'll be fine forever."

# 42

DECEMBER 2014

Roman used the time after the award ceremony in the Oval Office, and prior to discharge, to focus on rehabilitating his body. The therapists at Bethesda were the best. Rehabbing "wounded warriors" was their business, and they were good at it.

Roman thought, "No matter how you slice it or dice it, that's what I am. I'm a 'wounded warrior.'"

He spent hours each day in physical therapy to recover from the damage the sniper and shrapnel wounds had inflicted upon his body. The doctor's also ordered him to spend considerable time with a psychiatrist to deal with all the emotional issues coming up for him. He had flashbacks every night. Those nightmares were worse than walking with a cane, or the pain of his body healing and relearning its regular activities.

In his final week before discharge, Roman dreaded seeing his psychiatrist for the last time. He knew the counselor would continue to probe and expose the raw emotional wounds which Roman was doing his best to bury.

Doctor Davies asked, "How are you feeling?"

"Fine."

"Still having the nightmares?"

"Yes."

"How often?"

"Every night."

"Have you cried over Amber's death yet?"

"No."

"I see, let's try this a different way. What emotions have you felt since our last visit?"

"Numbness."

"Please expand on your answer. Give me more than one word, Commander. What else?"

"Emptiness," then seeing the frown on the Doctor's face, he added, "Looking at my emotions is like looking at the food on a refrigerator shelf. I see they are there, but I have no emotional connection to them. My feelings are numb, and I don't think that's a bad thing."

Doctor Davies said, "Not feeling your emotions is a bad thing for your future, Commander. This is your last visit before discharge. You don't seem to have many emotional issues with what you have seen and done in your career. You are, however, still struggling to deal with the deaths of your fiancée and child. I don't know how your fiancée and child died. But, I know you blame yourself. Your flashbacks are related to her death. You have a sense of failure and guilt over her death. Until you work through the issues surrounding their loss, I expect the flashbacks will continue. You can't ignore this or it will haunt you forever, Commander."

Roman's stomach tightened as Doctor Davies summarized his status. He thought, "I know that. I don't need him to tell me what I already know." Sitting ramrod straight in his chair, his face was expressionless.

The doctor continued, "You have told me there was nothing you could do to save her, and that your team did everything possible. You, however, are still internalizing her death as your fault."

"Shit," Roman thought, "What's this guy know about guilt? He sounds like he's reading out of a textbook."

Doctor Davies sighed as he took off his glasses, rubbed the bridge of his nose, and stared at Roman, "Look, Roman, you're the commander. You accept responsibility for all of your team. This is a great concept for the military, but it isn't serving you now as you heal and prepare to transition to civilian life. Your emotional health going forward will require you to accept responsibility for what you can control and to let go of the responsibility for what you can't control."

Roman said in a stiff voice, "Yes, sir, I know that, sir."

The doctor said, "You still don't trust me, do you? Your body language tells me you have shut this conversation down and are just going through the motions of this exit visit."

"That's not true, sir."

"Then, what is true?"

"What you're saying sounds good in the textbook, but how do I put all that to use in real life?"

"You're hard wired to serve and protect others. It is part of what makes you who you are. I suggest you quit blaming yourself and thinking about what could have been, and start thinking about what comes next. Stop focusing on what happened and internalizing those events by replaying them in your mind, because the outcome will be the same every time. Start thinking about what comes next. Shift your focus to others. Look outside yourself. Get engaged in other people's lives. Start looking for ways to help and serve others. Whenever you get stuck in a negative loop, I suggest you ask yourself a series of questions."

"What questions?"

Doctor Davies handed Roman a page full of typed questions. "I'm not giving you a prescription for any pills to take home. I want you to take this home and ask yourself these questions every day."

Roman started reading them out loud. "What is good about this situation? How can I help? How can I serve? What can I do for the people around me? What's my next step forward? What am I grateful for right now? Who do I love, and who loves me?"

Doctor Davies said, "I want you to read these out loud each morning and each night. Your thoughts will then move on to other things, but at the subconscious level, your mind will continue to seek an answer to the questions you've asked. My best advice is to ask a question which will have a positive answer, and an answer which will make you feel good."

Roman looked at the page again. He frowned at the doctor. "That's it? That seems too simple."

"Things that seem easy generally aren't."

# 43

Roman spent his time either in therapy or planning.

Roman thought, "People get so wrapped up in the doing of life, they don't have time to plan life. I have the gift of time. I should be wise in how I spend it."

He scribbled on several yellow legal pads. One pad was for each subject. The first pad was for his thoughts on how to integrate his money back into his bank account and community without triggering questions. The next pad was for his worries about his team and other veterans and how he could support them. There was a pad for his mother and sister and the best way to help them. The family business, Nelson Bait and Tackle wasn't producing enough income, and his mother was struggling with her finances.

Dr. Davies said he needed to allow himself to feel a range of emotions and to focus on generating positive feelings. Roman did his physical therapy as instructed, and he read his list of questions morning and night with the same discipline. He felt his first twinge of excitement as he started to dream about building a home. Feeling excitement was better than feeling numb. Intensifying his dreaming and planning grew his enthusiasm. He'd known for years where he would construct his home. His grandfather helped him pick out the site when he was a young boy. Sketching the house plan on paper, Roman asked himself, "What could go wrong? What're the worst things that could happen? How can I design my home for those worst-case scenarios?"

Going on the internet and doing a little research on his home state shocked him. Labeling a new yellow pad for each of the catastrophic events he found, which could happen in Oregon, he thought, "OK, crap can happen. Now, how do I prepare for it?"

Yellow pads piled up, dealing with fire and drought. Another tablet covered the risk of being snow or icebound on his mountain top. Roman even thought about earthquakes, floods, and landslides.

"What could happen, and how can I prepare in advance?" was his mantra.

He received a medical discharge on the first of December. He scheduled an appointment a few days later at the veteran's facility in Portland to discover the resources available to him. The president's assistant came by before his discharge handing Roman his itinerary, including his appointment schedule at the Portland VA. With the White House handling Roman's airplane tickets, lodging, and transportation to the hotel in Portland, Roman also received a personal message from the president, wishing him well.

Roman was hesitant to go home. It had been a few years since he'd seen his family. Emailing he'd been "banged up" in an incident, he didn't allude to the severity. No one at home knew about his discharge. A few days in Portland before heading home sounded good.

For the first time, he looked at where the president's assistant booked him a room. He whistled when he saw it was The Benson, in downtown Portland. It was within walking distance of the Pearl District, Pioneer Square, and all of downtown Portland. Constructed in 1913, it was the home away from home for presidents and CEOs when visiting Portland. The European style was luxurious, but the atmosphere was quiet wealth.

Roman emailed his sister, Alexia. "I'm headed home, staying at The Benson tomorrow night. How about dinner after you get done with the six o'clock broadcast? I'm sure The Benson has an attached restaurant. Can you make 7:30? Please don't tell Mom. I want to surprise her."

# 44

With a three hour time change flying from the East Coast to the West Coast, it was possible to leave Ronald Reagan International Airport just prior to 8 a.m. and have it still just be late morning as he exited the plane in Portland.

He thought, “I could get used to traveling first class.”

The president’s assistant booked him first class. It was a new experience for Roman. The seats had been bigger and more comfortable, but the walk from the gate where his plane landed to baggage claim was long and arduous. His pride wouldn’t allow him to call and ask for a porter with a wheelchair. Wherever he could, he used the moveable stairway.

He thought, “I shouldn’t have thrown away my cane before heading for Oregon.”

When he arrived at the baggage claim carousel, he found a limo driver holding a placard with his name on it. The driver got his bags and escorted him to a car, which was double-parked, waiting for him. They arrived at The Benson without incident, but as soon as the car arrived, a horde of bellhops descended upon him. Surprise registered on Roman’s face when he was told he didn’t need a credit card to check-in. The front desk person said, "No, sir. We will bill your room expenses to the White House."

The bellman escorted him to the presidential suite. When Roman protested the correctness of the room assignment, the bellman said, "The reservation is correct, sir. This is your suite. Thank you for your service."

Roman couldn't help thinking with a smile, "Maybe I should blackmail the president for another $50 million."

After making the dinner reservation for 7:30 with his sister, he figured before he could do anything else, he needed a truck to drive. With that in mind, he ordered an Uber to drop him off at a local car dealership. While at Bethesda Naval Hospital, he'd shopped the competing dealerships online purchase programs. He frowned at what new trucks cost, but with a grimace, he'd thought, "I've earned all the bells and whistles."

Roman had spent his career in the military wearing: desert camo, jungle camo, or nighttime black on black. It was time to come out of the shadows. He'd decided all his vehicles going forward, would be bright red; he ordered a beautiful F-250, XLT Super Duty, 4x4 Crew Cab.

The Uber driver dropped him off at the dealership's front door, where the internet sales manager was eager to show him his new truck. His vehicle was parked in a prominent spot by the door, the salesman said, "Isn't she a beauty?'

"Gorgeous"

"Why don't you get behind the wheel and I'll point out all the features."

Struggling to step into the truck, Roman thought, "This is so embarrassing."

The salesman was so busy pointing out and explaining all the features he didn't notice the effort it took Roman to get into the truck. "Drive it off the lot. I'll show you how everything works as you drive around. I've got your invoice here. It's got everything you ordered. You can see the gray leather interior you special ordered."

"Very classy."

Inside his head, however, he was thinking, "Wow. Amber would have loved it."

Roman drove through the neighborhood streets near the dealership. The salesman pointed out the integrated sound system, which could handle blue-tooth devices and multiple exterior cameras. As Roman pulled back into the dealership, the salesman said, "Drives like a dream, doesn't it?"

"Yes, although at the moment it felt like I was driving a big shoebox. I need to let you park it. I haven't worried about scratching a vehicle for a long time."

Roman told the salesman, "Keep your eyes open in a few months for an older 4x4 pickup, which could take the rugged use of going back and forth on a rough logging road. I'll be building my home on the top of a mountain, which only has a dirt track to the top. I'll want a rig that it won't bother me if I put a scratch in it, or dent a fender. That can wait until spring, for now, I just needed a big boy truck to go home in."

"Will do, I'll call you if something comes in."

Roman also wanted a few unique options added onto the truck. He arranged to have it delivered to him at The Benson on the day he headed home. He got a ride back to the hotel and, in exhaustion, lay down on his bed to relax. Sleep arrived in minutes.

When he awakened, it was to his phone beeping that he'd received a text. His sister was bringing her new boyfriend to dinner. Roman was curious. He followed his sister on social media. His computer alerted him whenever she was in the news. The gossip columns talked about her dating an actor, John Dunn. John was filming an action-adventure movie in Portland and taking Alexia to high profile events all over town. Cameramen spotlighted them sitting in the front row of the Portland Trail Blazers home games, or holding hands at an outdoor café. Roman also saw John Dunn's involvement in a physical scuffle at a local bar a week ago.

# 45

Arriving first, Alexia and John sat at their dinner table while waiting for Roman. As the waiter was leaving, John said, "We'll take two shots of Jose Cuervo while we're waiting."

Alexia said, "I don't want to start the night with tequila shots."

"If you don't drink it, I will."

John started complaining about The Benson, "I don't know why the studio is putting me up at such an old place. It's stuffy, and my suite is small. The presidential suite is enormous and over the top posh, but they tell me it's kept open for visiting dignitaries. My agent says this is the most prestigious place in town, but it's just ancient. I even heard the staff this morning saying they thought 'the ghost' would show up today."

Alexia said, "The rooms I've seen here have all been nice."

Ignoring her, John continued his tirade, "Look at this guy approaching us. He's clean enough, but he looks like a crippled up scarecrow. His clothes look like they are two sizes too large. I'll bet he tries to beg money from everyone."

Glancing up, it horrified Alexia to see Roman, "Oh my God." She ran to hug him and introduce him to John.

Alexia was expecting the brother she had known, and bragged of, to John. "What happened to you, are you ok?" she asked. Roman was gaunt, pale, and bent over. His movements were stiff and unsteady.

John said, "Yeah, you look like a street person. If you had a cardboard sign begging for a dollar, you'd fit right in on the street corner."

Roman faked a laugh, and with a grin said, "Well, I did get a little banged up, they tell me I've got a lot of work to do, but I'll be ok."

John replied, "What were you doing, drinking in a foreign port and wrap your car around a light pole?"

Alexia gave him a startled look and snapped at him.

At which point, the maître d' hotel came over, "Commander Nelson? Sir, it's good to see you. I heard The Ghost was in residence. I didn't realize Miss Nelson and Mr. Dunn were with you. Your table is over here. I think you'll find it more comfortable." He led them to a larger, hidden table.

IT SURPRISED Roman to recognize the maître d' was his radioman, 'Dink Lindsay,' from a tour in the Mid-East. As they were switching tables, the maître d' and Roman carried on a discrete conversation, which the others tried to overhear. "I heard a bit of scuttlebutt, sir. I want to give you my condolences."

"Thank you. I don't know what you heard. Just remember, whatever you heard is classified." Roman said, "But, thanks. That means a lot."

The maître d' waived over the waiter to get their orders and told the waiter to give them his exclusive attention.

Alexia was asking what the condolences were for, John was asking about 'The Ghost business,' and Roman was trying to avoid answering all questions. Roman found John tiresome, and his read of his sister was she did too. As they were finishing up dinner, John groaned, "Here come the autograph seekers."

# 46

Roman looked up to see an older, well-dressed individual with two clean-cut, young men a few steps back, approaching the table. The young men were quiet and respectful; each carried a menu and a pen.

The older man identified himself as the general manager of The Benson. "I was just informed that the dinner reservation for Roman Nelson was for Lt. Commander Nelson, our guest in the presidential suite. I want to welcome you to The Benson, Commander. Is your room adequate, and is there anything else you need?"

Roman laughed, "I don't know how, or why, I'm in that room. My entire team could sleep there and have room left over."

As he said that, he observed John Dunn bristling with frustration or rage. John's jaw was clenched, his knuckles were white, gripping his wine glass, and his glare was throwing daggers. Roman noticed Dink stepping to the general manager's side and the two young men, positioning themselves in front of the manager

With irritation in his voice, John asked, "That's a great question, why can he get that suite, and I can't?"

The general manager looked him in the eye and said, "Because sir, the president of the United States called me yesterday and asked me to give Commander Nelson a soft landing from his travels."

He turned to Roman, "Thank you for your service, sir, and wishing you a speedy recovery. If it's not an imposition, these two young men work here. They are both former military. Off duty today, they've been hanging around all day for the chance to meet you. They are hoping you'll autograph a menu. Would you have a moment to say hello?"

Roman struggled to his feet. Both young men stepped forward, hit Attention, and snapped a salute. "The maître'd told us about you, sir. It is an honor to meet you. Would you mind doing an autograph, sir? In case no one believes we met you?"

Roman asked, "What are your names?"

"Mark and Kelly, sir."

Roman started signing his name and rank.

Kelly piped up, "Sir, could you please sign it as 'The Ghost'?"

Roman nodded and continued signing Kelly's menu. His eyes, however, connected with Dink, who frowned and looked at John Dunn. Roman knew Dink was warning him of the trouble he could see developing. Moving to Mark's menu, he was thinking, "What does Alexia see in this guy? I can see him getting drunk and hitting her. There's no way I'm up to handling him yet. My physical therapy needs to gear up to another level."

John burst out with, "What's this ghost bullshit I keep hearing about?"

Both the young men sized him up, then Mark drawled, "Well, the way I hear it, sir. Commander Nelson moves like a ghost, you never see him, you never hear him, and he has a habit of turning other people into ghosts." Alexia blanched, and John got quiet.

WORRIED ABOUT HER BROTHER, Alexia, was finding it impossible to talk to Roman while John was with her. She was also contrasting the respect her brother was receiving and the paparazzi type of attention she received when out with John. John wasn't looking too good.

Alexia asked herself, "Where on earth am I supposed to meet a real man like my brother? It's not in the circles I've been moving in. I wonder if the men I've been meeting are attracted to me because I'm well known in the TV news business. I wonder if that's even true for John. They get their pictures taken when they go out with me. Hmmm, I've been thinking I'm getting my picture taken when I'm out with John, maybe it's the other way around."

With an audible growl at that realization, she organized goodbyes and asked Roman, "When are you going home. When can I tell Mom I saw you?"

"Tomorrow. I've been putting off going home, but I need to go tomorrow. Say nothing yet. I want to surprise her."

# 47

Roman was glad to see his old radioman, the maître d', Dink Lindsay, but it awakened memories of a few years prior and the last action in which Dink took part. The flashback hit as soon as he went to bed and closed his eyes.

He and his team were staged aboard a destroyer in the Arabian Sea. His team's specialty was insertion behind enemy lines, the rescue of hostages, and the elimination of the captors. His team operated in utter secrecy. The Navy didn't want the Taliban or any other group to know they existed.

Roman received orders from his destroyer's skipper to monitor an ongoing situation off the coast of Somalia. A small coastal oil tanker was under attack by pirates, its capture was imminent. Roman was curious why the boat was essential but was under orders to develop contingency plans to recapture the ship and to rescue any hostages.

Looking at the detailed satellite imagery, Roman thought, "Wow, this could be a beautiful resort if the place wasn't rife with terrorist training camps, pirates, religious fanatics, and out-and-out criminals. It has a beautiful beach, looks like fertile ground for agriculture, and has actual houses instead of huts. It's too bad the ordinary people don't stand a chance for a normal life as we know it."

The next day, the skipper of the destroyer ordered the team into action. Roman called the team leaders together for a pre-operation briefing. "Two days ago, pirates based out of Mogadishu hijacked an oil tanker with Sri Lanka registry. They have anchored just offshore and removed the crew to land. The pirates shot two of the seamen in the boarding process. The crew also killed several pirates as they boarded. Which leaves the captain and eight crew members now in captivity."

He projected an image of the tanker on the screen.

"As you know, piracy is an established business on this coastline. Pirates capture a ship and hold the crew as hostages. Sometimes it will be years before the ship's owners or the country of the company owning the vessel pay the ransom."

Pacing in front of the room, he saw heads nodding. He continued, "We've reason to believe in this case the pirates are unhappy. They were not expecting an armed crew to contest the hijacking. They'll be even unhappier tomorrow as they break the news to the family members of the killed pirates. The pirates could start executing people in retribution. Their executions are messy and involve beheadings."

He advanced several slides showing photos of the crew.

"Now, here's the sticky point. The captain is CIA, as are all eight of the other hostages. The ship may be a small coastal tanker, but it is also a CIA spy ship loaded with electronics. They have been delivering oil and gasoline in several of the small coastal harbors, but while there, they have been eavesdropping on whatever they could hear. The CIA was trying to keep tabs on the locals and see if any foreign jihadists show up."

He pressed the remote. The next image on the screen was an overview map, followed by a photo of the anchored tanker. The last picture was of a small house.

"Given who the hostages are, we know where they are. Each of them has a transponder implanted on them, giving us a fix on their location.

"The pirates have not had time to search the ship. When they realize it's a CIA spy ship, it's a certainty the pirates will turn the hostages and the tanker over to the local jihadists. You can then say 'goodbye' to the hostages, and who knows the problems which will come up from the treasure trove of information on the ship's computers."

Looking around the room at the team leadership, Roman asked, "Any questions so far?"

"No, sir."

"This is a complex mission. Two platoons will function on three separate fronts. If any of the three missions malfunctions, it could cause the other two to fail.

I'll lead platoon one. We'll focus on the rescue and recovery of the hostages. Chief Stockade and I'll take squad 1. Lt. Bush will take squad 2. Squad 1 will helicopter to the Fleet Aircraft Carrier, load onto an MC-130 Combat Talon II for a 500-mile flight ending with a High Altitude High Opening (HAHO) parachute drop just off the coast of Somalia as soon as full darkness hits. We'll exit the plane at about 25,000 feet, and if we are lucky, we won't get spotted by enemy radar or missiles."

Roman didn't need to tell the team the high opening of the parachutes was to keep anyone on the ground from hearing the chutes open, or that they would wear oxygen canisters and warm jumpsuits for the altitude.

"Petty Officer Baker, welcome back from training. Going forward, your secondary MOS (military occupational specialty) will continue as our team medic. Your primary MOS will now be as Brutus's handler. Since this will be Brutus's first operation with the team, I'd introduce him to everyone. For this mission, I will attach you and Brutus to squad 1. Brutus has just completed paratroop training. Do you think he is ready for a nighttime HAHO?" Roman asked.

"Absolutely, sir. We are looking forward to our first action together." Most SEAL attack dogs were Belgian Malinois. Brutus, however, was a massive, black, alpha male, German shepherd, trained to alert his handler to the positions of attackers. He also made an exceptional sentry. Andy Baker, in the training program, taught Brutus not to bark but to attack in silence. Brutus would also wear oxygen for the jump.

"Chief Stockade, silence is critical. Equip half of squad 1 with crossbows and sound suppressors on all firearms. You'll be in charge of planning and logistics for the HAHO." Roman continued.

"Yes, sir."

"We will need to drift with our parachutes and a full load of equipment about thirty miles, to a drop zone 10 miles west of Adale, Somalia. The drop zone is within striking distance of the target house, which is just west of Adale, and in the deep desert where no one will observe us.

Adale is about 100 miles north of Mogadishu on the coast of Somalia. We do not know why the pirates took them such a distance from the ship. From our viewpoint, it makes our job simpler because it's more isolated. The hostages are in a remote house about three miles west of Adale in the desert. Which is why we are dropping in instead of coming in from the beach. The beach is wide with white sand. We'll drop in the desert, hot foot it to the rescue point, and if everything goes as planned, make it to the beach for pickup before anyone discovers what's happening."

Again looking at Chief Stockade, he asked, "Questions, Chief?"

"No, sir."

Looking at platoon one's lieutenant, Roman continued, "Lt. Bush, you'll take squad 2. You must make a later High Altitude Low Opening (HALO), drop with three Zodiacs timed for our retrieval off the beach. Our team could all swim out to a rendezvous. Given the eight hostages and the possibility of wounded, I think we may need the capability of loading off the beach. You'll provide the retrieval vehicles, and covering fire as needed for our beach crossing. Any questions, Lieutenant?"

"No, sir."

"Lt. Clark, you'll lead platoon two. You'll helicopter to a Navy Cyclone Class Patrol boat waiting for you just outside the shipping lanes of Mogadishu. They'll have a Zodiac attached to a massive reel of cable on the patrol boat. You'll tow the cable, unreeling it, until you can position yourself out of sight of the tanker. Your dive team needs to continue to unreel the cable underwater until you can tie onto the tanker."

Looking at Lt. Clark, he said, "Take your underwater cutting torches in case you need to cut any anchoring cables. Someone will need to climb the ship and attach our tow cable to the front stanchion. Signal the patrol boat to tow the tanker as soon as the anchor cables are cut. Once it is moving, you should all board and prepare to resist the recapture of our ship."

Pausing for a breath and a sip of coffee, he looked at the assembled team leaders, "Questions before you're dismissed to start your preparations?"

Once again, "No, sir," echoed around the room.

"Then, you're dismissed."

# 48

**Roman's nightmare continued**

Radioman, Dink Lindsay, was the first man out of the MC-130 Combat Talon II, followed in seconds by the entire squad. Dink, as the radioman, ran all the electronic equipment, including the GPS keeping them on target for the drop zone. It was a clear night, with just a sliver of a moon. With their black on sand clothing and black parachutes, they were all but invisible in the night sky.

As they drifted down, parasailing about thirty miles, Roman couldn't help thinking of Africa.

"The United States, using the Army, Navy, or Marines, and now the SEALS has been coming to this damn sand patch since Thomas Jefferson was president. It's even sung in the Marines Hymn, 'from the Halls of Montezuma to the Shores of Tripoli.' Jefferson sent the Navy and Marines into Tripoli after pirates, then we chased Rommel all over North Africa in World War 2, and here we go fighting pirates again in Somalia."

Roman thought, "I don't know what the solution is, but this is crazy."

Everyone in squad 1 landed in the drop zone, gathered their chutes, and stored them in their packs. This put each of their packs, including equipment and ammo, at over 80 pounds, which was the weight at which they conducted their training runs. Gathering everything up was to eliminate anyone finding their parachutes and discovering the SEALS presence.

With Petty Officer Baker and Brutus running point, the squad formed two columns to jog down the dirt track. Chief Stockade and Commander Nelson were on either side of Brutus with their Digital Night Vision Goggles and crossbows with Thermal Scopes. With a column spaced behind each of them, they jogged forward in silence. It was 6.7 miles to the rescue point.

Special Operation Teams around the world trained with and used crossbows where silence was essential. They could fire a bolt (arrow) in close to total silence. A knife was the only weapon that produced no sound. Rifles and pistols with sound suppressors still produced sound. The movies would have you think with a silencer there would only be a small poof of air. That wasn't true. Sound suppression systems reduced the sound but didn't remove it. The crossbow for close-range work produced less noise, with only a small ping of the equipment release.

Petty Officer Lindsay ran the GPS to keep them on track for their destination.

When they were a half-mile from the target, Petty Officer Andy Baker halted and crouched next to Brutus. The entire squad dispersed into a skirmish line. Everyone was wearing helmets with an integrated communication system, allowing them to hear and speak to each other.

Petty Officer Baker was on the air, "Bandits to the right, Brutus has them pointed at 1 o'clock, sir."

Roman said, "Let me see what we've got," he moved forward. "It's a sentry outside the encampment smoking a cigarette."

Roman watched the sentry smoking his cigarette put his AK-47 down, and facing a bush unzip his trousers to go the bathroom. "Dumb, dumb, dumb," he thought as he fired the crossbow. The sentry went down without a sound. Roman went closer and filled the barrel of the AK-47 with dirt. He was hoping if a friend of the sentry picked it up and fired it without cleaning it, the barrel would explode.

Chief Stockade whispered into the CommNet, "Sentry two is down."

Roman gave the command to Petty Officer Baker, "Advance with Brutus, Baker."

With Brutus smelling out anyone, not on their team, they advanced into the encampment. Chief Stockade and Commander Nelson were moving in front of the squad eliminating all sentries. The crossbows were back on their shoulders. It was close contact knife work.

Roman watched as Chief Stockade directed the surrounding of the house containing the hostages. The chief placed microphones on the windows and scanned the home with thermal imaging. Body heat showing through the walls showed 11 people inside the house. The squad took up guard positions while the commander and chief strategized.

"I've got two additional heat sources, Commander. Petty Officer Lindsay, does the readout from the transponders show they are all here?"

"Yes, Chief."

Roman said, "Then we've two remaining sentries. It looks to me like they are in the first room just inside the door. How do you read it, Chief?"

Chief Stockade agreed, "The same sir, I'd say we go straight in the door, I go left, and you go right?"

"Agreed. On three, 1, 2, 3", Roman counted.

Roman tested the doorknob. It was unlocked. Opening the door, he and Chief Stockade stepped in and shot the sentries relaxing on a sofa.

Closing the door, he quieted the uproar from the hostages. Even with the sound suppression and subsonic ammo, the noise was loud in the closed house.

In a commanding voice, he shouted, "Quiet, U.S. Navy SEALS here. Captain, are your men all mobile?"

The hostage captain replied, "Yes, I believe so. They roughed us up, but there are no traumatic injuries."

"Good, then Captain, I want absolute silence from your crew. We will leave anyone who makes a noise behind. Is that understood?" Roman demanded in his command voice. The shocked hostages nodded.

"Ok, Captain," Roman continued, "As we leave, I want you in the front of your crew, your men single file behind you and inside a column of my men. Remember, not a sound. If we wave you to the ground, get down until told to move. Speaking of moving, we need to move now. We need to cross the beach before dawn. Let's go."

The hostages were all CIA, and to a large extent, they were in decent physical condition. When the encampment was behind them, Roman sent Petty Officer Baker with Brutus ranging further in the front; they picked the pace up to a jog.

It was the dark before the dawn, which lasted for just moments. The sun was about to break over the Eastern horizon, and the mosques would start calling people for morning prayers in minutes. Roman's now large group was on the edge of the white sand beach just south of Adale. The nearest house was a few hundred yards away.

Roman spoke into his hands' free radio, "Squad 1 ready for pickup with nine hostages. Make it soon, Lieutenant."

"Three minutes, Commander. Go ahead and cross the beach, we'll be there."

Roman turned to the hostages as Chief Stockade removed from his pack nine sand-colored ground cloths. They were close to the color of the beach. He got the hostages on their hands and knees, crawling for the water with the camo cloth over their backs. They spaced a SEAL to accompany every other hostage. Roman and the chief allowed the hostages a significant head start before they started crawling across the wide beach.

The tide was in, cutting the distance to crawl in half. Just as the first individuals reached the water, three Zodiacs paddled in. Spinning at the last second, they backed into the beach. Out of the Zodiacs jumped squad 2, in high alert. They were an intimidating sight to the uninitiated. The first two Zodiacs' were paddling away as Roman, and the chief stepped into the last one.

Gunfire rang out, and the SEALS returned fire on full auto. The pirates, jihadists, or whoever was shooting dove for the ground. The Zodiacs fired up their motors and left with a thunderous roar and an enormous rooster tail of a wake.

# 49

After rescuing the hostages and securing the tanker, the rescue team and the hostages were picked up by a Cyclone Class Patrol Boat. The boat delivered them at flank speed to Mumbai, India, for an in-depth debriefing of the operation.

With the debriefings completed, the Navy granted the entire team shore leave until transportation back to their destroyer was available. They were in a local bayfront restaurant bar eating hot Indian food and drinking copious quantities of beer.

Roman asked, "What happened when you retook the ship?"

To a large extent, they said, "No big deal."

The team cut the anchor cable at the stern with no problem. The anchor chain in the bow was an old fashioned chain with wrist-thick links. Looking like it would take too long to cut, Petty Officer Bridger, the team's demolitions expert, placed a demo charge on two of the links to blow the chain apart.

While they were waiting on the timer to blow the charge, the entire platoon went up the opposite side of the tanker. When the small explosion sounded, the team went over the side rails and dispatched the pirates who rushed to look in the water and see what the noise was. There was a token crew left on board. The team threw them overboard.

Once the tanker was undertow, the Navy sent a crew back to man the ship. The SEALS got back in their Zodiac and went to the patrol boat for further orders. The orders were to head for Mumbai to rendezvous with their team for mission debriefings.

Too much beer leads to one set of ground rules in men's storytelling. The first liar doesn't have a chance.

Squad 1 told the story of the rescue. Petty Officer Anthony Baker talked about the approach to the house holding the hostages. "These two are amazing," referring to Chief Stockade and Commander Nelson. Everyone got silent to listen to the story.

Andy rubbed Brutus's ears, "Brutus alerts on Commander Nelson's side. I look to see if he got the alert, and he signals he did, and then he's gone. I didn't see him walk away or crawl away. He was just gone. One minute he's there, the next he's not. I never saw him leave. Pretty soon, he's back. It was like he was a frigging ghost out collecting souls."

"And this guy," pointing at Chief Stockade, "it's the same with him, Brutus alerts. He signals he got the alert, and then it was like watching smoke disappear. You know how you can have a fire, there's smoke blowing around, and then it's just gone. That's how he was. I'd be watching him. He'd take one step, maybe two, and then just like smoke in the air, he'd disappear."

With one more round of drinks, they created a new identity. Smoke and The Ghost were now the unofficial names of Chief Stockade and Commander Nelson. The names were given in respect and never used when commanding officers were around. By the next day, however, everyone on the destroyer knew who The Ghost and Smoke were, and they'd heard rumors of how those names were earned.

# 50

EARLY DECEMBER 2014

**The Benson, Portland**

Roman's room phone rang, and the front desk said, "Commander, your new truck was just delivered to valet parking. It's a beauty. The dealership needs you to come down and sign for the delivery."

Prior to delivery, Roman requested several options be installed on his new truck. He was specific about what he wanted. The dealer installed a gun safe inside the console, which could hold any small arms he would ever need to leave in the truck.

Mounted on each side of the truck bed were two large, sophisticated chrome safes. They looked like a contractor's chrome tool chests. Roman called them gun safes on steroids. Five feet long, they were large enough to hold any rifles he would ever wish to transport. They were also ideal for safekeeping cash. No one would suspect they were anything other than a contractor's toolboxes.

The dealer installed a locking rifle rack in the rear window, and a winch completed the front bumper. The customized front bumper was a large black pipe affair capable of pushing small logs or small vehicles without damaging the truck. Roman knew, in his home town, the rifle rack and winch were standard equipment in a man's rig. He wanted to fit in. A question he'd pondered at Bethesda was how to become just, "one of the boys." He thought his high school buddies would like his new rig.

Before heading down I-5, he stopped at Brink's Armored Car headquarters to pick up a package. Brinks near Bethesda shipped his cash to Brinks in Portland for Roman to pick up. He put that into his truck safe.

The drive home was familiar, and yet, it wasn't. The roads were in the same place, but many of the buildings were different. There was new construction visible, and familiar buildings had aged. It had been several years since he'd been home. He could excuse it as deployments on the other side of the world, but he'd made his leave time choices to vacation around the Mediterranean and the South Pacific instead of going home.

Most of those times, he'd been with Amber. With a grin, he remembered, not always. Regardless of whom he'd been with or where, the truth was, he hadn't been home. He couldn't help feeling guilty over that. He wondered if part of the reason he hadn't been home was he'd known when he came home the next time, after his father's funeral, he would feel an obligation to stay.

Passing through Salem, he stopped at the office of Greg, his friend, who was an Investment Advisor. He completed the paperwork to set up the investment they'd been discussing over the phone. Completing the process didn't take long.

Roman didn't need his money to grow. He had plenty of money. He wanted to protect the principle and minimize the taxes on his earnings. Greg set it up for him to receive income each month. Roman figured if he couldn't live off that, his spending level was foolish.

As he went through Mill City and knew he was minutes from home, his heart rate increased. His knuckles were white, gripping the steering wheel. Excited, with butterflies in his stomach, he took a calming breath. His mind captured that moment, and he knew the butterflies and excitement were good. His counselor had worked with him on being aware of what his feelings were. Since the action in the Philippines and all the deaths which occurred, his emotions were numb. The counselor tried to put him on anti-depressants, but Roman refused. He knew they would help, but worried they would make his mind less sharp. First, he wanted to see if he could make it without the drugs. They had forced him to take too many pain pills while he was at Bethesda. Roman was trying to eliminate any which were not essential.

Roman's hometown of Gates looked a little older, and a little more decrepit than he remembered. He pulled into the empty parking lot of Nelson Bait and Tackle. The building looked deserted. Looking around, he realized, all the buildings in the town were 100 plus years old and dilapidated.

Gates was an old logging and farm town, founded in 1882. It hugged both the Linn and Marion County sides of the North Santiam River with a small bridge connecting the two sides of the city. Fewer than 500 people were living there when Roman was a boy, and thirty years later, there were still fewer than 500 people. Highway 22, passing through Gates, was the busiest of the State's five highways crossing the Cascade mountain range. It connected Salem, the state capital, sitting in the Central Willamette Valley with Central Oregon's High Desert playground.

Roman thought, "Let's see if I can get out of this truck without falling. I hope no one is watching." He did his best, holding onto the grab bar over the door. Forcing himself to stand straight and to walk without a limp, he made his way into the store. The door chimed. He could hear it ring in the small living quarters behind the store. While he waited for his mother to appear, he looked around. It didn't look good. Half the store's lights were burned out, and the store felt a little damp and chilly. The for-sale stock was sparse and looked like merchandise from a few years ago. All visible signs pointed to poverty.

Looking at everything with critical eyes, he thought, "I was already feeling guilty. I never suspected things were this bad." Feeling he had failed his mother, Roman's guilt level went through the roof.

He heard his mother, Rose, coming out of her living quarters and turned around. She gasped, and put her hand to her mouth, and started to cry. He wanted to cry with her, but couldn't so, he held her. She had aged. She was tall and slender, which is where he got his height. Dressed in simple clothes, her shoulder-length hair was now gray. She looked shopworn and tired. She cried, and he rocked her back and forth as he allowed his guilt to wash over him.

Rose asked, "What happened to you?"

"Mom, all I can say is I got a little banged up. Beyond that, the answer to all your questions will be, 'I can't tell you because the answer is classified.'"

"That's silly, were you in an accident?"

"Mom, how I got hurt, where I was, when it happened, and all the other questions you want to ask, are all questions I can't answer. I'm sorry."

"That's ridiculous. I'm your mother. I have a right to know."

Roman suggested, "Mom, could we go into the living quarters and sit? I'm not sure how long I can stand out here."

Roman knew the statement highlighting his fragility would stop her questions like none of his classified statements would. Sitting in his dad's recliner in the living room, Roman started asking questions about family members, the store, and the day-to-day life in Gates.

Part of him wanted to share with his mother about Amber and their child. Another part didn't want to discuss it. He knew she would have endless questions, none of which he could answer. Being truthful with himself, Roman accepted he didn't want to face the emotions churning inside him surrounding Amber's death. He was happy to bury them.

As the afternoon progressed, Roman knew he would need to pry to get her to discuss the state of her finances. Knowing how private a person she was, he thought she would be reluctant to discuss money with him. It surprised him when she opened up about her finances with just a few questions.

"Well, you know when the Great Recession of 2008 hit, your dad and I lost the big home we raised you in. It broke your dad's heart when we moved here, into the back room of the tackle shop. You know your father. He was always dreaming and trying to move forward. While he was alive, his old timber and fishing buddies would come by and spend a little money. They'd chat for a while and strike a deal on a few acres of timber. It was never big money, but enough to keep the wolf away. When your dad died, I knew nothing about the timber. Those little deals we relied on just went away."

She continued, "I've been living on the checks you and Alexia send each month. Every once in a while, one of your dad's timber buddies comes by and rents some of the heavy equipment we still have in the back of the building. They'll rent it for a few weeks, do a project, and then bring it back. None of them want to buy the equipment. It's too expensive. But it's good for them and good for me to rent it to them."

Roman hugged his mother, "Mom, I'm sorry. I did not understand things were this bad, or I'd have come home earlier to help. Please accept my apologies, but I'm home now, Mom. You never have to worry about money again. It's time for me to step up. I promise I'll make things up to you."

In his mind, his guilt level climbed another notch as he realized his ability to help his mother with her finances was, to no small extent, the result of his last action in the Philippines in which Amber died. If the operation had not occurred, he would have left the service with no retirement pay and none of the cash. He would have returned with no income and the need to find a job to support himself, Amber, their child, and his mother.

Roman felt excited about what he could do for his mother, and yet guilty over feeling excited. He thought, "Amber, forgive me. I'm happy for the good I can do with the money, but I'd rather be introducing you to my mother. My mother would have been over the moon to meet you and realize she would be a grandmother."

## 51

**Later that evening**

Alexia picked up a take and bake pizza, and showed up at her mother's home unannounced. The catching up with each other questions was over. They were approaching the point of talking about 'what now'?"

Alexia brought up last evening's dinner with John, "After you and I left, he continued to sit at the bar tossing back tequilas. The bartender cut him off after a couple of hours, which infuriated him. I think he believes he's the action/adventure character he plays in the movies. He forgets he has a stunt double, and someone else writes all his clever lines. Your maître d friend came over to calm everybody down, and John attacked him."

Roman groaned, "How bad was it?"

Alexia grinned, "John got a broken nose, a broken arm, and kicked out of The Benson forever. Oh yeah, and I told him I never wanted to see him again. Thank goodness I never slept with the bastard."

Mrs. Nelson was shocked, "Alexia, I've never heard you talk like that."

Roman winked at Alexia and changed the subject and said, "I've gone through the entire building this afternoon. You have been living here for several years, Mom, but it's not a house. It is a huge old warehouse with a store and living quarters in the front. The last time I was out back was when Grandpa Bill was teaching me how to drive a bulldozer. The store and your living quarters are just a small part of the building. It looks like the building is still in good shape. It's dry and solid, no matter how old it is. Which has been fortunate for all the logging and construction equipment stored in the back. Thank goodness, everyone around here is honest. There are several million dollars of equipment just sitting back there with the keys in them."

Rose said, "I know it wasn't smart, but I didn't know what keys went with what equipment. Your Uncle Russ came by and sorted them out, and I told him just to put the right keys in the right piece of equipment. I didn't think anybody would come in and drive off a dozer." She laughed and added, "And, it wouldn't be too hard to find them in this town if they did."

Roman grinned and said, "You're right. We've been lucky in lots of ways. Grandpa Bill put this property, the property across the road with the boat ramp, all that equipment, and the timber property into our family trust. Dad couldn't mortgage it. Therefore, he didn't lose it when everything collapsed. I think it's time for us to go back into business."

Rose shook her head, "How are we going to do that? We don't have any money to run a business. After you recover, maybe you can get a good job working for the state of Oregon. Something steady with benefits."

Roman looked at Alexia, who was also shaking her head and said, "I'm right. Our family made all its money by owning businesses, including timber. We need to do this. You know the Navy discharged me. I look like hell and move like an eighty-year-old man. But, if I continue with my physical therapy, they say I'll make it back to 100%. What you don't know is, with my discharge, I received a sizeable medical settlement. I get full retirement pay for life and have more money than I will ever need."

Alexia responded, "Good, I don't know how much you got, but I hope it's a bunch. Just looking at the pain you're in, and how difficult it is for you to move, I hate to think of the injuries you've suffered. I know you won't tell Mom or me what happened, but I think the Navy owes you big time."

Roman grinned at her and said, "I have confidence I'll be ok. It will take some work, but I'll get there. Back to the topic on the table, Mom, I can afford to buy you another real home. Where would you like to live? Maybe in Mill City or Stayton?"

"Save your money, Roman. There's no need to buy me a house. You may have gotten discharged with some money, but you shouldn't spend it on me. Save it for a home for yourself."

Roman grinned and shook his head, "Mom, I've got enough. I can get you a nice place, and have enough left for me."

"You don't understand. I don't want to leave here."

Roman and Alexia both raised their eyebrows and said, "What? Why not?"

"When we moved into the store, it was devastating for your father and me, but everyone in Gates made us welcome. You know we're related to half the town. I've lived nowhere this neighborly. My lady friends drop by every day. This may be a dump compared to our old home, but I have more contact with friends and family than ever. I don't want to move again. Maybe we can repaint a little and perhaps put down new carpeting, but this is where I belong. This is home now."

Roman couldn't believe it. The money to buy his mother a lovely new home was available, and she didn't want it. He also knew he couldn't leave her living the way she was.

Clarifying he asked, "Let me get this straight, you won't let me buy you a home, but you'll let me clean up this place a bit? Maybe new paint, any deferred maintenance, maybe a light version of the renovations I see on the home improvement show that's on your TV nonstop? That would all be ok? You just don't want to leave the store?"

"Roman, I'm just thrilled you're home. You don't have to do anything, but if you want to, that would be fine."

Roman continued, "Alexia, I'm not up to walking around for hours looking at home improvement stores. Could you take Mom into Salem tomorrow? Visit wherever you need to, but bring me back a bunch of paint samples. Maybe get an idea of what Mom likes in color schemes, fixtures, and materials? I want to inspect the old place and consider the ideas which are running around in my head. I'm thinking of putting money into both the Tackle Shop and the Timber Company. You two go shopping, and I'll walk around the warehouse and plot and scheme on my ideas." He said with a ghost of a smile.

The entire time Roman and his mother and sister were eating pizza and talking, the phone kept ringing, or people kept dropping by. The town grapevine knew was Roman was back, and his aunts, uncles, and cousins came out of the woodwork to say hello.

His mother was in her glory telling everyone, over and over, that yes, her prodigal son was home to stay, and the stories flying around town about his injuries were exaggerated.

Roman asked, "How do they know I'm back and hurt?"

Rose answered, "I don't know, they just do. I told your Aunt Alice, she told your cousin Dennis and Uncle Russ, beyond that, who knows?"

Touched, Roman drummed his fingers on the table, realizing he had another reason for feeling guilty. As a young man, he had joined the Navy and abandoned his hometown relationships. What was becoming clear to him was, he might have abandoned his small town, but his small town hadn't abandoned him.

Feeling the 'black dog' of depression sink its teeth in him, he thought, "Guilt, guilt, and more guilt."

Roman forced his mind to the psychologist, Doctor Davies. "What did he tell me to do when my emotions hit the skids?" Pulling the typed questions from his wallet, he looked at it in silence. He saw the questions. "OK, what is good about this situation? Well, I found out people in town still care about me. What can I do for the people around me? That's gotta be fixing my mom's living situation. How can

I help or serve? Who loves me, who do I love, and what's my next step forward?"

Grinning, he told his mother, "I'd forgotten how connected you are to everyone in town. I want to rent the Community Hall tomorrow night and have a 'pie and coffee' get together. You can invite everyone in town you think I might know. That way, I can see everyone all at once and get reintegrated back into the community. I'll even run into Costco in the morning and pick up pies so it won't be any work for you."

THE NEXT NIGHT he saw family, high school classmates, and people from around town who he hadn't seen in years. He displayed an interest in everyone, tried to catch up on what they were all doing, and who they married or divorced. He also paid particular attention to their careers. His cousin Dennis, three months ago, quit a sizeable architectural firm he worked for in Portland and started his own firm in Salem.

Roman asked him, "Could you pop by the store for a quiet conversation about a project tomorrow morning while Mom and Alexia go shopping?"

"Sure, what time?"

"How about 10 ish?"

When Dennis agreed, Roman added, "This is important. I need to ask you for total secrecy. I don't want anyone to know what I'm doing until the project's done. What I want to do will be a surprise for my mother. If your mother knows anything, she will tell my mother. If anyone else knows anything, they'll also tell your mother or mine. So, no one can know anything until we're done."

When Dennis showed up for coffee in the morning, Alexia was suspicious, but got her mother into the car and took her shopping.

Roman walked Dennis through the store, the living quarters, and then the connected warehouse and shop outback.

Dennis was in awe of the structure. "This building is enormous.

I've never been back in here. I don't think there's a glulam beam in the entire building. And, look at the size of those beams. Those aren't just beams. Those are trees someone dried and shaped as beams. The posts are 3-4 feet in diameter. I haven't seen a 2"x4" stud in the place, they are all 2"x6s" and 2"x12s," and they are all a full rough cut dimensional lumber. You can't buy those today. Roman, you could tear this place down and sell the wood for a fortune. I'll bet your mom's living quarters, and the store, have the same beams and posts up there, just covered over with old lath and plaster."

Roman could hear Dennis getting excited as he talked about the warehouse. When Dennis said, "It's too bad, this building is in Gates and not Portland."

Roman asked, "Why?"

"Because it has so many design possibilities. There are many ways to refurbish this building. All those huge open beams create a rustic look. It's just won't be cost-effective in Gates."

Roman explained, "Well, Dennis, you know my dad's side of the family has been in timber for generations. I'm not sure which family member built the building. I'm sure it predates Grandpa Bill. But, if you own an unlimited supply of trees and your own sawmill, you could season your trees and cut them to size, and all it would cost you is the labor. Cutting the lumber for the building probably happened in the off-seasons when they were creating work for the employees. We are just lucky today that it gives us the ability to build what we want inside it at a fraction of new construction cost."

"What do you want to do with it?"

As Roman explained, a shocked Dennis asked, "Let me get this straight. You're talking about gutting the store and your mom's living quarters, pushing her living quarters back into the warehouse, and building an entire house inside the warehouse?"

Roman nodded.

Dennis continued, "Then you want to redo the store and expand it into where your mom's living quarters are now?"

Each time he paused for a breath, Roman nodded.

Dennis clarified, "You want it all high end, top of the line? You want me to design it, and function as the architect in charge, hire the contractors, and supervise their work?" Again Roman nodded.

"Well Roman, as Grandpa Bill used to say, 'it ain't nuthin but money.' To pull all that off and do it in one month will take a lot of money. Have you talked to a banker about the project, and are you sure you want to drop that kind of money in Gates? You could never get your money back out if you wanted to sell."

Roman replied, "The big question for me is, are you up to the job? Do you have the skills and experience to run a project like this?"

"Absolutely."

"You remember you have pledged total secrecy?"

Dennis nodded, and Roman continued, "There's no need to check with a banker. I'll be funding this with cash. I may look like a wreck, but I'm coming home to re-engage with my family and community. Consider this your audition, Dennis. I plan on a major expansion of the store and the merchandise it sells. I'm thinking about building a showroom across the road for boats and quads. I'll be building a nice house up on the mountain on Hawkeye Ridge, and reopening Nelson Timber. There will be quite a few projects in the upcoming years. If I got my mother out of the house on January 2nd, could you be prepared to have crews working 24/7 and finish in a month?"

Dennis thought about it and said, "If I start the design process today, and work around the clock, I can have a preliminary drawing for you tomorrow. If that looks good, we can get permits. The bigger issue may be finding workers."

"Get the designs done, and get the permits. Plan on spending the day after Christmas with me. Maybe I can get you a crew of workers."

## 52

CHRISTMAS DAY

Alexia stumbled out of her tiny closet of a bedroom and headed for the coffee pot. Mrs. Nelson was busy fixing breakfast when Alexia noticed Roman's sleeping bag on the couch was empty.

Mrs. Nelson answered her question, "I think he's out in the shop exercising. He's out there all hours of the day and night doing strange exercises. I don't know when he sleeps. I have people every day tell me they've seen him out on the highway jogging up and down the canyon all night long in the dark."

She continued, "He claims he's doing his rehabilitation exercises, but I think he can't sleep. It's like an Asian restaurant. I think its Thai something, Tai Chi, Tai Kwando, something oriental. It looks like what I think of as Chinese ballet. But, whatever he's doing, he always surfaces about the time breakfast hits the table."

~

"It's Tai Chi, Mom," Roman said, walking in and gave them both a good morning hug.

His mother was right. Difficulty sleeping at night was the least of his problems. He awakened every night, out of breath and dripping with sweat from his nightmares. Roman didn't have a strength issue with his body. Flexibility was the issue. Disciplining himself to move his body, triggered excruciating pain.

He took long jog/walks up the deserted road at night. It was difficult enough walking, but he tried to simulate jogging. In the shop, he found a lot of large diameter rope, similar to ship hawsers. Hanging it from the walls and from post to post, he tried climbing the wall straight up using the rope. When he achieved that, he attempted to cross the room using the rope strung between the posts. It was agony. He would catnap throughout the day to make up for the sleep he was missing at night.

Roman, Alexia, and their mother hadn't shared a Christmas morning in years. Their small family had forgotten how to act like a family. After breakfast, they exchanged gifts.

Alexia handed Roman a small package. As he opened it, she explained, "When we were kids, there was always a knife on your belt or in your pocket. I haven't seen you use a knife since you got back. I hope you still like knives. Merry Christmas."

In his hand was a fancy new Leatherman Utility knife. Threading it onto his belt, Roman roared with laughter. It was his first heartfelt laugh in months. He thought, "If she only knew."

His gift to Alexia was a stunning diamond and emerald necklace and earring set. She gasped, "Oh my God" when she opened her present. He minimized the cost and told her she was so beautiful she deserved diamonds.

Roman sat on the edge of the sofa, balancing his coffee cup on his knees when it was his mother's turn to open a present. A slight grin flickered across his mouth as she struggled with the wrapping paper on the large package. A full smile made its way to his face hearing her gasp at a beautiful coffee-colored leather suitcase set from Coach. Each piece she opened contained another smaller piece. The last part held two envelopes. Inside the first envelope were reservations for herself and her sister, Roman's Aunt Alice, to a resort in Scottsdale, Arizona, for an entire month.

The envelope included airplane tickets for both and a BMW convertible rental car to use when they got there. Before purchasing the tickets, he had asked his Aunt Alice if she could clear her schedule to help her sister for a month.

Aunt Alice said, "You know I'd help her with anything, but what does she need?"

"She needs you to go somewhere with her for a month. I can't tell you anymore because she doesn't know yet."

"It sounds like an intervention thing you hear about, but Rose doesn't have any addictions. I'd know if she did."

"It's not an intervention, Aunt Alice. She is just going to need your help with something for a month."

"Well, all right," Aunt Alice said, intrigued.

The resort was all-inclusive. The plane tickets were for January 2nd, one week later.

Also included in the envelope for his mother were the paint chips she had chosen. Roman told her that was his way of letting her know he intended to do her home makeover while she was in Scottsdale, Arizona. He commented he was moving better but was still slow. He thought it might take him a month working at his pace to get all the painting done.

The second envelope contained twenty crisp $100 bills. Roman said that was pre-trip shopping money to make sure his mother and Aunt Alice had appropriate clothing for the resort. He didn't tell them there would be other envelopes on their pillows when they arrived for spending money.

Mrs. Nelson was crying and protesting all at the same time. She came up with all the reasons she couldn't go. "Roman, you can't do this. This is way too expensive. I can't allow you to pay for this. This is too much."

His response, "Mom, I can afford it, and I spent the money. There are no refunds. You both go and enjoy yourselves, or the money goes to waste."

She continued coming up with excuses, "I have nothing to wear to a fancy place like this. I won't fit in there. A small-town country girl like me will be out of place. I'd need a haircut. Do you think Cindy could get me in for a trim?"

Just then, the phone rang. It was Aunt Alice, hysterical with excitement. Roman had given her a set of luggage as well with duplicates of everything. Neither sister could have heard the other. They were both talking and giggling at the same time.

Roman, his mother Rose, and Alexia left for Christmas dinner at Aunt Alice and Uncle Russ's. His cousin Dennis would also be there with his family. Roman watched his mother and Aunt Alice race back and forth between the kitchen and Roses bedroom closet. The smells wafting from the kitchen confirmed Christmas dinner was cooking. He could see each trip into the clothes closet left them frustrated.

Roman's eyes twinkled as he heard his mother say to her sister, "We need to go shopping in Portland. I haven't had to have any dressy clothes for years. Everything from when Roman's dad and I would go traveling is out of style. I've got all kinds of rain gear for our Oregon winters, but nothing for sitting at a swimming pool."

The men were all gathered around watching the football game. Roman was standing in the doorframe, holding up the wall. Alexia came up to Roman and touching the new necklace around her neck, asked, "Can you afford all this? I'm hoping these are cubic zirconium and not real diamonds. A month in Scottsdale is pricey. I'm willing to chip in for half of everything."

Roman hugged her and said, "No need to worry, it's pocket change. The diamonds are real. You deserve them and wear them well. What I'll need is a lot of your help and guidance this next month. There will be a lot of activity at the old place while Mom's gone."

"What's going on?"

"You'll see when they leave, but I'll need a lot of your help," he said with a mischievous glint in his eyes.

~

Rose and Aunt Alice were scurrying back and forth. They'd spend time in the kitchen preparing Christmas dinner and setting the table. They would then rush into Aunt Alice's bedroom to continue picking out what she should take on the trip.

Rose confided to her sister, "I'm worried about Roman. I don't know what happened to him. I don't know if he was in a car accident or if someone shot him. He avoids answering anything and tells me what happened is classified.' He looks horrible. I'm worried about him. And where did he get all this money? Did you see the necklace he bought his sister? And this trip, oh my gosh."

Aunt Alice tried to calm down her sister, "You know, however, he came up with the money. It's legitimate. Roman is a good boy. He always has been. There isn't a dishonest bone in his body. He may not tell us where he got the money, or how he was injured, but we need to trust him and love him. Part of trusting him is believing him when he says he is will be ok. I've heard him tell everyone, if he does his physical therapy, he will be fine. We've got to believe that is true. We both know he is a driven personality, so he'll be motivated to do his therapy."

# 53

The day after Christmas, Rose and Alice headed for the shopping mall, and Roman took his cousin Dennis with him to the VA hospital in Portland.

The doctor welcomed Roman and commented, "You're moving better. Your range of motion is greater, and your overall mobility has improved."

After exchanging pleasantries, the doctor asked the obvious question, "Why are you here? Do you need help with something?"

Roman responded, "Yes, but not with therapy. Perhaps we can help each other. When I was in Bethesda, I discovered there were many Vets at the hospital in addiction recovery programs or physical therapy programs who would benefit from working while going through their programs, but there were no jobs available. Is that true here as well?"

The doctor replied, "Absolutely."

Roman continued, "I can help quite a few of them with a job if you can provide their supervision, counseling, and therapy after work hours."

"How's that? What kind of jobs?"

"I need a large group of men with construction experience. I'm hoping to find vets with framing, hand demolition, plumbing, electrical, and both rough and finish carpentry skills. They'll live inside a large warehouse while renovating it. I'll provide camp cots and food. Even though it is a warehouse, we'll have space heaters. It will be noisy since we'll be running crews, 24/7."

The doctor sat at his desk and said, "Let me make some notes."

Roman continued, "Let them know before they decide, I will run it like the military. The warehouse is inside a fenced area, and we'll have a guard dog patrolling for drugs. If that sounds too tough, the program isn't for them. Period. For those who accept, I'll pay wages, provide food and lodging, and you can provide counselors for those off shift. They could regard it as an in-patient treatment center where they also can work and get paid."

The doctor asked, "Where would this be?"

"It's in my hometown, a little community called Gates. It's a remote area, up the Santiam Canyon."

"I'm familiar with Gates. I go camping and whitewater rafting in that area every summer."

"You can tell them they'll have no visitors and no communication for about a month. I don't want anyone to know what the project is until it's finished. What do you think? Would anyone here have the skills I'm looking for, and would this be helpful for them?"

The doctor gave Roman a wide grin. "Commander, you know this would be fabulous. I'd have to scramble to provide staffing and cover their per diem costs for staying out of town, but it would be worth it for the benefit to the men in the addiction programs. I think it would be beneficial to get them working and earning while conquering their therapy and addiction issues. A man's self-worth, self-image, and self-confidence are connected to his work identity. If the ability to work is missing, it makes the recovery process that much harder. This could be a huge help. Why don't you and your cousin head over to the cafeteria for coffee and a cinnamon roll? I'll put an announcement out on the public address system for everyone to show up there. You can talk to them and see if they have the skills and are interested."

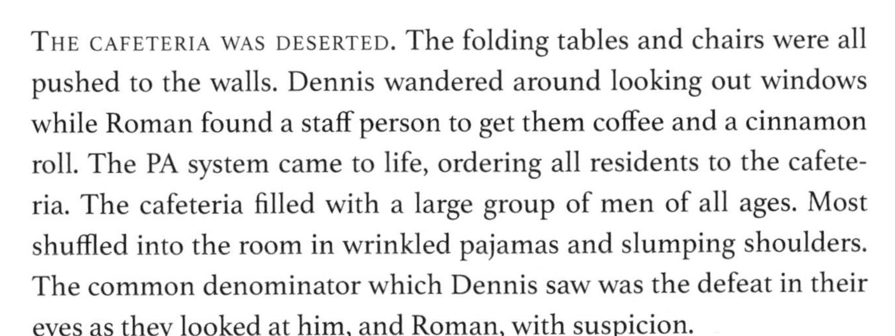

The cafeteria was deserted. The folding tables and chairs were all pushed to the walls. Dennis wandered around looking out windows while Roman found a staff person to get them coffee and a cinnamon roll. The PA system came to life, ordering all residents to the cafeteria. The cafeteria filled with a large group of men of all ages. Most shuffled into the room in wrinkled pajamas and slumping shoulders. The common denominator which Dennis saw was the defeat in their eyes as they looked at him, and Roman, with suspicion.

Seated at the only available table with his cinnamon roll and coffee, Dennis watched the disinterested group of men avoid his eyes and saw how a few of them looked at Roman out of the corners of their eyes. Looking at Roman, Dennis thought, "I hadn't noticed it, but even if Roman looks like a physical wreck, he still looks military. It can't be the way he carries himself. He's all bent over."

The doctor walked in and attempted to get the group's attention. The murmuring continued unabated. An older, more mature man watched Roman grin at the group of men acting like junior high school kids in rebellion. Putting his fingers to his lips, he gave a sharp whistle. Roman's smile widened, as the doctor said, "Thank you, sergeant."

Dennis saw the former sergeant nod and look at another individual in his forties who raised his eyebrows in a question and joined him in front of the doctor and Roman. Dennis's guess was this was another sergeant. He heard a quiet, "What's up?"

"I don't know. I just feel that guy is important."

The doctor announced to the group, "I have a special treat for you today. Years from now, you'll be able to tell your children and grandchildren that you met this gentleman who helped you break the cycle of addiction in your life. Gentleman, it's my privilege to introduce Retired Lt. Commander Roman Nelson, a former Navy SEAL, and holder of the Presidential Medal of Honor."

Dennis saw the two sergeants give each other a knowing look, and without a word said, they straightened up, got into a line, and stood at attention. One at a time, the room full of men stepped into formation behind the sergeants and stood erect.

Dennis also heard but didn't understand the repeated murmurings of, "It's him."

"It's The Ghost." "I heard a rumor The Ghost lived in Oregon."

He didn't understand but saw how the room full of men got quiet and paid attention and respect to his cousin, Roman.

Roman walked down the formation of men. He gave the men a little bigger version of the story he gave the doctor, "I'm home from the service. Just like you, I'm still struggling to rehab my body and my mind. I found my mother running our family business out of the back of a warehouse. It's better than it sounds, but still, it's not where I want my mother living."

Moving down the line, he made eye contact with every man he passed. "The shock of shocks is, on retirement, I have money in my pocket and can buy her a new home. Many of you would do the same thing if you could. The problem is she doesn't want a new home. She is happy where she is, but has agreed to a little 'upgrading.' She leaves on January 2nd for a month's vacation. When she returns, I want to have built her a new house inside the warehouse. She won't have to leave where she wants to live, but I get to have her living in a place she deserves. The challenge is it needs to happen in one month."

Roman continued stepping down the line, "What does that mean to you? My cousin Dennis is at the table. He is an architect and will run the project. I need a large team of guys to hand demolish walls, flooring, wiring, etc. Then, I'll need three teams working around the clock to do the construction. I'll pay you the going wage rate and provide cots inside a heated warehouse, food, and little sleep. The doctor will provide counselors and physical therapists for your off duty time. Retired SEALS and retired Navy guard dogs will provide security. There will be no drugs, no alcohol, no fighting, no sex, and no to anything else you can think of. One misstep and you're out of the program and on the bus home."

Again Roman stepped down the formation lineup. He stopped in front of a vet who was shaking, pale, and bleary-eyed. Roman looked the vet in the eyes for a long time. The vet straightened and struggled to meet Roman's eyes. Roman said to him, "You can do this soldier. This is a fight you can win. I want you in camp with us." Roman held out his hand, and after a long wait, the vet shook it. Squaring his shoulders, he saluted Roman.

Roman moved to the next rank and continued talking, "During the month, you can make big strides in your recovery program, make money, and feel good about what you're doing, instead of sitting here looking out the window watching it rain. If you're interested in being part of my project, Dennis will meet you at the table over there. He will talk to you about your background and what skills you can bring to the table to help him get the project done in less than a month."

Watching from his table, Dennis realized he had just witnessed a Commander review his troops, and the doing of it had instilled a feeling of hope in the room which wasn't there before. He did not understand what "The Ghost" whispers were about and didn't know what his cousin could have done to receive the Presidential Medal of Honor. He could tell, however, this group of men, who knew what it meant, were impressed.

The entire room moved over and got in a line to apply.

What no one knew was Roman had told Dennis, "Find a job for every applicant. If anyone wants to work, find them a job."

Dennis was coachable. He hired them all.

## 54

Roman and Alexia helped their mother load her luggage into the car. Rose asked, "Are you sure we should leave this early. I know we're spending the night next to the airport for tomorrow's flight, but it seems early."

"Not at all," Roman said. "It gets dark early, and you don't want to risk getting lost. Get there early and go have a nice dinner together."

"All right, if you think so."

Alexia and Roman gave their mother a big hug as she drove off to pick up her sister. The minute Rose was on her way, Alexia turned to her brother and said, "OK, what's going on? Why did you want Mom gone, and why did you confiscate their phones?"

"I took their phones because I didn't want them talking to anyone from Gates while they are gone. Mom may not want to move, but I'm giving her a new home. Let me show you Dennis's preliminary plans. I'd like to put you in charge of color schemes, fixtures, furniture, and decorator stuff. Dennis will run the construction crews and the day-to-day details. I'm the big-picture guy."

Alexia started turning the pages of the blueprints back and forth. "What is this, what's going on? I thought you were painting the walls and putting down carpet for her?" Getting deeper into the plans, she looked up with wide eyes, "This is crazy, Roman, can you afford this? You haven't been dealing drugs or anything stupid like that, have you? Is that why your body's a wreck, and you have lots of money?"

Roman took her by the hand and led her to his suitcase, "You can't tell anyone about this." He showed her his photo with the president and the letter from the president gifting Roman with any contraband cash in his possession as medical severance pay.

Alexia couldn't help asking, "How did you get it, and how much was it?"

He grinned, "That's classified. But know when I want to spend money, it is mine, it is legitimate, and I can afford it. No matter how crazy it may look like I am."

He continued, "Now, will you help me? We've got thirty days. I have a crew arriving in the morning at eight. We need to have your bedroom and Mom's entire house in boxes by tomorrow morning. We'll be knocking down walls in the morning. The storefront area won't get touched until the final days of construction. Who would, Mom trust to box up her stuff? I have a POD scheduled for delivery in the morning. If we can get everything in the living quarters boxed tonight, the crew can load it into the POD for storage during construction."

Walking around his mom's living quarters, he was opening drawers and cabinets, looking into everything.

He continued, "While you're thinking about that, who do you know who could help us cook food for thirty people working 24/7?"

Alexia asked, "Are you insane? You want nine meals a day? What have you taken on? How are you going to pull this off?"

Roman answered, "I don't know how much you remember Grandpa Bill? He always used to say, 'it ain't nuthin but money, son.' I think in this circumstance he's right. For the right amount of money, somebody will cook three meals a day for three shifts and do it for a month. We need a person who has the ability, and we need to find out what's the right amount of money. First things first, who would Mom trust to pack up everything in her house and who on earth can we find to cook?"

Alexia responded, “Do you know, Cindy, her hairdresser?”

Roman shook his head no, and she continued, “Cindy is about my age, but she and Mom are best friends. They talk every day. They do everything together. Bring her in on the secret, and she’ll be here all night packing. As far as the cooking, do you know cousin Darci and her partner, Gwen Delaney?”

At Roman’s denial, she continued, “She’d be your second cousin. They moved from Portland back to Mill City. They had big dreams of opening a restaurant and being able to run the lunch crowd during the day and have a fine dining trade at night. Mill City wasn’t prepared for hobnobbing with a lesbian couple as their chefs, no matter how good they were. And they were good. The business went down the drain, and I heard they are late on their house payment.”

Roman said, “See, he was right, ‘it ain’t nuthin but money.’ Can you get Darci, Gwen, and Cindy to come down here right away?”

“Now? It’s New Year’s Day.”

“Now.”

~

THE NEXT MORNING the veterans were up at 5 a.m. They were on the bus at 6 a.m. for a two-hour bus ride, from Portland to Gates, through beautiful farm country. When they arrived at the warehouse, everything in the living quarters was boxed and ready to move into the POD. The gallons of coffee, pancakes, and eggs waiting when they got off the bus impressed the construction crew.

Dennis arrived and started laying out the day’s work. Roman went into the shop and moved the heavy equipment into the fenced parking area, it would have to sit outside for a month.

A truck arrived from an equipment rental company and started setting up the rented equipment. It had cots, bedding, space heaters, portable showers, and rows of portable toilets.

The efficiency of the vets shocked Dennis, as the two old sergeants he’d seen at the hospital took the blueprints in hand and started walking through the store, living quarters, and shop area. By the time they returned, they had developed their plan. The two sergeants divided everyone into two ten-hour shifts, instead of three eight-hour shifts. They decreed everyone would have to work ten-hour shifts, seven days a week until they finished the job. They asked everyone what they were capable of and started them working. First, they hung a giant painter's drop cloth across the back of the store-front to keep the inventory from getting filthy. Which would also prevent all the Lookey Lou's from entering the construction area and interrupting the work.

Second, they started demolishing the walls which needed to come out. A third group grabbed pressure washers and started prepping the exterior for paint, and a fourth group got on the roof and checked the quality of the roofing material. Roman warned everyone to watch out for a hidden stash of gold in the walls. If anyone found it, the whole crew would get a finders bonus.

Dennis left them in charge and walked away.

Darci and Gwen worked as hard feeding the work crews as the men worked on the project. They set up a portable kitchen in the shop, brought in refrigerators, propane stoves, and ovens, and fed two crews three meals a day. Roman was amazed. They did all the work themselves. They had their old suppliers from the restaurant deliver supplies every morning.

Either Darci or Gwen was prepping food, cooking, or cleaning the kitchen around the clock. They slept on cots in the kitchen. The vets loved them.

While the veterans worked around the clock, Roman tried to stay out of their way. Dennis was supervising, and Alexia was worrying about all the color, style, and design choices. She was picking out cabinets and flooring and choosing all the new furniture. She was having a ball. It took a lot of her time. She used up a bunch of her accumulated compensatory time off. Her bosses grumbled but agreed it was better to give her the time off, instead of paying overtime on all her accumulated excess hours. She made it into her job two days a week during January.

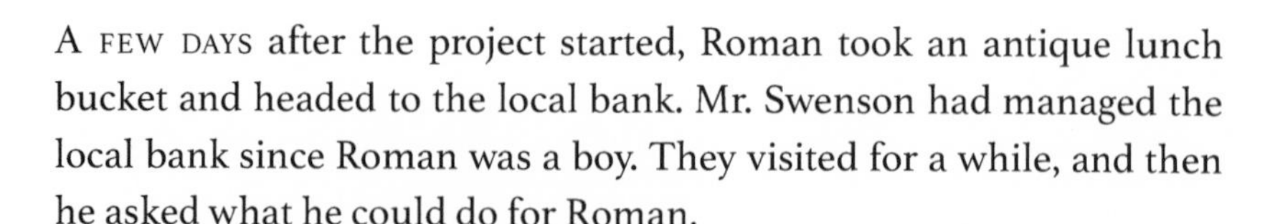

A FEW DAYS after the project started, Roman took an antique lunch bucket and headed to the local bank. Mr. Swenson had managed the local bank since Roman was a boy. They visited for a while, and then he asked what he could do for Roman.

"I want to open a local checking account to receive rather large deposits each month, which I can use as my short term spending money. But, my real question is, how do I convert this to cash?" He opened the old lunch bucket.

"I found Grandpa Bill's stash." Mr. Swenson's jaw dropped, but Roman thought, "That will explain to people where I get all my money." He knew the story would be all over town in a matter of hours.

# 55

Roman found the office file cabinet and started looking through the records. He discovered that years ago, his grandfather had gotten a federal firearms license for the store. Roman figured that had been just like the boat dealerships and fishing tackle. His grandfather's intention was to buy everything for himself and his buddies at cost.

His mother, however, had paid all the license and registration fees as they came due and had renewed the licenses all those years, even though she wasn't selling any guns.

Roman said, "Hey Dennis, I just found out the store has a federal firearms license. Will you redesign the store plans to include a large gun salesroom and a built-in, walk-in, gun safe? Also, is there enough space in the warehouse to add an indoor pistol range? And if so, could you soundproof it so Mom won't hear the shooting in her home or store?"

Dennis raised his eyebrows but included it on the warehouse plans wish list.

Roman spent a lot of time walking around, just looking everywhere. His body was healing, and movement was becoming easier.

The pain was diminishing. He kept stretching the limits of his flexibility and endurance. His emotions, however, were still numb.

He was going through the motions of doing what he knew he should do. Talking to people, helping others, staying engaged, instead of withdrawing, was necessary. However, even redoing Rose's home left him feeling empty. Knowing others expected him to be excited, he faked excitement, but inside himself, he felt nothing. He took a bunk and started sleeping with the other veterans. If he screamed at night, they understood.

The flashbacks of Amber and it was difficult for him even to say, his child, were unrelenting. He had never held his child. The child wasn't real to him but materialized in his dreams.

He killed Admiral Hayes and Ambassador Knapp a hundred times. The images of all he'd killed haunted him. It didn't matter the method. He'd killed, with sniper fire, by knife, by hand to hand combat, or by calling in an airstrike. He saw their faces and heard their sounds as they died.

By day, he pulled out his yellow pads and planning books and kept moving forward. He stood for prolonged times watching the traffic on Highway 22 or looking up the mountain, at Hawkeye Ridge behind the store. His lawyer training kicked in. He got out all the deeds and title policies on the properties the family trust owned. Next, he ordered, in large scale, plot maps and survey maps of all those properties. He pinned those to a wall in the warehouse. The table he always sat at to drink coffee, faced those maps. He started marking up the charts with colored markers.

It was January in Oregon. Which meant it was drizzling rain most of the time. It wasn't a downpour, but looking at the logging road to the top of the mountain, he knew it was wet slippery dirt. His truck would bury itself in the mud in the first 100 yards. He fired up the small bulldozer and thought about taking it up the logging road, but as heavy as the dozer was, he thought he might cause a landslide.

Since the remodel was proceeding well without him, he went shopping for an ATV. He was looking for an Argo he had seen with eight wheels and rubber tracks similar to the dozer. It even had a bed like a pickup for hauling small loads.

He decided if he was looking at ATVs, he should check out drift boats, snowmobiles, and Zodiacs. First, he went south to Eugene. Not finding what he was looking for, he headed north on I-5 through Salem, the Portland area, and wound up in Seattle before finding what he wanted. It took him three days to determine no one had a large inventory of anything he was looking for. He bought nothing. Instead, he called the factory on each of the brands he liked and asked about becoming a dealer.

They all agreed to send a representative by Nelson Bait and Tackle within the week. He thought, "I must be related to Grandpa Bill. Maybe, all I want to do is buy my toys wholesale." He asked the Argo representative to bring a demo model of the tracked ATV he wanted.

One week later, he signed papers for Nelson Bait and Tackle, becoming a dealer for the leading brand of jet skis, drift boats, Zodiacs, and Quads, both tracked and wheeled. He placed opening inventory orders for delivery on April 1st. But he wanted delivery of the demo model of the Argo Frontier 8x8 650 Tundra ATV today. It had the eight wheels, an optional set of rubber tracks, a winch, and was amphibious.

The salesman was resistant since that would leave him without a demo model, but Roman learned that cash didn't just talk, it shouted. He got his Argo that day.

He thought, "This is the ultimate boy toy." His next thought was, "That should be the name of the boat and quad division of the business. Boy Toys." Less than a minute later, he realized his mother, and his sister, wouldn't like the name. He continued thinking, "I can just hear Alexia having a fit. She'd be all over me about her girlfriends not going into a store with such a sexist name. Damm, she'd be right. Maybe I should call it Boy Toys & Her Toys Too."

# 56

Roman packed a lunch, put on his winter rain gear, and headed up the logging road to the top of the mountain. He thought, "The only way I'd get up this logging road without this machine would be on a mule, which would take all day. This dirt track may have been a logging road once, but that was thirty years ago."

There was a chill in the air when he left Gates. Gates sits at an elevation of 945'. Proceeding up the logging road, he could feel the temperature dropping with the increase in altitude. At the end of the logging road, he came to a meadow that sat on the top of the mountain. It was snowing at the meadow's 2000' elevation. The view was incredible, and just as he remembered. When he was a teenager, his grandfather took him elk hunting. They rode horses and brought extra mules for their camp gear and to take home any elk they shot. They had camped in this location for a week while they hunted.

His grandfather had said, "Look at that, boy, I'd love to see you build a home right here. It would cost a fortune. I don't know if you could do it, but wouldn't you like to sit right here, look at that view, and watch the seasons change?"

Roman had been hunting with his grandfather before, but this trip was exceptional in his memories. He remembered his Grandpa Bill telling him, "Your mother is a wonderful woman. Your dad outdid himself. She's got class and is a great lady. But, boy, you gotta remember where you are and who is with you. There will not always be a Kleenex available, nor will it always be appropriate to ask for one. You gotta be able to do 'the farmers blow' without getting snot all over you." Leaning forward with the wind at his back, he grabbed his nose and gave a hard blow.

Grandpa Bill said, "That's how you do it."

Another day, he talked about cleanliness, "You should always be aware of personal hygiene and sanitation. You need to pay attention to washing your hands around food, after going to the bathroom, or after you shake hands with anyone. But, don't be manic about it. Just remember, boy, 'you gotta eat a bushel of dirt before you die.'"

At dinner one night, as he picked a hair off his plate, he said, "A dog or cat hair won't kill you."

But over and over, he talked about the view. "Boy, look at that view. You'd need a pair of eyes out of those hawks circling up there to see it all." Or he'd ask, "Did you ever think about being one those hawks and seeing what they see?"

They started calling their camp the Hawkeye Ridge Elk Camp.

Roman had never forgotten the trip, the conversations, or the vision his grandfather cast of building a home, where he could see forever. A month after that trip, his grandfather passed away. Roman never forgot his lessons.

# 57

Roman sat on Hawkeye Ridge, with his memories until it started to get dark, and then headed back down the logging road with his lights on. He pulled into the parking lot as it was nearing full dark. Several of the off-duty veterans and his cousin Dennis heard him coming down the mountain and were waiting to see what he was driving.

As they "oohed" and "aahed" over the Argo, he took Dennis aside, "can you free up time tomorrow for a conversation?" They agreed on a time, and he told Dennis to bring his sketch pads.

The next day Darci kept their coffee cups full as Roman explained to Dennis what he wanted with a grin on his face,

"OK, you've passed the audition. This project is going great, and I'm proud of you. When we get done, you'll have earned your brag rights. Everyone in the town is dying to know what's happening here. We've had more people stop by the store to pick up a little knick-knack than we've had in years. It was a brilliant idea to post a copy of the blueprints of the store portion for everyone to see."

Roman paused for a breath, "The next step is by April 1st I want to complete another project."

As Dennis started talking about tight timelines, Roman said,

"You've proven you can manage large, complicated projects. It's a function of how many people you have working and how long you work them. Scheduling is brutal, but it is the secret for speed. Start now. I want to put a cyclone fence around our property across the road, which means we need to get it surveyed, so we don't fence in the neighbor's property. Make sure the fence is tall and sturdy, and we'll need to install drainage in the field and gravel it as a parking lot unless you think we should pave it. Behind the parking lot, I want to build a boat and ATV showroom, with an attached repair shop and living quarters for me upstairs. Next, I want to reestablish our private boat ramp and water rights out of the river. You may need to prove to the state we never relinquished either the boat ramp or water rights, both of which will have preexisting priority rights. You may need to hire a lawyer to litigate those questions, but I want those rights re-established, I'll have another use for them when I build my home."

Dennis started asking design questions, and Roman said, "We will have the best boat and ATV inventory south of Seattle. If we do this right, I think we can become the first choice of anyone wanting to buy a high-end new recreational toy. I want a showroom to equal that. Do it upscale. Also, there's still unused space in the warehouse behind the store and Mom's house. Plan on cleaning that up as additional indoor boat and ATV storage, just make sure you keep room for the pistol range we talked about. I think it will become an important addition."

Roman continued, "If we use up the existing warehouse space for the pistol range and indoor storage for the boats and ATVs, I'll need a place to park all the logging and construction equipment it now holds. It's all ancient, but valuable because it's always been stored inside. It's only exposure to the weather was on the job. We'll need another storage facility for the equipment. That can go up the logging road and around the bend, where it will be out of sight, later this summer. That will be a large metal pole building and doesn't need to be fancy. It will just be an equipment warehouse. But, I want it big, 200 feet by 400 feet, which should be large enough to keep all our equipment undercover in the winter."

Roman paused for a breath and asked, "How long before you can have preliminary plans and get started on building permits?"

"About a week."

"Good, as soon as you have the Boy Toys & Her Toys Too, showroom project moving, we need another conversation about project #3. I want to build a house on top of Hawkeye Ridge, behind us. We'll need more planning time for that since I have definite ideas of what I want. The weather needs to break at the 2000 foot level before we can start on anything except plans and permits. But, when the weather breaks, let's be ready to go. I'm not an architect, but I've sketched out a preliminary idea of what I'm thinking for a floor plan. As soon as you've got a few minutes, let's run up the mountain, and I'll show you where and what I'm thinking. When you see the site, I know your creative design wheels will start turning."

Roman handed Dennis the preliminary sketches. "Remember, you're the architect. None of this is to scale, as yours would be. These are just a starting point to jump-start your design ideas."

Dennis started flipping the pages of Roman's sketches. He was wide-eyed. "Roman, this is incredible. However, working at this pace is unheard of. To pull this off, I'll need to hire at least one draftsman as an assistant, perhaps two. I'll also need a supervisor to oversee the construction crews. Do you think the sergeants would stay on for the rest of the projects?"

"I don't know, can't hurt to ask them."

Dennis's voice was cracking, and he had tears in his eyes as he thanked Roman, Dennis explained why he was so grateful. "I had a great job, making big money working in Portland, but my wife and I didn't fit into the big city lifestyle. We're just country people at heart. I quit that job so we could come home and be close to our families. It took every dollar I had in savings to open my architectural firm. It was harder to get started than I expected, and we've been struggling to pay our bills. The money issues have brought depression and stress into our marriage. Just before you came home, my wife suggested we take a break in our marriage, with each of us going back to our parents to live."

Roman's project had solved the money issues, his wife was no longer stressed over money and, and she had just informed him she was pregnant. Dennis hugged Roman hard and said, "Thank you, Cousin. I have one favor to ask you. Would you honor us by being our child's Godfather?"

Roman was speechless before agreeing. Later that night, he thought about the conversation weeks ago in which his counselor, Dr. Davies, had urged him to get involved in other people's lives and to serve others.

He thought, "I can see the impact of what we've done already, the town of Gates seems to have hope again. The whole town is more vibrant. It's crazy, Mom's house isn't finished, neither is the store, and nobody knows what I'm planning, but I swear there's a different atmosphere in town. Is that what the counselor was talking about? I can see how Darci, Gwen, and Dennis will benefit from the projects, and how grateful they are. It's all so emotional for them. Why can't I feel that? Will I ever feel again, or are my emotions just dead?"

# 58

During the final couple weeks of construction on his mother's home, Roman sat at the makeshift table in the warehouse, looking at the property survey maps he'd mounted on the wall. He was watching the veterans work on her home, but his mind was racing.

Surveyors were marking out the property lines across the road, and snow covered Hawkeye Ridge. He asked Dennis and Darci, both of whom were his cousins, if they would pass the word around the family that he would like to talk to anyone who'd ever worked for his father or grandfather at Nelson Timber, no matter what their job had been or how long ago it had been.

Grizzled old loggers started showing up in the morning for free coffee and Darci's cinnamon rolls. They all wanted a look at the Argo. Soon, it was the talk of their morning coffee group. Roman sat with them for hours and took each of them for a ride up the logging road and back. He made sure the old guys were all strapped in and wearing heavy clothes before taking off. Several of them were in their mid-80s. They all loved it. Over and over, they said Roman's grandpa, Bill, would have loved owning one and would have been able to haul out a lot more elk. Everyone wanted to know if he planned on using it for next year's elk hunt.

"Nahhh, I don't think so. I hope I'm done with killing," Roman would answer every time.

Each of them told stories about logging and fighting forest fires with his father or grandfather. Standing close to the large scale maps on the wall, they ate cinnamon rolls and sipped coffee as Roman asked them where they had worked and what they could tell him about each piece of property. He got them to describe each fire they had fought and marked their answers on the large maps.

Roman asked each retired logger the same question, "If money were not a factor, what would you do with this forest to protect it and preserve it forever? What would you do to make and keep it a viable business? Not just what is cost-effective, but what would best practices be?"

He also asked them, "Do you know any out of work loggers, surveyors, or equipment operators? I'll be hiring. If there are any family members or people who worked for Nelson Timber in the past, I want to talk to them. I'll also be hiring clerks in the store for Mom, salespeople for the boat division, and mechanics for both the boat division and the logging equipment. Do me a favor, please, and put the word out around the community."

By the time Rose returned, Roman's plans were complete.

# 59

Twenty-eight days after starting his mother's project, Roman walked among the veterans and thanked them. Everyone was awestruck by their accomplishments. Pride radiated through the group. You could see it in their grins, in their eyes, and the way they stood. The counselors said the feeling of pride and self-worth was more valuable than their wages.

He acknowledged they had unearthed his Grandpa Bill's buried "stash." It hadn't been a bucket of gold, but a bucket of old silver dollars. He'd cashed them in at a Salem coin shop for today's value and divided 20% amongst them as a bonus. Besides their wages, he slipped each of them a prepaid phone card good for $100. He told them, "If you ever need a person to talk to, day or night, call me. Our Uncle Sam made us all brothers. We had each other's backs when we were on the front lines. Call me if you need me at your back in Oregon. I expect you to stay clean and sober, and to get a job, no matter how menial. Work has value to you, which is worth more than the money you get paid. I'll be doing another similar project next summer," he added, pointing to the hill behind them.

"I intend to build my home on top of Hawkeye Ridge. Make sure you stay connected to your counselors if you're interested in being a part of that project. We'll coordinate through them."

Alexia, Dennis, Cindy, and the chefs, Darci and Gwen, watched as the former sergeants called the group to order.

"TEN-HUT."

Everyone snapped to attention and saluted Roman, who gave them the honor of a crisp salute. The veterans drove away to everyone waving.

Roman handed the chefs an envelope filled with cash, "Can I give you a suggestion?"

At their nod, he continued, "Don't worry about your restaurant. Open a catering business. Lots of people will hear about what you did here. My mother will make sure of it."

He laughed. "You've made your reputation. You stepped in and helped our family, which will go a long way here in the canyon. People will quit thinking of you as the Portland girls slumming in the small town. You may not know it, but people here are about to claim you as their own. Keep your prices reasonable and maybe design a series of events and price points. Everything from summer barbeques and ribs, to weddings, maybe fancy dinners for two delivered, complete with thewine."

Darci and Gwen looked at each other and nodded. "I'll be your first customer. How would you like to cater a meal for my mother, Cindy, and all of us who helped with the remodel when they return this weekend? We can have a welcome home dinner for Mom and Aunt Alice."

The next day new furniture started to arrive. Alexia was busy pointing and directing the movers to show them where everything went. The store had quadrupled in size, encompassing the previous living quarters. There were rows of empty shelves, granite countertops, old fashioned wainscoting. It resembled a vacant store in a high rent district. Roman and Alexia had repainted the outside in an old-time theme, but it was fresh paint.

The living quarters were now inside the former shop/warehouse. It contained a suite for Rose and one for Alexia, including a bath and sitting area. It also included guest quarters and an office for Rose. The large open kitchen family room area and a formal dining room had windows looking up the mountain at the forest. Roman had even placed SolaTubes in all the hallways and throughout the store bringing natural light throughout the interior space.

The entire suite was open and airy, yet cozy, with rich, dark cabinetry. The counters were a light hard surface, and the light gray floor tiles heated the kitchen area. Alexia was opening boxes and putting away as many of her mother's things as possible when Roman stopped her. "Leave it for Mom. She will open boxes, throw stuff away, and rearrange for six months. Let her have that joy."

Alexia nodded and sat down, "Shall we go for pizza or have it delivered?"

Just then, the doorbell rang, and Darci and Gwen walked in, followed by Cindy.

"We'll cater the party this weekend, but this one's on us. How do spaghetti and meatballs and cheap red wine sound?" They started placing bowls of food on the counter.

The next day Rose's car pulled into the Nelson Bait and Tackle store parking lot. Rose and Aunt Alice started dragging their suitcases out of her car. Roman and Alexia came out to help, Alexia said, "Wow. Don't the two of you look hot?"

They both preened and spun in circles. They'd lost weight, toned up, and dressed in the latest fashions, with modern new hairstyles. Rose's hair had been "bobbed" into a stylish cut. No matter how she shook her hair, it always fell into place. It was now a light silvery brown with dark brown streaks and highlights.

Alexia took her mother by the arm and said, "Why don't we all go in, Roman can come out and get your suitcases in a few minutes?"

Holding onto her arm, Alexia guided Rose into the store. Rose was excited as she started telling Roman and Alexia about their trip. Rose made it several feet into the store before, stopping and gasping. Pivoting and looking around the room, she appeared to have difficulty breathing, as she kept gasping for breath with her hand covering her mouth.

The store now had a tile entryway, dark hardwood floors, granite countertops, and matching wainscoting. There were empty brand new store fixtures everywhere, which exuded quality.

There was a section with empty gun racks, one for fishing gear, another for boating supplies, and clothing. To one side, there was even a small grocery and convenience store.

Rose couldn't stop exclaiming in disbelief. "Oh my Gosh, I can't believe it. This is nicer than Cabela's. What have you done? How did you pay for this?"

She kept walking around, touching everything. She asked, "Why all the empty racks, this store has never sold enough to fill up these racks."

Roman responded, "I thought the three of us could go to Buyer's Market and lay in a bunch of stock. I think it's time for Nelson Bait and Tackle to expand. There are several thousand cars a day going past the front of this store, headed to Central Oregon, or a recreational campsite. I think it's time we get them to stop here to go to the bathroom, instead of the state rest stop down the road. If we've got what they need, we can make this store a destination shopping stop on their way to wherever they are going."

As he was talking, the store was filling up behind her. Cousin Dennis and his wife were the first to arrive, followed by Cindy, Darci, Gwen, and Uncle Russ.

Alexia said, "Mom if you like the store, you better hold on to Roman's arm as you go into your home."

Roman walked her into her living quarters, with everyone following behind. She stopped, her eyes large, and her mouth open as she surveyed her new home. With Rose's hand on his arm, Roman walked her through the rooms. Tears were streaming down her face by the time she'd seen it all. Alexia, Alice, and Uncle Russ were also tearful. Roman wished he could cry with them.

# 60

Two days after her return, the family sat down for dinner. Alexia was down from Portland, and Rose was arranging and rearranging everything in her big new kitchen.

Rose asked, "What else do you have up your sleeve? I see survey stakes across the road, and there's a constant stream of 'old geezers' your dad or grandad's age coming around to talk to you. It's like watching Marlon Brando as The Don, in the movie The Godfather, except you are way too young for that role. I swear every woman in Gates has been by the house with a 'housewarming' gift hoping to see the remodel. None of them seem to know what you're up to, but they are all excited about what you're doing."

Continuing to open drawers looking for her utensils, Rose kept talking, "You haven't been around to see them, but in case you're interested, all of them with single daughters brought them. A group of girls from your high school class came by to welcome you home. They were all pretty. You're a rare commodity, a single, handsome male who looks like he has money. My friends made it clear their daughters are interested in coming by. They want to meet you and welcome you back to town. If the subject comes up again, what shall I tell them?"

Roman laughed, “Be nice, but tell them I’m damaged goods, and their daughters are better off without me at the moment.”

Rose sighed, “So much for grandchildren, which brings us back to the Godfather question, what are you up to now?”

He answered, “I’m glad you asked, Mom. I want to talk to both of you about my plans. Let’s start with the obvious. The store is almost empty of inventory. Like I mentioned the day you got home, I think the three of us need to go to the Buyers’ Market. We need to order a lot of stock. We need fresh, cutting edge stuff. Do you know when and where the next market is? Aren’t they held in half a dozen cities? When are they? Which one should we go to Seattle, San Francisco, Dallas, or maybe, Chicago?”

“Seattle is closest.”

Alexia asked, “Don’t they have one where it’s warm?”

“Well, there is a show in Dallas and Las Vegas. But, Roman, you’ve already spent a fortune on the store, which I don’t think you’ll ever get back.”

Roman said, “Mom, there are thousands of cars passing by here every day. I’ve ordered a new sign. It will read, Clean Bathrooms, Open to the Public, and be installed on April 1st. I guarantee people will prefer to stop at a warm, clean bathroom instead of the state’s highway rest stop down the road. If we have fresh, enticing inventory on the racks as they walk by, I’m betting a bunch of it will walk out the door with them. I don’t think we need to worry about being the cheapest. We need to carry the best. The stuff they can’t find down the street. They are going by here to play in the mountains or in Central Oregon. Let’s have the things they need to make that play enjoyable.

“I hope to have a Grand Opening in mid-April. So, we need to get the merchandise ordered right away.”

Alexia piped in, “I vote for Dallas, it’s warm, and I won’t want to just hang out at the pool like I would if we went to Vegas.” They discussed locations and dates and planned to attend the next Dallas show.

# 61

Roman said, "You asked what else I'm planning. Quite a bit, I've been sitting here for a month watching other people work. All I could do was make plans, which brings us to what's going on across the street. The trust owns the property, which is producing no revenue for either of you. It's just sitting there, costing us money in taxes each year. I want to open a boat, Jet Ski, and ATV sales lot. I don't think either of you is interested in investing a few million in inventory. Here's what I propose. I have opened another business in my name. Let's call it the boat division. The boat division is building a showroom across the street. It will pave the parking lot, etc., and buy the inventory. It will hire the staff and carry all the liability. The family trust will continue to own the property free of any debt. The boat division will pay rent to the family trust which will then distribute your share to you. That's my way of giving you, Alexia, and Mom a guaranteed income. You can keep working because you want to, not because you have to."

Rose stopped rearranging her cabinets and said, "Roman, you can't just keep spending money. You've already spent a fortune on us. I love my home, but I'm worried you'll wind up in the mess your father got into if you keep spending money like this."

Alexia stepped into the conversation, "Is this all part of the 'classified money' you can't tell us about?"

Roman nodded.

"Mom's right, we don't want you to go broke or lose what you've got. Do you have enough to do all this?"

Roman nodded again.

"Are you sure you don't want to take all that money and go sit on a warm sunny beach and drink Mai Tai's?"

Frowning, he shook his head, "I've done that. Now it's time for me to use what I've got to help those I care about, and to protect what we already have."

Walking over to Roman, Alexia gave him a long hug. She looked at her mother, "I trust my brother. We need to quit second-guessing him and start helping him in whatever he wants to do."

After discussing the details of the boat division for a while, Roman said, "which brings us to the timber division, Nelson Timber. All those 'old geezers' you mentioned Mom, represent perhaps 60 years of the institutional memory of the forestry industry here in the canyon. A handful of those 'old boys' fought the massive forest fire of 60 years ago. Even Dad read about it in the history books. Those guys experienced it. They have a lot they can teach us before they die if we will listen. Their bodies may be too old to log, but in their minds, they're 20 years old and vibrant. I plan on reopening the timber division, not as a full-scale logging business, but on a smaller scale. My goal is to mitigate forest fire risk. If we can sell enough timber to cover the costs of minimizing our risk of fire, it's a huge win."

Rose continued being practical, "But Roman, what do you know about logging?"

"Nothing, but I'm betting there are people in the community I can hire, who will know what I need to know."

She nodded, "Probably. Is that why you're talking to all the old guys?"

"It's one reason, the next is, I intend to build a home. It will be on the top of Hawkeye Ridge at Grandpa Bill's old elk camp. If either of you wants to take a ride in the Argo, I can show you where. It will be a cold ride. There's snow on the ground up there. Dennis is already working on my preliminary plans."

They both jumped at a ride in the new toy they'd heard everybody talking about. He got them dressed for a cold trip. Even inside the canvas-topped Argo, with the heater going full blast, it was cold. Alexia loved the ride. His mother kept telling him to go slower, but they both were awestruck with the view when they got to the top.

Rose, however, was the practical one, "Honey, this is beautiful, but how are you going to get up and down in the winter? You can't be going back and forth in an ATV. And, even if you grade it out with a dozer, it is way too rough a road for wintertime driving."

Roman drove them over to the other side of the meadow. He pointed the nose of the Argo downhill, and they could see Nelson Bait and Tackle at the bottom of the hill, "I'm putting in a chairlift."

"You're doing what?"

He grinned, "You heard me. I'm putting in a chairlift. It will be an enclosed chairlift. It's not all that expensive and will handle the winter access question. Also, in the event of a catastrophic dam failure upstream at either Big Cliff Dam or Detroit Dam, you could get out of the canyon, Mom, before the water hits Gates."

# 62

MAY 2015

Roman sat in his Argo with the top off and watched the construction. He took his Argo everywhere.

The project Dennis was overseeing intimidated him. He said, “I can design it, envision the finished project, and oversee all the steps to completion. It’s no big deal to tell the contractors what to do. But when you see the size of the holes in the ground and how big the piles of dirt are, it gives you a different perspective. Your veterans are doing a great job. I’m glad a lot of the crew from your mom’s remodel came back. Those two sergeants are a Godsend. I may put them on as a permanent crew.”

On the ground were gigantic mounds of dirt. The piles of dirt hid the vast holes out of which they came. It was a maze of giant ditches connecting three enormous holes. One hole was the dig out for a daylight basement home with an attached three-car garage. Another hole was for the separate five-car garage, an airplane hangar, workshop complex, and the last hole was for the geothermal heating system.

Roman’s home and garage complex were semi-buried. Clerestory windows rose high above for light. Covered with sod, the roof featured natural plantings. The design with the south-facing windows was such that the need for heat and air conditioning would be minimal. The primary feature, however, was a significant fire could burn across it with negligible damage.

Trenches were going everywhere. Enough ditches crisscrossed the mountain top to mask the fact that one would contain an underground tunnel. The tunnel would go from the safe-room in the home to the garage complex.

Roman had told Dennis, "I want the ability to enter or leave my home in safety with no one knowing what I'm doing."

The tunnel wasn't on any of the plans or permits. Dirt piles masked it in such a way the inspectors never recognized it for what it was. The home would be wide across the back, which was all glass looking downhill at the view. Visitors reached the front door, on the uphill side, by walking through an atrium with a glass ceiling.

A guest would pass through the greenhouse/atrium entry to the carved double doors leading into the entry foyer. Upon entering the home, they would look straight through the foyer and through the open living room at the fifty-mile view. The entrance would hold a four-foot crystal chandelier.

All rooms faced downhill to the view. Where appropriate, the hard surface flooring contained heating coils. The floors would always be warm. Floored with aromatic cedar, Roman's master closet off the master bath was a walk-in, cedar chest. It was also a work in deception with several hidden features. A secret passage led to the safe room/gun room on the ground level. Out of the safe-room, Roman could exit into the tunnel leading to the garage/hangar complex.

Roman planned to model his library after a library he saw in a castle in England. He stipulated a floor to ceiling wall of books in dark bookcases. The tall shelves required a moveable ladder. He wanted the colors done in hunter green and a rich burgundy with leather furniture. Alexia disagreed with his color choices, but Roman was adamant. "I saw a library like this in England and fell in love with it. I told myself that someday I would recreate the look."

Alexia and Rose were engaged in picking out colors, carpets, countertops, and hardwood floors. His primary criterion was he wanted a rich, masculine feel. He wanted lots of dark woods, luxurious leathers, and to Rose and Alexia's surprise, crystal light fixtures. Dennis consulted with the chefs, Darci and Gwen, on the design of a dream kitchen. They wanted the kitchen set up for entertaining and the ease of cooking multiple entrées at the same time.

Roman was more engaged in planning the outdoor living area. It was on the downslope side of the house with a view to the Southwest, which was incredible. He could see west down the canyon to where it opened into the Willamette Valley. He had a large fire pit in the center of the slate patio. The outdoor chairs were all heavy. They wouldn't blow away in the mountain top storms and were weather resistant. A large propane BBQ was off to the side. It was all comfortable and masculine.

The roof of the covered portion of the deck had two massive posts as the support uprights. The posts were, in fact, two matching kiln-dried cedar tree trunks. Three feet in diameter and thirty feet tall, they framed the patio entry and added a WOW factor.

Dennis was becoming accustomed to coordinating Roman's around the clock construction projects. Breaking ground on April 1st, he promised to finish it by Thanksgiving.

Rose told Roman, "Perfect. It'll be ready in time to host Thanksgiving dinner. We can invite your Aunt Alice, Uncle Russ, Cousin Dennis and his family, and Alexia."

Darci and Gwen were fixtures in catering family events to which they became guests when the meal was ready. Alexia brought her latest boyfriend. Roman called her string of boyfriends the tall, dark, and handsome flavor of the month.

~

WITH THE HOUSE COMPLETED, Boy Toys & Her Toys Too, up and running, and Nelson Bait and Tackle becoming a mandatory stop on the way to Central Oregon, Roman's attention turned to the logging business.

He hired all the experienced, out of work, loggers he could find who had ever worked for Nelson Timber. He wanted people already experienced on his property, and who knew how to use his ancient equipment. The old loggers knew where his property was better than he did. Finding a mechanic, who had worked on the equipment years ago, and knew how to keep the machinery going, was a huge help. Mechanic's fresh from new training schools had no clue how to work on the old stuff. Roman hired his experienced mechanic, three new apprentices, to train and transfer the knowledge to the next generation.

Once Roman hired everyone, he gathered the men together. He told them, "I don't want to lose money, but I'm not worried about big profits. Our primary focus is on being a good steward of our forests. Timber companies clear cut for efficiency, leaving a narrow band of trees at the edge of the property. That screens the clear cut from the view of any roads, and leaves 'seed trees' at the edge of the property for reseeding."

Roman said, "We will not do that. What we will do is clear cut the edges of our property, back say 50 to 100 yards from our property lines. We will clean up the area we clear cut, and then we will enter the rest of the property, and thin it. Which should allow the remaining trees to grow taller faster. While we do that, we can limb up all the low-hanging branches and remove the scrub undergrowth, which is just tinder in a fire."

The loggers looked at each other with raised eyebrows.

"What I want to do is clear out all the fuel inside our forest, and put a firebreak around all our properties. When most companies log their property, all the slash goes into piles for burning. Which is the cheapest way to go, and in difficult terrain, that is what we'll do. The problem is burning the slash contributes to air pollution and global warming. It also removes the nutrients which would, over time, re-enter the soil. Slash burning also leaves the soil more subject to erosion and runoff."

He pointed across the shop at all the machinery, "I have purchased two large wood chippers, the heavy-duty industrial style.

Instead of burning our slash, I want to chip it. We'll be producing mountains of bark chips. If anyone wants to buy it, we'll sell it. But, what I want us to do is load those chips into a truck that has a hose and spraying system. You should be able to chip the slash, then spray it right back onto the ground in the area it came from. The chips will slow rainwater runoff, which will slow erosion in the clear-cut areas.

"I know it's a small gamble. If a fire comes through soon, the bark chips will burn, but they will be at ground level. If, however, we don't have a fire for a while, those chips will disintegrate into the dirt. Anybody have questions so far?"

One of the crew said, "Sounds expensive, and it will be a slow process."

Roman agreed, "I know. At the moment I'm not expecting a profit. What I want to do is protect our forest. I'm expecting a major fire here in the canyon. When that happens, everyone will attempt to create firebreaks to stop the fire. I want to put our firebreaks in now to keep a fire, which may start elsewhere from spreading into our forest. I don't want to see anyone else's forests burn, but if they do, I don't want mine to burn with them."

# 63

With all his plans progressing, Roman could pause. He had people in place running the boat division, Boy Toys & Her Toys Too, and people running the timber division. His mother was running the store, which was becoming busy. She was employing several Gates locals who wanted part-time work. People who wanted to work a second job on the weekend or evenings, or people that needed flexible work schedules. Nelson Bait and Tackle, Nelson Timber, and Boy Toys & Her Toys Too were now the largest employers in Gates.

Roman had three cords of wood delivered to the side of his patio for his fire pit. He sat there with a fire going, even in the coldest weather and read. His reading included the Bible, and the writings of the Roman emperor, orator, and philosopher, Marcus Aurelius. Religious or philosophical materials from various viewpoints were his constant companion. Most of the time, however, he just sat there, fed his fire, and watched the seasons change as his Grandpa Bill had mentioned.

He thought about all the people he had killed. He remembered the men on his team, lost in actions all over the globe. His heart and mind ached with the memories.

Thinking about Amber, he remembered their first weekend together at Annapolis. Their vacations, around the world, screamed for memory. He could see her coming out of the water and lying on beaches in Australia, Hawaii, and above all, Bali. He remembered making love to her in the water in Bali.

The emptiness continued.

He remembered his counselor at Bethesda telling him, "It's in your personality to help others. So, do that. Be engaged in other people's lives. You need to focus on helping others."

He thought, "I've done all that, and I still hurt. That's not correct. I don't hurt, I just don't feel. I'm still numb."

He tried to analyze the numbness. Was guilt causing it? Was it guilt over all the blood on his hands? Was it guilt for not being able to save Amber and his baby? Perhaps it was a sense of loss over the death of his fiancée and their child? He couldn't tell. None of those emotions were overpowering. That was the problem. He didn't feel much of anything.

"Hell," he thought, "Who knows what it is? I sure don't."

He got up, fixed a sandwich, and came back to watch the seasons change.

# 64

The view from the patio was spectacular as the leaves turned color. Douglas fir trees covered the foothills of the Cascades, along with numerous maples, oaks, and alders scattered throughout. The yellows and reds of the leaves contrasted with the dark green of the fir in a way that changed every day.

The temperature dropped. It was drizzling rain in Gates with high temperatures in the mid-40s and low temperatures in the low 30s. In the mountains, the elevation affects the weather and creates microclimates unique to the area. Roman hadn't heard the term, snow level, anywhere other than the mountainous west.

The Willamette Valley of western Oregon is 100 feet of elevation or less. Although the locals complained about the rain and chilly winter temperatures, Roman knew the weather was mild compared to the other parts of the United States that he'd seen. The valley seldom hit the freezing mark.

Long-time locals referred to the Santiam River Canyon as, The Canyon. The Canyon was the entry into the Cascade Mountains with a gradual but steady climb in elevation as Highway 22 passed through Gates. With Gates sitting at 900 feet of elevation, it could be spitting snow, scaring the travelers headed over the mountains. Many would stop at Nelson Bait and Tackle to pick up gloves, hats for the kids, and chains for the steeper climb up the mountains, which was just beginning. The summit of the pass was at 4817 feet above sea level and was 54 miles east.

On Hawkeye Ridge, the elevation was about 2000 feet. Many mornings Roman awakened to fresh snow. He put his Argo to good use, traveling in all kinds of weather with what he considered his ultimate boy toy. Many times the salesmen at Boy Toys & Her Toys Too would call him to take a prospective purchaser of an Argo for a ride. It was seldom the prospective purchaser didn't take one home. Veterans always got a discount.

For weeks he sat next to his fire and read his books. He started attending programs for veterans at Chemeketa Community College. It was a way to connect with individuals who could understand what he was going through. Every once in awhile, he would get a phone call from a veteran to whom he had given a prepaid phone card. Most times, they just needed to talk. They knew he would understand. If he needed to, he would drive to where they were, and help get them out of a tough spot and back into treatment.

As soon as Dennis completed the construction, and while the weather was still beautiful, Roman sent out an open house invitation. He invited all his SEAL buddies who retired at the same time to a weeklong barbeque. Twelve of them showed up. They ate lots of red meat, drank too much beer, and discussed what was happening in each of their lives. This was a group that had been to war and back. They would always be there for each other.

Darci and Gwen catered. Darci told Rose, "They are a warm, outgoing group of men. They're easy to cook for, as long as the main ingredient of the meal is meat.

Andy Baker drove in with Brutus. He was a tall, 6'3" Irishman with black wavy hair. Like many of them, his memories haunted him. He, however, turned his memories into songs over the campfire. He had a beautiful tenor voice and would sit, strum his guitar and compose songs by the hour. Sitting by the fire, he would pull a small harmonica from his shirt pocket and start producing mournful haunting music. He'd carried that harmonica all over the world on his assignments. Several of the men remembered him playing the same harmonica at a forward base in Afghanistan. Brutus would sit with his head on Andy's lap with his eyes focused on the man he loved.

"Crap, Commander, this place is everything you said it was. I fell in love with Oregon, just driving in. This whole area looks like western Pennsylvania, where the mountains drop off into Ohio, but without all the cities and pollution. It's beautiful, and I like all the people I've met. Do you think the people around here would accept a city boy like me, who would like to turn into a country boy? And, the big question, will they accept Brutus?"

At the mention of his name, Brutus thumped his tail.

At Roman's assurance, Andy said, "I'm gonna find a Realtor tomorrow and start poking around."

About that time, with the loud roar of his 4x4 Chevy, Jim Bridger showed up. He jumped out of his rig to yells of welcome. Andy tossed a beer in his direction. Bridger had a dark tan, brown hair hanging over his collar, and looked a little softer and heavier. He was wearing a loud print shirt, cutoffs, and sandals.

Andy ribbed him, "You don't look 'fit to fight,' Bridger. You look like you have a six-pack on your abs all right, but it seems like the kind you drank."

"Maybe so, but I was fit enough to chase the women around all the beaches of the world." He laughed and said, "I even caught a few of them."

Since discharge, almost a year ago, he'd been traveling from one sunny beach to the next.

Bridger asked, "Where's Smoke?"

Roman replied, "He couldn't make it. He took off about a month after discharge and then went to work for President Myers on a serious of 'special projects.' He's turned into a real workaholic."

Andy commented, "Well, Smoke is like the rest of us. None of us ever need to work again, but we're all keeping busy. I think it's because we don't want to have time to think about the visions that haunt us. I have nightmares of the action in Somalia where I had to send Brutus in to locate and attack the sentry. He did a great job, but I hated having to tell him to attack and rip out that guy's throat. I think Brutus has flashbacks over it. You can hear him whimper at night. You guys know what a big pussycat he is."

Bridger said, "Every time I close my eyes, I can see that school bus in the Philippines, loaded with kids, dropping into the river when the bridge blew up. I've stayed busy trying to drink the 'beer river' dry all over the world. No matter how much beer I drink, or where I am, I still see the bus. It doesn't go away until I drink myself into a stupor. It doesn't matter if it's beer and women. Or if it's women and beer, none of it works. I may as well stay here and drink as anywhere else. At least here I've got a few friends and speak the language."

He looked up at Roman's big house, "I don't need anything fancy, just the opposite. I think I'll pick up a small travel trailer and park it in that little campground I saw down by the bridge. There's no sense in me getting a lovely house when I have no one to share it with. Besides, I get claustrophobic indoors. I'll use the trailer for toilet facilities and cooking, but I think I'll sleep outside under a tarp." More than one guy nodded in understanding.

One after another, the former team members bared their souls. It was Andy who looked at Roman and said, "OK, Skipper. No need for the tough guy role with us. We all know how tough you are. You've been just as busy as the rest of us. We are all your brothers. What's going on with you?"

Roman replied, "Not being able to save Amber and our child haunts me."

They all nodded in understanding.

Andy, however, would not let him stop. "What else? You can talk to us. You've saved each of our lives, and some of us have saved yours. You can speak the truth with us when no one else is around. I can see it in your face, what else has you tied in knots?"

Roman looked at each of them before speaking. "Everything surrounding Amber is the big thing. But if you need a list, the deaths of so many of the men I've been responsible for across the globe is at the top."

The team was silent as Andy nodded and said, "What else?"

"The cold-blooded killing I've done bothers me. My parents raised me to believe in the biblical commandment, 'thou shall not kill.' Will God forgive me?"

Again the team was silent, but many nodded their heads. Andy prodded again, "You're on a roll, Skipper. You know the shrinks at Bethesda told us to get it out, to talk about things. We may not have answers, but we can listen. What else has you tied in knots?"

Roman eyes were moist, but no tears ran down his face as he said, "I wonder what my life can be like, given what I've seen and done. Do I still have a decent human being inside myself? Will I ever be able to have a relationship and family with another woman? If I let a woman know what I've done, how could she love me?"

Everyone was silent while Andy hugged Roman. Andy then said, "Let's put our wrists together with our brothers." Everyone gathered in a circle and placed their right wrists together, one tattooed seal with a bloody knife, above the other. Andy then prayed, "May the God who guards all sailors, protect us, heal us, and give us peace."

"Amen," resonated around the circle.

BY THE END of the weeklong barbeque, half a dozen of the team decided to stay in the area. Former Petty Officer Roger Harper loved Oregon. With Roman's encouragement, he enrolled at Oregon State University in Corvallis to finish his accounting degree. He joked with everyone about passing his CPA exam and becoming an official 'bean counter.'

Roman told him, "Get your degree because you want to. But, I know how good you are. I have trusted you with my life and know I can trust you with my money. You can go to work right now as part-time CFO of Nelson Enterprises, while you go to school. You can set your work hours around your classes. I need your help running all these businesses."

They agreed upon a part-time schedule and a base salary, plus a small share of the profits.

All those who were staying were excited to hear their buddy, Dink Lindsay, was about an hour away in Portland. They agreed to get together once a month for conversation, exercise, and SEAL training. As a group, they had enjoyed the conversation and camaraderie but noticed they were no longer in peak physical condition.

Even though they were no longer active duty SEALS, they thought it would be good for them to remain "Fit to Fight." That was a military phrase dating back to The British Royal Army Physical Training Corps. A phrase used for over 150 years by many military services as a response to any query of a soldier's current status.

They all wanted to remain able to say, "Fit to Fight, sir."

# 65

JANUARY 2017

*Donald Miller Compound*

"Mary Beth," Donald hollered from his recliner.

She came in from the kitchen, "Yes?"

Bruce said you got a letter from Little Charlie today. When's he gonna be home?"

"He says at the end of the month."

"Good, it's about damm time. Everything's been on hold long enough."

Spitting his tobacco into an empty Coke can, he continued. "It's all your fault we've had to wait. If you hadn't turned him over to the police for making up to that little girl, he'd have been home a long time ago."

Mary Beth said, "But Donald, he'd knocked her unconscious, raped her, and was about to burn her with the soldering iron. I couldn't ignore that."

"So what? After the boys and I talked with her and her dad, neither of them would have pressed charges, and Little Charlie would have been home when we needed him. It's your fault we had to wait."

"But Charlie,"

"Don't but me, when he gets home, don't you go hanging around listening to conversations that are none of your business. Stay out of the barn. What we talk about is none of your business. Understood?"

"Yes, Donald."

## 66

JULY 5, 2017

Governor Stan Anderson and his wife, Margaret, were leaving the historic Timberline Lodge on Mt. Hood on the morning of July 5. Thirty-five years before, on July 4th, they had gotten married on the lodges beautiful deck. After the festivities, the entire wedding party had changed clothes and gone skiing. At that time, Timberline had the only year round skiing in the United States.

Back then, it had seemed a hoot to go snow skiing in a bikini on your July 4th wedding day. Those wedding photos didn't go in the public areas of their home, but they looked at them every year. Stan was wearing cutoffs and reflective sunglasses. Standing next to him, Margaret wore her skimpy bikini with pride, sipping her champagne glass for the photo at the top of the Palmer Glacier Field.

Margaret had searched for the perfect location for their outdoor wedding and kept coming back to Timberline Lodge. It was a depression-era, Works Progress Administration (WPA) project. Upon completion, Franklin Roosevelt dedicated the Lodge. Filled with artwork from a bygone era, the old world craftsmanship could not be replicated today. The small hotel rooms and knotty pine-covered walls were quaint and old fashioned by today's standards. At the time they built the ski resort, it was the 2nd chairlift in the country.

Both were avid snow skiers, and they had developed a 35-year tradition of sking the Palmer Glacier field, at the 8500-foot level, on their anniversary. Spending the night in the old nostalgic hotel, they still had fun pretending they were newlyweds. Stan reflected the years had been kind.

Margo, as her friends knew her, looked classy, and worked out with a personal trainer three days a week to keep her 56-year-old body toned and fit. She had another appointment every week at the spa and beautician to maintain her looks. Her hair wasn't the same blond color, but it was still blond. She didn't want to give her husband an excuse for a 'wandering eye' like had happened with too many of her friends.

Stan's success softened him up a little. He had a few extra pounds from eating too well and getting too little exercise. Claiming the 210 pounds on his height didn't look bad, just solid, he knew, he was a bit pudgy. His full head of hair was more silver than brown.

Timberline Lodge was a little challenging to get to. From the governor's mansion in Salem, it was close to a three-hour drive. The road for the last 6 miles from Government Camp to Timberline Lodge is steep. In the winter, mountains of snowfall and the snow blowers create an open-topped tunnel as they clear the road.

In July, however, the sky was clear, and the weather beautiful. Faint-hearted drivers were panic-stricken on the drive. The winter snow at the side of the road, which kept cars on the highway, was gone, and so were many of the guardrails. The roadway was carved out of the rock wall of the mountain, and the steep climb zigzagged up the hill with sheer cliffs on the outside.

Stan and Margo were holding hands as though they were still newlyweds. He helped her into their ski rig. With their daughter grown, they didn't need the room of the Suburban, it just felt right to take the big SUV when they went skiing.

Pulling out of the parking lot, Stan headed into the first steep downhill drop and touched his brakes before the first hairpin curve. With a sinking in his stomach, he realized the brakes felt soft and mushy. Pumping the brakes, he felt them lose all pressure as he swept into the first turn.

Margo started yelling, “Honey, slow down.”

“I can’t. We have no brakes. Pull your seatbelt tight.”

Stan tried downshifting to a lower gear. The massive Suburban was gaining speed as Stan squealed the car around a turn with no guard rail on the cliffside. Margo screamed as the car kept picking up speed.

Margo was praying for divine intervention, “Help us, Lord, please protect us, and take care of Julia.”

Stan yelled at her to get her attention, “Press your head against your headrest. Put your hands in front of your face to protect it from the airbags. It will be better to crash uphill than to go over the cliff downhill. Hold on. I love you.”

With that decision made, Stan said a prayer and drove the car into a large abutment. Both forward and side airbags deployed in a millisecond battering them, but saving their lives.

Arriving in minutes since they were part of the Timberline Lodge ski rescue team, the first responders were loading Stan and Margo into the Life Flight helicopter as Trooper Metcalf of the State Highway Patrol officer arrived at the scene.

TROOPER METCALF’S license plate scan of the car had already informed him that this was the governor’s vehicle. Trying to stay out of the way of the first responders, he still asked what happened. Stan gasped, “No brakes.”

No one was allowed to leave until the trooper interviewed everyone who had seen the accident happen. The car following Stan and Margo had parked next to them in the parking lot. Trooper Metcalf asked the driver to show him where both vehicles had parked. Both the witness and the trooper stood there, looking at a puddle of brake fluid. Pondering what he was seeing, the officer made a call to have the Suburban delivered to the police impounds lot and requested a crime scene investigator to check out the parking area. He marked the parking area and crash site off with tape as potential crime scenes.

# 67

SIX WEEKS LATER, MID-AUGUST 2017

It was mid-August. Salem was having its typical, perfect summer. The temperatures were in the high 80s, the humidity was low, and the sky was a gorgeous blue. Stan was leaving the governor's mansion, Mahonia Hall. Towering Douglas firs and Oregon maples with their huge leaves surrounded it. The trees provided shade for the flower beds to flourish. The flowers were in full bloom. Mahonia Hall was a Tudor mansion, designed and constructed in 1924 by the founder of the University of Oregon Architecture School for a wealthy hop farmer. The state acquired it in 1988 as the official residence of the governor of the State of Oregon. When built, it contained a pipe organ and ballroom. Today, it was still elegant.

Stan had recovered from the accident, but Margo was still receiving therapy from her injuries. She wanted to make sure there were no mobility issues down the road.

As a young married couple, it took both their jobs to pay the bills. They struggled, living paycheck to paycheck, as young couples do. Owning his own business had always driven Stan, and his natural talents led him to the development of computer software. Every young kid thought he could write computer code, but few could, and even fewer could market it.

Stan, however, could and did. He developed Anderson Technologies Inc., a software firm specializing in gaming software. His timing was perfect. He sold his firm and its patents to an industry giant for undisclosed tens of millions of dollars, stock, and royalties.

~

STAN WAS in his early 40s at that point. He thought, "I'm too young to retire and do nothing, even if I have the money. I'd be bored to tears." He turned his attention to politics.

Running for the legislature from Oregon's wealthiest district that encompassed Lake Oswego and West Linn, he surprised everyone by running as an Independent and beating both the Republican and Democratic candidates.

His constituents adored Stan's plain-spoken and direct manner. Socially liberal and fiscally conservative, he told people, "I don't care what you do in your bedroom or who you love. But I think you should work and pay taxes. If you need help, we should do everything we can to help you, but I think you need to do your part, no matter what it is."

His belief was justice should be fair for all but fast. He thought the district attorney's offices relied too much on plea bargains, and defense attorneys relied too much on appeals. That created a process that allowed the time frames for sentencing to drag out for years.

Stan had a personal example of that issue. Before selling his business, he and his family lived in an upscale neighborhood in Lake Oswego. One evening gunshots awakened them. Going outside, he watched as the police arrested a broke hillbilly for killing their neighbor and wounding his wife.

Stan persuaded the police to allow him to take the victim's daughter, Samantha, his daughter's playmate, to his home. Samantha stayed with the Andersons until they released her mother from the hospital. He watched the mother and daughter dealing with the emotional trauma and loss year after year as the killer's family made appeals, keeping the death penalty postponed. Their wounds stayed fresh for decades as they were forced to relive the events of that night for each appeal process. Stan felt the judicial system ignored the victim's family and made the grieving process so much more difficult. One of Stan's campaign promises was to work at fixing those issues in the legal system. After a few terms in the Legislature, he ran for governor and won in a landslide.

When Oregon voted to allow the death penalty, he was a vocal proponent. While in the legislature, Stan attached a rider to a bill allowing the governor, in an emergency, to approve the death sentence by a means other than lethal injection. The amendment didn't draw much attention. The current governor had declared a moratorium on the death penalty, and no one foresaw any situation that could require its implementation.

No one made a political fight out of it.

On this beautiful day in the Willamette Valley, Stan was taking an air-tour of the Cascade Mountains and the Coastal Mountains. The two North-South running mountain ranges helped define Oregon's diverse ecosystems. For 175 years, people had been making fortunes logging the vast forests. Firefighters had been attempting to preserve those fortunes by fighting forest fires for just as long. Wildfires that would sweep through the forests every few years, clearing the underbrush and creating healthy forest ecosystems, were fought while they were small.

Tinder-dry underbrush filled today's forests, which hadn't burned for decades. Brush, low-hanging branches, dead and down trees, and fallen branches filled the forests. One dropped cigarette or lightning strike could set off a fire. Half a dozen major wildfires were raging. It would take a freak weather system to put the flames out before the rains started in November.

Stan and his pilot planned to fly down one mountain range and back up the other. Stan wanted to see the fires firsthand before he started pressing the federal government for help in fighting them. He had already mobilized all the National Guard forces at his disposal. The continuous blazes had exhausted Oregon's resources.

The plane left the Salem Airport and followed Highway 22 up the Santiam Canyon and over Detroit Dam and Detroit Lake. He could look down and see hundreds of people camping, fishing, and water skiing. They headed up and over the top of the pass to observe a significant fire on the east slope of the Cascades. His pilot started climbing, gaining altitude to clear the jagged peaks and the upcoming smoke plume.

They were over Hoodoo Ski Resort observing the large plume of smoke to the east when the pilot started cursing and banked the plane back the way they had come. Stan could hear the motor sputtering and saw smoke coming from the engine.

Stan asked, "What's going on?"

The pilot replied, "We just got shot at, we are going down. I think I can make it into the dirt firefighter's landing strip back at the junction. You might want to put out a mayday call."

Stan grabbed the microphone and triggered it to send, "Mayday, Mayday, this is Governor Anderson, we have an in-flight motor failure. We are attempting to land on the firefighting strip at the junction of McKenzie Pass and Santiam Pass. Mayday."

A female voice broke into his call, "We've got you spotted, Governor. This is Alexia with Eyes in the Air News. We'll keep Eyes on you until you're down. Wishing you a safe landing."

The pilot was ex-military and skilled at landing on a dirt strip. When he was sure they would make the field, he turned off the smoking engine and glided the plane in. He had no sooner gotten stopped before the news helicopter landed next to them.

A raven-haired beauty jumped out of the copter and raced to open the door of the small plane. Wearing casual slacks and an attractive top, she looked camera ready.

"Are you ok, Governor? My pilot says he saw someone shooting at you."

"Nonsense, Alexia, we just had an unexpected motor failure,"

Governor Anderson said as he gave his pilot a look that said that's the official story.

Alexia, however, was walking around the small plane, inspecting it.

Skepticism showed in her voice, "Yes, sir, if that's what you want to say, that's what I'll say. It sure looks to me like six bullet holes in your wings and fuselage and three in the motor. But I guess that qualifies as unexpected motor failure."

The governor couldn't help but grin at her, impudence, "Thank you, Alexia, I owe you."

She returned his grin and said, "It's not a bad idea to have the governor owe you."

"I have to ask, Alexia, why were you so close?" Stan asked.

"Easy sir, your out of office agenda is always have posted on your website. I always check to see if you're doing anything newsworthy." She answered, "I thought your inspecting all of our forest fires was newsworthy. If you said anything, based on what you saw today, great. If you didn't, we would have new footage of the fires, and I could do a story on them. We were hanging back, shadowing you, sir."

"Hmmm," Stan said, "I think posting my calendar on my website may not be smart."

"Yes sir, that's what it looks like to me," she nodded.

As Alexia flew away, she wondered what was going on and hoped the governor was OK. She thought, "I like him. He seems like a regular person, with real compassion for the people." She contrasted that to the politicians she had met who focused on narrow ideological agendas and didn't appear to care how their agenda impacted the average person.

Later that evening, after a long conversation with the Oregon State

Police Investigator, Stan sat with Margo and discussed the shooting and the car wreck. Neither of them could come up with a list of enemies who would be angry enough to want to shoot him. Margo was crying, and Stan was angry. Neither emotion gave them an answer to who was targeting them or why.

Stan said, "My business dealings are years in the past, and I did nothing that would cause anyone to want to shoot me. I don't know how, but I know it involves politics. I've looked back year by year at my political career. There are decisions I have made which various groups opposed, that cost people money. But, I can't see any of those decisions causing someone to want to kill me."

Margo asked, "What about the execution of Charlie Miller? His family was vocal and threatening the entire time he was in prison."

His reply, "I don't see it, the timing is wrong. That was years ago when I first came into office. If that were it, why wait for so long?"

"I don't know the answer to that, but wasn't the judge that presided over Charlie Miller's trial killed a few weeks ago?"

Stan looked at her for a long moment and said, "Yes, he was. He and his wife died in a house fire."

"Was it arson?"

"The report I read said he had linseed oil-soaked rags in his garage near his old paint cans. They went up in flames because of spontaneous combustion. Once the fire started, the paint cans, propane tanks, and lawnmower gasoline exploded like a bomb. I understand flames engulfed the house in minutes."

"Back to the question, could it have been arson?"

Frowning at her, he said, "I don't know. It sounds like a good idea to ask the investigators to take another look at it."

# 68

MID-AUGUST

***Home of Donald Miller***

I thought you said you could shoot that plane down. That didn't work any better than the car crash," Donald Miller exclaimed.

Bruce Miller was defensive in his explanation to his father, "I shot it down, and I caused the car to wreck. I didn't count on them surviving a car wreck or a plane crash."

"Well, enough of trying to do this from the background," Donald said. "It's time to quit pussyfooting around and get this done for your brother."

Donald walked to the refrigerator and grabbing several cans of generic beer, he walked back into the living room and started tossing them to the men in the room. "Little Charlie, I want you to track the girl. Figure out where she lives and works. Figure out who she dates, everything she does. The rest of you, I want the governor covered every minute of the day. When you see anything that looks like an opening, let me know."

He continued to rant, "Also, I want him terrified. Charlie lived in fear for over 20 years. He was afraid he would die every day. He didn't know if he would get executed or stuck with a homemade knife in the showers. I want the governor to know that fear. Start sending those letters we talked about. Whenever you can take a shot at him and get away with it, do it. I don't care if you hit him, that would be a plus, but I want him scared shitless."

# 69

MID-AUGUST

***Mahonia Hall (the governor's mansion)***

"Honey, Alex is on our private line," Margo said as she carried the phone to Stan.

Taking the phone, Stan said, "Thanks, Sweetie, I wonder what he wants?"

He answered with, "Hi Alex, are you coming out to go fishing?"

President Alex Myers said, "No, I wanted to find out what the hell is going on out there, and why you haven't told me?"

In a worried voice, Stan answered, "Well, I don't know what's going on, except it looks like someone wants me dead. The state police are involved, but they don't have a lot to go on."

President Myers said, "When they took a shot at you in your airplane, it became a federal case. The FBI is already coordinating with your state police. They'll get him or them. Let's hope it's before they get you."

Stan sighed, "That would be a good thing."

"I'd like to offer a little extra help. I have an individual who holds a U.S. Marshal's status but works on special projects for me doing VIP security work. He could show up as your private bodyguard. Let him coordinate your safety with his contacts in the private security business. You have deep enough pockets. You can afford the people he puts in place. They can keep you safe until the FBI figures out who is after you."

Margo, who was eavesdropping, nodded her head. Stan agreed, saying, "Thank you, Mr. President, how do I reach him?"

"I'll have him reach you. His name is Jimmy. You can trust him. Give my love to Margo," President Myers said as he hung up.

~

TWO DAYS LATER, Jimmy showed up on Stan's doorstep. Taking charge, he asked to meet with Stan and Margo in their private quarters. As Jimmy talked and asked questions, Stan paced back and forth.

Jimmy wanted to know, "What are you doing about security now?"

Stan replied, "Not a lot other than what the State Police provides the governor."

Jimmy started talking about the situation, "It's a piece of classic good news, bad news. The good news is, whoever is after you is an amateur. The bad news is, by his actions, he is telling us you obsess him, and even amateurs can kill you."

Ceasing his pacing for a moment, Stan interrupted, "With no disrespect, what can you do that our investigators can't?"

"You must be good friends with the president. My job isn't to find out who is doing this. He told me to keep you safe while other people figure out who is trying to kill you."

Margo gave a low moan at that thought.

Jimmy said, "The president has a fleet of armored cars pre-staged around the country for whenever he flies into an area. The sport utility kept for his use in Denver is in transit. It should arrive tomorrow. I'll be your driver, that's how you should introduce me into your life. Tell people I'm your driver and personal assistant. I have a large team of private security showing up tomorrow. They are all former special ops in the military. The president said you could afford the best. That's what you're getting."

Stan resumed his pacing. He couldn't sit still. Walking to the window, he looked out into the darkened yard and then turned back to the wine bar. Picking up a glass of Oregon pinot noir, his pacing was brisk.

Jimmy said, "Starting tomorrow, a team will surround you no matter where you go. We'll have mobile teams in front of and behind you as we drive. We'll have teams deployed outside the mansion and your office down at the State Capitol. The special teams will be unobtrusive and blend in wherever you're going. I suggest you step up the visibility of the State Police. Your shooter expects evasive action from you. You need to let him think you're doing that. Remember, my job isn't to find your shooter. My job is to keep you safe."

As he said that, a shot rang out, and the window exploded, showering them with glass. Jimmy threw himself at Stan and Margo, knocking them to the floor.

Margo screamed.

Moments later, they heard a loud motorcycle roaring away.

Jimmy stood up and made a point of closing all the draperies, "As I said, an amateur, it's good you were pacing. A professional wouldn't have missed. I think until you can get bulletproof glass installed in all the windows, we should at least close the draperies."

# 70

PRESENT DAY

**Student Union**
**Chemeketa Community College**

Julia was looking forward to the day's photography class. She'd rearranged her job as a volunteer preschool instructional assistant to allow her to take an outdoor photography class.

She enjoyed working with the children, many of whom were from disadvantaged families. Julia had never experienced the range of issues the children she worked with dealt with every day. Julia came from a loving, supportive family and was close to her parents.

She talked with her parents about the immigrant children living in fear of separation from and deportation of their parents. They spoke about single mothers having multiple children from different fathers. Most received no child support. They talked about the blatant racism the children in her class were exposed to every day and the lack of resources and role models in the children's lives.

Julia asked the hard question, "How does it get fixed, Dad?"

Julia knew she had led a storybook life as a 'trust fund child.' She didn't need to work to support herself, but enjoyed her volunteer job and felt like she was making a difference. The work was, however, challenging for a person who had never experienced the 'gritty side of life.' For her, she knew it was an opportunity to learn what others went through. Her mother and father had always been protective of her. He had worked hard and provided his family with everything they needed.

While she was still a young child, her father sold his business and deposited a significant sum into a trust fund for Julia. With the help of an Investment Advisor and her father's input, that trust fund had grown to a substantial amount. She now lived off the income of her trust fund and could work or volunteer because she wanted to, not because she had too.

Julia talked with her mother about her feelings. "Mom, I know I'm blessed, thanks to you and Dad. I have a nice condo, and you and Dad have made sure I'll never worry about money. But, I feel depressed. There's nothing wrong I can pinpoint. I can't see a reason for it, but I feel a low level of unhappiness permeating my life."

Her mother said, "Honey, you're lonely. You want a man you can love and respect. And one who will love and respect you in return. You've had a bumpy ride with men. You need to look at how you're picking them. Think about what attracted you to the relationships you've had and why. Maybe use your head more and your hormones less, when you meet a man you're attracted to."

Julia knew her mother was right. She was lonely for a meaningful relationship with a man worthy of her.

The preschool also had awakened her mothering instincts. Julia longed for a child of her own.

# 71

PRESENT-DAY

***Friday, September 8, 2017, 8 A.M.***
***Student Union Food Court***
***Chemeketa Community College***

Roman was enjoying the morning. His wounded body had recovered, and he felt like he was making progress on the emotional front. He'd been involved in many PTSD counseling sessions. Now he was the leader of a small group of veterans who met once a week for an early morning program. It wasn't counseling. It was just a place where vets could stay connected to others with similar experiences. He hoped he could help them talk through issues when they came up. Roman still felt numb, but he was no longer having continual flashbacks. Because he startled, and jumped, at loud noises or personal contact, he tried to always pay strict attention to what was going on around him. He didn't enjoy embarrassing himself or others with inappropriate responses.

It was a beautiful day, and he'd ridden his motorcycle this morning. A friend in his counseling group asked if he could borrow the bike for the day. The friend had a date with a girl he wanted to impress.

Roman said, "Sure. I've got research to do in the library anyhow. That'll take all day. Why don't you put it in parking lot B when you get back from your ride? I won't need it until 5 p.m."

He thought, "I must be getting better. It has been several years since I noticed a woman." He glanced in vain across the coffee shop for the beautiful woman he'd seen.

Moments later, feeling a tap on his back, his instincts kicked into overdrive. In his mind, he was no longer in the Student Union having coffee. Instead, he was under attack from the rear. His training and reflexes kicked in. Spinning and placing one foot behind his attacker, Roman pushed on his attacker's chest to take him down backward. While doing so, he grabbed the throat of the attacker to rip out his windpipe and permit no sound.

Except, as they were falling, his senses picked up her fragrance, the firm softness of her breast, and her terrified green eyes. Horror-stricken, he twisted, so she landed on him, and he jumped to his feet.

It mortified Roman to know he had been within seconds of killing her. He also hoped she didn't know that.

He had a strong belief that everything happens for a reason. Moments prior, he was holding her up as his vision of the woman he would like in his life. Now she was in his arms. Well, she was in his arms to the extent that he was trying to clean her up after her fall.

JULIA SAW her attacker being solicitous, as he requested dry towels, etc. He appeared in command of the situation as two of the three baristas ran to his bidding. She thought, "His concern would be sweet if my throat didn't feel crushed, and my breast didn't ache from his grip." She started to shake as she remembered the chill of his eyes and thinking they were the eyes of the angel Gabriel, death's messenger.

Maneuvered into a chair, she could hear the conversations around her as she gasped for breath and felt herself shaking.

Through a fog, she heard, "Here, please sit. Put your head

between your knees. Try to slow your breathing. Bob, can you get us a paper bag and something to wrap around her? I think she is hyperventilating."

The barista, Bob said, "No wonder, sir. I saw her approach you from the back. What was she thinking? She is lucky you didn't hurt her."

"She has no idea how lucky. Why don't you get her another drink? Do you know what she ordered?" She saw her attacker hand Bob his credit card for the new drink.

He asked her name, and she gasped back, "Julia, I can't breathe."

Minutes later, Julia found herself breathing into a paper bag with several towels, and his jacket draped over her shoulders. Forcing herself to calm down, her hands quit shaking.

~

WHAT SHE COULDN'T hear was him thinking, "No, Bob, I'm the lucky one. I have enough ghosts that I deal with already. I don't need another beautiful woman to haunt me. I would never forgive myself if I had harmed her."

# 72

Forcing herself to relax and focus, Julia heard the man with the piercing black eyes speak, "Once again, I'm sorry, I should be more careful. I turned and knocked you down. I'm such a klutz. My name is Roman."

Julia realized the explanation was an attempt to put the unpleasant situation in the past. She also knew she had witnessed, firsthand, extraordinary martial arts moves designed to eliminate an enemy attacking from the rear.

She couldn't help her response, "Bullshit. I had five years of martial arts training when I was in junior high and high school. My dad wanted me to learn self-defense. Even though I never won any major competitions, I had good training and know what just happened. I don't know if that was taekwondo, krav maga, or karate. But, I recognized the move and experienced firsthand how expert you are. I know I approached you from the rear and startled you, but you were seconds from killing me. What was that all about? Just because I touched you?" As she asked that her voice raised at least an octave.

Roman couldn't look her in the eye. He looked at his hands, which she saw were shaking. He put them in his pockets, "I'm sorry. It had nothing to do with you. It is a flaw of mine, and you are the one who suffered. I wish I could take that moment back and have a 'do-over.' Again, I apologize. I hope you can forgive me?"

Julia looked him full in the face for the first time. Studying him, she saw a strong face with a firm jaw, full black eyebrows, and long eyelashes. His furrowed brow expressed anguish over what had happened. The 'angel of death eyes' had disappeared. She wondered where they went, and part of her longed to know the story behind those eyes. "He's the most handsome man I've ever seen, and I love his voice. It's so rich and resonant." She thought to herself.

Concern was clear in his voice, and she thought his face showed the fires of personal trauma. His eyes looked haunted. "I wonder why he looks so distressed. I don't think it's what just happened, there's something else."

After a long moment, she said, "Yes, you're forgiven. I do not believe you meant to hurt me."

Lingering, on the verge of hyperventilation, Julia couldn't hold her hands quiet. Picking up a towel, she started drying her fancy camera. The camera was waterproof, but it had gotten soaked with the spilled coffee. She could see Roman watching her and looking awkward and unsure.

"I hope I didn't ruin your camera or your blouse. If I did, I'll reimburse you."

"Don't worry about it," she snapped.

Taking her camera out of her hands, he handed it to Bob, who was still hovering in the background. "Bob, do you think you could ask in the food court for a bag of uncooked rice to pack her camera in?" Looking at Julia, he explained, "That will pull all the moisture out of it."

Minutes later, Bob was back. "Callie, the owner of all the food booths, is here. She says she will find the rice and pack the camera herself. That way, she says she knows it'll be done right." Both Roman and Bob smiled.

Julia, however, still getting over her initial shock, had stopped shaking, and her curiosity was now in full gear.

"Why does everyone here jump to your orders, and why does

everyone call you, sir? They appear to stand at attention around you. Who are you? What do you do?"

He replied, "I'm nobody special. I help with my family businesses a little, and I do volunteer counseling with veterans here at the college. That's where I know most of these guys. I spend the bulk of my time finishing up my mountain cabin. It seems like a never-ending project. I'm just your basic guy, trying to get down the rocky road of life without too many bruises."

He paused, "I'm much more interested in you. What brings you here at this hour, are you taking or teaching a class?"

"Can anybody jump into this conversation?" A large, middle-aged woman with an air of being in charge interrupted. "You must be the Julia I heard about. I'm Callie. Here's your camera. It's a beautiful piece of equipment. Make sure you keep it packed in rice for a week before you open it or try to do anything with it."

Handing over the camera, Callie pointed at Roman, "I couldn't help but hear Roman give you the 'Aw Shucks' ma'am, I'm just a poor country boy routine. In another minute, I'd have believed it myself. Now you need to know he is the nicest man around, donates his time at any hour of the day or night to help vets that are having an issue. They might be dealing with flashbacks, PTSD, homelessness, disability paperwork, whatever. What I can't tell you about is his history or anything personal. Whenever I ask about that, I get a stupid grin as he tells me he's classified. Just don't let him BS you that he's just Joe Average, he's not."

Callie winked at Julia and strolled away as Roman laughed, "Callie, get out of here, or I'll sabotage your deep fat fryers."

# 73

Feeling both attracted to Roman and yet terrified, Julia allowed Roman to help her out of her chair, as he said, "Why don't we go outside? Just walk around for a few minutes and get you a little fresh air. You still look a little shaky."

Feeling warm and on the verge of throwing up, she agreed to walk around the flower beds in the Commons. Besides, it didn't hurt to have a handsome man giving her his undivided attention. Despite the morning's event, she had to admit to herself she could feel her attraction to Roman growing.

Julia could hear her mother's warning echoing in her to use her head, and not her emotions, or her hormones. Slowing her breathing helped her regain control. Shocked at her response to this morning's experience, she started gasping for air again. "I've done lots of high energy, high adrenaline sports, and never reacted like this morning. Why am I doing this?"

"I terrified you, I'm sorry. Try slow, deep breaths."

She brought the conversation back to Callie's comments. "You know, I've got a lot of experience in recognizing when a politician or anyone else answers a question by not saying anything. You were evasive when I asked about you. Is there any reason, or are you just evasive by nature?"

HER BLUNTNESS SURPRISED ROMAN. He knew a lot might depend on his answer. Hesitating, he questioned how much to say to a woman he had just met. He also thought about the cosmos bringing into his arms the first woman he'd felt attracted to in a long time. "I ask for a relationship with a woman like her. Minutes later, she's here. I can't tell her much about me, but if I don't, I may never see her again."

He answered, "There are several reasons that I would prefer not to go into with a beautiful woman I have just met. None of them are about you. They fall into the category of more personal information than I am comfortable sharing at the moment."

He continued with the first grin she had seen on his face, "I'll make you a promise. If in our getting to know each other, we decide we want to move forward, I promise I'll be as open and truthful as I can be."

When she raised her eyebrows at that, he grinned again and said, "Remember, as Callie said, I'm classified." When he smiled, his entire face lite up, and she had trouble remembering this was the man who had the 'angel of death eyes,' a short while ago.

She couldn't help but laugh, but responded with, "Am I to assume, then you want to see me again without coffee stains on my blouse?"

There was a brief pause before he said, "Yes."

She wondered about his hesitation, "This has been a mighty strange way to meet someone. OK, I'll put off my questions until later, but you better be on the up and up."

"I am," he said with a smile. "Now, Julia, I want to know about you," said Roman shifting the conversation back to her.

"Well, the reason I was here at this early hour was to meet my outdoor photography class for a carpool. I'm sure the class has already left without me. That's the most disappointing thing about this. I was looking forward to this week's outing."

"I'm sorry. Where were you going? I'll try to make it up to you."

She replied, "It was a raft trip of the North Santiam River. I'm sure it's too late for me to catch up with them. It's a rare opportunity since they are letting all the water out of Detroit Dam for an inspection. I understand, with the water level change, it will be an incredible photo opportunity. I'm sorry to miss it."

In an instant, Roman went from appearing relaxed and laid back, to laser-focused and in a command role. He started firing questions faster than Julia could answer.

He asked, "What guide service were you using?"

She responded, "None."

"Did the college approve this trip?"

"No, it was just a little side trip we arranged as students."

His next question, "How many rafts?"

She answered, "Five two-man inflatable kayaks."

Without a breath, he asked, "Where were you putting into the river?"

"Packsaddle," she answered. Roman knew Packsaddle was a campground on the North Santiam River rafters used as a launch point.

Again he asked, "When did they leave?"

"Stop, you're scaring me. Why are you interrogating me?"

"I'm sorry, that's not my intent. This is important. When did the group leave?"

"About half an hour ago, we were meeting here and arranging carpools. We were planning on being on the water around 9ish."

"Who was the idiot that suggested this?" Roman kept questioning.

"Charlie, he's why I came over to talk to you. Why did you look disgusted when you saw me talking to him? With everything that happened, I forgot, that was the whole reason I came over to talk to you."

"Oh, that worm. He reminded me of several of my sister's ex-boyfriends. They all have the tall, dark, and handsome routine down pat with a scruffy three-day-old beard, an earring, and a macho tattoo. It always looks like they are trying to duplicate prison or gang tats. To me, they look slimy. All their body language says to not turn your back on them. "

Roman face got severe and quiet as he looked her in the eyes and said, "You need to trust me on this, I need your help. It is likely those nine friends of yours are about to die. No promises, but if you and I leave right-now, maybe we can save them. I need you because I need a crew member. Your car is necessary because I rode my bike this morning, and loaned it to a buddy who wanted to impress his girlfriend. And before you ask, yes, I'll call the police, but they can't get there fast enough."

## 74

Shocked, she asked, "You're kidding, right? Please tell me you're kidding."

"No, sad to say, I'm not... everyone up the canyon has known for weeks to stay off the river today." Roman said, "It's a death trap."

He paused and then asked, "Yes or no? Are you going to help?"

Julia had a premonition that this was a pivotal point in her life. Without knowing why she knew, this decision was the proverbial fork in the road of her future.

As she looked into Roman's eyes, they no longer looked like the eyes of death she had seen earlier. She realized that she trusted this man she had known for moments and would do whatever he needed to help save her friends.

Without saying a word, she stood up and handed over the keys to her Mercedes AMG C63Coupe. It was her pride and joy, with a 469 Horsepower motor paired with a seven-speed automatic transmission. She'd never sampled its full power for more than a few seconds, attempting to do so, scared her. She just loved its brilliant blue metallic color and the way she felt behind the wheel.

"Good, set your fastest pace to your car, I'll drive," Roman said.

Julia was in training for the Portland Marathon. She knew she was in great shape. She took off at a quick run, thinking, "I'll bury this cocky guy."

However, when she arrived at her car, he was right next to her and wasn't even breathing hard.

ROMAN GOT in and took a quick look around to familiarize himself with the car while adjusting his seat and mirrors. Tightening his seat belt, he took another long look around the car and at Julia as she strapped in.

Julia looked up as she heard him whistle and say, "Beautiful. Nice ride."

From the way he was looking at her, she wasn't sure if he was talking about the car or herself. She couldn't help but comment, "That was my thought when I saw it sitting on the showroom floor with the spotlight shining on it."

"Your car tells me a lot about you."

"Like what?"

"Most people's cars reflect how they see themselves. Your car is sporty, fast, luxurious, and has a vivacious personality when the light hits it. I bet she's an independently minded female, requiring a firm hand on the wheel and my full attention. I bet she loves to drive fast. If we met in other circumstances, I'm sure you're just as much fun. What's her name?"

"What makes you think I'd name my car?"

"A car like this deserves a name."

"You'd laugh."

"No, I wouldn't. That wouldn't be nice to her."

"It's Miss Blue."

She could see Roman struggling to hide a grin as he handed her his phone. "You can get the numbers we need out of my contacts. Hook my phone to your Bluetooth or dial on your phone, but I need to talk to several people on speakerphone as we drive."

Julia said, "I'll use my phone. It's already hooked to my Bluetooth. Do I need a password to get into your contacts?"

"No"

Exiting the parking lot, Roman turned on the car's emergency flashers and said, "Call my sister Alexia."

"This is Alexia," came through the speakers with a lot of background noise.

"Alexia, it's Roman."

"Roman? Who is Julia Anderson? That's who showed up my caller ID. Are you holding out on me, bro'? You got a friend you haven't told me about?"

"Later, can you put Uncle Russ on the line?"

Julia grinned, as a disembodied voice, came through the speakers, "Oh no, you always dig the info out of me about my boyfriends. It's your turn. You have something going on the side you haven't told me about?"

Shaking his head, Roman said, "She's just a friend. You'll meet her in a few hours. Get Uncle Russ on the phone. This is urgent, put it on speaker if you can."

"She already did, what's up?" Uncle Russ said.

"Some idiots are attempting to raft the Santiam today. It sounds like they are all amateurs in little funky two-man inflatable kayaks. There's a whole group of them. I'm leaving Chemeketa Community College and headed to pick-up a boat. Then I'll put in at Packsaddle. If they're lucky, I'll catch up with the rafters before they get into serious trouble."

The entire time Roman was chatting with Uncle Russ, Julia was white-knuckled as Roman raced in and out of traffic on Cordon Road. Emergency lights flashing, passing cars as though they were standing still, he was fast approaching the on-ramp to Highway 22. It terrified Julia, wondering what speed they'd be driving when he hit the open road. She was even more concerned when she heard Roman ask Uncle Russ where he and Alexia were, and could he get Roman a police escort.

Uncle Russ said he was showing Alexia the Willamette River.

They'd put into the river in Salem and were about at Buena Vista Ferry, sightseeing and videoing scenery for Alexia's news show.

Uncle Russ said, "We'll drop what we are doing and head to the falls at Mill City. You know I can't take the jet boat upstream past the falls."

Julia asked in a low tone for Roman, "Where are they in relation to where we are going?"

Uncle Russ, however, heard the question and answered, "By boat, it's a long way. We need to continue south on the Willamette to where the Santiam drops into the Willamette. Then we will head east up the Santiam until it splits into the North and South Santiam Rivers. After that, we will continue up the North Santiam to the falls. Even at full speed, that's a long trip by jet boat. You and Roman will be on the river before we get anywhere close to the activity. Roman, can you still hear me?"

"Yes, Uncle Russ."

"My deputy is crewing for us. He's on the radio right now ordering a police escort for you. He says they'll be on the Aumsville on-ramp waiting for you. There's no need to stop, they'll merge with you. Alexia is calling her station right now to get 'Eyes in the Air' to help spot the rafters. The police want to know what you're driving."

"It's a bright blue, Mercedes sports car."

Julia said, "She's a brilliant blue."

Julia was listening to the rapid-fire conversation, trying to understand what was happening. She was clenching her door handle and pressing her foot onto the non-existent brake pedal. She heard Uncle Russ say, "As soon as I hang up, I'll call my coordinator at the Oregon National Guard unit for a medevac helicopter. The question is, will my coordinator get it approved in time?"

Julia interjected, "If there's a problem, maybe I could make a call." Roman gave her a quizzical look

Feeling a sudden speed deceleration, Julia glanced at the speedometer. It was dropping to 80 mph to allow the police cruiser to enter the highway in front of them at Aumsville. Working hard at controlling her breathing, Julia refused to look at the speedometer.

The police car, with sirens blaring, roared down Highway 22 with the mighty AMG Coupe chewing on its tailpipes. It amazed Julia to see police blocking the access ramps until they passed. Their lane of the road was clear.

Thinking about what was happening, she thought, “I don’t know who this guy is to have the clout to get us a police escort. If he hadn’t tried to kill me earlier, I’d be excited. Who am I kidding? I am excited. I may never get another high-speed police escort anywhere, I’d better enjoy it.”

As soon as Uncle Russ hung up, Roman asked, “Can you connect me to my mother?” He gave her the phone number. Julia couldn’t hear the name she answered with, but it was a business name. As soon as Roman identified himself, the tone changed, and just like Alexia, she wanted to know who Julia was. Julia couldn’t help chuckling at the curiosity of Roman’s mother and sister.

“Mom, not now. You’ll meet her soon. There are several raft loads of idiots on the river who may die if we don’t get to them first. Who is around the store that can help crew?” He asked.

“Nobody other than Bridger, that drunken friend of yours, who sleeps under the bridge,” was her answer.

“Urghhh.... ok, tell him what’s going on. I need him to pull out that new drift boat and get it hooked up to the GMC. I need ten life jackets, a propane tank hooked to the heater, that new air gun that shoots life preservers, and the boat defibrillator. Also, I have a young lady with me. I’m guessing a size 8? She needs everything from skin out, The Warm and Wet long underwear, a drysuit, and the boots that go with the drysuit.”

“What size boots?”

At Roman’s hesitation, Julia said, “Seven.”

Julia felt irked without knowing why. “What's bothering me? Is it that a man I’ve known for minutes is guessing my size or the fact that he has the experience to be correct? I wonder if he has gotten around to guessing my 38 D bra size. I’m sure he has. There’s no question he had a firm grip on my right breast. I’ll be black and blue tomorrow.”

As the flurry of phone calls slowed down, Julia asked, "Why haven't you called the police for help?"

Roman gave her a puzzled glance and then said, "That was the first call to Alexia and Uncle Russ. Uncle Russ is a Marine Deputy for the Marion County Sheriff's office. I knew he'd be on the river today with my sister. She's a news broadcaster with a Portland TV station. She was doing a ride-along today with a cameraman."

Roman continued, "Uncle Russ's plan for today was to cruise the Willamette River, looking for people in trouble with the expected increase in river flow. Nobody expected rafters on the Santiam River itself, because of the massive publicity campaign warning everyone to stay off the river. We'll be coming downriver hoping to find anyone in trouble. Uncle Russ will come upriver, God willing, between us, we will find all the rafters."

The police officer pulled into the parking lot of a business in Gates that had an old Nelson Bait and Tackle sign with a picture of a drowned earthworm. There was also a newer looking sign that advertised "Clean Restrooms, Open to the Public."

Paying strict attention, Julia realized, it was a large sporting goods and boat complex. There were several cars in the customer parking spots. The police officer waved goodbye and headed back the way he had come.

The exterior of the old building gave every appearance of having served the fishing community for decades. Noticing the small details, Julia realized, "This building has fresh paint, but it's done, so the building looks like it's been here for years. Maybe it has."

Stretching as she exited the car, and turning in a circle to see everything, she was impressed. The complex spanned both sides of the highway. On the riverside of Highway 22 were about 2 acres of boat parking and a newish boat showroom. It appeared to have living quarters above the showroom with a tall cyclone fence surrounding a parking lot filled with boats, quads, and snowmobiles of all kinds. The Bait and Tackle Store was on the mountainside of the highway. It also appeared to have about two acres surrounded by a cyclone fence.

The Nelson Bait and Tackle property also had several outbuildings. As strange as it was, it appeared one was the landing for a small chair lift. Julia couldn't think what else it could be since she saw a single line of poles going straight out of the back of the property and up a steep mountain. She couldn't imagine why anyone would have a chairlift at this elevation. It was too low for consistent snow, and besides, she couldn't see any ski trails in the thick forest other than the clearing going straight up the hill that contained the poles and line.

## 75

Julia unclenched her knuckles from the grab bar above the door and climbed out of her car. She saw what looked like a dirty, bearded, homeless person throwing up at the side of the parking lot. She heard Roman shout to him, "God Bridger, how can you get that drunk? Never mind, do you have the boat hooked up and loaded?"

"Give me another five minutes to get everything loaded. You go change."

Roman grabbed Julia by the hand and dragged her into the store. He introduced her to his mother.

With raised eyebrows, his mother shooed Roman off to change and took Julia through the store and into the living quarters. The quarters were more beautiful and extensive than Julia was expecting. Regardless of the dilapidated exterior, everything inside the building was brand new and top quality.

Inside the stores' entrance, was a large sign directing people to the restrooms and free coffee. There was also a barista offering espresso based drinks. Julia couldn't help but smile as she noticed the route to the bathrooms and free coffee required people to walk through the entire store and past all the merchandise.

She thought, "Smart, I'd bet money those bathrooms are immaculate. Any woman who ever stops here on the trip to Central Oregon will stop on every trip."

Rose was tall and slender. Her silvery brown hair had a stylish cut with dark brown streaks. Well dressed in slacks and a casual top, Rose looked a year or two older than Julia's parents.

Rose said, "You can change in here while we talk, or rather while I talk. I can see from your expression you aren't sure about the need to change. You look beautiful, and what you have on is gorgeous, but Roman is right. The clothing he had me put out for you is more practical for what you'll be doing. The long underwear will keep you warm, even if it gets wet. Over that, you put the drysuit, which keeps you dry and functions as a flotation suit. The boots are so you can step on the jagged river bottom without hurting your feet, and the soles are weighted. That way, you'll float with your feet down and head upright. What I want to say is I don't know who you are or how long you have known my son, but thank you."

Julie responded, "There's no need to thank me for anything. I just met your son this morning. We ran into each other by accident."

"That may be true, but I saw more life in his eyes a few minutes ago than I have seen in the two years since his return," said Rose with tears in her eyes.

Rose continued, "To quote Roman's grandfather, 'there are no cosmic accidents.'"

"Mom, Julia, We gotta go," was Roman's loud shout.

"Roman," his mother said, "You know I taught you not to yell in the house. We're in here. Your new girlfriend and I have been having a great time getting acquainted."

Both Julia and Roman reacted to the girlfriend label, but Mrs. Nelson just waved them off. Each of them, however, was thinking they wouldn't mind its being true.

Julia noticed the appraisal in Roman's eyes as he saw her in the form-fitting Spandex type outfit. She was happy all the hours in the gym had paid off, but hoped he couldn't see her scoping out his fit body and all its bulges. He wore an all-black dry suit, including a head covering and had wicked-looking knives and obscure paraphernalia hanging off him.

As they exited the store, he hollered at his drunken buddy, "Bridger, jump in the boat."

They were out of the parking lot in minutes, pulling a trailer with a new drift boat.

The knot in Julia's stomach was loosening as Roman drove the truck and trailer at a reasonable speed on the winding road. She knew her eyes got wide when he pulled past a barricade and backed the trailer down to a boat ramp. Julia had never been here, but could tell the river was in full flood stage. Lying off to the side, she saw a kayak with her name pasted to it. The problem was, it appeared half flat.

JUMPING out of the drift boat, Bridger started inspecting the kayak with great care. He waved them over and asked Julia, "Do you have any enemies, any ex-boyfriends who wish you ill?"

While asking Julia the questions, he was showing the leaking kayak seams and a puncture to Roman. Bridger and Roman were both suspicious and listening to her answers. Julia was close to tears as she denied having an ex who would wish her ill.

Roman said, "OK, let's be frank, Julia. I know nothing about you. If you can't think of anyone who might wish you harm, what about your parents? You drive an expensive car, you dress like, look like, and smell like money. Who are you? Could someone be targeting your parents through you?"

"Doubtful," she answered, "but my dad is Stan Anderson. He founded Anderson Technology Inc. He's also the governor."

"Holy shit, I'll bet that's it, Bridger," Roman said. He was quiet thinking for a minute and then asked Bridger to explain to Julia how all the equipment in the boat worked. He needed to make a few phone calls before they got on the water.

# 76

Julia found herself talking to the dirtiest, foulest smelling individual she had ever seen. His hair and beard were long and filthy, and his clothes were mud-encrusted. She remembered her first sight of him had been his throwing up at the side of the store parking lot.

Regardless of appearances, he sounded polite, respectful, and educated, "This strange-looking gun is like the gun they use to shoot T-shirts into the stands at the Volcanoes baseball games. Instead of shirts, it shoots life preservers. It's powered with compressed air. You load the preservers here like this. Notice the lightweight line with a carabiner at the end of each preserver. You attach that end to the boat before you fire it. That way, you can drag the guy with you if you need to. Here's how you fire up the space heater. It also runs the little cooktop for hot tea or soup. This boat's got everything on it. It's the Cadillac of drift boats. I'd love to own it."

Positioning herself upwind, Julia held up a hand, "Stop, Bridger, why a stove and a heater?"

He explained, "Well, it may be a nice warm morning, but that river is snowmelt. If you've ever been in water as cold as this river without the proper clothing you would know, it will sap all the heat out of your core in minutes. When that's gone, you lose your energy and the ability to move. The heater will warm the outside, but The Ghost and I found our Brit buddies favored tea to warm the core."

"The Ghost?" she asked.

"Oops, sorry, Roman." Bridger answered, "We used to call him The Ghost. You never saw him moving at night, but when he did, a 'bad guy' died. You, of course, didn't hear that from me. He would tell you that was a classified story."

Julia added that to her file of what she was learning about Roman. She thought, "That may explain a bit, it sounds like he's been in combat. I've heard about PTSD reactions. I wonder if that's what happened back at the coffee shop?"

Julia continued her questioning, "Bridger, I can see Roman trusts you. I've got several questions. They are none of my business, but I want to know the answers. I'll ask them fast while we are waiting for him to get off the phone. If you don't want to answer them, just say so."

"Ask away."

"Why aren't you acting as his crew? Why are you living under the bridge? Why are you willing to live addicted, and what are you addicted to? You appear intelligent, under all that hair and filth, you may be handsome. Yet, you reek to high heaven. There's not a woman out there that would get within five feet of you. What gives?"

Bridger winced, "That's harsh, but I know the truth hurts. In fact, that hurts a lot. Alcohol and marijuana are my friends when I need to forget. All addicts tell you they are not addicts, but I'm more of a drunk than an addict. As far as the rest, just like Roman, neither of us has been on the water since we mustered out two and a half years ago."

Roman jogged back over with a hurry-up look on his face. He asked Bridger to guard the kayak as though it were a crime scene until a Marion County deputy arrived and afterwards to take his truck and trailer back to the store. Over Bridger's protests that the deputy knew his driver's license was revoked, Roman tossed him the keys and pushed the drift boat into the river.

# 77

**The Santiam River**

Julia continued explaining that she didn't have any vindictive boyfriends, and the Outdoor Photography class was just that. She now realized it might have been a stupid decision to go out on the river today but couldn't believe there was anything sinister. All at once, she looked around and realized she was in the middle of a large river, in flood stage, in a small boat.

The boat wasn't small, but compared to the size of the flood, it was like a fly walking on the back of an elephant. The aluminum boat was 17 feet long, had high sides, and both the stern and prow were taller and pointed. It had four rows of seats. There was one small seat in the rear. The largest position was in the middle for the rower, and there were two forward seats. The seats rotated, allowing them to face either forward or backward. Just in front of the rower's seat, was the space heater, Bridger had been explaining. Under each seat was a small locker.

Julia commented, "OK, this is serious. I hope you know what you're doing. What do I do other than freak out?"

He asked, "Have you ever been in a drift boat?"

At her denial, Roman explained the boat's balance points, and how a drift boat worked. He explained step by step what to watch for and how to use the specialized equipment.

"Bridger already reviewed how to use the equipment with me."

Rowing the oars backwards, Roman said, "I know, let's review again. We are sitting here, almost stationary, talking. When we start moving, I want you comfortable with what we will be doing. Once things begin, everything will be in hyper speed. There will be no time for questions."

He explained, "The drift boat works just opposite a canoe or rowboat. In a canoe or rowboat to control direction, the rower attempts to go faster than the speed of the river. Sometimes they'll row backwards for sudden steerage. In the drift boat, I'll almost always be rowing the boat backward against the current. This slows the boat down, allowing the fishermen to fish, or in our case, for you to get a life preserver to someone. A good rower can hold the boat close to stationary."

Julia was facing Roman as he explained the boat. When he finished, she asked, "What is the noise I'm hearing? I thought a ride on the river would be quiet. It's not."

He replied, "Part of what you're hearing is the oars banging on the aluminum boat. You're also hearing small trees and logs bumping against us. This is a flood. There is a lot of debris the floodwaters have picked up."

"No, no, what's the rumbling, grumbling, banging sound I keep hearing?"

His answer shocked her, "The rocks rolling down the river. In full flood stage, the water is fast enough that the rocks on the bottom are rolling downriver bumping against each other."

Julia pointed towards the bank, "There's David." Hanging from a tree branch was a middle-aged, overweight rafter. He was soaking wet, had blood dripping from his scalp, and appeared only semi-conscious. Roman backed the boat up against the flood. Julia brought up the compressed air gun and shot a life preserver which snagged in the tree David was clinging to. With Roman and Julia both shouting instructions, David got the life preserver fastened. He didn't jump into the water, letting go of the tree, he fell into the water with a splash, which allowed Julia to drag him to the side of the boat. David had no strength left to help lift himself into the drift boat. Julia struggled to keep him hanging onto the edge of the drift boat. She couldn't get him inside. She yelled in a panic, "I can't do it. I can't get him in the boat. He's too heavy."

Roman was doing his best to keep the boat stationary as Julia's efforts rocked it side to side. Roman said, "Sit still and don't rock the boat any further." He stood, and as the boat started to spin, grabbed David by his shirt front and jerked him into the boat. Jumping back to his rowing seat, he stabilized the spinning boat.

David's shivering was out of control. Julia got him positioned in front of the space heater and fixed a cup of tea to warm him. As they were looking for the next rafter, they heard the unmistakable "thump, thump, thump" of the Oregon National Guard medevac helicopter arriving. A news helicopter shadowed it.

She heard Roman mutter, "No matter what country I'm in, the Blackhawks all sound the same."

Julia thought, "Another tidbit of information, he's heard Blackhawk helicopters overseas. I wonder where. Again, that's consistent with prior or current military service. So does the veterans counseling Callie mentioned. Hmm, I'll bet I'm right. If he's suffering from PTSD, that could explain this morning."

Roman was on the radio with the pilot. The pilot and Roman both attempted to hold stationary while the crew lowered a harness to lift David. The harness flew in the helicopter's downdraft. After two failed attempts, a medic lowered on the line. With Roman crewing the boat, Julia helped hook up the harness on the medic, for a "buddy" lift with David. David was no sooner dangling in the air than Roman started working his way across the river with the TV crew directing him. The "Eyes in the Air" news chopper could see someone hanging to a boulder.

For the next hour, with the TV helicopter acting as a spotter, the drift boat searched for and rescued seven rafters. A series of National

Guard medevac helicopters ferried people to the hospital about 40 miles away. Everyone was suffering from hypothermia, cuts, and bruises. A couple had broken arms and legs, and a few had concussions.

Allowing the boat to drift with the current, Roman and Julia searched the river banks for the remaining two rafters. Julia said, "We have to find them, Charlie is the guy who suggested this trip. The other person, we haven't found is Bethany. She's a single mom who struggled to find the money for the camera she needed to take the class. She has a little girl in second grade."

Julia was using the seat just in front of Roman as her work station. She could feel Roman's eyes on her the entire time. Turning and making eye contact, a big smile lit up both their faces. They were in a perilous situation, but she felt alive, and to her surprise, safe. They broke long periods of scanning the river for people or rafts with short, intense rescue efforts. In the quiet moments, her curiosity was raging. "Who is he? Why was he at the college this morning? Why is he so good at what he has us doing on this river, this is scary stuff?"

Looking back at Roman one more time, she found his eyes focused on her. She thought, "I wonder if he has a girlfriend. He said he wants to get better acquainted, but maybe he's married or something. He's the most handsome guy I've seen in a long time. I'm getting hot and bothered just knowing he's checking me out. I wish I knew if he was for real. He seems too good to be true."

Julia thought about it and realized they were in danger every minute they were on the river. Watching Roman maneuver the boat, and handle all the tricky situations, she was amazed at his skill. He never faltered in his command of the action.

She thought, "If he's putting on an act, it's a darn good act. This guy's good at what he's doing. I don't see him faking anything."

Roman kept up a steady commentary, telling her what to expect and how good of a job she was doing. He wasn't only familiar with the twists and turns of the river, but he appeared to have X-Ray eyes on what was below the river surface. He would warn her when they were about to go over a rough spot or perhaps hit a boulder she couldn't see.

She thought, "Other than the incident in the coffee shop, which I'm guessing was PTSD, he has been polite and in control of what is going on. The macho types I have dated would yell at me to sit down, not rock the boat, and to call 911. They'd also be doing it in a loud voice, so I'd know they were in control. This guy appears unflappable. Roman has me standing in the prow of this bumpy boat shooting life preservers to people or dragging them into the boat. He's like a fireman racing into a burning building while everyone else is fleeing. And, he has me going into the burning building with him. What's crazy is, I'm doing it. I think the reason is, he acts like he expects I can. A lot of what we are doing is insane stuff, and he's got me doing it like it's no big deal."

NEITHER JULIA nor Roman realized the TV station had preempted scheduled broadcasting. They were broadcasting the entire rescue live.

As tricky as rowing the boat against the flood was, Roman felt exhilarated. A huge smile was on his face, and for the first time, in a long time, he felt at peace with what he was doing. Watching Julia, he felt pride in her actions. He saw Julia jumping in and doing her job like a "pro." Roman had pushed his body's rehabilitation since discharge, and he was using all those muscles to keep the boat under control in the angry river. He felt alive for the first time in years.

While he was rowing, his eyes were on Julia the entire time. She was sitting in front of him. He couldn't help thinking, "She is amazing. She's everything I ever dreamed of and hoped Amber would become."

Guilt over thinking that thought made him analyze it, "I loved Amber, but I knew she wasn't athletic or adventurous. I always hoped once we got to Oregon, I could teach her to enjoy the outdoors. I could never get her away from the pool or the beach at the resorts we went to."

Julia stood to peer under a tree. While standing, she stretched and arched her back. She then bent at the waist and touched her toes, holding the stretch for a minute. The drysuit stretched over her buttocks and thighs. Roman grinned to himself, "She did that on purpose. She knew what I'd see."

Straightening, she groaned and said, "This has been exhausting. You could never have told me a few hours ago I would stand in this tiny boat as it bobs around, or that I could do what we've done."

Being male as he watched Julia, he thought, "She is just smoking hot. I wonder if she has a boyfriend or husband. I should have asked earlier, now's not the time to ask."

Then he thought, "If I don't ask, I'll never know."

At the next pause in the action, he asked, "I should have asked you earlier, do you have a husband or boyfriend hiding in the background?"

She turned to look at him as she answered, "No, how about you?"

He flashed a grin, "No, I don't have a husband or a boyfriend."

"OK, wise guy, how about a wife or girlfriend?"

Julie heard his voice crack, "Not any longer."

His next thought was, "I wonder if she's as good in bed as I think. I'd bet money she is."

***

JULIA HEARD the pain in his voice when he said he had no girlfriend or wife and wondered.

# 78

## Mill City Falls

The flood was increasing as the two dams upriver continued to release water. The current was fierce and swept the drift boat towards the falls at Mill City. Julia spotted Bethany hanging in a tree branch with her collapsed kayak hanging below her. Julia stood in the back of the boat and shot the life preserver just as they went over the falls. As they hit at the bottom of the falls, Julia fell hard to her knees but stayed in the boat. Holding onto the life preserver, Bethany came flying over the falls. But, as she went over the falls, she lost her grip on the life preserver and sank into the maelstrom at the base of the falls.

The falls were the remnants of a small old dam. Typical water levels would have six inches of water flowing over the broken top and dropping ten feet. There was a small pool at the base of the waterfall. Divers reported it was twenty feet deep, and the falling water created air bubbles that swirled in every direction. It was easy to get disoriented and lose track of which way was up.

There was a notch or chute on one side of the dam, which carried the bulk of the water, rafters used on normal days. It gave passengers an exciting ride but was safe enough for experienced rafters. Today, with all the water, there was no notch or chute for the rafts. The Santiam was running bank to bank and going over the dam in a torrent. The standard six inches of water overflowing the barrier and dropping ten feet was now a dangerous three to four feet of water shooting over the dam twenty to thirty feet horizontally as it made its plunge. It was like looking at a river dropping at a forty-five-degree angle for thirty feet.

It was into that maelstrom Bethany disappeared.

Roman jumped to the back of the boat and released the anchor to keep the drift boat from continuing down the river. Stepping onto a seat, he made a beautiful swan dive into the base of the waterfall. The water pounding into the pool at the base of the falls was frothy white with air bubbles.

JULIA THOUGHT, "That stuff would be like swimming in milk. How will Roman know which way is up, how can he find Bethany? What if he gets disoriented?"

Peering into the water with her heart pounding, Julia did not hear the low growl of a jet boat pulling up next to them. She was too engaged counting how many seconds, and then minutes Roman was underwater.

As she felt the bump of the sheriff's jet boat, she looked up into a beautiful face she saw every night on the evening news and realized a cameraman had her in his focus.

Unaware of her gesture, Julia brushed her hair off her face as she straightened, and saw Alexia smile. Alexia jumped between boats, and grabbing the oars, stabilized the drift boat. Her swift actions were confident, showing she knew what she was doing on the water.

Roman appeared with a limp Bethany in tow. Julia and Alexia helped drag her out of the water and into the boat. Roman turned her on her stomach and pressed hard on her back to pump the water out of her. Bethany spewed water from her lips with feeble movements and a weak moan. Her lips were blue, and she appeared unconscious. Checking her carotid pulse, Julia shouted, "She has no pulse. Bethany, come back, you can't die. You have a young daughter."

Roman grabbed the boat's cardiac defibrillator, "She can't die now, not after that. I didn't think I'd find her. Everybody stand clear."

Applying the heart paddles, he pushed the button for the electrical jolt and said, "Everybody say a prayer."

Moments later, they had her in a rescue litter being lifted skyward to the medevac helicopter.

Julia struggled to stand erect. The boat was rocking side to side and swinging on its anchor. Water was splashing over the sides. She saw Roman reach out to her. She melted into his arms as he gave her a huge hug and a kiss that lingered. Letting her go, he said, "I'm proud of you. You performed like a SEAL."

Julia could feel her juices flowing after the kiss and thought, "I'd better get control here. I was about ready to jump all over him."

Alexia stepped in, "Sorry to interrupt, Bro, but I've got to go. We need to follow everyone to the hospital."

She turned to Julia, "Roman's not much on introductions. I'm his sister, Alexia. I'm counting on seeing you again soon and getting acquainted."

Stepping closer to hug Julia, she whispered in her ear, "I love you already for what you've done for my brother. His eyes are alive again. Thank you. What's your name?"

"Julia Anderson"

"As in Governor Stan Anderson's daughter?" Alexia asked.

"Yes," Julia answered.

"I thought so," Alexia said, "I tried running the name which showed up on caller ID when Roman called on your phone. There were two Julia Andersons. The other one was 80 years old."

"That would be my great aunt," Julia laughed.

"Well, tell your dad and mom to watch tonight's news," Alexia added with a wink.

Alexia jumped into the jet boat and asked her uncle to get her across the river to the news helicopter waiting for her on the ground. Julia wasn't sure if Alexia had heard her mention she couldn't call her dad. Her phone had gotten wet in the rescues.

# 79

**Nelson Bait and Tackle**
**Gates, OR**

A quiet Bridger pulled Roman's old GMC and trailer into its parking spot, ready for an easy exit to pick up Julia and Roman when they finished. It was Roman's father's old work truck. He had driven it for years around all the logging roads. But, when Roman found it in the warehouse with all the construction equipment, it had less than a hundred thousand miles on it.

Roman took it to a mechanic who cleaned it up and did any necessary maintenance. It wasn't fancy, but it got the hard work done, without getting his newer truck abused on logging roads.

Bridger looked around the fenced compound at all the boats. He stopped for a long time, looking at a Zodiac LE2800 with twin Evinrude Outboard 250s. It was the Law Enforcement model, used by all five services. To him, it looked like an old friend calling his name.

Bridger stood outside Rose's store for several minutes before he walked in and found Roman's mother. "We've spoken little, Mrs. Nelson, but Roman and I are friends, and I let him down this morning. He is in what could be a life or death situation, and I let him go with an untrained girl for backup. That can never happen again. It doesn't matter what happened in the past. The past is the past. Please forgive my vulgarity, but it's time for me to get my shit back together. Would it be ok if I used his apartment, took a shower, and maybe borrowed a pair of scissors to cut my hair and beard? My wallet is at home, but I also need new clothes. Roman knows I have the money, and I'm good for it."

Rose said, "I know Roman considers you a good friend, and he would want you to use his apartment for a shower. Why don't you pick out whatever you want from the store, and I'll give you a key to his apartment over the boat showroom for a shower? I could call Cindy. Maybe she can get you in her beauty shop to cut your hair and trim your beard?"

"I wish I could, but I can't. Cindy threw me out of her shop. She told me I was a filthy beast and not to come back. When I first arrived in town, I fell for her in a big way. The problem is, I also fell into the bottle. She said she didn't want to see me again until I'd cleaned up my act. I think I have a lot of proving to do."

"You go get your shower. I'll see what I can do about a haircut for you," Rose said.

Half an hour later, Bridger's clothes were in the garbage can. He'd had his shower and put on new clothes. He was eyeing his beard and hair when Cindy opened Roman's apartment door above the boat showroom and walked in. The bathroom door was open. Cindy just stood there looking at him in the mirror.

Bridger saw tears in her eyes as she watched his reflection in the mirror for the longest time. He returned her look.

"I understand you need a haircut."

"That's not all I need, but we could start with the haircut," Bridger replied.

"That's all you're getting today and for a long time to come."

Three pounds of hair disappearing off his face and head made a considerable difference in appearance. When Bridger walked into the store with Cindy in tow, he was unrecognizable. Bridger had a sharp look, erect carriage, and a spring to his step. His haircut was trendy, and he sported a short, trimmed beard. Cindy was holding his arm, smiling.

He asked, "Mrs. Nelson, can I borrow the Zodiac? I need to get Roman. I expect they'll need a pickup soon."

A surprised Rose said, "Sure, are you certain you don't want to take the truck and trailer down to the boat ramp?"

"No, ma'am, the boat ramp is next to the bridge, and I've seen enough bridges. I'll drop down to the waterfalls and give him a tow back. It's not far if I go out the back of the boat lot and into the river."

He picked up several coils of rope and walked out. Opening the back gate, he tied one line to a tree and the other end to the prow of the Zodiac. Positioning it on the edge of the river embankment, he jumped in and, with a loud yell, rode it to the bottom. The Zodiac plunged into the river and swung wildly on the rope. Bridger got the twin 250s fired up and idling, and cut the Zodiac loose leaving about a dozen feet of line attached to the prow.

He took off racing downstream for the waterfalls. When he got there, he started circling above the falls, scoping out what was below him. He caught Roman's eye and headed upstream 100 yards. When he got there, he spun the Zodiac in a tight spin and raced for what he had set as his takeoff point. As he neared the lip of the waterfalls, he let out a loud shout and rocketed over the dam riding the falls on the way down. Spinning tight circles and spraying rooster tails of water on Roman and Julia, he pulled up. With a big grin, asked, "You guys worn out, or are you up to a tow home?"

# 80

Alexia was in the news helicopter, 'Eyes in the Sky,' fast-forwarding through what had gone out on the live feed all morning. With everything that had happened, it was hard to realize it was still early afternoon. Her station had preempted regular broadcasting and live-streamed the entire series of rescues with the pilot and cameraman providing the only comments.

As she forwarded through the broadcast at high speed, the actions of her brother and the attractive woman doing all the actual rescue work riveted her. Julia was handling the life preservers, getting people into the boat, and up the skyhook to the medevac unit.

Alexia thought, "This is incredible. Roman and Julia look like a Coast Guard unit doing another day's training exercise."

The last clip was of the final rescue with Roman walking the boat over the waterfalls in slow motion and Julia standing in the stern firing the final life preserver. Alexia had been there. She saw it happening live, and her mouth was still in her throat as she watched the video.

The pilot was running through a checklist before lifting them off for the run into Salem Hospital. Alexia wanted to check on everyone pulled from the water, especially Bethany. Alexia's cameraman had gotten an excellent video of Bethany, as she was drug from the base of the waterfall and resuscitated.

The pilot called out, "Hey, Alexia, something is happening."

Alexia looked up as Bridger was circling upstream. She yelled to the pilot and cameraman, "Lift and film."

Alexia wasn't sure what was going on but thought it would be newsworthy. The cameraman flipped the switch to cue the producer for a live feed once again, and they went live as they lifted off the ground.

As the Zodiac went airborne over the falls, everyone in the helicopter was yelling, "Holy crap, did you see that? Did you get that on film? Please tell me you got that on film? Oh my god, what's he doing now? What's happening?"

It was an exhilarating moment. Alexia started live commentary for the viewers. The producer was cueing her to cut and return to regular broadcasting, but she kept talking and indicated she wanted to stay live for a few minutes. Everyone watched as Bridger tied a long rope to the front of the drift boat. She could see him pull a short line from the prow of the Zodiac and tie it around his body. Without hearing the words, she could tell from the body language that Roman was offering to put Julia on the shore with the TV crew. Everyone watching understood her refusal without hearing a word. Alexia could then see him instructing Julia. She knew he was telling her where to sit and how to hold on before he climbed into his own seat as the oarsman.

Alexia kept up her newsroom commentary, filling airtime until Bridger started the Zodiac forward, letting out the line. When the drift boat started moving behind him, Bridger circled faster, picking up speed. It looked like the child's game of 'crack the whip.'

Alexia got excited and asked her pilot, "Can you get us higher for a better camera shot? Hurry! That's it."

Talking to the cameraman, she asked, "Can you focus three different cameras at the same time? Can you get one on each of their faces for close-ups?"

Bridger had the boats racing around the flat area below the falls and, at the far end, straightened out and made a beeline straight at the waterfalls. Alexia heard herself gasp on live TV. Bridger poured full power to the twin 250s and threw all of his weight backward on the rope attached to the nose of the Zodiac. As he did, the nose rose in the air, and the powerful motors clawed their way up the waterfalls and over, dragging the drift boat behind.

"Oh my God, oh my God. That was amazing," Alexia said.

Everyone was chattering on her open mike. Her producer was asking, "Who was that?"

Alexia's response was, "That was my brother and his buddy, two ex-Navy SEALS playing at the end of the workday. I think that was their version of 'happy hour.'"

She turned to the pilot, "Skip the stop at the Salem Hospital. The producer can send a local reporter to the hospital for the follow-up."

Alexia wanted to get back to the studio right away. Texting her producer, she asked him to schedule a thirty minute "special report" at 7 p.m. covering today's activities. The next call was to her mother, "Mom, do whatever you have to do to keep Roman and Julia at the store when they get off the river. When I'm done, those two will be the biggest heroes the State of Oregon has seen in years. I may get a Broadcaster's Emmy out of it. I need to go edit for a while. Then I want to come back to interview them. I'll have a special report on the air at 7p.m."

"When will you be here? I won't be able to keep them forever."

"It's about 1 p.m. now. Roman and Julia will get back soon and want to get away from the publicity. Please do whatever you have to do to keep them there until I get back. All I know is my brother looks alive again, and I want to help that continue. I think I know how."

# 81

Cindy and Rose were glued to the TV watching everything live, as were most people in the state. They were talking about how to keep Roman and Julia from leaving once they got off the river.

Cindy said, "Easy, where is that fancy car I heard about?"

"It's across the road in the boat lot."

"What about all of Roman's wheels? Are they there also?"

Rose responded with a grin, "Yes, they are."

They ran across the road, locked the gate, and then started making calls on the local family gossip network. They put out the word, "We're having a spur of the moment potluck to celebrate the rescues. Call everybody you can think of and tell them to park in front of the boat gate."

LOUNGING IN HER SEAT, Julia relaxed and laughed as she listened to Roman and Bridger arguing. Circling in the river opposite the dirt boat ramp, Bridger was still playing 'crack the whip' towing the drift boat. Bridger was trying to get Roman to sell him the drift boat and the Zodiac, which had seen action all afternoon.

Bridger said, "I wanna buy both these boats."

Roman said, "No way, Bridger. We trashed both these boats today. The drift boat has rock dings all over it, and the aluminum bottom on the Zodiac is a mess after the beating it took going over the falls. I can get you two brand new boats within the week. They won't have a scratch on them."

Bridger was adamant. He didn't want a shiny new one. Bridger swore up and down, "I want the boats we used today. They have a history now."

Julia was quiet, listening to the two friends wrangling over the boats. It started again when Bridger declined a "used" discount. He insisted he would pay full retail, and refused to take them to shore until Roman agreed.

The rope Bridger had cut off earlier was still hanging off the bank. He hooked it to the prow of the Zodiac and tied another cable from the stern of the Zodiac to the drift boat. Holding onto the tow rope, they climbed the hill. Julia discovered Bridger had preplanned his exit. He had the rope tied off to a winch, which pulled both boats into the parking lot.

When Bridger, Roman, and Julia climbed the bank, they found the boat showroom already filled with people. There were mountains of food arriving, and cases of beer were icing in tubs. They walked into a rousing cheer, and their buddies handing them beers. Roman raised his eyebrows in surprise, as Bridger turned down the beer.

Bridger was talking non-stop to Cindy, and waving his hands for emphasis. She took him over to an aging baby boomer with long gray hair and a ponytail, and said, "Chase, this is Bridger."

Chase said, "I know who he is, but he looks a little different today."

Bridger laughed, "I imagine I smell a little better too. Cindy says you're the best guy in town with an airbrush."

"Yup."

"Did you see the video of Julia standing in the back of the boat firing the life preserver at that gal as they went over the falls?" Bridger asked.

"Of course, everybody in the place has seen it. It's on all the channels."

"Good, I want you to spray that profile of Julia shooting the gun on the nose of the drift boat and the Zodiac." Bridger said, "But, I want you to make the profile look more like Cindy than Julia. You know, way bigger boobs and flaming red hair. I want you to label them Lifesaver I and Lifesaver II. I'll pay extra if you can do it today."

"For extra, sure, let's go get my tools." The two exited without saying a word to anyone.

~

KNOWING ONLY ROMAN, Rose, and Bridger, Julia had time to herself to sip her beer and wander around the boat showroom, checking it out. She thought, "The name on the sign outside is perfect for this place. It's filled with expensive toys."

What she was interested in doing was observing Roman. Showing on the showrooms large screen TV was a replay of the live broadcast from earlier in the day. Watching from across the room, she saw Roman engrossed in watching the video. Approaching him, she offered him a sip of her beer and said, "Your mom must have recorded that live. It looks like it is on a loop."

Roman grinned at her, sipped the beer, and then put his arm around her and stood there watching the replay for a long time. Dennis brought them both a plate of food and smiling at Julia said, "You need food if you're drinking beer. I'm his cousin, Dennis."

Roman said, "I'm sorry. I should have introduced you as soon as you came up."

Dennis said, "That's all right. You were pretty focused on the video. I'm married, but I still know how to introduce myself to a pretty lady. Come with me, Julia. I'll take you around and introduce you to everyone. When Roman gets focused on something, bombs could go off next to him, and he wouldn't notice."

"Not true, I always heard the bombs," Roman said with a grin.

Dennis asked, "What are you doing, critiquing your performance? I don't know if you impressed yourself, but you impressed everyone else. That was a tricky job of boat handling in extreme conditions."

"That's not what I'm watching. I'm watching Julia. Her competence and composure, as she risked her life to save others, jumps off the television screen. I was there, I saw her doing everything, I know how scared she was, and how insecure, but she did what needed doing. She blew me away. But, you're right, Julia forgive me please, for being rude. I'll introduce you to everyone."

"I just did what you told me to do. I knew if I didn't, I might die, or someone else might die from my incompetence."

Julia watched Roman's interactions with the large crowd of people. He was comfortable with them without being cocky. Friends with a broad cross-section of people, he introduced Julia to everyone, regardless of their age or social strata. Treating everyone as his equal, she could tell, everyone loved and respected him.

Rose came up to both of them and asked, "Do you think you should go get cleaned up? You're both still wet and muddy. I'll bet you'd feel better with a shower and clean clothes." She pointed around the room to people who were snapping photos of the two of them with their phones.

She reassured Julia, "Don't worry about having clean clothes to put on. We can find you something to wear in Alexia's closet. You're about the same size."

Realizing photos were being taken, Julia groaned and said, "Great idea."

# 82

As the 'Eyes in the Sky,' helicopter headed back down the canyon towards Salem, Alexia told her producer she needed to make a short detour. She asked him to find out Governor Anderson's location and to alert him she was coming by.

"Please let him know it's a courtesy visit, with a message from his daughter."

She also requested their Salem reporter meet her at the airport to give her a ride to the governor's location.

The producer said he could do all of that. The helicopter could drop her off, but it couldn't wait on her. They needed it back in Portland for the rush hour traffic reports.

Minutes later, she was pulling into the parking area of the governor's mansion, Mahonia Hall. It surprised her to see the visible State Police presence. Exiting the news wagon, the press crew presented their credentials.

A State Police Trooper reviewed their ID's, and then said, "Miss Nelson may enter. I need to ask everyone else to wait in the vehicle."

Escorted to the entry foyer, Alexia was met by a well-dressed young man with short blond hair parted on the left. He appeared close to six feet, perhaps 5'11" was her guess. He wore a charcoal cashmere sports coat, a black dress shirt she was sure was raw silk and tailored gray slacks. She was confident nothing he was wearing was off the rack, with the possible exception of his underwear.

She was sure the fancy tailoring hid a myriad of shoulder holsters and weapons.

As he checked her identity papers, he looked her over from head to foot, "Any weapons?"

Alexia said, "Now, you and I both know you don't think I have any weapons. If you thought I was armed, you already would have me up against the wall."

"Please come with me. The governor has vouched for you."

As he led the way, Alexia thought, "Well, he's not tall, dark, and handsome, but tall, blonde, and handsome is good, and he exudes danger." Which she had to admit to herself was a little exciting.

Watching him move, she thought, "He moves like Roman, I've never thought of Roman as dangerous."

He escorted her into the library where Stan and Margo stood waiting for her. Stan shook her hand as he introduced her to Margo. Margo responded to all the questions about her recovery from the car accident on Mt. Hood, but asked, "What's the message from Julia?"

A flush crept across Alexia's cheeks, "I'm sorry. It wasn't my intention to worry you. I could have told you over the phone that Julia is fine. I'm sure you have seen our broadcast all morning. Her phone got wet during the rescues, so she can't call herself."

Taking the seat the governor pointed at, she continued, "The reason I wanted to come by was to give you the courtesy of letting you know about my special report airing at seven tonight."

The governor asked, "It's that bad? What did I do now?"

Alexia laughed, "No, sir, just the opposite. It's nothing you've done. I've got to get out of here in a few minutes to beat the rush hour traffic, so I can get to my studio in Portland, in time to finish editing. Then, hurry back to my mother's store. I am interviewing Roman and Julia for tonight's broadcast. If I can do everything fast enough, we'll be broadcasting within minutes of getting the editing done. If the interview and editing go as I expect, Roman and Julia will be the biggest heroes this state has seen in years. Right now, not many people have tied Julia to you. By the time the show is over, every reporter in the state will call or show up at your door, asking you for a comment. I wanted to give you a heads up."

Margo hugged Alexia and said, "Thank you, dear. Today has terrified us. We didn't understand what was going on, or why she was on the river."

In a voice cracked with emotion, the governor said, "Thank you, Alexia. We appreciate the news. You mentioned rush hour, the big issue for you in this scenario is all the driving and traffic?"

She agreed, "Yes, sir, that's why I need to rush. I'd be remiss though if I didn't ask what's going on? You know I'm here regularly, sir, and I've never seen the police presence like tonight. This well-dressed man standing in the shadows oozes expensive private security. I presume he is your bodyguard. He may be polite and dress like a male fashion model, but I know lethal when I see it. If anyone gets near you, he will take them down, perhaps permanently."

"You're good, Alexia. You have always been respectful and helpful. I mentioned the last time we were together, you were racking up IOU credits." Stan answered, "This dangerous gentleman is Jimmy Stockade. I cannot confirm any of your suspicions tonight. Let's tell anyone who asks that Jimmy is my security consultant. My promise to you is when I'm able to announce anything, if it's possible, you'll get the scoop. Now, we need to deal with the traffic issue. Jimmy, you've been checked out on my personal helicopter, haven't you?"

"Yes, sir."

"Here are the keys," Stan said as he handed them to Jimmy. "Take Alexia to her studio, wait on her to perform her magic, and then fly her back up the canyon close to her mother's store. She can have her crew meet her there and take her to the store. We can't use the state helicopter, but there's nothing in the ethics laws which says I can't use my money and helicopter to do a favor for a friend."

"Yes, sir. With your permission, sir, I have a question." Jimmy asked, "Alexia, where do you think Julia will stay tonight?"

"What? I have no idea. Why is that any of your business?

"It's my job to keep her, Stan and Margo safe. If she's with Roman, she's safe." Turning to Stan, Jimmy continued, "Sir, I think we need a team at Julia's house. Also, Roman needs a heads up. Could you text him for me, Alexia?" Jimmy asked.

"Yes"

"Tell him. Smoke says, beware of bogeymen."

"Ok, are you Smoke?" she asked.

"Yes, to a few select friends. Now, let's get you to Portland. Where is the closest heliport to your office?" Jimmy wanted to know.

"On top of our building."

"Well, that's convenient."

As they were flying north in the small two-person helicopter, she thought about the power his wealth and political position gave Stan Anderson. She couldn't help but contrast his use of that power with several other wealthy people she had known or dated. She felt in her experience, money, and authority made good people better and bad people worse. Stan and Margo were two good people.

Jimmy was piloting the small helicopter with skill. They were approaching her office when she realized she liked him. He was quiet, respectful, wore his fancy clothes like they were second nature, and, besides being dangerous, was flat out handsome.

She couldn't help asking, "Is there anything you can't do?"

With a grin, he replied, "Dance."

Later in the afternoon, Jimmy circled the parking lot at the Mill City Falls until the sightseers cleared a landing spot for him. "Lookey Lou's" filled the parking lot, watching the divers attempt to find the last rafter. The divers couldn't find his body, and they couldn't find a name for him other than Charlie.

Alexia turned and gave Jimmy a dazzling smile, "Good luck with protecting the governor, he's a good man. I hope I get to see you again." She was happy seeing Jimmy at a loss for words as she exited the helicopter. Alexia grinned at rattling Jimmy's composure.

Waiting for her in the news programs minivan was a producer, a cameraman, and an editing crew. With the satellite uplink, they could upload to the studio and broadcast moments later.

# 83

Alexia and her cameraman strolled into the party to a rousing cheer. In the eyes of the small town, Alexia was a fantastic success story. In the minds of her hometown people, she was an essential part of the day's rescues, and responsible for the world seeing what happened.

She found Roman in his apartment upstairs, getting cleaned up. She headed back to the small suite, which was still hers when she was in town. Sure enough, Rose was there helping Julia sort through Alexia's closet. Alexia held several items up, and said, "This one, Mom. I'll help Julia. I think Aunt Alice is looking for you."

When her mother left, Alexia said to Julia, "First, your dad and mom said to take care and have a good time tonight."

With a grin, she added, "We both know those instructions sound contradictory. I want to interview you and Roman for my special report tonight. To make that happen, I will need your help. Knowing my brother, he will try to get out of it. You need to know that what I want to do is in his best interest. He has been home for two-and-a-half years. During that time, he has shown little interest in life. He goes through the motions, does everything right, but there has been no fire in my brother. Today, I saw fire again in his face and eyes. I think you are part of it. Life always looks better when there's hope in the hormones. But, another part is what you both did today. Roman is hard-wired to serve, to help, and to protect others. It is why he went into the Navy. I want to do an interview which will give him a chance to protect others. He needs an opportunity to use his knowledge and skills to guide others. If he feels he has a purpose, maybe, we can keep the fire in his eyes."

Then with a smile, she added as Julia blushed, "Of course, you and the hormones need to do your part."

As they grinned at each other, Julia responded, "That is a challenge I may accept."

A few minutes later, Alexia waylaid her brother with the request for an interview. Julia was holding onto his arm and distracting him as he kept trying to say no to Alexia. She listened for a while then said, "Honey, why don't you ask her what questions she wants to ask?" As she called him Honey, she squeezed his hand.

Alexia said, "She's right, Roman, what I want to do is ask you to go through what you guys did today. Describe the various situations you were in as I show each rescue. What I want to focus on is all the equipment you guys used. You were using equipment the vast majority of people don't know exists. And, you were doing it in a drift boat. What I saw is a lot of your rescues wouldn't have happened if all you were doing was throwing the life preservers the law requires boats to carry. You were successful because of your skill, but also because of your preparation and equipment. How about sharing all that information? It might save someone else's life."

Roman, who had never been successful in refusing Alexia anything, agreed.

The minute he said, "OK," Alexia went into her professional mode. She rearranged the furniture so the three of them could sit and look at the TV on the wall while being filmed by her cameraman. Everyone in the room was quiet and enthralled at being part of the special report. Several people volunteered to go on camera when Alexia told them she would come around the room for comments.

Alexia set the agenda, "I'll show you a video of various rescue scenes. Roman, I'll want you to describe what was happening. Julia, I want you to describe your emotions as the events were unfolding. Can you do that?" They both nodded, and she continued, "Julia, I want you to describe all the equipment you had to use, and how easy or difficult it was to operate. When we're all done, I want to go out to the storage lot and get a close up of the two boats."

With Roman and Julia standing in front of the big-screen television, Alexia said, "Let's start with what will be the last question after this is all edited."

Cueing them she was ready to film, Alexia said to Roman, "We've just watched an amazing series of water rescues. I couldn't help but notice, as you described each of the rescues, to a large extent you were using equipment the average person has never seen, and which the law does not require on a boat. Why do you think that is, and should everyone have this equipment?"

Roman hesitated for a moment and then responded, "People are the same all over the world. In whatever situation we are in, we always expect nothing bad will happen. The law requires all watercraft to carry life vests. It doesn't matter if it's a small fishing boat or a large car ferry. The boats are required to have enough vests for every person. The problem is, in a disaster, no one knows where they are or how to use them. I think the operator of the boat is afraid discussing that upfront would scare people away. What you get on a big commercial boat is a prerecorded message which no one listens to. On a small boat, the owner-operator seldom even mentions it."

People all around the room were nodding their heads.

He continued, "I'm an incredible optimist and believe good things will happen. I also, however, am always looking at what's the worst-case scenario? That way, I can prepare in advance for both eventualities.

"Do I think the state should require the equipment we used today on small boats? No, I think it would do more good to get people to learn how to use the safety equipment, which is already required. Most people don't know how to put on their current life preservers.

People need to look around their lives and ask themselves, how could I make my family's life safer? What's the best way to get people talking about this? I don't know."

Alexia's producer was exclaiming in her ear to pick up the pace as she turned to Julia. "Ok, here's the first rescue, I think his name is David. Can you walk me through what you were thinking and feeling as you saw him hanging in the tree and worked to get him on board?" The party was at a dead stop as everyone in the room listened spellbound.

FINISHING the inside portion of the taping, Alexia asked Julia and Roman to walk her out to the boat and explain the life preserver gun and boat defibrillator. As they approached the drift boat, Roman started laughing. On the prow was a stylized image of Julia going over the falls, shooting a life vest. However, the profile was buxom with flaming red hair blowing in the wind. Stenciled on it were the boat's new name, Lifesaver 1, and a phone number.

Bridger and Cindy stood next to the boat. Bridger beamed into the camera and told everyone, "I've been the town drunk and lived under the bridge. Today changed everything. I've quit drinking, and I'm going into business. I know I can stay sober, but if any of my brothers see me drop off the wagon, you have Cindy's permission to kick my butt."

Roman gave Bridger a resounding high five.

Bridger continued, "Bridger's Guide Services will offer photo and nature tours on all the valley rivers. We'll not be competing with the fishing guides. I want to focus on the beauty around us on the rivers."

Bridger pointed at first the drift boat, and then the Zodiac, "I bought Lifesaver 1 and Lifesaver 2 from my military brother, and they'll be equipped as you saw on TV."

Bridger turned to Cindy, "If anyone wants to know my motivation, tell them I found a reason to live again. I want to convince Cindy to marry me. First, I know I need to prove myself to her by staying sober."

The producer was screaming to Alexia for a wrap. "You couldn't get a better closing, stop there."

# 84

After Jimmy dropped Alexia off in the parking lot of the fall's in Mill City, he returned to Mahonia Hall. Entering the governor's office, he found the staff hard at work, attempting to get background information on Roman.

Jimmy interrupted the process, "Sir, that's an exercise in futility. Roman's records are buried deeper than your people can search. What you'll find is a sanitized biography with no important information other than he grew up in the Santiam Canyon. You'll find his family trust owns thousands of acres of timberland, but his dad went broke. Hundreds of people 'up the canyon' could tell you he went to Annapolis after high school. A few may know he was a Navy SEAL. Beyond that, he's classified at such a deep level that even his medals are classified. If you must find out about him, there's only one person who can give you any information."

Stan asked, "Who's that?"

Jimmy said, "Your buddy, President Alex Myers."

# 85

Roman and Julia walked back into the showroom. It seemed like the entire population of the small town was now at the party. Alexia joined them and asked, "Did you get the text I sent you with a message from your buddy, Smoke?"

Shaking his head, he pulled out his phone. His entire demeanor changed. Without another word, he collected Bridger and his retired SEAL buddies. He showed them the text. Julia heard a tall man with black hair, who had been introduced as Andy, ask, "Brutus?"

At Roman's nod, they all exited the party. Roman headed upstairs to his apartment. Minutes later, they were all back. Each had slipped into black clothing from a 'go bag' in the trunk of their car along a variety of weapons. Now dressed in all black, Andy had Brutus, a huge German shepherd, on a leash.

Roman suggested Julia start saying goodbye, that he and his buddies would take a stroll around outside to make sure everything was ok. Andy and Brutus had already gone out. They were checking the perimeter of the property.

As Roman came up to him, Andy said, "Everything appears ok, Skipper. Brutus alerted when I first arrived in the back corner, but I think whoever it was, took off."

Roman went back, and collected Julia, and gave his mother and Alexia a hug goodbye. As he hugged his sister, she rubbed her hand up and down his back. He felt her fingers pause over the shoulder holster. She whispered, "Be careful."

As THEY EXITED, Roman handed Julia back her keys. She waved them off and said, "You drive. Today has been a momentous day. No one in your community knew me, but everyone enveloped me and made me feel as though I were part of them. Never in my life have I had so many hugs in such a short time. I loved Alexia and your mom. You drive. I want to sit back in the seats and process the emotions I'm feeling." She sat back in exhaustion and laid her hand on his knee as he drove.

It had been an eventful day, filled with high energy and wild emotional swings. It started with what she thought of as her 'near-death experience' at the coffee shop, followed by the huge adrenaline rush of the river rescues. The day's activities and emotions were unprecedented in her well-structured life. Meeting and being accepted by Roman's family and friends had been pleasant and overwhelming at the same time. The day had enveloped her. She took a deep breath and looking at Roman allowed the emotions of the day to wash through her.

She thought, "He is handsome, but there are lots of handsome men. He seems in total control of himself and everything around him. Without being obnoxious or aggressive, he always takes charge of the situation. He always seems confident, which is a turn on. Can he be for real? What do the shadows I see in his eyes hide? Do I want to know his secrets?"

Roman drove below the speed limit, and without conversation until he pulled into a deserted roadside rest area. He backed into a parking spot at the far end where he could see all the cars coming and going as travelers made a late-night bathroom stop on their trips back and forth across the Cascades.

He was quiet for a long time, staring off into space. Julia said nothing, she just waited. At last, he started talking, "You asked me about me, and I put you off. I think you have earned the right to know more."

Julia's attention sharpened as he said, "You're an attractive woman. I'm sure you have heard that your entire life. I'm certain you can feel my attraction for you. But that attraction is surface level. What we went through today exposed your real character. All the façade gets stripped off when it is life or death, and today had quite a few life or death circumstances. I feel like I have known you more than today. I'm comfortable with you and feel an unexpected connection to you. To be fair to you, if you would like to spend time with me, you deserve to know more about me. I'll tell you what I can. There's a lot I'll never be able to share with you. It's the truth when I say I'm 'classified.'"

Julia waited without speaking. Her hand was still on his leg. Her heart was pounding.

She thought, "That's it, it's what I was chewing on all day. His character was being exposed to me. Not the games we all play, in a new relationship, but who he is. I don't think I need to worry about macho games from him, or his trying to control and dominate me. I saw the real him, raw and unedited, there wasn't a question in his mind, he knew he was in control of what we were doing. He was risking his life, and mine, on his ability to rescue people he had never met. Wow, I need to process that thought, it's presumptive. Am I ok with it? "

Roman jiggled her car keys back and forth in his hands as he continued, "My family had an original homestead grant of 320 acres generations ago. They homesteaded timber property here in the canyon. Each successive generation expanded the holdings. Whenever anyone in the area, who owned property, was going broke or wanted to sell, my family would buy their land. Today there are several thousand acres in our Family Trust, which checkerboard both sides of the canyon. The beneficiaries of the trust are my mother, my sister, and me. I have managerial control of the trust since the death of my father. Over time my family made a lot of money. We had a small sawmill here in town, and everything else we needed to log and turn the trees into money."

Julia said, "Wow, you're a logger?"

"My family was. I guess I still am, but I couldn't cut a big tree down if my life depended on it."

Roman turned her car onto auxiliary power and started fiddling with all the gadgets. First, he opened the moon roof and then started playing with the sound system. Taking a deep breath, he continued, "About 60 years ago there was a big fire. It destroyed a lot of timber. My grandfather was a logger who turned into a conservationist at heart. He replanted and started to manage the forest as an agricultural crop. He opened Nelson Bait and Tackle Shop as a hobby, and so he and his buddies could have the latest fishing gear and always have fresh bait. The rumor was he hid buckets of gold coins in the walls of the store as he built it. He was an original conspiracy theorist and believed in the upcoming collapse of the economy."

Shaking his head, he said, "My father was just the opposite. He believed everything he touched would turn to gold and never prepared for disaster. Mortgaging all of his properties to invest in the stock market and the mortgage securities bubble, the collapse of 2008 devastated him. He lost the sawmill, the commercial properties around the valley, and everything else he owned, except the beat-up store and the timber property, which was in a trust. Dad was distraught, and about a year later, he died of a broken heart. It was a bleak time for Mom. They'd lost the big fancy house, in which they raised Alexia and me. Mom was now living in a shack of a room in the old store. I had already gone into the Navy, I sent support money every month, but I knew it wasn't enough."

Julia made sympathy noises, "How awful for your mother."

"Yeah, it was bad. The worst part was I wasn't here to help Mom when she needed me."

"I'm sure she understood. Mothers do. I have lots of questions, but I have to ask something."

"What?"

"Could we hit pause? I had three beers, and nature is calling."

Laughing, he started her car and drove to the front of the bathroom. As she began to get out, Roman motioned for her to wait, "Just a minute, let me walk you to the entrance. When you get in there, make sure no one else is there, please. I'll run into the men's room. Please don't leave the bathroom unless I answer your call."

Julia froze for a moment and looked at him as he walked around to open her car door. Her internal alarm system was vibrating as she asked him, "Isn't that over the top controlling? Telling me to not come out of the bathroom unless you're here?"

She scrutinized him as he answered. He frowned and looked like he was trying to understand her question. "Remember the text from my buddy, Smoke? Beware of the bogeymen."

She nodded.

He gestured at the dark parking lot and the forested area surrounding the bathroom, "This is bogeyman country. Careful is better than dead."

Julia relaxed, "OK, I get it now, but I still can't believe someone wants to kill me. Let me check it out. I do need to go."

Minutes later, as he parked in the same spot they were in earlier, she said, "I'm sorry about a few minutes ago. I've had bad experiences with controlling men. You don't strike me as a controlling, male-dominant kind of guy. Are you? Because, if you are, I'm done."

"Not unless I'm in a command role, a life or death scenario like earlier today. The good news is those rarely happen in civilian life."

"Believe me, on the river, I was more than willing to let you be in command and tell me what to do. If I hadn't, somebody could have died, and it might have been me. I'm sorry for interrupting you to use the bathroom. You were telling me about yourself."

"I grew up in the forest with my grandfather." Roman continued after taking a centering breath. "I did a lot of hunting and fishing with my father. The fishing was drift boat fishing here on the Santiam, most of it where we were today. That's why I know every inch of the river. In high school, swimming was my favorite sport. I still hold two state records for distance events."

"You seemed to know every twist and turn of the river before we got to it."

"That's why. My granddad, father, and I drifted the river hundreds of times. When I was growing up, my family was prominent. Dad and Granddad had the connections to get me an appointment to Annapolis. I started working towards a law degree, thinking I would become a member of the JAG Team, but I was also on the swim team. A recruiter for the SEALS came and talked to the swim team. Being a JAG couldn't compete with the allure of being a SEAL. I got all the requirements out of the way for my law degree, but I never took the Bar Exam. I was too busy with back-to-back deployments to hotspots around the world. Those are all classified and are not only top-secret but for presidential access only."

Julia nodded her head. She was getting a better feel for this man. No wonder he was at home on the water.

Roman continued. Julia could tell he didn't see her nodding her head. She thought, "He's deep inside his head, thinking about what he's saying. If he didn't respond to my questions and comments, I'd think he was in a trance talking to himself."

"I fell in love with a fellow sailor. Her name was Amber. She and our unborn child were killed 90 days before the wedding." Roman's voice choked as he spoke.

Julia moaned and took his hand.

"I can't tell you anything about that," Roman said, again speaking in a quiet, measured tone.

"I can say, because of that action, our entire SEAL Team was given and accepted early retirement. They advanced each team member in rank to the rank the navy would expect them to hold at their twenty-year retirement point. We received full retirement benefits and Honorable Discharges with classified medals. They also gave each member of our team a medical severance bonus. Several members decided they wanted to stay together in a slower-paced environment. They returned to the canyon with me. Some of them are here in Gates like Andy Baker and his dog, Brutus. A couple are down in Mill

City and Stayton. You saw several tonight. They may look a little scruffy, like Bridger, but each of them is worth millions."

Julia said, "None of that made the news did it?"

He shook his head.

"Does your mother or sister know all this?"

"No, everything I told you is classified except for the early local stuff you were trying to pull up when I saw you googling me on your phone. I still can't give you any significant details. Part of me says I should not have shared any of that with you. My mother and sister know nothing about any of it, and I need to ask you not to say anything to them. I felt you deserved to know why I reacted to your touch like I did this morning. Or why I may be emotionally unavailable. I hope that isn't the case, but it's been three years now, and I have yet to cry over Amber or our child. You're the first woman I have even had an interest in talking to."

"Thank you for being open with me. Perhaps it's time you opened up with someone. I'm honored you feel safe enough to talk to me, and I will keep what you've shared to myself. Is there more you would like me to know about you?"

Roman's floodgates were open. All his barriers were down. He told her about his flashbacks and how he would walk for hours in the middle of the night to exhaust himself. He talked about his PTSD reactions revolving around loud noises or someone touching him without warning.

Julia asked, "That's what happened this morning, isn't it?"

"Yes, when you touched me, on my back, my instincts kicked in. In my mind, I wasn't at Chemeketa. I thought I was on patrol in Somalia. I'm still sorry about that."

They talked for over an hour. It touched Julia how he shared about himself, and the anguish, she heard in his voice, broke her heart. She found herself teary-eyed listening to him.

She thought, "This is a good man. He's been through a hell I can never know, but he is still at heart a good man, and somehow, he held onto his humanity through it all."

Julia reached out and held his hand, "Would you do me a favor, Roman?"

"Of course, anything."

"Take me home. Part of me wants to say, take me home and make love to me. Spend the night. I cannot think of a better way to end such a spectacular day than to have you make love to me."

Roman reached down and started to turn the car on, then stopped as she continued talking.

"As much as I want to say that, I think I should just say take me home. I'm attracted to you. It would be easy to invite you in, but I think we should go a little slower. I have made a lot of bad relationship choices in my past. It's been a year and a half since I've been involved with anyone. I'm working hard on making my choices with my head, and not my heart, or my hormones. The hormones are screaming, yes, my heart is willing, but my past traumas tell me to go slow. Do you understand?"

He turned on the car, "I do. I'll take you home and get you settled in and leave. I need to check with Smoke about his bogeyman comment."

The exasperation showed in her voice, "Who is Smoke? And, why is a comment from him so significant."

"His name is Jimmy Stockade. I need to check to be sure, but I think he's running your father's security detail."

"Jimmy? Jimmy is my dad's new combination driver, personal assistant, and all-around flunky. Although I will say, Dad is dressing better since Jimmy arrived."

Roman roared in laughter.

# 86

Julia gave him directions to her condo overlooking the Willamette River. Approaching her unit, they realized news trucks from three television stations lined the street in front of it. There was a horde of reporters with microphones yelling at them as the garage door went up, and they pulled down into a basement garage.

Julia jumped out first and stepped towards the reporters, looking photogenic as the cameras flashed. She looked to her side and realized Roman had disappeared. Watching for him as she spoke to the reporters, she saw him ghosting in the background. He was checking out everyone and all the vehicles.

The reporters were attempting to outshout each other, hoping to get their question answered. Alexia, however, had asked all the same questions on her special.

The primary question was, "Is it true you're Governor Anderson's daughter?"

"Yes."

Coming from the female reporters, "Who was the hunky guy you were with?"

"That would be Roman Nelson, here he is."

"Is he your boyfriend?" Alexia's most significant competitor on the evening news, Rebecca, asked.

"No, we just met today," Julia said with a demure smile.

ROMAN AND JULIA answered the repetitive questions until each reporter was on film, having a question answered. Each news crew then left for their studios. Roman and Julia waited until everyone left. Then, she walked him into her condo. As soon as the door was closed, they wrapped their arms around each other and enjoyed a passionate kiss. Feeling his body's reaction as her tongue explored the inside of his mouth, she held him tight. His hands rubbed her back and dropping to her buttocks, pulled her tighter. Their groan was mutual.

"I agreed to leave, but I think I should be asking where the bedroom is."

"I know. It's hard trying to think with my head when my emotions want to rip your clothes off. As much as I want you to stay, I think you should leave."

There was a loud knock on the door, "Julia, it's your dad. I need to come in."

Preceding Stan into the room was Jimmy. He gave Roman a half-hearted salute and said, "Howdy, Skipper. Have you cleared the premises?"

"No, I didn't think I needed to," Roman replied.

With a grin, Jimmy replied, "Yeah, you were a little distracted. Anybody standing outside could see straight through the sheer draperies the way you were backlit. That's not like you, sir." He grinned, "With everyone's permission, I'll clear the house."

The governor came over to Roman with a grin and introduced himself. "Sorry to interrupt you a moment ago, but I thought I shouldn't wait."

Frowning, Julia stomped her foot as her face flushed in embarrassment, and said, "Dad!"

Governor Anderson said to Roman, "I wanted to thank you for saving my daughter's life and taking such good care of her today. I also wanted to meet you in person and see if there is anything you need that I could assist with."

"No, sir," he replied. "I'm in good shape, and it was my pleasure."

"I'm guessing you two don't know how big a deal you already are in the news. Over the next few days, I'm certain you'll think you're in the eye of a storm. All the reporters will try to humanize you." Governor Anderson said.

"No one should find much on me, sir," Roman said.

"I know. I've been looking for information on you all afternoon. You both have clean backgrounds. Don't be surprised though if the reporters keep digging trying to find some dirt."

Roman shrugged his shoulders.

Julia realized her father was sizing up Roman. This was more than a casual conversation. Jimmy reappeared and said, "The condo is secure. Julia, there will be a security team outside your unit tonight."

Roman looked at Jimmy, "You don't show up unless there's a big problem. What's going on?"

Jimmy glanced at the governor who nodded, before Jimmy said, "There have been three assassination attempts on the governor's life, and today's incident looks suspicious. The crime lab is still analyzing the kayaks used by the rafters today, which divers have recovered. The puncture marks in each appear similar."

Jimmy told them about the cut brake line on Stan's car, the bullet holes in the airplane, and the shots fired through the window of Mahonia Hall.

Julia's eyes widened, and her heart started pounding at the thought of losing one or both of her parents. She started machine-gunning questions to her father, "What are you talking about? Why would anyone want to assassinate you? I thought you just had a car accident and a motor failure on the plane."

She started to cry, and her father pulled her into a hug. With the pitch of her voice rising, she continued. "Why didn't you tell me about all this? Why is somebody shooting at you? Is Mom ok?"

Receiving assurances that both her mother and father were ok, Julia's panic lessened. Looking at Jimmy, she asked, "Are you saying my friend's inflatable kayaks all had punctures? They were all sabotaged?"

"That's what it looks like."

Julia asked, "What about the last rafter, his name is Charlie? Have they found him yet?"

Her father replied, "The sheriff's divers will continue searching the river for a body tomorrow. However, be careful. Everything looks suspicious. One ripped kayak might be an accident; all of them having a puncture is not an accident."

Jimmy said, "We have not established an identity. You say his name is Charlie. Do you know his last name or anything else about him?"

"I think I have a photo of him on my cell phone," Julia replied, pulling out her phone.

As he looked at the photo, the governor's face grew grim.

He asked, "Would you email the photo to the crime lab for facial identification? Maybe he has a record."

Jimmy also explained, "Besides the actual attempts on his life, your father has been receiving death threat letters every three days. The letters come from different cities, but the message is always the same. 'You're guilty. For that, you shall die.'"

As the governor left, he apologized again for interrupting them, and with a grin, urged them to pick up where they left off.

Roman acknowledged the grin but said, "I think I'll be leaving in a few moments."

The governor's last remarks to Roman were cryptic. "I've got phone calls to make tomorrow, but if everything turns out the way I expect, I would like to meet with you soon."

He continued, "I may have a project for your special skills."

Roman replied, "I would do anything to help you, sir. But, I'm not looking for a project, and I don't need a job."

The governor said, "Jimmy has made that point clear."

After Jimmy and the governor left, Julia wanted to talk. Roman, however, thought it was best if he left. He knew the governor would get a report from Jimmy's security team about what time he left tonight.

Roman also said, "If I spend the night, the reporters will notice. I don't think either of us wants a video of me leaving your home on the morning news cycle."

She compressed her lips, and while frowning, nodded her head.

"I'd like to suggest an alternative. I'll take a late-night conditioning run to the parking lot where my friend who borrowed my bike this morning, promised to park it. Why don't I pick you up in the morning, on my bike, for breakfast at about 9 A.M.?"

"That sounds like fun."

He continued, "If you want, you could bring a change of clothes in a backpack. We can take off after breakfast and do whatever we want. If we want to get rooms somewhere later, we can. You might even decide you want just one room. We can do whatever we want, and no one will know where we are."

With a kiss, she agreed.

All night long, she tossed and turned, thinking of the day's activities and the news about the assassination attempts on her father and mother. The question which had her staring at the ceiling was, "Do I want one room or two tomorrow night. Dare I trust him?"

As she drifted off to sleep, she smiled, "I think Dad likes him."

THE NEXT MORNING while packing a small backpack, she was still conflicted. "After I had that disastrous affair with the car salesman, I decided, enough. Never again would I let a man take me to bed until I knew him and was sure my head and my heart agreed. I told myself I wouldn't let my hormones fool me again. I've known Roman for one day, and already he has me all hot and bothered."

Opening a drawer, she pulled out a skimpy pair of black panties and a sheer negligée. She held both up to her image in the mirror. "Damm. Why is it so hard to know what to do?" She put the negligée back in the drawer but pulled on the skimpy panties.

She continued speaking out loud to herself, "I know I'm rationalizing and justifying. But, if I met a guy, and we went out for dinner and drinks, I'd spend three or four hours with him. If we went out once a week for a month, I know I'd be thinking about making love with him."

Choosing a pair of skin-tight jeans, she sat down on the bed to pull them on. She kept talking to herself, "I met Roman yesterday, but I spent fourteen hours with him. That's equivalent to at least a month of dating. I'll be spending another twelve to fourteen hours with him today. I know I'm making excuses, but that's equivalent to two months of standard dating, before, I have to decide one bedroom or two."

While applying her makeup, she looked into her eyes in the mirror and asked, "Mirror, mirror, on the wall, what should I do?"

## 87

Leaving her condo, Roman drifted into the shadows and searched the area. A security guard stepped out of the blackness and said, "Looking for me, Commander?"

"Yes, making sure everything is secure before I leave."

The guard replied, "All clear, sir. Don't worry. We'll keep her safe."

With the skies clear and temperatures in the low 70s, it was a perfect night for a run. Roman took off on the seven-mile run back to the Chemeketa Community College parking lot to pick up his Flaming Red Ducati 1098S. Roman appreciated its brute power but had never approached its 169 MPH upper-speed rating. He was too aware of all the deer and elk which crossed the back roads he liked to cruise.

He had been out of the navy now for a few years but still tried to maintain his SEAL conditioning. The seven-mile run was a distance, but not one he considered challenging. A bigger concern was the memories. They had come back in a rush as he talked with Julia. He started running and, his body on autopilot, allowed the memories to wash over him. Roman expected his flashbacks while he slept, but tonight, they came as he ran.

Scene after scene flashed in front of his eyes. He saw himself talking to President Myers, taking the Zodiac onto the beach, listening to the rebel leader Juan Alvarez shoot the sailors, and ordering Amber captured. Roman saw the blood spurting as his knife flew into Ambassador Knapp and the sound of Admiral Hayes neck-snapping.

For the last year, his flashbacks always stopped there. He'd killed the admiral and the ambassador a thousand times. He no longer had visions of anything which happened after he was wounded, and no longer of other earlier actions.

It relieved Roman to arrive in the parking lot and find his unvandalized Ducati waiting for him.

THE MEMORIES HAD RETURNED as though everything had happened a moment ago. Roman was fearful other memories might surface. He had submerged them for a long time, but tonight everything felt fresh. He was looking forward to getting back on the bike. It was a tricky enough ride that he knew he needed to give the motorcycle his full attention. He hoped the memories would fade into the background.

He debated driving back to Gates and decided it was too far to go, given he would be returning for breakfast. His solution was to drop into Fred Meyer's, a 24-hour grocery and department store, and pick up what he would need for the next couple of nights. He got a package of underwear, socks, and shirts that he could roll into his bike's luggage container along with shaving cream, toothbrush, deodorant, and toothpaste.

Believing in preparing for all eventualities, he picked up a box of condoms.

Shopping took all of 20 minutes to accomplish. He then checked into the hotel closest to Julia's condominium.

# 88

At 9 A.M. sharp, the Ducati pulled into Julia's driveway. As Roman looked around, a guard stepped into sight and chatted with him for a few moments. As the guard retreated, Julia walked down the stairs from her condo with a small backpack.

Roman thought, "She looks like a fashion model dressed for a motorcycle ride." She had on tall designer boots, a form-fitting leather jacket, and skin-tight jeans. All he could think of was getting her out of the clothes and naked beneath him.

With no hesitation, she walked up, gave him a hug and a brief kiss, and looked with surprise at the Ducati.

She walked around it, admiring it, and then said, "It's sexy. I expected you to show up on a Harley. Is it as fast as it looks?"

"Faster. I fell in love with the Ducati while serving in the Mediterranean. Jimmy and I'd rent them when we had shore leave. We rode them all over Europe. They are incredible on the German Autobahn."

"Where are we going for breakfast?" she asked, "I'm starved."

He answered, "I thought we'd take a ride through the country to Silverton. There's a little place the locals go which overlooks Silver Creek and has a great breakfast."

He pulled another helmet out of the small luggage compartment and showed her how to link the two helmets through Bluetooth. They could talk, listen to music, and even send voice text messages. As he pulled out of the driveway with her holding on tight, he nodded at the security guard who spoke into his radio.

Roman proceeded at a slow pace through the city streets, acting like a biker familiarizing a new rider with how to ride a motorcycle. He circled the block, making exaggerated turn signals, etc.

Julia asked, "Why are we going in circles?"

As she asked that, they circled past another security guard who gave them a "thumbs up." Roman sped up, "We were waiting on his all clear. I was making sure no one was following us."

Roman left town and headed to Silverton. Even with the population explosion which had occurred in Oregon, they were still driving through beautiful farmland. The harvest of various grass crops was in full swing. Combines were everywhere, and it didn't take much imagination to visualize wagon trains arriving on the Oregon Trail and pulling into the rolling hills. It was easy to imagine the settlers thinking they were arriving in the biblical Promised Land.

Julia was leaning into him and holding on with a firm grip. With her arms wrapped around his waist every few miles, she would sit up and rub his back or shoulders, and then wrap her arms around him again. Roman wasn't sure if she was rubbing her breasts on his back on purpose or if it was just because of their size. The combination of her rubbing on him and the vibration of the Ducati was causing his jeans to become tighter. He thought if anyone were watching, it could be an embarrassing moment when he got off the motorcycle at the restaurant.

Silverton was a former logging and farming community that had transformed itself into a beautiful, quaint, little 'artsy-crafty' kind of town. Art galleries and knickknack shops were side by side with old fashioned barbershops and small restaurants.

As Roman held her hand and led her to a window table, she exclaimed, "I would have thought you had enough water yesterday."

The old building sat on tall pilings over Silver Creek. The creek flowed below them.

They had a relaxing breakfast. The large portions of the meal would have been perfect for a logger or farmer's breakfast. Perhaps that accounted for the restaurant's popularity. Soon the matronly owner came out and gave Roman a big hug. Roman introduced Julia, who also got a hug.

Roman said, "I'm related to almost everyone in all the little farming communities on the east side of the valley."

He told her with a grin, "When I was a teenager and thinking about girls, Dad told me I couldn't date anyone from Silverton, Stayton, or any of the towns up the canyon. When I protested, Dad pulled out old genealogy charts and showed me I'm related to a good portion of the girls in the area. Second and third cousins, including the owner of the restaurant who just hugged you, are everywhere."

They lingered over coffee and had the ordinary conversations of people getting to know each other. Julia asked, "What else is on the agenda for the day?"

Roman's replied, "Unless you want to do something else, I thought you might enjoy going to the Oregon Gardens. It's just up the road."

"That sounds like fun."

"I'm looking for landscaping for my mountain cabin. The Gardens are an eighty-acre demonstration project of the Oregon Nurseryman's Association. Twenty demonstration gardens encompass several miles of trails, creeks, water displays, and thousands of trees and flowers."

"I knew it was big."

"If you haven't been there before, I suggest we start with a ride on the open-air tram around the property to check it out. Then we can get off where ever we chose and walk the trails. I want to check out the Conifer Garden, the areas with Native Flowers and Shrubs, and the Rhododendron Gardens. The challenge in adding color to my home landscaping is finding flowers or shrubs, which are deer and elk resistant."

Julia said, "I've always heard about the Gardens and wanted to go, but I've never been there. It sounds great. However, I'll admit, it's hard for me to imagine the macho guy I was with yesterday, suggesting we go walking through a flower garden."

Roman replied, "I'll have you know, I've walked in flower gardens around the world. I love the Butchart Gardens in Victoria B.C. If you haven't, you need to see the gardens in England, France, and Italy. Many of them are centuries old."

With a big grin, she asked, "Is suggesting the Gardens your way of showing me you have unsuspected levels of complexity and substance? Or, are you just trying to lower my defenses by getting me to think how sweet an idea it is?"

"If either of those works, I'll plead guilty," he grinned back.

IT WAS JUST a short ride up to the garden entrance. While the Ducati idled up the entryway to the nearby lodge, Roman said there was one other option on the table if she wanted. "We could check into rooms at the lodge for the night. Get out of our leathers and boots and put on more comfortable walking shoes before we go into the garden. Later we could have a wonderful dinner in the lodge and spend the night."

With a throaty tone to her voice, she said, "I think one room sounds like a great idea."

Roman checked into the lodge. Playing over the front desk person's shoulder was a soundless news broadcast. It had several clips of yesterday's rescues, and on the closed captioning, he read about one person, Charlie, who was still missing. The news clips showed Bridger ferrying Marion County Sheriff's divers to various search locations in his new Zodiac, Lifesaver 2.

Roman requested a room at the far end of the building. When they arrived at their hotel room, Roman and Julia carried their helmets and small bags into the suite. As Roman closed the door,

Julia just stood there looking at him. It was a lovely suite with a fireplace and Jacuzzi tub, but the most prominent object in the room was the king-size bed. It was a bit of an awkward, tentative moment.

Without a word, they were in each other's arms, having a kiss that wouldn't end. As they came up for air, Roman started helping her off with her clothes. They continued kissing and removing items of clothing as they backed to the bed. Both their shirts were off, and Roman was nibbling and licking her nipples as she groaned.

Julia sat down on the edge of the bed. She held up her feet for him to help her off with her boots. As he pulled her calf-length boots off, she lay back on the bed and started to push her jeans down. He grabbed them by the legs and ripped them off. She scooted back on the comforter and lay there waiting for him. He kept watching her as he kicked out of his boots and jeans. She lay there with only a pair of skimpy black panties he planned on removing in moments.

Roman said, "I've been thinking of this since I first saw you across the room getting coffee."

He played with her breasts, kissed her, and slipped a hand between her legs as he positioned himself on her. She moaned and rose to bring him into her. They were made for each other. Their passion repeatedly rekindled until it was time to take a break.

They started cleaning up and becoming presentable to walk around the Gardens. The lighting had been dim in the bedroom, but with all the lights on, Julia inspected the scars on his body. "Oh my God, what happened to you? What are all these?"

He tried to brush it off with a grin and saying "classified," but she wasn't having it, "What's this one?" as she pointed to scar after scar. "A knife wound." "Sniper fire." "Shrapnel."

They dressed in T-shirts, shorts, and running shoes for a slow walk around the gardens. Hours later, they were back in the bedroom, the fireplace flickered, the music was on low, and they made love over and over throughout the night. They were drifting off to sleep when he warned Julia, "I hope I don't have any flashbacks tonight. When I first returned from the navy, I had them every night.

It has been several months since I experienced any, but I had one last night."

She gave him a tender kiss and said she would be there for him.

# 89

## FLASHBACK

*The Oregon Garden*

With Julia in his arms, they both drifted off to sleep. Einstein once said time and space were relative. As his breathing became rhythmic and his sleep deepened, Roman was propelled back in time to the South Pacific. Once again, everything was happening as though it were in real-time.

He was on the same mission, and Amber was killed. He knifed the ambassador and snapped the neck of the admiral. But, tonight's flashback ended with a first time experience.

Julia spoke to Roman in a soothing voice and awakened him. When he came to, he was sobbing in her arms. With tears running down his cheeks, he cried and cried as she stroked his head.

EXHAUSTED and embarrassed the next morning, Roman awakened full of desire for the beautiful woman sleeping in his arms. Instead, he got up early while she was sleeping and took a shower.

He was still processing the night's flashbacks and his anguish over

Amber and their child when Julia put her head behind the shower curtain.

She asked, "Do you want company?"

Without waiting for an answer, Julia climbed into the shower with him. He thought, "There goes my introspection," as she soaped him down. Later, he thought, "The shower sex was a little tricky with the soapy floor but well worth it."

They packed and went back into the lodge for a magnificent all you could eat country breakfast buffet. It was delicious. The seating in the beautiful fine dining restaurant overlooked the Oregon Flower Gardens and the Willamette Valley. All of that, proceeded by a night of the best sex he could ever imagine. Life was good.

Roman told her, "I'm embarrassed by my flashback. It is one reason I haven't had a date since getting out of the service. I don't know what caused me to cry, I've never done that before."

Julia held his hand and told him, "It's ok. I'm proud you felt safe enough with me to cry."

Roman said, "I can't tell you what happened. What happened is classified. But, in my nightmare, my fiancée, Amber, and the child we were expecting died."

She continued to hold his hand.

Julia addressed the death of Amber, "Have you talked to a counselor about what happened?"

"Yes, to the extent that I can."

"Good because it's not good to bottle up emotional pain and loss. You'll never be whole and healthy for either yourself or another relationship until you deal with and accept the loss of the last one."

Roman said, "I know that, but it's been hard to do. I have so much guilt over her death, and over how long we put off our relationship because of our careers. We decided to get married, get out of the service, and have a child. We were so excited, and then she was just gone, and so was our child."

Squeezing his hand, Julia said, "Regardless of how we met, my heart tells me, you're a good guy. If you can get over the wounds of your past, it may be possible for you to find a new love in your future. If you do, you can still have a child."

They continued the conversation for a few more minutes before he asked, "Would you like to run up the canyon and spend tonight at my cabin?"

"Yes, I'd love to."

With no warning, his phone rang. Roman looked at his caller ID and said, "It's your dad."

She groaned.

# 90

**The Miller Compound**

Donald Miller asked his boys and grandson, "What's the latest on the governor and his rich bitch daughter?"

Bruce, Charlie's brother, said they were mailing a letter to the governor every three days from various places around the state. The message was always the same, "You're guilty. For that, you shall die."

Little Charlie, his grandson, said they had lost track of the daughter for now, but had coverage on the sporting goods store in Gates. All the recent news portrayed Roman as being her new boyfriend, and something connected him to the store. Little Charlie was sure she would turn up there.

Little Charlie reminded everyone that when it was time, he got the rich bitch for his own for a while. He'd make her pay for the "sins of her father."

Donald smacked Little Charlie across the face and said, "You don't deserve her. None of you do. Bruce, you swore you could kill the governor, and no one would know. None of those attempts worked, all you did was alert him. And you, Little Charlie, how many kayakers did you put in the water without killing any of them? What a bunch of losers. Do I have to do everything myself?"

Donald asked again about the governor.

His son, Bruce, said the governor's security team had the governor on full lockdown. "Short of a mortar strike, we'll not be penetrating the governor's mansion. They've closed the curtains, the state police are out in force, and I just feel whenever I go by there that other people are watching, but I see no one. I walked by there the other night, and I swear I could feel eyes on me.

"However," Bruce said, "He can't stay locked down forever. He's not that kind. We've got all the boys staking out his mansion and office. When he moves, we'll know it and follow up. An opportunity will come up."

Donald ruled his clan like an old-time patriarch. He was narrow-minded, racist, anti-government, and dictatorial. Others might have referred to him as a "skinhead" or "Aryan," but Donald would never accept those labels. He wasn't joining anything other than the Klan, and he hadn't been to a Klan meeting since leaving Alabama.

The cause he believed in was his family. He had a full head of hair, and wouldn't think of either shaving it or wearing a ponytail. Donald told his boys, "Tattoos are for sissies who want to look tough. When times get tough, it's not the size of the tattoo on your arm. It's the size of the club in your hand."

While still in 'Bama, he had gotten a mail-order ministers license. Everyone thought it was for the tax benefits, but he had evolved his own strict belief in the Old Testament version of the Bible. He believed in "an eye for an eye" and "justice is mine saith the Lord." Donald thought he was the Lord's instrument of vengeance.

Donald preached the patriarch had the responsibility to marry the daughters of his sons or brothers when they came of age. He had two young wives besides the older one, Mary Beth.

Donald was adamant, "We've got to get this done. All Big Charlie was trying to do was provide for his family, just like I taught him. His baby was hungry and needed food. It's not right what the governor did."

Donald didn't know Mary Beth had divorced Charlie. Several years ago, she coaxed him into getting married by a local Justice of the Peace. The legalities of the marriage didn't matter to him. He didn't care if she was also married to Charlie. Donald married Mary Beth to shut her up.

Donald thought Mary Beth was a better cook than she was a lover. She served him a large rasher of bacon with his eggs each morning, a fresh cake with buttery icing was on the table every week, and Southern sweet tea was available all summer long. Her cooking featured high fat, high-carbohydrate foods, even though both were taboo with his diabetes and high blood pressure. His pills for both issues had rendered him impotent. Neither Mary Beth nor the young girls he called wives had to service him any longer. He blamed the women for his inability to perform.

# 91

Roman answered his phone, "This is Roman."

"Hello, Roman, this is Stan. I hope my daughter is with you and just has her phone off?"

"Yes, sir, she is with me, and she is safe." Roman said, "Would you like to speak to her?"

Stan replied, "No, I was just nervous and hoping she was with you. Jimmy assured me she was and was safe. The reason I'm calling, Roman, is I want to meet with you. Today if I can. I need your advice and help on a project. Can I break you free from my daughter for a conversation? Perhaps you can bring her here to the governor's mansion where it's safe, while we talk?"

Roman thought about it for a moment, then said, "May I suggest you come out to my home for dinner, sir? I'd like you to meet my mother and sister. Perhaps we could have some social, get acquainted, time?"

Stan was quiet for a moment, processing that thought. Julia looked shocked. Stan answered, "Great idea, can we bring anything?"

"Yes, sir, I assume you have a large SUV?" Roman asked.

"Yes?"

Roman said, "Why don't you bring the SUV, and I would take it as a personal favor if you would invite Jimmy Stockade to join us. Let him know I said a little 'night work' is always a possibility. Shall we meet at my mother's store at three p.m.?"

As he hung up, Julia said, "You're kidding. You want our families to meet?"

"I told you I was serious about you." Roman grinned at her and said, "Now I need to call my mother."

They ordered another cup of coffee. Roman asked what Julia's parent's favorite foods were, and then called his mother. Rose about panicked when he said he had invited the governor for dinner. He asked her to call Darci at Darci and Delaney Catering and ask if she could cater the meal. He suggested drinks and hors d'oeuvres at 4ish and dinner at 6:00.

Roman asked, "Could you also call Alexia and ask her to take tonight off and come to dinner? Don't let her weasel out of it. I want her to meet my best friend."

When he said that Julia whispered, "Jimmy?"

He nodded, and she smiled.

They left the restaurant and headed for Gates. She still held on, but he grinned as he thought she was more relaxed in her grip after last night's activities. It was a beautiful country drive as he took the back roads. Before she realized it, they were pulling into the store.

He parked the Ducati in the fenced parking lot, and they went into the store. Rose gave Julia a big hug and told her with a laugh, "I'm just a nervous wreck, worried about meeting your parents. That's before, for heaven's sake, I found out your parents are Governor and Mrs. Anderson. Roman, why didn't you tell me earlier? You should have given me enough time to go buy a new outfit."

She kept babbling over what to wear, but said, "Thank goodness Alexia will show up in a few minutes. She can help me get dressed."

Rose took a calming breath, "Darci has been by in a dither about what to serve, but she's got a menu prepared. She hopes it will be ok. Roman, she wants you to look over the menu, and if you want something different, please text her. Darci is at the grocery store right now and heading up to the house in the next hour to cook. She also wants to know if you need her and Delaney to serve, or just prepare everything and leave."

Roman grinned and said, "I think Julia and I might have fun serving."

Roman asked his mother, "Would you and Alexia mind showing Stan and Margo how to get to my cabin?"

That puzzled Julia, "I thought you lived above the boat showroom?"

Rose gave her an indulgent grin and said, "No, honey, his cabin will surprise you."

Roman took Julia by the hand and led her out the back of the store to a small shed at the rear of the property. When they walked in, he flipped a switch and motors hummed to life.

She watched in shock as a small ski chairlift pulled up. It wasn't an open chairlift, but a glass-enclosed double lift capable of seating four. It even had a steel-plated floor. They stepped in and got seated. Roman pushed a button on a remote control device, put it in his pocket, and up the hill, they went.

ROMAN GRINNED at Julia's amazement, as she peppered him with questions. When she asked how much the chairlift cost, he minimized the expense, saying it helped in the construction process. The lift allowed the work crews to go up and down much faster, saving time. The lift poles went straight up the hill, and the timber was cut back away from the lines about 100 feet. When she turned and looked over her shoulder, and down the mountain, the views were spectacular. Off to the side, she could see what looked like a steep logging road winding up the hill.

Roman pointed at it, "That's the road everyone else will come up. It's a rough dirt road and takes a bumpy half-hour in a 4x4."

"I've been on lots of chairlifts, but this one is the quietest I've ever been in."

His response stilled her, "It's got bulletproof glass and a steel-plated floor."

When they crested the hill and started dropping toward the shed, which was the upper terminus for the chairlift, she looked off to the side and saw the house. "Oh, my God. Is this your idea of a little mountain cabin?"

She couldn't believe what she was seeing. "This is like a mansion you would see in a magazine for the rich and famous. Walk me through everything I'm seeing. I know this is incredible, but I can also tell I don't even know how nice this is. Tell me about your home."

She could tell he was sheepish about the pride he felt in his home. "Well, first, turnaround and look at the view. Can you imagine looking at that every morning over breakfast?"

"I think I'd like to have that opportunity," she smiled at him.

"This was the site of my Grandpa Bill's elk hunting camp. He called it Hawkeye Ridge Elk Camp. Deer and elk wander around up here all the time. Part of it's obvious. The house sits in the middle of Nelson Timber forest land. But, in case of a forest fire, there are no trees close by." He pointed at all the cleared space around the house, chairlift, and outbuildings.

He continued, "The house itself is half-buried in the earth on three sides and has a sod covered metal roof. I have a 1000 gallon gravity fed water storage tank up the hill. It feeds an irrigation system on the roof. A fire could burn across the top and do negligible damage."

He pointed at the house itself, "With the reflective glass, and the way it's positioned on the property, it is next to impossible to see in from outside, and the glass doesn't reflect the sunlight to let people know the house is here. I installed a geothermal heating and cooling system and my own solar-powered electrical system. In an emergency, I can be off the grid and still power my property."

He pointed further to his right, "Over there's the garage and airplane hangar. It is semi-buried for insulation like the home. From the air, nothing is visible. The airstrip is a grass field behind the garage, but it's kept groomed, and has hidden beacons I can turn on at night if I need to."

"My God, Roman. How much money do you have?"

"More than I'll ever need."

Julia couldn't help thinking, "It doesn't look like I need to worry about him wanting me for my money. My trust fund is pocket change compared to what this is worth."

"Ok, show me the inside. I grew up with my father's friends having nice houses, but this is amazing."

He escorted her towards the house. Outside the three-story, south-facing windows was a large flagstone BBQ/fire pit area. They walked around to the front, to enter a greenhouse atrium. A small recirculating creek wandered through the atrium with a rock waterfall at the far end.

At the far end, near the waterfall, was the actual entrance into the home. When she opened the double doors, she stood still, looking up. Her jaw went slack. An enormous crystal chandelier hung in the entryway. She could look straight through the foyer, across the living room, and through the rear windows at a view that went on forever. A masculine old-world charm emanated from the homes library, which was filled with dark wood paneling and floor to ceiling bookshelves. The kitchen/great room was open and inviting, and the dining room had another magnificent chandelier over a beautiful handmade table that seated twenty.

Julia jumped as an alarm sounded. Roman glanced at a panel near the door and said, "I forgot to tell you, I also have a military-grade alarm system and sensors throughout the property. When I was in Bethesda, I met a vet who had lost his legs to an IED in Afghanistan, Brian Beatty. He inspired all of his with his dedication to his physical therapy and how excited he was about restarting his life."

"Oh, how sad."

"Yes, it is. It's happened to way too many guys. Anyway, Brian planned on creating an electronic surveillance security company. He had excellent ideas but no money. I put up a few dollars for a small piece of the company he wanted to start. When I was planning my home, I shipped him the topographic maps of the mountain and the plans for my home. The house is a test site for all his ideas. His biggest challenge up here was to figure out how to get the system to recognize a real threat versus picking up the bear, deer, and elk, which wander around everywhere.

Brian had a good idea, he's a technology wizard. I tried to help him out with some business concepts and a little seed money. I didn't expect much return from my seed money and was prepared to lose it. Instead, his business has exploded nationwide. I get dividend checks every month, and he's talking about doing an IPO. I'm thrilled for him and his success.

That alarm was my cousin Darci arriving to prepare dinner. Why don't you give yourself a tour of the home while I get her set up in the kitchen? That way, you can show your mother around later."

"You want me just to wander around?"

"Sure, poke into anything you want to see. Before you do, let's set you up a passcode for the alarm system. I'm hoping today isn't the only day you'll be here. It's sensitive. If you're ever here and someone drops a glass, you can turn off the system before sirens sound."

"It goes off with just a broken glass?"

"Maybe, I haven't tested it with a glass. It will for sure if any of the windows break. Right after I moved in, while I was unpacking, I dropped a big pitcher. It sounded like a war zone until I got it turned off."

# 92

Jimmy drove the armored Suburban into the parking lot of Nelson Bait and Tackle Shop. He helped Stan and Margo out of the rig and escorted them into the store. They both seemed a little surprised at the visible high-end quality on the inside of the building. Alexia was there, and as she introduced her mother to everyone, commented to Jimmy, "See, we meet again."

Leaving the store, they all climbed into the Suburban. Jimmy drove. Alexia sat next to him in the passenger seat, making small talk. Rose jumped into the third row, leaving Stan and Margo in their original positions.

Alexia directed them out of the back of the store parking lot and up a dirt logging road. As they left the parking lot, she had him stop to shut and arm the gate to the dirt road.

She suggested to Jimmy, "I'd shift into four-wheel drive. The road is rough."

Everyone oohed and aahed over the views as they kept climbing. There were several hairpin curves with sheer cliffs on the way up. Margo screamed twice, and even Stan was white-knuckled.

Alexia was grinning until Rose mentioned, "I expect this is a difficult ride after the recent car accident, I read, you were in."

Both of the Andersons agreed.

Jimmy made one last sharp uphill turn, and they were looking straight at Roman's home. Jimmy stopped the car to look and couldn't help himself, "Well son-of-a-bitch, would you look at that. Roman told me about it, and I've seen pictures from the team who came for a barbeque he had. But my imagination didn't do it justice. That is amazing."

The governor and Margo were exclaiming over the beauty of the house and property as the Suburban pulled to a stop next to the fire pit. Roman had a fire going, and he and Julia were relaxing in front of the fire with a glass of wine.

Everyone walked up to the fire pit and exchanged hugs. Julia acted a little nervous around her mother and father, but Mrs. Nelson just walked up to her and gave her another hug.

Roman walked up to Jimmy and gave him a bear hug. He then turned to everyone and said, "I know you have all met Jimmy, but I want you to know this is my best friend. I can't tell you how many times he has saved my life."

Julia walked up to Jimmy and said, "I've seen the scars. Someone had to have saved him from the scars I've seen. Thank you."

Alexia also hugged him and whispered in his ear, "For saving my brother's life, I could love you. Thank you," and kissed him on the cheek. Jimmy wasn't sure what to think of that.

Roman poured the Oregon wine, and Julia offered the hors d'oeuvres. Margo said, "Wine is ok, but I have to see this house." Roman grinned and waved Julia forward to do the tour. Stan and Jimmy said they wanted to see it.

When Stan and Jimmy said they wanted to join the tour, Roman could see Alexia deciding she needed to see it again. The whole group took their wine, and Julia led the way. She walked them around and entered the home from the front, through the atrium, just as she had. She didn't know why she felt proud of showing off Roman's house.

# 93

After dinner and over crème sherry, the governor told the group, "This dinner originated from my desire to get Roman's input on an important issue. I hope you all can forgive me for talking shop, but I'd like to get Roman's comments before we head back. There's nothing private that we will talk about, I'd appreciate everyone else's comments as well."

Roman said, "Let's take our drinks into the library where it may be a little more comfortable."

With everyone seated, the governor set the stage. "I'm supposed to do everything in my power to protect the people of Oregon. Part of that is protecting us from ourselves, in the form of politicians, criminals, and just plain idiots. Protecting Oregonians from natural disasters is also essential. I have read the recommendations of several committees, but nothing seems practical. I watched Alexia's interview on TV along with everyone else. Roman, your level of preparedness struck me as well thought out. To the extent we can, I want to apply that thinking to the entire state. If you were governor, what natural disasters do you think we need to prepare for, and what preparations can we make to minimize the loss of life and property?"

Roman pursed his lips for a moment and raised an eyebrow at the governor's question. He replied, "It's interesting you ask that. When I was thinking of building my home, I gave a lot of thought to those issues. I also read the reports of those commissions. They identified lots of problems but did nothing to help anyone prepare for a true emergency. I have binders of research, which I did. You're welcome to look at them."

He pulled several binders off his library shelves and started leafing through the pages. "Many of the design features I built into this home are preplanning for my family to survive a catastrophe. If you want a list of possibilities," he said, dropping a binder on his desk, "I'd say the most significant risk for mass fatalities is the 'Cascadia Subduction Zone Earthquake.' That event is past its average time for an occurrence off the Oregon coast."

Stan nodded his head.

Dropping binder after binder on his desk, Roman read off their titles. "Other risks would include tsunamis, volcanic eruptions, and accompanying lahars. You can't forget forest fires, river flooding, and dam collapses either from natural causes or terrorist activity. Global warming and climate change, salmon extinction, the terrorist activity I mentioned a second ago, but not limited to, dam collapse, and don't forget incoming missiles from a rogue nation like North Korea."

Roman took a sip of his sherry and looked at Stan.

Stan asked, "What do you think will be the biggest event?"

"Ranked by devastation and death, or by the probability of occurrence?"

"Both."

"Without a doubt, the Cascadia Subduction Zone earthquake deserves its nickname of 'the big one.' Cities a thousand miles inland will feel it. The event will devastate everything west of the Cascade mountain range, and wipe out most of the towns on the Oregon Coast. In order of probability, I'd say it also gets a high ranking. It's coming, maybe tomorrow, maybe in 200 years. The odds, however, are very high that it will occur in the next 30 years. Most people, however, believe forest fires and river floods to be more likely."

Alexia said, “I don’t like this conversation. I love the coast, and you’re scaring me.”

“Sometimes, scared is good. It can force you to be smart.”

Margo said, “I agree with Alexia. I don’t enjoy talking about this stuff.”

Rose said, “Neither do I.”

Stan replied, “To a large extent, that’s why nothing happens. Nobody wants to talk about it.” Getting up, he walked over to the library bar and poured another glass of sherry. Tipping his glass to Roman, he asked, “What else?”

Roman asked, “Is this a test?”

“Kind of, what else do you see as potential disasters?”

Pausing for a breath, Roman looked at the women and, closing his last binder, laid it on his desk. “It’s easy to come up with a bigger list, but those are the immediate issues I see. If you want to dial down into any of those and discuss them, we can, but this may not be the time for that. The details can be graphic.”

The women were all in agreement, “We don’t need the details.”

Roman grinned at Stan, “Did I pass the test?”

Looking glum, he replied, “Unfortunately, yes.”

## 94

EARLIER THAT DAY

"Thanks for taking my call, Mr. President."

"Stan, you never called me that when you were stealing my beer out of the fraternity house refrigerator. You know it's Alex. What's got you up this early in your time zone, and how do you like Jimmy Stockade?"

"Well, he's a great guy, and he must be doing a good job because I'm still alive. I gotta say he dresses better than any man has a right to."

With a grumble, the president said, "Well, the son-of-a-bitch can afford to. What's up? They briefed me on what was happening with Julia yesterday."

"What can you tell me about the guy she was with yesterday, Lt. Commander Roman Nelson? Jimmy says you're the one person who can talk to me about him?" Stan asked.

"He's as big of a son-of-a-bitch as Jimmy Stockade, maybe bigger. If he hadn't blackmailed me for a large sum of money, I'd introduce him to my daughter."

The president added with a laugh, "Which it seems you have done. Why do you want to know about him?"

The governor explained what he had in mind.

President Myers said, "He's perfect. He and Jimmy are two of the deadliest men you'll ever meet. I can't tell you what he did, but I can tell you he and his entire SEAL Team were in the Oval Office for a top-secret presentation of the Presidential Medal of Honor. Lt. Commander Nelson pulled the United States out of a bad situation. He tied up all the loose ends and did everything in total secrecy. His conduct in this situation created goodwill for the U.S. but came with a great personal expense. He almost died from the wounds he sustained, and his fiancée and unborn child did die in the action."

Stan was silent for a moment, processing what he'd heard before saying, "That's awful."

"It was. Commander Nelson also walked away with a significant amount of cash. Understanding the political ramifications of what he and his team did, he knew it would be more expedient for me to give the money involved to him and his team than it would be for him to return it up his chain of command. That's why I joke and say he blackmailed me. He helped me solve a big problem, and I was willing to give his team the money. Commander Nelson is discreet, sharp, and a lawyer by education. He's also perfect for what you want. Tell the bastard I said hello, and I'm glad to see he's recovered from his injuries. I've worried about him and owe him big time Stan, so does this country. Treat him well."

# 95

PRESENT-DAY

"We got him, Papa," said Bruce Miller as he came into his father's house. "I knew staking out that store would pay dividends."

Donald asked, "What do you have?"

"Julia showed up on a motorcycle. She was with that Roman guy she was with on the river. They disappeared up the mountain on a chairlift, and just a few minutes ago, the governor and his wife showed up. I don't know what's up there. The dirt trail out the back of the parking lot has a locked gate. I didn't want to cut the bolt until we are ready. Let's send Little Charlie's drone up to see what's there."

Donald smiled, "Sounds perfect. We've got him bottled up. All we've got to do is take out anyone on the chairlift, or on the road out as they leave. Big Charlie will rest easy in his grave."

Little Charlie remarked he wouldn't rest easy until the rich bitch was groveling for him. "I want her to suffer and scream for a while first. It's only right."

# 96

PRESENT-DAY

***After dinner***
***Hawkeye Ridge***

Stan was enjoying his crème sherry and pacing the room. "Well, thanks for scaring the crap out of everyone with your disaster analysis. Let me tell you the situation, as I see it, what my plan is, and what I would like to ask for your help with, Roman."

Roman nodded in curiosity.

Stan pointed at Roman and Julia, and then at Alexia. "Thanks to what you did, and thanks to Alexia's news coverage, the two of you are the biggest heroes this state has seen in decades. The term hero doesn't mean much to people anymore. It's been overused and trivialized. But Alexia, you stuck their actions in everyone's face for hours yesterday. First, you did it with your streaming live coverage and later with your special report. I read the reports. You had the highest ratings, for a news program, your station has ever received. You humanized the heroes and the victims."

He gave a self-deprecating shake of his head, "Many times, the victims were visible on the television screen before the two of you could see them from the boat. I know I found myself yelling at Julia and trying to point out someone hanging in a bush. It embarrassed me when Margo reminded me Julia couldn't hear me or see where I was pointing. I'm sure I wasn't the only one who was engaged in the action."

Ceasing to pace in front of Roman and Julia, he looked at them and said, "People around the state and country saw the two of you, risking your lives for others and moments later hugging and kissing out of excitement. Everyone wants to relate to you or be your friend."

Roman was frowning and shaking his head while squeezing Julia's hand hard. He was squirming in his chair, uncomfortable with the praise.

Julia asked, "Where are you headed with this, Dad. I know you. You're flattering us to set us up for something. What do you want from us?"

"You know me too well. Next week, I would like to have both of you in my office for the first-ever presentation of The Governor's Hero Medal. I want everyone in this state to know who you are and what you did."

Roman cleared his throat and said, "That's unnecessary, sir. I'm not big on being in the limelight. Besides, what did all the questions about disasters have to do with the river rescues?"

Stan shook his head. "Sorry, Roman. This time you don't get to stay in the shadows. There's a reason I want to publicize you as heroes. I'll get to that in a minute. Friday night, I said I needed to make a few phone calls to check you both out."

Stopping at Roman's desk, he picked up the disaster-related binders. Holding them in his hand, he continued pacing the room while looking at Julia. "I may have known you since birth, Sweetie, but I had to put you through the same vetting process as Roman. Jimmy warned me there was one person who could talk to me about you, Roman. That is President Alex Myers.

"Few people know, Alex and I were, and will forever be, fraternity brothers. Alex said to tell you hello, Roman, and he still has a job for you if you get bored. He couldn't tell me a lot, but I'm sure I know more about you than your mother or sister. Alexia, this is a classified conversation and not for TV. Did any of you know Roman earned the Presidential Medal of Honor and received it in the Oval Office?"

Rose said, "No, it sounds important. How did you get that Roman? You never told me you'd met the president."

Julia looked at Roman with wide eyes, and Alexia nodded.

Stan said, "I didn't think you knew. How and why he got it, is classified. The fact he got it isn't. Roman, you dodged the spotlight the last time you were a hero because of National Security issues. In this case, you don't get to dodge the spotlight. Alexia's news broadcast put you in everyone's living room. I hope this time you use your hero status to help the people of Oregon. It is in Oregon's best interest for everyone to know your credentials, and for you to have high profile recognition. My hope is, if people know you, recognize you, and respect you, they will follow your advice, and we can make real change."

Ceasing to pace, he tapped Roman's disaster planning binder. "This is why you need to step into the hero role. Oregon faces critical natural disaster issues, just as you outlined. We've had one planning group and commission after the next. Nothing gets done. No one is prepared for anything. Once everyone knows and respects you, I want to appoint you as Statewide Director of Natural Disaster Preparedness. As the director, you can forget about the legislature. Nothing is getting done there. Use your reputation to connect with leaders in our local communities. I want you to get the local communities involved in solving the local community's disaster needs, by starting dozens of local preparedness groups. Your state needs you, Roman."

An alarm interrupted the governor. Roman frowned as he spoke to a voice on the other side of the alarm for a moment. He then opened a concealed gun case masquerading as a bookcase. He handed a BCM-RECCE 16 KMR-A reconnaissance rifle to Jimmy and took one for himself. Both knew the U.S. Navy SEAL armorers developed the Recce rifle.

Jimmy held the rifle with familiar ease and asked, "How the hell did you get these?"

Roman winked at him, "I have my ways."

He turned to everyone else in the room, "There may be nothing to worry about, but our bottom gate has opened, and there's a drone approaching," Roman said as he walked out onto the flagstone around the fire pit. Everyone followed him.

Jimmy looked at Alexia and whispered, "If you have a camera, you might start recording. This could be good." Everyone stood behind Roman and Jimmy as they first could hear, and then see, a small object in the sky. Roman lifted his rifle, tracked it for a moment in the scope, and fired.

It exploded. Roman and Jimmy looked at each other. They both then looked at the governor. Jimmy ran down to the smoking drone and brought the pieces back. Examining it, Roman said, "Functional, but not sophisticated."

Jimmy asked the governor, "Could you get a trooper to come to pick up the pieces and take them to the crime lab. Perhaps we'll get lucky and find fingerprints."

Roman, however, said, "Why don't you get ahold of the pilot of the guard chopper who's sitting on the ground down at the falls in Mill City. He's just sitting there waiting on the search boats to find somebody for him to pick up. That rafter will never surface. I'm sure he's long gone. Have the chopper stop up here, pick it up, and get it to the crime lab in minutes instead of hours."

He pointed up the hill to his landing strip. Minutes later, the wreckage was airborne.

Julia had her arms around her mother and father. They were all distraught.

# 97

A few minutes later, Julia walked her mother to a quiet spot on the patio, "Mom, what do you think of Roman? Am I wrong to like him?"

Margo laughed, "Honey, you haven't asked me about a man since junior high school. I'll tell you what your Uncle Alex told your dad. 'Tell Julia she's got three weeks to get a marriage proposal out of him, or I'll be sending my daughter, Kathleen, to Oregon for a little competition.'"

They both laughed, then Margo added, "But, you'd better figure out what you want. You know I'm good at reading people. Roman doesn't realize it himself, but he's head over heels in love with you. It shows in the way he looks at you. He's a man of action. Once he realizes he loves you, he'll take action."

"That's kind of scary. I'm not sure I'm ready for all it implies."

Giving her daughter a big hug, Margo added, "You've been drifting for a while. Roman is for real, Honey, and just maybe, he's the man for you. I don't know what else your Uncle Alex told your father, but he hasn't stopped talking about him. When the time comes, if he is the right man, you will know it."

ROMAN SUGGESTED they go back inside. He kept looking at the alarm system and talking to his friend, Brian, on the other end.

He approached everyone, "If you all want to spend the night, I have enough bedrooms. You could then leave in the morning. Jimmy, however, would like to get you back to Mahonia Manor as soon as possible. We could fly you out in a helicopter tomorrow, but Jimmy and I are both most comfortable with your safety if we move you in the dark. Your car will be a slow-moving target going downhill. If we wait until daylight, the advantage shifts to whoever is after you. Our suggestion would be for you to go down in the chairlift tonight. Jimmy and I would lead and follow you down to make sure you were safe. Jimmy could then take you home in my truck, which is at the bottom of the hill. "

Margo piped up, "I'm more comfortable with a chairlift in the dark than I am going down the dirt road in the dark. Let's do it."

"Good, Jimmy is changing clothes right now. I'll step into the bedroom and change. We'll take off as soon as it is pitch black outside." Roman said.

A few minutes later, he and Jimmy stepped into the library. Everyone gasped. Dressed in black and draped in weapons, they looked frightening. Roman had half a dozen knives attached to his torso. They wore wearing strange-looking helmets, which they said had a built-in communication system.

They had strapped .45 caliber Sig Sauer pistols to their chests and were wearing a strange zipline harness. Each was also carrying what looked like fully-automatic rifles. They were, in fact, H&K MP5s. Jimmy and Roman looked like something out of a war movie, wearing the weapons and combat gear with complete ease.

Roman approached Julia and took her to a small room he described as a safe room. Roman asked her to stay in it until he returned. She frowned but agreed.

Kissing her on the forehead, Roman said, "You can get out, but no one can get in. I'll be back as soon as we get your parents headed to Salem."

Roman turned off all the lights both inside and outside the house. He slipped on the digital night vision goggles and escorted Alexia, Rose, Stan, and Margo to the chairlift. Jimmy had already done a perimeter search. Roman took the remote control for the chairlift and stuck it by Velcro to his front, along with everything else. Roman fiddled with the chairlift cable for a few minutes, and Jimmy lifted from the ground. He was now hanging from the wire in front of the chair.

Roman explained, "Jimmy will be about thirty feet in front of the chairlift, running downhill on a zipline. I'll be about thirty feet behind the chair. Each of us has a braking mechanism to bring us to a stop and rappelling rope to drop off the zipline to the ground."

Roman got the governor and Margo in the front seat and his mother and sister in the back seat. Before closing the door, he explained to the governor, "The chairlift bubble is bulletproof glass, and the floor is a tempered steel plate. Our sensors picked up at least six, maybe eight bogeys." He added, "It may get a little exciting for a few minutes. But you should be safe inside the chairlift unless they have heavy weapons, which I doubt. Just sit tight and try to relax, it may be stressful for a few minutes, but Jimmy and I will get you home unharmed. For your family's safety, sir, these attacks need to end."

He nodded as Alexia pulled out her video camera with a questioning look.

The night was dark, with just a sliver of a moon in the sky. There was a slight breeze causing the chairlift to rock. The sound of the wind in the trees was loud. On the chairlift, once they were in the forest, everything was black on black.

Roman and Jimmy were wearing digital night vision goggles. For them, this was second nature. They had done night work across the globe, against people their team referred to as the "bad guys." Comfortable with the night action, they had discussed taking everyone down in the governor's sport-utility. It was one of the president's armored cars, he had sent with Jimmy, to protect Stan. The problem was whoever was after Stan would still be out there. Roman was uncomfortable using his family as bait but was confident in their safety. The primary desire of Jimmy and Roman was to control the point of attack on the governor and his family. They felt the advantage was theirs if the attack occurred in the dark, in close quarters.

Tonight, Roman and Jimmy felt in command. They knew an attack was coming, and the target was as safe as possible. The enemy attack points were limited, and their response was preplanned. If they didn't end it tonight, who knew where the next attack would come from, or what form it would take?

Roman controlled the speed of the chairlift, allowing it to move at a slow walking pace. Jimmy and Roman were all but invisible. They had only gone a hundred yards, when Roman's heard in his earpiece, "Bandits to the right."

Gunfire erupted from the right with the bullets bouncing off the chairlift. The flashes were bright, as were the ricochets from the chairlift's steel floor. The shooters were spraying the chairlift car with shot after shot. Roman could see Alexia filming. Jimmy dropped off the zipline at the first shot and was on the ground returning fire. Jimmy killed three of the attackers with his first three aimed shots. A large man wearing bib overalls stepped out from behind a tree and was drawing a bead on Jimmy's back when Roman's gun cracked. Blood spewed from the bib overalls, as the powerful bullet knocked him to the ground. Jimmy turned and gave Roman a thumb's up.

Roman could hear brush crunching as the remaining two attackers ran downhill in the dark. What the attackers didn't know was the alarm company had already called the Marion County Sheriff and the State Police, as the attack involved the governor. Waiting at the broken gate were, Bridger, Roger, and two of the other former SEALS.

# 98

Julia knew she had agreed to wait in the safe room. Fifteen minutes seemed like two hours. Bored, she replayed her time with Roman in her head. It was easy to see Roman impressed her parents.

"He seems perfect. He's almost too good to be true. I tingle with excitement when I'm with him, he treats me with class, and the bedroom is incredible. I'm gun-shy and don't want to think about all my bad experiences with men who were duds once I got to know them. Although how Roman could be a dud, I can't even imagine. For heaven sakes, he's out there now playing Rambo protecting my parents."

The more she thought about it, the more she started questioning if there was anything to protect her parents from. "I can't believe someone is trying to kill dad. I'm sure there's a reasonable explanation for everything." Convincing herself it was silly to wait in the safe room when there was so much cleaning up to do in the kitchen, she walked out of the safe room and into the kitchen. Turning on the lights, she started rinsing plates and loading the dishwasher, humming a happy song.

A PIERCING SCREAM from the house sounded in the night, and the alarm siren started blaring. Roman dropped off the chairlift. Tossing the remote control for the chairlift to Jimmy, Roman took off up the hill at a dead run.

He reached the flagstone area and slowed to a cautious, but purposeful walk. His goggles allowed him to see as though it were daylight. Moving towards the kitchen, he saw two assailants attempting to rip Julia's clothes off. He recognized one as the man he had seen in the student union, Charlie. The men's backs were to him. He approached without a sound. Julia made eye contact with Roman over Charlie's shoulder. She continued to scream, covering any noise Roman made. Roman reached around Charlie's head and snapped his neck.

When he did, the other man jerked back in surprise. Julia grabbed a butcher knife off the counter and stabbed him in the stomach. He started screaming. Roman looked at her and said, "Unless you want to deal with him again, I'd stab him a little higher."

In a panicked frenzy, she stabbed him again and again, before leaving the knife in place and collapsed sobbing into Roman's arms.

"I'm sorry, it's my fault. Boredom hit, and I left the safe room to clean up and do the dishes. That's what I was doing when they broke the window and jumped in."

The wounded man on the floor was moaning, "Aren't you going to help me? You can't just let me bleed out."

Roman said, "I don't see why not. Unless you were on an operating table right now with fluids running into you faster than what's flowing out, you're done. I'd use the next minute to ask forgiveness of your sorry life from whatever God you believe in."

He gave the man a towel, "Press this on the wounds that are spurting blood, so we can say we tried to stop the bleeding. Let's go outside, Honey, and wait for the police to get here. They should be on their way already."

Not letting her go clean up or put on other clothes, he took his phone and started taking detailed photos of her torn clothes, her bruises, and cuts.

Roman responded to her request to clean up with, "No, you can't clean up or wash your face. You need to go to the hospital for a full rape kit workup, including the scrapings from under your nails. Your entire body and everything on it is now evidence."

ALLOWING herself to be led outside to the patio, Julia began to shake as the reality of what happened sank in. She knew she had killed a man. Ferocious shaking racked her body at the thought. She allowed Roman to gather her into his arms and hold her close.

Still sobbing, she could hear Roman murmuring how brave she was, how proud he was of her, and telling her he would keep her safe.

His words penetrated her sobbing, and Julia realized she did feel safe. She felt safer than she remembered feeling for a long time. Her shaking subsided as she stood in Roman's arms, feeling secure.

ROMAN FELT AT PEACE. He knew this would be a long night of interrogation, but understood the necessity. What gave him peace was killing Charlie in the same way he'd killed the admiral. It felt fitting that in Amber's case, he'd been unable to protect the woman he loved, and in the next situation, he had. Without knowing why he felt like his nightmares might be over.

# 99

Alexia was still filming as Jimmy took the remote Roman tossed him. Reconnecting himself onto the zipline, Jimmy delivered the chairlift car and its passengers to the bottom of the hill.

As everyone unloaded from the chairlift, Jimmy demanded, "Where're the keys for the Argo?"

Alexia said, "Not unless I get to go with you."

"You better hold on then, girl. Let's go."

She was hanging on for dear life, as Jimmy raced straight up the hill under the chairlift. She still had her camera on a strap around her neck. Arriving just moments later on the chairlift were the governor, Margo, and Rose. They waited until the two remaining assailants had been captured at the bottom and then started back up the chairlift to make sure Julia and Roman were ok.

As the various police agencies started to arrive, Jimmy took control. He identified himself as a member of the U.S. Marshal's office on special assignment from the president. He, as a federal officer, had been the primary shooter on the chairlift shoot out. To everyone's surprise, he also identified Roman as a member of the Marshal's office. Therefore, his killing of Charlie was also an officer killing an individual in the middle of a crime. The one person killed by a non-officer was the man knifed by Julia in self-defense.

As the questions started to fly, the first involved Roman's having a badge appear on his shirt. To the small family group, he explained, "While I was at Bethesda, I met the president. He enjoys playing poker."

Stan laughed and said, "Yes, he does."

Roman continued, "Well, a few days after I met him, he showed up in my room one evening with a deck of cards and a bunch of Secret Service agents. We played poker for hours. Several times, after that, while I was waiting for discharge, he had the Secret Service pick me up in the evening and escort me to the family quarters. The chairman of the joint chiefs, Admiral Seastrand, showed up, and we played until late in the evening. We played for jelly beans, never for money. One evening, the stakes were on my becoming a reserve deputy available for presidential activation in the marshal's office. He won. I agreed to activation in Oregon if I felt I could contribute. After he discovered my connection to you through Julia, Governor Anderson, he called and asked me to accept activation."

Roman looked at Jimmy and shrugged his shoulders, "Jimmy, I'm not sure how I do it, but I'm resigning from that activation. Julia, with your permission, I would like to act as your lawyer until you can get one."

"Of course, why do I need a lawyer?" she asked.

"For the same reason Jimmy and I will need lawyers, there are a lot of bodies on the mountain tonight. All these police officers will have lots of questions for all of us."

He turned to the police, "Gentlemen, my client will have no comment until we have taken her to the hospital. She has gone through a traumatic event and is cold, shivering, and traumatized. Two individuals attempted to rape and kill her. To make sure we protect all the evidence establishing her innocence of any crime, I must insist you rush her to the hospital and treat her in a way that preserves the chain of evidence."

Roman paused until the officers agreed, he then continued, "As her interim lawyer, I'll be by her side until her release from the hospital. At that point, she will be ready to talk to you. I'll answer all your questions about my part in tonight's events after I have her in the hands of the doctors. The fastest way to the bottom for us will be in my truck since both the Argo and chairlift will need analyzing for evidence, bullet markings, etc. Who is prepared to ride downhill with us in my vehicle to protect the chain of evidence? You can have an ambulance meet us at the store, and I'll turn my rig over to you if you need to analyze it."

An officer stepped forward and got into the backseat for what would be a bumpy ride. Roman said, "Before we get started, I need to discuss something with my client. We will stand here where you can see her, but this will need to be a private conversation."

Closing the truck door on the officer, Roman spoke to Julia, "You know I have graduated from law school, but never passed the bar in Oregon."

She nodded.

"Ok, until your actual attorney turns up, let's act like I am your attorney."

"If this weren't such a horrible night, that would be funny. Can you get in trouble for impersonating a lawyer?"

"Let's not worry about that. I want to coach you on how to answer all the questions which will come up.

AS SOON AS THEY LEFT, Jimmy took Stan aside and said, "Now would be a good time to call in any IOUs you have. I suggest you call the best attorney in the state. He needs to be at the hospital when Julia comes out of her exam. If you have any other attorney friends, it might not hurt to get one for Roman and one for me. We can afford the best."

# 100

Overhearing the requests for lawyers and having seen too many innocent people railroaded into prison for crimes they didn't commit, Alexia decided to help.

Knowing the power of public opinion in the prosecution of crimes, she went into Roman's library and accessed his computer. She figured if public opinion could force a prosecutor to pursue a weak case, it could also cause a prosecutor looking to pursue charges against a "victim" to proceed with caution.

"I'd better make sure the prosecutor doesn't railroad Julia, my brother, or his friend Jimmy, for his own political career."

Typing a "Breaking News- Assassination Attempt on Governor Anderson" story and attaching the video file of the zipline shootout, she hit send. It was a fantastic video, Alexia was in the chairlift recording, and the screams of Stan and Margo were crystal clear. The night was black, and you could see the muzzle flashes, and see the sparks as the bullets hit the chair they were in.

It was easy to hear Margo crying and asking, "Who is doing this, and why is this happening?"

Alexia sat in the library, waited five minutes, and sent another "Breaking News, attempted rape/murder of the governor's daughter."

She attached a series of shots of Julia weeping with ripped clothing. She didn't show the bodies but showed the wreck of the kitchen and the broken window access point.

Alexia waited another five minutes for her station to get the scoop of the breaking news bulletins. She then sent Carl and Rebecca, colleagues at each of her competitors, a text to their personal phones. It said, "I'll be available for an interview at the Salem Hospital while Julia undergoes her testing. Expect more announcements. This is a big story."

She continued with another text, "You can tease a headline of additional assassination attempts on the governor and his family. Details at hospital interview."

Alexia wanted a sympathetic media frenzy and was sure she would get one.

She walked out of the library as Jimmy was claiming jurisdiction over the Marion County Sheriff's office. His suggestion was until they established authority, everyone should leave. A U.S. marshal's agent could secure it until the next day when crime scene investigators could process with the proper authorizations.

He was claiming federal authority tonight because of the shooting at the plane and the use of the mail to send the death threats. Both actions he claimed, gave him federal jurisdiction. Jimmy didn't care about any of that. He wanted to limit access to the area of the deaths only. He didn't want people wandering through Roman's home. Who knew what they might find which they shouldn't.

When everyone agreed to leave, the next question was how to get everyone off the hill. After the home was locked and a guard posted outside, Alexia turned to Jimmy, "Roman said you could fly about anything."

He responded, "That depends on what you've got."

Taking charge, she turned to the police, "The governor and his wife need to get to their daughter's bedside in the hospital. They will be leaving. Could one of the police officers give my mother a ride down to her home? The only request is you do not question her about what happened until tomorrow when lawyers will be present."

A young trooper said, "Yes, ma'am, I'll give her a ride down the mountain."

The police agreed the interviews of all parties would be the next day, with lawyers present. Alexia opened Roman's garage, flipped on the landing lights for the dirt runway, and escorted Stan, Margo, and Jimmy to a small single-engine plane.

Looking at Jimmy again, she asked, "Can you fly that?"

"Yup. Cakewalk."

As everyone climbed in, she asked the guard left behind to safeguard the scene, "Would you please close the door and turn off the landing lights once we are in the air?"

After Jimmy did a thorough preflight check, he lifted the plane off the dirt runway and headed for the Salem Airport. The governor made a call to have a car waiting to take them to the hospital.

Alexia turned to the governor and said, "Well, sir, I think now would be a good time for the scoop you were talking about. There will be a huge amount of publicity over this. We need to manage how the information is distributed. We want to make sure it helps, not hurts, you and your family. What is going on? Who were all those people, and why were they trying to kill you?"

His reply was, "I just got it figured out after the attack on the cable car. The Oregon State troopers searched the bodies for ID. Believe it or not, they were all carrying driver's licenses."

Jimmy commented, "Like I said when I first met you, they were amateurs."

"It all goes back over twenty years. Julia's playmate, Samantha's, father was killed, and her mother shot by a broke hillbilly who was burglarizing their home. We cared for the child for weeks, took her to her father's funeral, and took her to her mother's bedside every day until the mother's release from the hospital. I watched the mother and daughter suffer for years because of the murder. They both had to deal with the trauma of the brutal death and loss of their father and husband. The mother also had to deal with the physical aftereffects of the gunshot. It traumatized everyone in our neighborhood.

"The shooter was Charlie Miller. He was found guilty and

sentenced to death. I was naïve and thought he would be executed soon after he arrived in prison. Nothing was further from the truth. Year after year went by, appeal after appeal delayed the carrying out of the sentence. While I was in the legislature, I advocated for prompt carrying out of sentences. I added an amendment to a bill which allowed the governor, in an emergency, to approve an alternative method of carrying out the death penalty if lethal injection were not possible."

Margo interrupted, "I remember that. You were excited about your success."

"Maybe I shouldn't have been. A month after I became governor, twenty years after the killing, Charlie Miller had used up his appeals. All of them. I'll be damned if the drug companies didn't step in to save him. The state supplier of the lethal drugs sent the state a letter. In the letter, they claimed the current anti-death penalty political climate was creating an emergency they had not foreseen, and they were invoking their right to cancel their supply contract, because of an emergency clause in their contract with us. The head of the Department of Corrections came to see me at 5 p.m. with the letter."

Stan tried to twist in his seat to see Alexia, "I called our state attorney to come over, and we all reviewed the amendment. The letter from the drug supplier fit the wording of the bill. It was almost word for word."

Continuing to turn to see her, he said, "I drafted an executive order authorizing an alternative method of execution and stipulated the order be carried out without delay. At 10 p.m. the same evening, a firing squad executed Charlie Miller. The next day his family went ballistic, and if you remember, there was a big furor in the press. What I did was quick, and it was abrupt, and it gave no notice to anyone for additional appeal time. There was a considerable uproar the next day, but when all the dust settled, what I did was legal."

Alexia said, "I remember, that was on the news for days."

"It was. When everything started to happen, I considered the Miller family. They had been vocal and vitriolic. The investigators and I discounted them since the conviction was many years ago. We thought if they were going to try to kill me, they would have done it a long time ago."

As they were nearing the airport, Jimmy piped in, "One reason they waited was Charlie Miller Jr., the one who was assaulting Julia, hasn't been available until a short while ago. He was in the Navy brig at Miramar Naval Air Station outside San Diego, for attempted rape of a servicewoman. The Navy gave him a dishonorable discharge and released him about six months ago. Charlie Miller Jr., Charlie's son; Bruce, his brother; and Donald, his father, were all killed tonight. I know we also picked up two other brothers, Hank and Larry, as they tried to escape. Hank had an opportunity to meet Brutus," he said with a chuckle.

He continued, "The other bodies didn't have any ID on them, it will take a while to identify them."

Alexia once again took charge, "I'm not your press secretary, sir. But, I'd like to suggest you and Margo rush into the hospital with 'no comments' until you have seen your daughter. Try to stay out of sight for a while. I'll take the scoop you promised me and get everything on my channel right away. I want to manage public perceptions of your family and mine. With your permission, I'll brief the other stations on everything."

"That would be fine," Stan said.

"By no fault of yours, as Roman told Julia, there are a lot of bodies on Hawkeye Ridge tonight. We want everyone feeling sorry for you, thinking you're lucky to be alive, and feeling proud to know you both. Like it or not, Jimmy may find himself a public hero this time."

Margo spoke before Stan had a chance, "Honey unless I'm mistaken, we will all be family before too long. You do whatever you believe is best to protect your family and those of us who may become part of your family."

Stan couldn't resist adding, "Maybe I should have you as my press secretary, Alexia."

## 101

Their driver dropped everyone off at the front door of the emergency room. Television trucks were double-parked in the front parking lot. Camera crews were filming as they walked in. Once inside the lobby doors, a horde of news people descended upon them.

Stan stopped, faced all the news people, and said, "We've been through a terrifying experience and are anxious to check on our daughter and make sure she is ok. I've asked Alexia to share with you information which, for our safety, has not previously been disclosed. We have no further comment at the moment. Thank you, and please pray for our daughter."

Stan and Margo rushed through the swinging doors into the hospital. Alexia knew her way around the hospital. She asked the reporters to each bring one video cameraman with them and go to the hospital's public service room, just down the hall.

Alexia saw with surprise that Jimmy had dropped off the governor's arm and was now shadowing her. "Aren't you supposed to be with the Governor?"

"Governor and Mrs. Anderson are with Roman. They'll be safe. I thought I'd stick with you for a bit."

Carl and Rebecca, Alexia's two primary competitors from the big Portland stations, had made it to Salem in a mad dash after receiving her text. Both came up to her with hugs and concern. They had seen the Breaking News Videos on Alexia's station. They couldn't believe Alexia had been in the shootout with bullets flying.

Rebecca, an attractive brunette newscaster, offered Julia a makeup kit before going on air. Alexia declined, "After what I've been through tonight, I'm not concerned with my appearance. Let everyone see me the way I am. Tonight was a harrowing experience which no amount lipstick can disguise."

It was, however, instinctive for Alexia to run a brush through her hair before looking at her audience. "If everyone is ready, I'm prepared to give you the governor's statement and to give you the details I witnessed tonight."

She made sure everyone was set up and their cameras ready before she began. Looking at her peers, Alexia said, "You know of two life threatening incidents the governor has experienced in the last few months. What you don't know is there were also other events. Many of you have questioned the series of accidents. They were not accidents. They were assassination attempts on the life of the governor and his family."

The entire room gasped and then started to shout questions.

Holding up her hand for silence, she continued, "You can get the details later, but the car accident on Mt. Hood was a cut brake line. I was there and saw the supposed motor failure of the plane at the top of the pass. It wasn't a motor failure. I witnessed someone firing a rifle at the governor's aircraft, causing the emergency landing. For the safety of his family, I agreed to suppress that story until now. Also, he has been receiving two death threats a week by mail. Each said, 'You're guilty, for that you shall die.'"

The reporters were exclaiming and trying to shout questions. Alexia quieted them and continued.

"Just days ago, we all witnessed my brother and the governor's daughter rescue eight people from sure death on the Santiam River. They made it look easy, but if you remember, I was on the river in the sheriff's jet boat. That was a major river in full flood stage. It was as close to death as any of those individuals will want to come until they say 'Hello, Jesus.' Five of those individuals are still receiving treatment in this hospital. What we learned tonight is the assassins plotted the entire incident to cause the death of Julia, the governor's daughter. It is by pure chance she ran into my brother and missed being on the raft trip."

There was a gasp from the reporters, most of whom were scribbling in their notepads. One reporter, Carl, was waving his hand to ask a question.

She continued, "Tonight, there was another attempt on the lives of Governor and Mrs. Anderson and Julia. I was there with my mother for dinner with our families. The alarm system warned of intruders. U.S. Marshal James Stockade, hiding in the corner back there, and my brother, who holds a reserve appointment as a marshal, decided the safest way out for the governor was on the chairlift you saw in the video."

Carl was still waving his hand at Julia, she said, "Give me just a minute, Carl. Let me finish my briefing. I'll try to cover all the questions you have. If not, I'll do my best to answer them once I'm done. Ok?"

"Ok, Alexia, just because it's you. This is an insane story, and we'll have lots of questions."

"You all can see the attack in the video. I started filming at the top of the ride down. Four of the attackers were killed in their initial attack. They were not expecting Marshal Stockade and Marshal Nelson, or their level of skill with nighttime action. You can hear Julia scream and Roman's house alarm siren in the video, and see my brother drop off the zipline and race back uphill to get to her."

Alexia was starting and stopping the video, punctuating her story. She wanted the reporters to understand what they were seeing.

"When Roman got there, two attackers were attempting to assault Julia. My brother, Marshal Nelson, killed the primary attacker. Julia grabbed a knife and stabbed the other attacker. You can see in the photos and video I just sent you the wreckage in the kitchen and the broken access window. You can also see the photos of Julia and her ripped clothing and bleeding face. I ask your discretion as you use those photos on your broadcast, as they are graphic. Please be respectful and don't sensationalize her."

Carl asked, "Who was making all these attacks, and why?"

Alexia turned on her voice recorder and let Stan's earlier explanation in the plane explain it all. She told them the recording would be edited for clarity and sent to their newsrooms.

Carl and Rebecca came up to her afterwards and thanked her for the detailed briefing. Rebecca asked why she was so transparent in what was a major scoop.

In answer, she pointed to a team of high profile lawyers the reporters all recognized. The attorneys had just walked in the door and were asking for Julia, Roman, and Jimmy.

"That's why. I need your help getting out the true story about what happened. Public opinion needs to be on the side of the victims in this story and not focused on the body count. Those high profile lawyers shouldn't be necessary for my friends and family. For heaven's sake, my mother and I were involved in the shootout. They attacked us on private property while we were having dinner with friends."

Carl and Rebecca looked at her and then looked at the lawyers. Carl commented, "This must be important to you."

Alexia said, "Of course it is. It's my family, Carl. Roman is my brother. Julia is his girlfriend. I was in that chairlift with bullets bouncing off it. It scared the crap out of me. Roman and Jimmy saved our lives. Hearing Julia scream terrified me. She killed a guy trying to rape her. I think every woman out there will say more power to her."

Rebecca said, "AMEN to that."

Carl said, "Understood, and you got it. Watch our broadcasts. We've got your back."

Both her competitors hugged her goodbye as they raced for their trucks to get back to their stations. The cute brunette, Rebecca, however, had time to ask about Jimmy, "Is he from around here? Is he single? He's just so cute."

Alexia looked at Jimmy and said, "I'm hoping he's taken."

# 102

Roman stayed with Julia until her parents arrived, and the doctors had all the paperwork to do a complete rape kit test. She protested, “There’s no need to do a rape kit, they weren’t successful in raping me. Thank goodness you arrived when you did.”

Roman explained, “It’s not just about the potential rape. I talked to the technicians. The police will ask them for a rape kit. I told the technicians what happened, and what I, as your lawyer, want them to look for. They’ll look for evidence which shows Charlie and his friend were engaged in assaulting you and that you were fighting back.”

She nodded. Roman also asked the doctor to keep her overnight for concussion observation since she had received blows to the head during the attack. Leaning close, he whispered in her ear, “I’m buying time for your real attorney to go into action before you’re released and interviewed by the police for killing your assailant.”

He told her he was going back to Gates for clean clothes and to get a vehicle. Looking at her parents, he asked, “Is it OK for me to pick her up in the morning and take her to Mahonia Hall? I think it would be best if you asked all the various police agencies and attorneys to meet there and interview everyone at once."

Stan said, "That's a great idea. Do you think they'd do that?"

"I don't know, but you're the governor, it doesn't hurt to ask."

Besides a big hug and a kiss from Julia, he got a bear hug from Stan and Margo. They were both holding Julia's hands and crying in relief that she was safe, and the terror of the night was over.

Roman texted Alexia and tracked her and Jimmy down. They were sitting in an all but deserted hospital coffee shop. They both stood to hug him, and Jimmy pointed at Alexia, "She's good Skipper, damn good. She had those news people eating out of her hand. We're just waiting on the early news broadcasts."

Roman asked Alexia, "I'm about to get a ride out to Gates. Do you want to go along, or do you have other plans?

Her glance lingered on Jimmy for a moment, "No, I think I'll wait and see the news with Jimmy and then get a ride to my condo in Portland. It's about the same distance. I'll see you in the morning at Mahonia Hall for the questioning."

On the Uber taxi ride home, Roman called and talked to his mother for a long time. When he arrived, she came out to make sure he was ok before going to bed. They agreed on a time for breakfast, and he went to his apartment above the boat showroom.

As he went to bed, Roman was at peace with the day's events. He didn't enjoy killing Charlie or anyone but understood the necessity. If it came to killing Charlie or allowing Julia to die, there was no question in his mind that he did the right thing. He said a quick prayer for the souls of those who died. He wept as he asked forgiveness for being an instrument of the assailant's deaths. And, he gave thanks for being there with the necessary skills, and in time, to save the lives of the people he loved.

He went to bed thinking of Julia. His mind was replaying all their interactions. He tried not to think of their sexual activity. Now wasn't the time to replay those scenes. But, he couldn't help thinking about it. He realized his sexual activity with Julia was the best he had ever experienced. It wasn't any wild new positions, it was that they fit together perfectly, and their passion levels were in sync. With a groan, he realized all he had to do was think of her, and he would get aroused.

He thought of Amber. It was difficult. Julia's face kept erasing Amber's. Forcing himself to remember his times with Amber, what they had done together, what they had said to each other, he tried to remember how he loved her.

In his final analysis, he realized yes, he would always love Amber. Part of the love was the years and memories they had together, which made them comfortable with each other. A part had been he was at a point in his life where he was ready to accept love in his life and get married. He felt a peace come over him with that answer and then released her memory to move on.

Crying, he said to an empty room, "I will always love you, Amber, be well."

He no longer felt haunted. For the first time in years, he felt peace and love in his heart.

~

THE NEXT MORNING, his mother again raided Alexia's spare clothes closet for Julia. Rose told Roman, "Get this to Julia right away. Tell her it's a 'care package.' It's got makeup, hair spray, clothes, etc. Julia will want to look good for the cameras, which will be waiting for her when she leaves the hospital."

Mrs. Nelson refused to ride to Mahonia Hall with Roman. "You'll want alone time with Julia before the day begins. I'll take my car and meet you at Stan and Margo's." Roman thought it funny that yesterday, she was afraid of meeting the governor and his wife, and today it was Stan and Margo. Then the irony struck him, "I guess getting shot at in a chairlift together could remove barriers."

When he pulled his pickup into the parking structure at the hospital, he got a taste of the media frenzy waiting in the lobby. He texted Julia for her room number, he wanted to avoid asking for her at the information desk. When he walked into her room, she was still in bed. Her explanation was she had no clothes. They had confiscated everything as evidence. She squealed with happiness when she opened Mrs. Anderson's care package. She had underwear, sandals, pants, and a blouse, but no bra. Roman, being male, commented she could pull off the no-bra look and be right in fashion.

She made Roman turn his back while she got dressed. While dressing, she talked about last night and this morning's newscasts. After they did all her tests the night before, she had nothing to do but watch TV. She had watched Alexia's remote Breaking News announcements followed up with the broadcasts from her channel. Then she switched to see what Carl and Rebecca had said on their station's coverage.

She commented, "I don't know what Alexia said to them, but you couldn't have hired a public relations team to do more for us than they did last night. All three news channels portrayed us as two of the biggest victims, the biggest heroes, and the nicest people. My nurses all think you're handsome and wouldn't quit talking about you until I told them you were my fiancé. And, Dr. Pritchard still asked me out."

Roman laughed out loud.

With poise, she faced all the reporters in the lobby, showing them her black eye and cut lip. She even allowed the video photographer a close-up.

She told everyone, "I can't give you a comment until the police question me. Why don't you all come out to Mahonia Hall? I'm sure my father will have a comment later."

Roman asked, "How many of you have been here all night?" A good portion of the reporters waved their hands.

"The governor can't give you anything. But, there are no ethics rules for me to worry about," he said with a smile. "If, on my way to Mahonia Hall, I picked up coffee and donuts and left them in the bed of my truck, how many of you would help me eat them before the birds found them?"

Everyone laughed and waved their hands again. On their way to Mahonia Hall, Roman picked up two gallons of coffee and three dozen donuts.

When they first got into Roman's truck, Julia gave him a long hug. As he turned on the truck, she asked with a trembling voice, "Could we have a serious talk while you drive? It might be the only private time we get all day."

Roman looked at her and nodded.

"I didn't sleep well last night."

"That makes two of us."

"In less than a week, you have saved my life not once but twice. We've been in high drama, life, or death situations, and I have walked through flower gardens with you. I have experienced situations ranging from intense to laid back, and speaking of laid. I have been well laid." She added with a big smile.

"I feel like I know you better than anyone I've ever known. I feel 100 percent safe with you. The entire time Charlie and his buddy were assaulting me last night, I knew if I kept fighting and screaming, you would hear me. I knew when you heard me. It would be ok. You would protect me."

Squirming in the passenger seat, she readjusted the seatbelt, which wasn't working well with the no-bra look.

Looking at Roman as he drove, she said, "I thought about this a lot last night. I think all my life I have been searching for you."

She twisted her hair into a knot, "You heard the story of Charlie Miller killing my friend, Samantha's father. I was young, but it made a big impact on my psyche. I think ever since I have been searching for the male figure with whom I would always feel safe. My father kept me safe that night, but no one else has given me that sense of safety and security until you. I have made bad choices in my relationships, hooking up with the male macho types who exuded strength, but they were all abusive or phony."

She undid the knot in her hair and then redid it, "I know we've known each other just a few days, but I know I love you. Not because you saved my life, not because I feel safe with you, but because of how you treat me. And because of how you make me feel when I'm around you. I tingle. I'm yours, Roman, I'll take whatever you can give me. Do you think it will ever be possible for you to have the feelings for me you had for Amber? Would you ever consider a family with me? Is there a possibility of a future for us?"

She got quiet and, looking scared, tried to hold her hands still in her lap. Roman pulled in the parking lot and, with a grin, motioned for her to wait. He got out and putting the coffee and donuts on the tailgate, asked the reporters, "Do you guys suppose we could have a few moments of privacy before we've got to start dealing with the day?"

Everyone backed off.

Roman climbed back in the truck and turned toward Julia, "Well, I didn't sleep either. You know I have dealt with a lot of flashbacks. Last night, every time I saw Amber, something superimposed your face. It was difficult for me to remember her. I tried hard to remember the feelings of love I had for her. I loved her, but I also question whether I loved the idea of love, marriage, and family as much as I loved Amber. Were she and I convenient for each other when the timing was right in each of our lives?"

Holding her hand, he paused before continuing, "I thought about it all night. I knew her for years. But, we never had long periods of time together. We spent a lot of our time making love in romantic, exotic locations. It's hard not to fall in love in those circumstances. What I wonder is if our time had not been cut short, would our love have survived the ordinary day-to-day rituals of married life. If we weren't on a beach in Bali but were trying to get down the rocky road of life together, would we have stayed together? I don't know."

Julia asked with a saucy grin, "If I promised you wild sex in any romantic, exotic location you chose, do you think you could fall in love with me?"

Feeling at peace with his past, he replied with a smile, "I already have."

# EPILOGUE

*Six months later*

A late-model, red, Lexus pulled into Mary Beth's driveway. A tall, overweight, black man got out of the car. He appeared to be in his 40s and was wearing a well-tailored dark blue suit. Stepping to his trunk, he opened it and withdrew a medium-sized cardboard box. The lid was closed on the box, which appeared heavy.

Carrying the box, the man walked to the door of the trailer. Mary Beth opened the door, and he entered, placing the box on the kitchen counter. She poured him a cup of coffee, and they sat at the small table. She fiddled with the thin wedding band on her right hand, which had a diamond chip in it.

"Thank you, William. This was kind of you. You have been a huge help in this whole process. I'm grateful Biggie introduced us."

"That was a long time ago, and you're welcome. It's been my pleasure throughout the years. This is the last of the unpleasant details. It took the county and state agencies quite a while to release the bodies for cremation." Opening the box, he pointed to black garbage bags containing the ashes of Donald, Bruce, and Little Charlie.

He said, "The wives of all the other men had their husband's bodies moved to funeral homes. Nobody claimed Bruce. It was good of you to assume responsibility for his remains. Are you planning on spreading their ashes on the property before you sell the lots?"

"No," she said with a sad look at the box containing all that remained of her son.

After an awkward pause, William said, "Mary Beth, I know it's none of my business, but I'm dying of curiosity over something."

"What's that?"

"I've known you now for years. I know how rough your life was and how broke you were. How did you come up with the money to handle the cost of subdividing the property to reap all the profits from the lot sales? I expected you would sell the acreage to a developer, which would have been good. But you'll make much more this way. Where did you get the money for all the upfront costs?"

Mary Beth grinned, "Life insurance. Right after you helped me get the divorce from Charlie, I got married to Donald."

William nodded.

She continued, "He still thought he'd be getting sex every night from a young, naïve girl. I demanded a life insurance policy. He never thought he would die, but I figured eventually, someone would kill the bastard. I sold eggs to pay the premium on a term life insurance policy."

William chuckled, "I understand you're leaving later this week. Where are you going, and will I see you again?"

"I'll see you at least once a year when I come back to bake Biggie his cake. For now, I'm flying to Palm Springs and checking out one of those fancy resorts. With a hundred and twenty lots to sell, I'll have a good income for twenty years if I sell six every year. I'm only forty. I've been in the gym every day since they killed Donald, and I've lost thirty pounds. When I get to the resort, somebody will help me figure out how to dress and what to do with my hair. Maybe I'll learn how to play golf or tennis."

"I wasn't going to say anything, but you are looking hot," he said with a kind smile.

She grinned at him, "Thank you, William. I leave on Friday. I've sold my car, and I'm leaving everything. If you know any folks, who could use anything that's left here, tell them to take anything they want from the house and the buildings. They can have the chickens if they promise not to use them for cockfighting. I've donated the buildings to the fire department to burn down for practice. Everything here will go up in flames."

"Everything?"

"Everything. I want nothing from that horrible family but the money from the property. They owe me that."

THE NEXT DAY she took the garbage bags of ashes to the chicken pen. Before entering the pen, she looked up at the sky. "Charlie, if you can hear me, I hope you know I loved you." She played with the ring on her finger he had given her so many years ago.

She continued, "I know you killed that Trailblazer. But, I know you didn't go there intending to kill him. You were never an evil man, Charlie. You did some bad things and paid a heavy price for it. But, our son was a different story. You know your dad was a monster, and he raised our son with his evilness and no boundaries. I did the best I could. If you'd been here, maybe things would have been different."

She walked around, scattering the ashes on the ground for the chickens to eat. Since no one could hear, she spoke out loud. "I know I'm supposed to say a prayer for the three of you, but I can't. Little Charlie, I loved you like a mother loves a son, but you quit being my son and became Donald's when you cut the head off the first chicken. I'm glad you didn't kill any of those people. Bruce, you should have left the family when you were of age, but you stayed under Donald's rule. And, Donald, you were just evil. You're better off dead," she said, spitting on Donald's ashes.

Emptying the last bag, she said, "Ashes to ashes, dust to dust, I hope you don't make the chickens sick."

She walked away without looking back.

# ACKNOWLEDGMENTS

*My wife, Lisa, heads my Gratitude list. This series would never have started without her love and encouragement that continued every step of the way. From the first, "What are you doing, writing a book?" To the daily proofreading and critique, thank you, Honey.*

*Peggy Lowe, of Authorgraphics.com, deserves a large thank you for her eye-catching artwork.*

*Kathy Saviers, Co-chair of the Salem chapter of the Willamette Writers Guild, was invaluable as I started Hawkeye Ridge. She took the time to explain to an excited new writer, what I didn't know. Proofreading my first book, Hawkeye Ridge she gave me an example of the exhaustive work involved in revising your work. Thank you, Kathy.*

*My step-daughter, Terah Haslip was invaluable in her editing and critiquing. Going far beyond what was expected, she helped make Hawkeye Ridge a book I am proud of. Thank you, Terah.*

*Chris Patchell, USA Today Bestselling Author and co-chair of the*

*Willamette Writers Guild, gave me the final invaluable assist in moving forward. Thank you, Chris.*

*With a grin, I thank our Himalayan cat, Rosebud. She did her best to sit on my lap or lie on the keyboard while I typed the entire book. She donated her hair coloring and name to Rose Nelson, Roman's mother.*

# ABOUT THE AUTHOR

*As a child, I escaped into the magical world of fiction. The small-town library became my refuge. A Vietnam era medic in the USAFR, I've always owned my own business. I worked my way through college as a barber, have been a Real Estate Broker and owner of a Real Estate School, and have spent 37 years in the financial services industry. A book was always nearby.*

*On vacation, I became disgusted with the books I had with me. Muttering, "I can do better than that," I opened my laptop. Hawkeye Ridge escaped onto the pages.*

*You can learn more about me and my work on my website:*

https://www.gdcovert.com